SHIVER IN THE DARK

SHIVER IN THE DARK

A Collection of

Eerie Tales & Novellas

BY
C. A. PORTNELLUS

⫼BookBaby

Published by **Book Baby**
Pennsauken, New Jersey, USA

Published by /**BookBaby**
7905 N. Crescent, NJ 08110
https://bookbaby.com
Ordering Information:
For details, contact csparrow.bliss@yahoo.com
First Edition

Images compiled on the cover and in the book are purchased from Adobe Stock or the author's artwork.

ISBN: 979-35092-931-7 (sc)
ISBN: 979-35092-932-4 (ebook)

Printed in the United States of America on SFI Certified paper.

TABLE OF CONTENTS

About The Stories

What is more fun than camping and telling creepy stories by the fire with the kids? Recalling many such yarns spun by adults and children often enhanced our evening and maybe fueled some dreams. Although the stories in this book are for mature audiences, they are spicy treats. Some are *Sideways Tales*, using characters from the book series—*Sparrow Wars in the Garden of Bliss*. These are original works by the author, C. A. Portnellus.

Shiver in the Dark was written during the **NaNoWriMo** 2016 challenge held annually in November (and a few other times a year). **https://nanowrimo.org** **N**ational **N**ovel **W**riting **M**onth. It was challenging to write only 50,000 words, completing a novel in thirty days. I have never had a problem continuing to write. But to be focused and use restraint was also the key, thus creating a complete book in only 50k words. This latest work has more than 50k because I have added three more stories for your enjoyment.

Thousands of writers worldwide were engaged in their own goals for this challenge. We had local groups to chat with and meet for technical writing and continued encouragement. I finished days before the end of the challenge with 51,000+ words for my *Shiver in the Dark* prequel. If you enjoy writing, consider taking the NaNoWriMo challenge; you may work on previous stories or books or create something new.

I have expanded my *Shiver in the Dark* collection with new bonus novellas.

Bring out the S'mores for these tall tales.

THE LAMENT OF THE LADY IN WHITE

(Madame Coeur)

(Mademoiselle Berthe Deroche)

1

જ

Chapter 1—Pauvre Chérie Liliana

Baton Rouge, Louisiana
Sunday, February 11, 1872

Liliana Bonté lay naked under a damp linen sheet, her body soaked in sweat. The mound of her belly seemed to move on its own. Crying in pain, she gripped the sheet in her fists and tried to sit up to push. Then, exhausted and panting, she dropped back against the pillows too soon.

"It is no use. The mother and child will die if the doctor doesn't come quickly." The governess, Mademoiselle Berthe Deroche, said *en Français* to the upstairs maid, Eunice.

"But Berthe, what should we do? *Le Maitre, il n'est pas ici. Mais*—" Eunice complained in French, "The master will be angry and beat us if—" but was interrupted and roughly shaken by the tall, robust governess, stopping Eunice's whining complaint.

"For pity's sake, stop blathering, you little cow." She set aside the younger mulatto woman to step around the curtained bed. Berthe commanded, "Pick up these soiled nightdresses and linens. They only breed disease." She kicked at the bloodied items.

"*Oui*, Berthe." The maid curtsied and bent to work.

Adjusting her cap, tucking in the frizz of sweat-dampened curls, Berthe Deroche leaned to her charge. Pressing a damp cloth again against Liliana's fevered crimped brow.

"*Ma Coeur*, Liliana, you must sit up. Here, have some tea... it will refresh you and ease your pain." Mlle Deroche held the china cup to the young woman's lips, but Liliana did not respond.

"See there, Eunice? This girl is half-dead from exhaustion. What an inopportune time for her labor to start! And what with the party tomorrow evening and Lucien not here... it is ill timing!"

"Start? But it began yesterday before lunch." The maid responded as she picked up the soiled bedding. "Look at her... she is so weak, no food, no drink for two days, it is a wonder *la maîtresse* is alive!" The maid crossed herself

3

and kissed the silver crucifix at her collar to continue her lament.

"This is terrible... evil... bad juju. You should let me bring Maman. She knows what to do. And you did not put a silver knife under the mattress. I told you it eases the pain! May the Holy Mother save Liliana's soul if she dies." Eunice wept, making odd signs. "Oh, but the tiny *bébé*... we cannot let the Devil get him!"

"Fool! Get out of here. Stop speaking nonsense." Berthe grumbled, shutting the door on the maid's noisome wailing exit.

"I want Lucien!" Liliana cried out, "Where is he?"

Berthe rushed to the bed and gripped Liliana's flailing hand. "You know he is traveling. He has business in New Orleans. He will be here later tonight." She declared, telling a lie.

Liliana, at this moment, did not need to know that friends yesterday had observed Lucien visiting his mistress in the Latin Quarter of New Orleans. A Creole woman of mixed races, stunningly beautiful and talented in the theater and among the social circles. Abigale Gagner held too many men in thrall for her own good.

Not only was Lucien being entertained by another woman, but he was engaged in the Rex Krewe. This year, the society of businessmen involved in the Rex Krewe for the Mardi Gras scene and parades was a new threat to the town's traditions. The young idiot, Lucien, was behind some of the financial backing and the intrigues of being a crazed entertainer for the long holiday. But, for personal reasons, Lucien couldn't be here in Baton Rouge and doing the same thing. It was beyond Berthe's ken. In Berthe's eyes, all the pomp and *frou-frou* silliness were unworthy of her *maître*. The ne'er-do-well boasted about his new Rex Krewe position to several friends weeks before. Berthe had overheard it all. "Foolhardy fop!"

But the incident pointed another accusing finger at Lucien Bonté and his comrades' hedonism, vanity, and self-serving attitudes. If something did not propel him to feel sated gluttony, find sex, or gain more riches, Lucien would seek other avenues for pleasure. Then, he usually forgets about his lonely wife, child, and home. Yet everyone at home waited faithfully until he returned.

A ball and Mardi Gras gala was planned at the Bonté home tomorrow night, followed by everyone going to the streets to party. The guests, including Lucien, would travel to New Orleans for Tuesday's more fantastic parades and festivities. So, no one here might see Lucien for another week!

Berthe sighed and swept the long, dark chestnut tresses from the girl's face. "Such beauty and a life wasted... and promised to a man with no heart." The governess whispered, holding the girl's languid, clammy palm.

Then, pressing a hand to the mound, hoping to feel movement or a kick, Berthe laid her head on Liliana's abdomen. "*Rien. Quelle domage, chérie.*" Berthe said after a minute, sitting up to pull the bedsheet over the young mother again.

"These men only want their fun, but never the responsibility of their consequences." In anger, gripping a fist, Berthe rose to her feet, then yanked on the servants' bell by the bed and waited for Eunice or one of the other young girls to appear. She had missed two meals so far today because of this untimely birth. The baby was coming too early, so Berthe worried for Liliana and the child.

She walked to the arched casement window to peer through the sheer curtain, noting the bleak, vacant cobblestone street beyond the property walls. The long drive to the gate was empty—no servants preparing for the *fête* tomorrow night. Berthe wondered why nothing was happening for the ball or the dinner. Yet she had no orders, and neither had most of the staff heard anything about the plans.

The Bonté property was extensive, with no neighbors other than opposite street ends. The mansion faced southwest, which caught the afternoon heat, baking the three-story red brick and fieldstone-clad home and its occupants.

A year before the 'War Between the States,' Lucien's father had ordered removing many of the century-old trees so the slaves could not hide or use them to escape over the walls and iron fences. As a result, everyone in the household and farm was held prisoner for the selfish Claude Lucien Bonté's pleasure. He was never a good man, in Berthe's opinion.

As a young woman, Berthe had served in this same house as a maid, nanny, and then private handmaid to Claude's two successive wives. The beautiful young women were useless other than to produce offspring—only sons. The ladies were only little fandangles on Claude's arm at parties.

Any daughter mysteriously disappeared after birth or died within days. Of the seven children produced by the two wives, a pair of twin boys had survived—Maurice and Dominic, their half-brother, Lucien, and his half-wit brother, who lived until nine. Reggie fell from the sleeping porch roof one summer and died. Berthe had suspected foul play rather than Reggie's clumsiness.

For the years Berthe served in the Bonté home, she watched the battles between the young brothers vying for their father's favors and inheritance. There were now two remaining adult half-brothers, Lucien and Maurice, the solitary twin. Although born of different mothers, the men still physically resembled Claude, including his callous attitude, roving eye, penchant for gambling, and selfish escapades.

Claude died some years ago under mysterious and nefarious causes in a duel. He should have won it, settling the argument. Berthe had suspected it was a death debt. Soon after Claude's death, cruel men invaded the mansion, taking many fine things: artwork, crystal, silverware, jewelry, and furniture. Berthe also surmised the theft was to pay Claude's creditors.

That had been a bad day.

Lucien and Maurice had also fought, thrashing each other in the front yard on the walkway. It was good that the house and yard had high stone walls, so no one passing by would see them brawling. Finally, the cleverest and most merciless brother, Lucien, defeated his elder nemesis half-brother in a duel with a derringer wound in Maurice's shoulder.

Maurice soon left Baton Rouge and settled among his friends in 'the ton of New Orleans.' He currently owned a saloon and upscale *cat house* from the gleanings of his shared inheritance.

"Too many lives gone to the Devil. A beautiful house wasted, too," Berthe commented with sadness. "This home should have happy guests, children, and loving families. But no, it is only a Lothario's play castle. A rapscallion who says he wants and needs sons yet rarely acknowledges them. Atavistic for his money and foolish pastimes." Despite the heat of the afternoon, Berthe shivered at the terrible memories.

She looked toward the bed, observing that her charge had not cried or called out in pain for some time. She suspected the infant was dead, and perhaps so was Liliana.

Closing the heavy dark blue velvet winter drapery to hide the room from the afternoon heat and sun, Berthe said a silent prayer for her charge.

This was the third child for Liliana and Lucien. The first infant girl was lost, miscarried at five months, only three months into their hasty marriage. At least Lucien had married the girl! But then, last year, Liliana bore a son, Randolfe Claude Édouard. Then suddenly, Liliana was pregnant again with this one. And to think, if she died now, perhaps Lucien's mistress Abigale Gagner in New Orleans would be the next wife and Randolfe's stepmother! The situation made Berthe cringe, finding it all sordid like a two-penny trashy novella.

Candice, the downstairs maid, burst into the bedroom. She gasped and breathed in to say, "*Docteur Vincent est ici!*"

Berthe gave a sigh of relief, ordering, "*Vite!* Bring the doctor here now. Your mistress is lying there nearly dead in her childbed!" Her French was sharply accented, like knives striking the poor maid.

Hearing the older gentleman clomping up the many stairs to the third floor, taking a breather at each story— Berthe could only grit her teeth in impatience at the slow progress. It was no wonder the doctor was so tardy, nearly a day later, after being called upon by Andreas, their carriage driver. The negro servant had returned two hours later without the doctor to report that Dr. Vincent Thomas was on another call. Even the money offered to the physician wasn't a significant enough bribe to bring him sooner.

Berthe glanced at the miniscule timepiece pinned with a ribbon to her blouse and shook her head. "Doctor, please hurry. Madame is fading quickly," she called to him.

Heaving a great sigh, the doctor stepped onto the landing. Then, entering the bedroom, he snappishly inquired, "Why are these drapes drawn? I need light! Bring me hot water and clean linens." Then, stepping over to the canopied bed and drawing back the curtains, he commented, "Now, Liliana, you cannot expire so soon. I am here. Let me see how you are progressing." He dropped his bag, rinsed his hands in the nearby basin, and lifted the sheet.

Liliana only moaned as the doctor examined her. Eunice and Candice returned with the requested items, gently setting them near the bed and removing the other pan of cooled water and bloodied rags. Afterward, Eunice lit two nearby oil lamps, bringing the dim room into brighter, rosy colorfulness.

Without a look at the women, the doctor requested, "Bring me a cup of meat broth, some whiskey or cognac, and put two spoonfuls of this powder in a cup of hot water." Doctor Thomas passed a small cloth bag to Candice. "Now be quick." He put on his spectacles, stripped off his suit coat, and sat on the bed with his patient. Taking her hand, he whispered, "It will be over soon, my dear."

"I know... I am dying. I think I saw my mother... Maman looked like a beautiful angel." Liliana murmured as she pressed a hand to her abdomen. "Please tell Lucien I am sorry."

"Nothing to be sorry about, my dear." He gently thumbed away her tears to say softly, "Your baby is not positioned correctly, so after you have some tea, you will relax, and we shall have a child before you can yell again." Dr. Vincent said with a wink and a smile under his bristly, waxed silver mustache. He folded back his shirtsleeves and, from his medical bag, took out a rolled towel with implements.

Berthe closed her eyes and said, "Thank the lord, we finally have a man of science to help us." She stepped to the bed and laid her hand on Liliana's fevered head to say, "Eunice was fussing about earlier, spewing bits of gloom and doom from her mother, who is supposedly a midwife or healer. But most of the mid-wives around here are nothing but charlatans or old superstitious hags. So let's put leeches on everything or bleed them! Or a concoction of nasty-smelling weeds for an emetic cure-all!"

The doctor made a face and said, "I wouldn't be so quick to dismiss everything they do."

He smiled up at Berthe. "You were delivered by a midwife and lived. So were many other children in this house and around our fine city. We don't have enough physicians to deliver all the babies. If you had a midwife, the baby would be here already."

The doctor sighed and said, "But now, I am here and will see our dear girl to the grand finale." He glanced at his pocket watch. "I predict if Liliana drinks her tea, then in perhaps thirty minutes... or more, *Maître* Lucien will have his second child. And a happy little mother as well."

Minutes later, the maids returned with the items requested. The doctor bathed his hands again in the new basin of hot water, followed by a splash of whiskey. Then he took the tea, added whiskey, and stirred the contents of a vial into the cup. The tea changed to an oddly muddied color.

The maids held Liliana up as she drank the bitter concoction, then rested her against the freshly plumped pillows. Vincent's hands were hot and firm inside and on her abdomen, as the doctor massaged the girl's belly. Then, amid a few cries of pain, Liliana suddenly fainted.

The women gasped.

"Is she dead?" Eunice squeaked, "*Mon Dieu!*" and made a cross upon her breast.

"No, just very relaxed. Now watch this." After more manipulation and movements under the sheet, the shape of Liliana's belly changed, and the lump elongated downward. Many minutes later, Dr. Vincent pulled out a blue baby. He unwrapped the umbilical cord from the infant's neck, swiped a finger into its mouth, and then lustily blew into the baby's face and nose. The infant drew its first breath after several brisk rubs and thumps on the back. Soon, it wailed like a weak cat.

"We have a boy!" the doctor cried as he vigorously wiped the infant of the bloody placenta, tied and cut the cord, then passed him to the nanny, Berthe. "See if our girl will awaken with a little smelling salt. She needs to hold her baby, not take a nap."

He continued to work, expelling the rest of the placenta, and passed the soiled rags to Eunice, "Burn these immediately." He noted Eunice took the umbilical cord, hiding it in her pocket. He shook his head at her curious tradition, finding it macabre.

Berthe held the tiny infant. His color was returning—instead of blueish, he was scarlet and in the throes of a violent screaming tantrum. His little arms trembled as his body arched and went rigid as he screeched. Berthe wrapped him tightly in swaddling cloth, yet the baby howled. "Liliana, your baby needs you." She held the child out to Liliana, who seemed finally to awaken.

"Please, dear God, let it be a boy." She cried. "I cannot bear to go through this again! Tell me if it is a boy."

"You have a boisterous, loud, demanding son, just like his father." Dr. Thomas said with a modicum of humor as he swabbed Liliana's thighs and belly, cleaning away the blood.

Berthe watched as the young mother clutched the baby and kissed his dark, damp curls. "I was there too when Lucien was born, all piss and vinegar, right out of the womb," Berthe mumbled.

The doctor chuckled. "Yes, I recall that day. Unfortunately, I was late for his birth. Thank goodness for a midwife, then. But I was glad Lucien had a healthy set of lungs and kidneys... since he screamed and peed on me. The lad was and is still irritable whenever I must attend to him. But alas, that is Liliana's lot now." The doctor stood, cleaned his hands in the water basin, and took a cloth to dry them.

He then gave the cup of broth to the mother. "You need a little sustenance." She sipped weakly, then more when Candice held the cup for her.

Eunice picked up the whiskey bottle. "And this too?"

"No, that is for me. *Mon Dieu*, it has been a long day." He swallowed the drink and grimaced, "Woof, that potent stuff makes me want to howl." He winked at the women. "Now, if everyone is fine, I shall take my leave. I'll see myself out. *Bonjour*."

Berthe rushed after the physician. "Your bag, hat, and coat, sir."

"Ah, yes. My wife always said I had a head full of wool. Can't remember much these days. *Merci*, Berthe. Please tell Lucien he owes me more than his worst bottle of wine." He chuckled. "Cheapskate."

Berthe walked the man out to the hallway and stairs. "Will you be attending our gala tomorrow?"

The doctor put his spectacles in his coat pocket. "Oh? A gala? I am unsure if I should come. Lucien never mentioned it to me, nor did I receive an invitation. Besides, this was the third birth in two days I attended. At some point, I need rest, too. I'm not young anymore."

"Neither am I. But perhaps you could look in one more time in the afternoon on the Bébé and Liliana. We were so sure they were dying. But you are the miracle worker, breathing life into your patients again. That tea was a marvel, too. Only modern medicine and a man of science can do such a thing." Berthe tapped his arm. "I wish I could be a skilled physician like you to save people."

"You are mistaken, *ma chérie*. That tea and the 'breath of life,' as you called it, are methods I learned from an old Choctaw midwife, who helped *my* Maman bring me into this world almost the same way." Then, wagging a finger at Berthe, he scolded, "Do not place your trust in everything that is only modern. Some old methods are the foundations of what we know for actual medicine."

"But surely it was a miracle for Liliana."

"It was only raspberry leaf tea, black cohosh, and a little laudanum. All to help the mother relax her tense muscles, breathe better, and let the baby come easier in more efficient contractions. She was hysterical and ready to die. I only helped to turn him into place once she relaxed."

Taking Berthe's arm, the doctor steered her onto the stairs. "See that Liliana has some bland food—broth, maybe an egg or custard, and plenty of peppermint and chamomile teas. She and the infant need to bond. Do you have a wet nurse if Liliana cannot feed her child? Or will not?"

"Yes. I will see to everything Liliana needs," Berthe said as they approached the second-story landing. "Now, as to you... Might I have the cook prepare you something? Since Blanche passed away, you are thin as a chewed string. You must take better care of yourself, Vincent. And you must come to the party. Who else will dance with me?" She said, arriving at the main floor's foyer.

The doctor smiled. "Ah, true. Who can say no to such a fine woman?" He put on his coat, "I shall see you at five-thirty, then look in on the mother and child. Perhaps we can chat then."

"And have our dance, too?"

"Are you sure Lucien won't mind?"

"Doubtful. The idiot is in New Orleans with his lady friends and his new brotherhood of Rex Krewe."

"You mean he knows nothing about his wife and the birth of his child?"

"I imagine most of Lucien's time has been spent visiting friends and on the Rex Krewe business more often over the last two months of his wife's pregnancy. So poor Liliana is overly worried."

"Hm, it is no wonder that Liliana had the child early then. The infant might have died if Liliana hadn't gone into early labor. Although early, the baby is over-large, so he might have been too much for her to bear in more weeks. She is such a tiny, frail creature. Who is to say? Any trauma to the mother can mean possible death to an unborn child. I have yet to understand why men must take young women barely out of childhood and impregnate them. Then cry foul when the girls are physically too weak and die bearing their children."

Vincent shook his head. "No one deserves to see a dead child, bear an unhealthy one, or lose a beloved wife. Perhaps it is time for a *tête-à-tête* with Lucien. I'll set the cad straight. It is one thing to have a little excitement on the side sporadically but not blatantly act like that. Nor should any wife be neglected or overly used. The poor girl is not a brood mare!"

The doctor made a noise of disgust. "I never can understand a man who holds other women's love interests. *Moi*, I am faithful like a hound."

The pair continued to the front door, with Dr. Vincent taking Berthe's hand and kissing it lightly. "Until tomorrow." His dark eyes were intent upon the tall woman. He whispered, "If only our lives were different, and I were not so decrepit, I would openly court you, Berthe. You are an astounding and resilient woman. You should have been married and a mother yourself." With that insightful comment, he put on his hat and left through the front porch screen door.

Berthe watched Vincent step up into his covered surrey and click to his horse, "*En-y-va, Pomme!*" The old, dappled, gray carriage horse sighed, shaking his mane, and stepped out leisurely. Dr. Vincent tipped his hat as he passed the stable boy and girl, then tossed each child a coin.

Berthe sighed, murmuring, "Vincent is a generous gentleman, a rarity these days." Then, closing the front door, she caught the cook's apron and skirts flying as Esmeralda hurried into the kitchen.

Chapter 2—Charité

"**I** saw you! Spying on me, were you?" Berthe paced after the heavyset woman. Both women were light on their feet despite their girth, age, and full skirts. "Aha! You do not fool me, Madame!" Berthe announced, arriving in the kitchen.

"But, Berthe, I was not spying. I meant only to give *le Docteur un petit cadeau... un gâteau riz.*" Flustered, the cook spoke brokenly in English and French and held up a wrapped rice cake.

"*C'est vrai?*"

"*Oui.* I made an extra rice cake this morning for when he came." She said loftily, "You are right. Dr. Vincent looks worn out. *Peut-être...* I should make him better food than sweets. Yes?"

"Maybe. Although, unless the kind doctor is a dinner guest, I don't think Lucien and Vincent would like the charity aspect. You understand? Lucien has no regard for the indigent. While the doctor is not poor, he could benefit from kind treatment. But that is not for me to say."

Esmeralda's eyes widened. "Who would say anything? You know the last lady, Lucien's mother, was kind that way. She insisted I give any remaining tidbits to the servants. And the extra preserves or produce we gave to the parish church. Père Pierre Auguste always needs such things. So I feel sneaky, donating anything these days. It's worse now with Lucien's new locks."

Berthe pulled out a chair at the kitchen table, sat with a sigh, and held out her swollen feet, turning them about and easing the pressure of the tightly laced shoes. "Right now, I would welcome some charity. My feet and back are tired. Birthing babies is not for the weak or old, even if one is assisting!"

"Did I hear a baby cry? Please tell me it was a boy."

"*Oui, un grand garçon.*"

"*Ça promet! Luciene promet ses monts et merveilles.*"

Berthe took a deep breath, then pressed a hand to her heart. "We can only hope that Lucien will keep his promises to his wife. With a new son, they have a chance now. But a bit ago, I was sure we would lose them both. The babe is a couple weeks earlier than expected, but the doctor seemed to think *L'Enfant* was healthy enough."

"What about Liliana? It was days of hard labor for her. I will make her some soup with herbs to ease her pain."

"Let her rest for now. I could use a meal, though. Whatever is in the larder is fine." Berthe sighed and lifted her *pince-nez* from her nose, letting it fall to her bosom on the black ribbon. "Weak, am I. Perhaps it is good that I never had children of my own. Birthing babes is only for young women, I think." She said wearily, rubbing the bridge of her aquiline nose.

"Ha, I've had six in my time, all healthy, and you know the last one was only four years ago." Esmeralda said proudly, "I am only forty-two this year and not ready for the grave. I still have three at home to raise."

"Lucky for you, Esme, your husband Henri is a good man. But I worry about my Liliana. Lucien is not proper husband material. He is always gadding about. Both Madeline and Henri saw Lucien with that tart, Abigale Gagner. She is the ruin of men like him."

"Tsk. *Quelle domage.* So Lucien has another pretty fish on the line, then? I did not want to believe Henri." As she pulled items from the *garde-manger*, Esmeralda worried aloud, arranging food on a blue patterned plate. "I am sometimes ashamed that I work for Lucien Bonté when I hear the gossip in the shops. But you and I have been here for many years. At least he pays me well. And I believe you are beloved, having been Lucien's *nounou*. So, you are valued as well."

Berthe shook her head. "I make a pittance in money since I live here. You at least can go home to your family. My 'family,' such as it is, is only here. I have no one else." She accepted the cup of cream-topped *café au lait* from Esmeralda. "Sometimes, in my heart, I feel you are my sister. So maybe I am lucky in that regard."

"As do I." The cook set a plate of bread, cheese, *saucisson, confiture des abricots*, and a peeled hard-boiled egg before Berthe. She paused for a moment to grip the woman's shoulder.

"You are the best mother the Bonté children could ever have. You have raised them all well. These pampered women don't even feed or nurture their children. The babes are only playthings to show off in ruffles and velvet clothes for others to say, 'What a pretty baby.' Ultimately, only you and their fathers have a say."

Shaking her head, Esmeralda returned to the counter to crack eggs into a crockery bowl and then, whisking them fast, commented, "No, my dear, any child born here is your baby. Count on that. You raised Lucien better than Claude's other boys."

Although feeling taciturn and tired, Berthe ate her meal lustily as Esmeralda talked about the latest master's crazy lifestyle.

After a time, Berthe, feeling refreshed from the respite meal, pushed aside her plate and rose from the chair. "I must see to Liliana and the Bébé."

"Oh, wait, take this egg and rice custard for Liliana. It will help her feel strong again." She passed a warm bowl to Berthe. "Oh, and did she name the Bébé yet?"

"I do not know. But thank you. I know you are probably busy preparing for the gala tomorrow." Berthe eyed the heavy-set cook and wondered aloud, "But I do not see any girls here to help you. Why?"

"Hmph! Lucien said to me two weeks ago, 'No food for the party.' How can you have a Mardi Gras party with no food? There should be a feast. Anything less than that is a sin! If he had been here these past couple of weeks, my kitchen and I would have been overworked, sure thing, for at least four meals a day for guests and the family. Something is wrong with that man!"

The cook shook her head and pulled a spoonful from a steaming pot on the stove. She sniffed and tasted the creation, then salted the bubbling broth. "*Non, le maître* said I was too old for all that fuss. Imagine that! So, he says he will only provide drinks, and someone will bring the rest. But who? And where does it come from?" Esmeralda fidgeted with her apron ties, looked at Berthe with concern, and attacked again.

"With the Mister gone, who can say anything? So, I have my plan. I made sweet tea biscuits and cream cakes and took extra cheeses, jam, smoked fish, and bread from the bakeries. I will bake fresh croissants for tomorrow morning. I also ordered more milk and cream since our cows cannot make enough in time, and I will make a syllabub. Most people like that."

The woman nodded and smiled. "The La Barres, you know, near St. Francis Ville? They were happy to provide what I ordered and brought it all early this morning. They even gave us extra eggs and a pot of their best honey for half the price! What a kind family they are. I do hope Lucien invited them." Esmeralda took a deep breath as if she had been running, but smiling, she went on.

"There will be canapes, dainties, and sweets. At least those can be made at the last minute. You know everyone gets hungry after dancing." Esmeralda puffed up with pride, "If the Mister refuses it all for the party, our staff will have the lion's share! So why should we not have a treat, too?"

Berthe darkly eyed her friend. "Oh, dear. I hope it all goes well. Because no one seems to know anything about the plans. The parlor and front room are still full of furniture. How can there be dancing there?" Berthe worried aloud.

Then she squeezed Esmeralda's warm hand to say, "Well, no more worries. We have other pressing details for today. I must care for Liliana and the babe now. Please ask Girard to send his wife Bibi if Liliana cannot nurse her baby or use Hilde. Then, have Henri take a message to Lucien about the baby. Perhaps Lucien will come home earlier than tomorrow. We can address some of these concerns with him."

"I do not know why," Esmeralda shook her head in disgust, "but I feel something twitching in the dark, like a dangerous viper in the shadows. I think Lucien's poorly planned *fête* is doomed."

Chapter 3—Un Jour De La Fête

(Lundi Gras) Monday, February 12, 1872

Henri stomped up the steps onto the back porch, slammed the kitchen door, and announced to the busy room, "*Le maître... finalement, il vient aujourd'hui. Mon Dieu!*" Then, sweating heavily and nearly panting, he fell into a chair at the kitchen table. "*Mon Dieu, je suis ancien...*" he groaned, rubbing a knee.

The trio of girls helping Esmeralda squealed at the surprising intrusion.

Esmeralda rushed to him, "*Ma Coeur! Tu es malade!*" She put her arm about him and searched his face.

He held up a hand, "*Non, non. Je suis fatigue,*" then sighed to grumble in a mishmash of French and accented with Cajun epithets, "I am not sick, just too old to run around. That wretch. I searched between here and New Orleans and left messages for Lucien everywhere I stopped yesterday and this morning. And what happens? On my sad return, I was only five miles from home, and he was on the road! If he had not been in the company of his friends, I would have given Lucien hell for it! The brat!" Henri swiped the sweat from his head and face with a kerchief, then pocketed it in his coat. "If he was a boy and his father was here, he'd suffer a red ass." Henri gripped a fist.

"I hate running about like a crazed chicken on a fool's errand!" He spat a foul word *en Français*.

Esmeralda kissed Henri's cheek and reached for the plate on the counter, "Here, eat something. You probably never ate a thing since you left yesterday." She passed him a fresh, warm croissant and the butter crock.

"Not true. I ate the bread and cheese you gave me yesterday and drank the cider. But then I had to pay someone to take a message at *le club privé,*" Henri rolled his eyes and made a derogatory gesture, "so I had no money left for supper or breakfast or any decent place to stay the night. Can you believe I slept with the damn horse on the road?! This morning, we ate the berries we found in thickets along the way."

He held up a mud-encrusted foot, "I slipped in the muck and almost got bit by a baby gator. But I clobbered

19

it with a stick, and Poppy and I ran away before Big Mama could get us."

"*Mon pauvre p'tit agnelet!*" Esmeralda cooed and petted his curly dark hair as Henri shrugged away.

"*D'accord. Ma femme! Laisse-moi! J'ai faime.*" Testy Henri demanded another croissant.

Instead, Esmeralda slid a quickly prepared plate with a slab of corncake, a dry, scorched sausage, and a honey dish before her husband. "You eat. So, when is Lucien coming home?"

"Lucien could be here in minutes if he does not stop or dawdle along the way. There were twenty gaudily dressed idiots in his entourage—" he replied between bites and chewing, then slurping coffee.

"Were there women? Oh, I hope not."

"*Bien sûr.* Several, mostly with husbands or such."

"Was that woman with him? You know, Abigale?"

Henri shook his head. "*Non,* I did not see her like what happened last week. But there were four fancy rigs, a coach, and at least three carts. So, I am unsure what Lucien is bringing home today."

"Did he speak to you about the party? How many guests will we have overnight? Or, the good Lord forbid, longer?"

Between bites of crumbled corn cake, Henri answered, "I only think two couples are staying tonight—one daughter and a son. So perchance we are lucky there won't be a houseful. But, since the idiot let go two maids, your *sous-chef* and Valente, the houseman, we are shrinking and short-staffed. So Lucien said I would act as *Le Portier* tonight instead of tending the horses and carriages like usual. *Il etait hurluberlu—Quel idiot.*"

Esmeralda pulled Henri's head to her chest and petted her husband to mollify his ill temper. "Don't speak like that, my lamb. It is too bad for the fool. I am still worried, though. Will we have enough food? There have been no proper preparations for dinner, a ball, or anyone staying here."

"*Non?*" Henri squinted at his wife, "But what has been going on since I was gone?"

"*Rien.* Nobody knows a thing. But I am cooking just in case we need it. It would be shameful if Lucien suddenly announced a feast or grand reception and I had nothing. I can only hope that the cellar is well-stocked. I do not know if we have enough wine or rum or anything since Lucien only keeps the key these days. The last time it was open, I snuck a few bottles of burgundy, sherry, and rum for my cooking."

"*Ma femme! Qu'est-ce que tu fous?* You will get sacked for stealing. Or beaten!" Angry, Henri half rose from his chair with a fist. "I will beat you myself if they catch you!"

Esmeralda stepped a few paces away but did not cower at the threat. "I stole nothing. How can I cook and feed the household if I cannot do it properly? We barely had enough whiskey for the doctor yesterday."

"I like Dr. Thomas, but I hope you didn't give him the bottle."

"Of course not. Only a sip for Vincent and Liliana. I am no fool; the doctor and Lucien can drink anyone under the table!"

Esmeralda took the empty plate, saying, "If you are finished here, then the girls and I have better things to do than hear your complaints. Go watch out for Lucien. *Adieu!*"

The cook silently watched her angry, tall, brawny husband leave and limp across the back lawn toward the horse barn. She assumed Henri had to tend the horse he took for his trip, poor old Poppy.

Turning about, she addressed the girls, "*Mes filles...* Eunice and Corine, you must prepare three rooms, one on the second and two on the third floor. The green room near the nursery should be fine for the children. While up there, see if Berthe or Liliana need anything. Nobody rang for breakfast today. Perhaps we can prepare a tray for their tea and supper later."

Corine asked, "Will Madame attend the party too? We need to make only a plate for Berthe, then."

Esmeralda shook her head. "*Non.* Do as I ask, lazy girl. After childbirth, *La Maîtresse* is too ill to dance and carouse with Lucien's lot."

"*Oui. Pauvre Madame.*" Corine replied with a bob of her capped head. She side-eyed her cousin, Eunice, then whispered, "You take the third floor, and I'll do the rooms for *le maître* and the guest on the second."

Eunice hissed, "Why must I clean the top floor? I usually have the second *étage*. I do not wish to bother the lady."

"Better you than me. The lady threw her slippers at me the other day."

"That was because you spilled tea on the coverlet." Eunice sneered at her cousin. "Besides, the lady was in labor already. I would throw a piss-pot at you if I was in her condition."

Eunice cast a wary eye at the cook, busily stoking the cast-iron oven. Then she whispered, "There is something wrong with the lady. She was dead, and the doctor revived her with that medicine tea. He saved the baby, too. Mama would have burned herbs to keep the devil away. Since he didn't do that, he probably invited Satan in. We are doomed, cursed maybe—"

Corine's lighter *café au lait* skin flushed hotly as she whispered, "She was dead? Truly?"

"*Oui.*"

Corine genuflected and kissed her tiny silver crucifix. She turned about to call the other girl washing dishes. "Psst! *Allo!* Sandrine!" She waited for a response. "*Viens.*" She rolled her eyes and jerked her head.

Cautiously eying the cook, the girl stepped away from the soapstone sink. "*Oui?*" She dried her hands on her apron, no longer crisply ironed but damp and stained with butter and crusted flour.

"Hey, you must trade with Eunice. She needs to stay here and help the cook. You can clean the top-floor guest rooms and bring food trays to Berthe and our mistress."

"*Non*, that is your job. But, you know, I only clean the downstairs with Candice and help in the kitchen. Besides, what do I know of the Lady? I have not seen her leave her rooms in months."

Corine gripped the girl's thin arm. "You will do as I say."

"But Cook said you two—" Tears sprang to her eyes, "*Lâcher prise... tu me fais du mal.*" Sandrine twisted away to yelp, "*Madame! Esme!*"

The cook spun around, one fist on a wide hip to bark, "*Qu-est-que vous faites!*" She glowered at the trio—Sandrine in tears, the other girls looking suspiciously ornery.

Corine then let go of Sandrine's arm. Finally, with no patience left, Esme demanded, "Why are you crying?"

"*Les oignons. Puis-je... être excuse pour le cabinet de toilette?*" Sandrine asked. Then, seeing the cook nod, Sandrine sped away outside, the screen door slamming with a gunshot report as she high-tailed it toward the outhouse.

"That girl is always crying over something. Stop tormenting her. Why are you two still here? Enough onions for now, and no more whipped cream. Go prepare the rooms. *Vite! Le Maître* will be here soon." Esmeralda shooed the young pair out of the kitchen.

She turned to inspect the mess they had created. "Sandrine is the only worthy *fille* here. Maybe I'll ask Lucien for another girl to train and have a nice pair in my kitchen. Eunice and Corine are too clumsy and never listen to me." She lifted the whisk with a frown and moaned, "The cream is curdled and halfway to butter!" She grabbed the bowl and dumped the contents into a crockery bowl. "I'll use it for sauce."

꙳

The day progressed with at least a modicum of impromptu plans, everyone to a task. Then, when finished, the staff of the Bonté house waited for *le maître* to return home. Like in the past celebrations, greenery garlands hung on the front gate and upon lantern-topped posts along the front walkway. Flowers were placed in the foyer, the parlor, the dining room, and the living room. An urn of fresh greenery greeted guests on the landing posts of the staircase on each floor. The kitchen and stables were the busiest. Many of the estate's working horses were put in the pasture behind the barn to make room for the party guests' rigs and animals.

By late afternoon, the house staff had become testy, worried about the clean and decorated mansion's presentation, as they waited for Lucien.

Henri wisely remained in the horse barn, seeking peace and neutrality among his animals and staff. But vexed that his word was doubted. Lucien was tardy. Had Lucien received the messages about Liliana? Or was flighty Lucien still gadding about without caring for his family and home?

Suddenly, the gate bell rang at precisely four-thirty, and various bells echoed through the house and stables. Then, putting on and smoothing his waistcoat and a final inspection of his shoes, Henri stepped into the sulky and set the horse to trot down to the big house. Coming around to the front gate, he parked the sulky. Then, he opened the front entrance gate with his stable boy, Petit Poche, dressed for the event in a velveteen gray coat and breeches, with polished shoes and brass buckles.

A coach waited in the street with two carriages and an overflowing cart that the mule could barely pull through the gate. The coach and carriages rolled up along the front walkway, the lanterns already lit as the sun set, casting lavender dusk about the property. The front of the house was ablaze, each window illuminating the walkway and lawn. Henri opened each door and stood aside as Andreas appeared to hand down the passengers.

Everyone was dressed in velvet and satin, dark purple or bright green, with gold trims, some wearing gaily painted and jeweled masks, each descended from the conveyances already boisterously engaged in conversation. Yet, Henri, Andreas, and Pocket did not see Lucien among the arrivals.

The jolly guests ambled onto the porch and through the front door, greeted by the downstairs maids who took coats, wraps, and capes to hang in the closet under the stairs. Henri hot-footed it into the house, helping the guests, seeing them seated in the various front rooms, where tables laden with the party fare awaited them.

After nearly a half-hour, the loud clatter of horses and wheels startled everyone as a carriage careened through the gate and up the drive toward the house. Red-faced and winded, Lucien jumped down and ran up into the house. He shouted, "*Non!* We are outside tonight! Everyone outside!"

Confused guests blinked and grumbled as they were led outside again. Several wagons and carts were being emptied there, and a team of men quickly erected a tent and laid down boards on the lawn. Soon, a festive party began outside on the expansive front and side lawn. The tent kept most guests occupied. As if by magic, the food and drinks were quickly arranged.

Meanwhile, as the guests talked and paraded about the tent and lawn, another tented pavilion was set up with a dance floor and chairs, and an awning linked the two structures. The entire yard and driveway had many carriages and carts being unloaded as other serving and cook staff prepared three large braziers with skewered portions of meat. Festive paper lanterns lit the way among the red and gold striped pavilions. The impromptu tents were a good idea as a light rain began as the guests danced to the newly arrived band.

Unsure of their roles for the evening, the house servants grumbled and were like anxious cats, afraid of punishment for their earlier deeds. But the party outside seemed to go well, and they were forgotten.

Esmeralda came from the kitchen, expecting to see guests, but glowered with the news that the party was outside the house. She grumpily stared out the front windows. "Fine. It serves them right! Go ahead, have a party in the rain. Hmph! After all, we did!"

She looked around at the glum faces and then caught Corine and the stable girl, Didi, snitching tidbits from the tables. She made an announcement. "Corine and Eunice take these trays of cream cakes and meringue pies to the kitchen and the cold fruit and aspic salads, where the staff can eat them. The rest of the food is hardy enough for the overnight guests should they come inside from the rain. Put the chocolate and fruit tarts in the guests' rooms. Later, we will bring them tea or coffee."

Soon, the front rooms were less welcoming; the tables were rearranged into small groups and left for whoever would return to the house.

☙

Exhausted from the trying day, Henri sat on the front porch to watch if anyone came to the house or needed their coach. His eyes wandered over the haphazardly parked buggies, carts, and carriages, disliking their disorder. Lucien had a muscular giant man and bull mastiff stationed at the closed gate, should anyone else arrive. But it seemed most guests had come and were enjoying the party.

Already sated from the rich food, Petit Poche (Little Pocket) dozed on a chair and Andreas on the wicker lounge. Henri nibbled a plate of treats and tiny anchovy and leek tartlets while sipping the milky syllabub, enjoying, as his wife called it, "His lion's share." Considering the craziness of the last few days, he deserved the exceptional food.

The aroma of the wood smoke and cooked meat was enticing, causing his mouth to salivate. The raucous laughter and music were invigorating—his foot tapping to the contagious beat, humming the tunes.

It had been years since he and Esmeralda had gone to a party or danced. Sometimes, they ate the leftovers from such events or dared a few swings about the kitchen or back lawn when the guests were asleep or gone.

Munching a tiny morsel of chocolate-covered fruit cake, he was glad his life had a purpose. He had a handsome, happy wife and plenty of children to be proud of—the eldest had already been sent off to school with their savings.

His wife, the talent and force of nature in the kitchen, kept the Bonté home humming, as did the servants. Between Berthe, Esmeralda, and himself, he proudly knew the Bonté home was maintained well, and its servants dutifully did their work.

After today's rigorous outpouring of good deeds ensuring a beautiful and delicious party, Henri was proud of all they did. He roused Andreas and Poche to help him bring the horses and carriages to the barn, not liking that the poor animals were getting drenched by the rain and cluttering the drive and yard.

Now, the staff could sleep easier tonight, knowing all was well.

☙

Chapter 4—Les Petites Catastrophes

Lucien smiled mildly at the inebriated crowd, now glad for his decision to have the large party outside. The tents were primarily dry inside despite the rain. The guests had a terrific time in the unusual venue. The food was simple Louisiana fare: grilled pork, chicken, *boudin saucisson*, bread, and small cups of rich soup spiced like jambalaya, except not spicy enough for his taste. In honor of the Grand Duke, many portions of meat were seasoned and skewered in the Russian tradition. Tiny sugar-glazed almonds and sugared dried fruits were set in bowls for snacks among tiered plates of petit fours, champagne bottles, and porcelain bowls of rum punch. But the food was not for Lucien's taste but for his guests.

He wanted to impress these people, for some were the Russian Grand Duke's entourage members. There was a rumor that Alexis Romanoff might grace one of the many parties tonight in Baton Rouge, even his own! And, of course, tomorrow, His Grace's plans were to be among the honored guests at the Carnival festival parade in New Orleans.

These past weeks had been a whirlwind of activities to prepare for Mardi Gras and the Grand Duke's visit. Lucien's new role as an investor and part coordinator for the Rex Krewe had been tasking. He was no longer attending university and wasn't used to such drudgery or mind-consuming sums and paperwork! In addition, he had accountants for his estate, and for the past month, they had griped about the excessive monies going out of the accounts to creditors for the festival and Lucien's party tonight.

There had not been such grandiose expenditures since Claude's reign. Although Lucien would not allow a repeat of his father's gambling misfortunes to befall his estate. But to help pad the books and expenses, Lucien let go of several non-essential workers at home and kept the wine cellar locked, knowing some servants weren't above helping themselves. Some of the best champagne, wines, and liquor had been gleaned earlier in the month and set aside for tonight's party. In addition, he had reserved several rare vintage cognac bottles for the Grand Duke if he visited or stayed at the Bonté home.

But the Grand Duke, while overly zealous, charming, and making 'acquaintances' everywhere, had over-promised his time. So Lucien doubted he'd experience the duke's presence in his home. The duke was effusive when pleased and conversely surly and taciturn when over-burdened or upset. But trying to keep a smiling countenance, Lucien hoped the man would find his hospitality exceptional tonight—should he arrive!

Today had been chiefly a comical farce of mishaps and miscommunication. Thus, Lucien was relieved that the Duke had been absent from the entourage coming from New Orleans. The tent men were supposed to set up at Lucien's home yesterday. But the previous renters' party had been overlong, and the crews were late.

Costumes and the parade floats were not ready for tomorrow's parade. Currently, a team of people feverishly worked until completion.

Then tonight's chef had to be resupplied with fresh goods, as his cart tipped over after breaking a wheel hub, and the food was spoiled on the muddy road. Some urchins and wildlife ate the spoils of the disaster. Finally, the original musical quartet was over-engaged, and another had to be bought from a theater in New Orleans.

Then Lucien got a garbled message at the club that his wife, Liliana, demanded he come home, or she would divorce him! He felt harried along the way home today, as other people were looking for him with messages to go home!

"How dare she say such a thing to me?" Lucien gulped down the warm, buttered rum punch. The sweet sugar and spices warmed his soul, which had gone cold these past few months.

Liliana had proved to be a whining, weepy, and sad little woman. She was far from the sunlit fairy and coy enchantress of their courtship two and a half years before. Liliana always threatened to poison him or kill herself if Lucien did not play her way. But, of course, she was a beautiful and calculating cat and often got her way. But when pregnant, she was horrible to be around.

Thus, armed with this previous knowledge and experience of his wife's pregnant moodiness, Lucien ignored her. Instead, during the past weeks, still burdened with the tasks of the seasonal festivities, Lucien had sought other *femmes* and friends who were the carefree and delightful company needed to lighten his heart.

Today's messages only angered him—wishing never to come home or darken Liliana's bedchamber again. He mumbled a foul name for his cruel young wife and stepped away for a dance with the charming older but safe Eleanor Dumont—a judge's wife.

Lucien sometimes felt guilt for his escapades and mild infidelity. But most times, it was only to keep his spirits lightened and glean information or favors. He was, at heart, atavistic and not sorry for it. His estate and affairs were fully restored these days, better than when his father, Claude, had reigned. He wasn't afraid to work a little, currying or exchanging favors for the betterment of everyone, especially his purse.

And despite his previous feud with his elder half-brother, Maurice, they were on speaking terms. They passed along information and business contacts, helping each other to succeed. They had both agreed that if each had a fruitful life, neither man would be a burden on the other. Lucien had even considered having the fête at Maurice's club, sending some business his way. But then, selfishly, Lucien acted independently to have the party at home in Baton Rouge.

Of course, Lucien had surprised everyone tonight with the outside venue. He didn't need to burden his servants or have the house in disorderly chaos before and after the event. Nor did he want to engage his sniping and whiny wife!

Earlier, Lucien had been so busy providing the guests' needs that he had never visited his family. Such as it was. Unfortunately, nothing was in place for his too-early guests when he tardily arrived to finish setting up. However, his entourage and the team of paid workers had set up the festivities in no time. That is what money was for, wave it and get what he wanted *toute suite!* He was grateful the Grand Duke Alexis had not been one of the earliest guests!

Lucien felt as if his timing was off for several days. Plus, he felt spying eyes upon him. Today's mishaps and messages everywhere might prove him correct.

Apologizing for stepping on his partner, he finished the dance and guided the woman to her husband with a courtly sweeping bow to the pair.

Needing fresh air, Lucien hurried across the pavilion floor to the exit. His ebony curly hair fell lank and damp against his neck and face. The tent felt too warm, and he inhaled the rain-fresh air with relief. The marital noose also lessened as he left the tent, loosening the tight cravat and relieved himself.

Deep in thought, Lucien walked among the wet greenery and rose bushes near the house, slowly removing the restricting clothes of gloves and cravat, then mopped his face with a kerchief.

Of the many properties his father had owned, Lucien preferred the Bonté mansion in Baton Rouge. It had an elegant simplicity. Lucien loved his bedroom on the second floor near the sleeping porches. But as a child, he believed ghosts haunted the home. Sensing spirits from people long ago, especially some from the last war, disturbed the place. Most of the time, people living here seemed unhappy. As if there were a dark spirit looming over everyone. Or maybe, at one time, it had been his father's vengeful shadow that kept everyone fearful. Yet Lucien loved the old house despite the ghosts, dark natures, and his volatile father.

Most marriages in his recent family had been battlefields. His mother, Paulette, was a second wife and only needed to bear children and aid Claude with her wealthy familial connections. Claude Bonté, at first smitten by the lovely teen, had swept her away from family and school to make her a kept wife like Eleanor of Aquitaine.

Lucien never knew if his father ever loved his wives, but his striking handsomeness had charmed them into his bed enough times for several children each. Sometimes, the wives were invited to the theater or parties. Yet Claude was a rogue, always with an entourage of beautiful women and men about him, ready for any amusement.

It was from this type of oddness that Lucien grew up quickly. Mostly, he preferred a single life doing as he pleased. But before his father died, Lucien was betrothed to Liliana Cachet to marry when she was of age. She came to him at sixteen, and they courted for several months.

Lucien was at first pleased by his father's choice. However, Lucien immediately married the girl when she became pregnant.

But since then, Lucien felt the noose tighten, no longer free to entertain or travel around the countryside when he wanted. His last trip to France had been during his late teen years, with a year at the Sorbonne. He sorely missed the people and the connections he had made, including many of the young coquettes. Then, tragically, he returned to a war-torn city and his broken family.

Lucien had wondered if his family had a curse like the La Barres of St. Francis Ville. Longtime friends and business associates, the La Barre family, were influential in this parish and theirs. Their third sons were often incredibly talented and handsome people. But some rotten to the core of their sour apple hearts—rogues, cheats, philanderers, outlaws, or skillful gentlemen in high places who could callously steer the fates their way, no matter the cost or consequences to others.

The La Barres always hoped to break their curse, often destroying their family through recent wars and centuries. Yet a few of the La Barre men were luckier than most, having remade their fortunes, and the last generation of third sons were better men, possibly able to break the centuries-old curse.

Like the La Barre family, Lucien aspired to attain enough wealth to gain what was rightfully his without delay. So far, everything was that way. It was hard work, but the victory was solely his.

Tonight's gala proved the affair was a success despite the failures of his original plans and inept hired help. But, again, money was the answer, affording him the quaintrelle's lifestyle and appeasing his whimsical moods.

Tonight's only sadness was that he was alone, walking off nervous energy and feeling like the Sword of Damocles dangled perilously overhead. He couldn't imagine why or what he had done, that he should be punished or burdened by the frightening image.

The sounds of the party became distant as he rounded the house, then passed under the sleeping porch—a place Lucien had rarely gone since his brother Reggie died here.

He knew the secret behind the boy's death—it wasn't any sibling, but a servant paid to push the child off the porch roof. The children always sat on the railing and atop the enclosure, sometimes daring each other to climb up the pitched mansard roof to the garçonnière windows near the attic and the catwalk, but it was only for fun. After Reggie's death, the children were not allowed up there on the porches, and the catwalk along the backside of the third floor was closed.

Lucien stepped around where Reggie died, the bricks still darkened as if stained with his blood. Lucien loved Reggie, even though the boy reacted oddly and slowly. They had great fun pulling pranks. Lucien would step up for the beating, taking it for Reggie. Their father, Claude, despised the slow-witted boy, wanting to put him in an asylum, but Paulette fought for her son. For that, Lucien held more affection for his dear departed mother.

Lucien's half-brothers, Maurice and Dominic, were relentless bullies toward Reggie. They were the first accused of the child's death, but after being severely punished, a newly hired youth admitted he was paid a silver dollar to push Reggie. He would never tell who had put him in such jeopardy, but he was let go after a beating, no longer a member of the closely related servants. No one else came forward, so it was just a sad week in 1863.

Lucien often imagined his ghostly brother visiting him, but he told no one, afraid of ridicule and censure.

As Lucien walked toward the back porch of the kitchen, he continued to reminisce. This was a recent addition, as the former kitchen was a separate wooden building behind the house, but it was destroyed during the war. He could smell food and wondered what his staff was doing, for there were many voices in the brightly lit kitchen, and a pair of shadows smoked on the porch and played the concertina.

Not wishing to be seen, Lucien veered away toward the stables, a favorite spot with his horses since he was a youth. Several wagons, a coach, and a surrey were parked outside. He wondered briefly where the drivers were. Most had horses still hitched, a few were soaked from the rain, some were tied at the posts under the barn's overhanging roof, while the surrey's dappled gray gelding wore a wool blanket.

Lucien stepped quickly to pet the familiar dappled horse. "Hi, old fellow. What are you doing here tonight,

Pomme?" He stroked down the white blaze as the horse nibbled at his fingers. Lucien fumbled in his pocket for a handful of the warm, sugared almonds he had put there earlier. The horse gobbled them and nosed him for more. "Sorry, fella, *je n'en ai plus.*"

Lucien now wondered why Doctor Thomas was here. He never invited him. But then, a sudden thought came to him. *Was someone ill?* From the sounds in the kitchen, it seemed a cheerful affair.

He usually allowed his servants to have families and brief times for amusements or rest during unneeded times. He never discouraged romance among them, even though Claude had. Lucien knew Doctor Thomas's secret—the old man was enamored with Lucien's *nounou*, Berthe Deroche. Sometimes a harridan, but still a handsome woman.

While many former masters had allowed their people to breed like rabbits as an extra income to sell off those not needed, Claude had once kept a tight count on everyone, especially after the war. Some people stayed as paid servants, while many left the Bonté house and farm far behind to seek their fortunes after liberation. It was a difficult time.

By 1872, life in Baton Rouge had returned to mild prosperity and a sense of normalcy. There were no more dark times, daily war losses, extreme poverty, or lack of food and goods in Lucien's home. Life was mainly peaceful again. He was glad he'd missed most of the war since Claude sent him to family in France. But now, the Southern states were slowly recouping their massive losses, failures, and defeats. While this estate wasn't a big plantation like others along the river, it was residential for several families, especially during the war. It once was a refuge for many.

Because of Lucien's careful hand, he had put the Bonté family back on the road to success with many irons in the fire for investments and prospects. He was proud of what he had accomplished following the war and his father's death in 1867.

Lucien's attention was diverted from his musings and old Pomme.

"*Maître* Lucien! *Où êtes-vous?*" Andreas, shouting from the back gate by the house, caused Lucien some alarm.

He didn't like scenes with the hired help. And refused to yell across the property. Annoyed, Lucien stepped away from the horse, crossed the yard to the lane, and headed to the gate. Coming closer out of the darkness, Lucien startled the departing Andreas.

"What is it, Andreas?" he demanded *en Français,* for his servant spoke poor English, only conversational French, German being his native language, once enslaved to a German wine importer. Lucien knew only a handful of Germanic phrases that were rarely appropriate.

Clutching his chest, Andreas spun around, gulped, and sighed, relieved. "Oh! You frighted me, looking like... *der Geist* coming out of the dark."

"Why are you yelling for me?" Lucien stopped at the gate, the two men eye to eye in height, one very slim like a reed, in striped trousers and a long wet coat. Andreas's crème Brulé mulatto countenance was already flushed from running, his damp wavy hair askew and hanging in his face; he swept it back.

Lucien looked like the society gentleman tonight in his evening coat, dark trousers, and new white lace-edged cravat dangling from his collar, while his servant appeared sloppy and sweaty. Lucien sniffed affectedly in his perfumed handkerchief, hiding his nose from the man's sour sweat.

"Good God! Haven't you any decency or sense? You smell like horses! You'll offend the ladies looking like a ragged mess and smelling foul." He remarked unkindly in French.

"Sorry, sir. But I have been searching everywhere for you. Someone arrived and is asking for you."

"I don't care. You don't run about willy-nilly like a buffoon. Have a care, man." Lucien let out a weary exhalation. "So, who is it?"

"Sorry, but I did not get a name... only that I must find you."

"Well then, let's go. *En-y-va!*" Lucien flung a hand out, chastising the flustered servant as they walked. "I don't understand why you are flapdoodled and positively a mess. You'd think the King of France was here, or— wait—" Lucien grabbed the man's sleeve, "Is it the Duke? Oh, I hope it is Alexi... let us hurry!"

"*Non.* I don't think so. *Dies ist eine Fräulein?*" Andreas shrugged and made a face.

The pair walked swiftly to the front of the house. Lucien then spotted a black, shiny coach with a team of four tall ebony Percheron horses parked along the lane.

Lucien stopped. "*Merde! Fous!*" He drew back near the rose bushes. "You must do me a favor, Andreas."

"*Oui? Pourquoi?*" The man now peered closely at his boss. "What is it?"

"You must tell Henri that I left for the evening."

"But that is not true... your carriage is still here. Henri said that many at the party have been looking for you. Some wish to leave for the Carnivale in town."

Lucien hissed, gripping the man's sinewy arm and responding in terse French. "Tell anyone who asks, including this uninvited guest, I have been called away. Henri will know how to settle the situation. Everyone else can stay as long as they wish." Lucien swept a hand across his brow, now feeling slightly bilious. "Those staying tonight have Henri aid them. No questions... asked or answered. Understood?" The pairs of dark eyes assessed each other briefly until Andreas nodded obediently.

"*Ja. Oui. Monsieur.*"

"Go! *Maintenant!*"

Lucien turned away, striding with angry steps along the lane toward the barn again. "My God, what is she thinking, coming here? How did she ever find me? I'll thrash the idiot who told her where I live."

Arriving at the stables, Lucien seized an English saddle and neck reins. He went to the stall of his prized Arabian, Noire, stroked his long nose and released the gate. "*Viens, mon ami,*" Lucien cooed to the stallion as he quickly saddled the animal.

Lithely, he swung up onto the horse's back. Then, with a click, he urged Noire forward to the doorway. After surveying the empty yard and lane, Lucien spurred the horse to the road, urging it to fly over the closed gate, clatter quickly around and past a few wagons, and then came to a sudden stop as the black carriage swung out in front of him.

Noire reared and screamed, flailing his front hooves at one of the Percherons. The carriage horses shied, and one bucked in its harness, nearly upsetting the team and carriage. Screams came from inside the coach.

Lucien reined his animal down, more worried about harming the horses than angry about the near accident. Then, attempted to ease the agitated Percheron, coming near, grabbing its bit rein. "*Reste.* Sh-sh. Easy boy." With Lucien still gripping the bridle, the carriage horse calmed enough for the driver to move the team to the side of the lane again.

"Lucien? Is that you?"

"Damn." Lucien let go of the animal as the carriage came up even with him and stopped. He swept back the damp curls from his face. Lucien cast a look at the carriage's occupant. "*Bonsoir*, Abigale."

"I was told you were not here."

"*Oui, je partais tout juste—mais,*"

Noire shifted restlessly, stamping a foot. Lucien eased the rein, sitting back in the saddle. He still wanted to escape but must address his problem now, choosing not to lie.

"Why are you here, Mademoiselle Gagner?"

৵

"Why did you not invite me to your *fête*? I was in town and heard about it. So here I am. Maybe I should be hurt that you did not think of me." Abigale made a coy pout and fluttered her lowered eyelashes.

She found Lucien exciting, with wide-set shoulders in his sateen coat, sleek clad muscular thighs, looking virile sitting atop the powerful, prancing black Arabian. The animal was nearly as tall as her Percherons. But with the elegant slim legginess of its breed. She knew well-bred horses, and Lucien's steed was among the finest. Abigale pridefully acknowledged her team and coach cost her nearly a small kingdom!

But seeing handsome Lucien, another prized stallion, her heart beat crazily against her rigid stays as if to leap out of her chest. Abigale fanned herself suddenly as a surge of heat inflamed her cheeks.

"So, may I stay on? I am interested in your party. Rumor has it the Duke might be here. I truly want to meet him. I hear he is the most charming fellow. Do you have dancing? Because you owe me two, as I recall." She coyly fluttered her lashes again and smiled at Lucien.

She was then pleased to see the ruddy flushing of his face. Yes, he was still a playmate. Perhaps she had *un amant amusant pour la nuit*. She shivered in anticipation of Lucien's exciting lovemaking.

Abigale waited for a response, but seeing him reining in the antsy horse, she asked, "Might I at least ask for respite and hospitality for my journey here? You are not near any inns or hotels. Perhaps I could stay a night here. We could then travel together tomorrow to New Orleans. It seems... um... that I am suddenly all alone." She glanced to the side of the carriage, where a shadowy dark form slumped.

ॐ

Lucien caught the perfume that arose from Abigale. It made his nose twitch—not his most recent gift of the expensive rose oil from Provence. Whoever she came with probably was drunk and senseless. It hardened his heart, as did Abigale's wanton choice of a rhinestone-decorated emerald green costume with a plunging neckline barely covering her rosy nipples. The pink wig's tresses curled seductively about that lovely ample bosom—a veritable playground. But not his tonight.

Feeling sensibilities and anger return, Lucien replied curtly, "*Non*. You may have your coachmen tend to your team, water only, and you may use the... um, cabinet and have a refreshment. Then you must go. I must go." He reined his horse away from the coach.

"*Au revoir, mademoiselle.*" He bent his head, then spun his horse about despite Abigale's indignant shout, spurring Noire down the lane to the front gate. Half the gate opened as if by magic by the watchman as Lucien raced onto the cobblestone street.

The rain-slicked stones and large puddles of water splashed them both. Noire's hooves slid, one leg went out, and his hindquarters bunched up to stop. Lucien, unexpectedly unbalanced, was thrown over Noire's head. The panicked animal slipped and stepped on his leg, falling and rolling over Lucien.

Lucien screamed. He would later swear he heard more than his scream in that mishap. Maybe it was Noire!

Before he could move, the gateman and dog ran to him. Andreas was also there, pulling at the terrified Noire's reins, settling him away from Lucien. Winded,

Lucien looked up to see a circle of faces hovering in the
dark as a lantern held by Petit Poche came closer. The
boy's usually cherubic smiling face peered worriedly at
Lucien. "Is you hurt, Master?"

"Everyone stand back. Give the man some air." A
husky voice said as Henri appeared. The tall man kneeled
in the wetness. "Lucien, how are you? Can you walk?"

"I am... winded. How is my horse? Please make sure
he is not injured!" Lucien exhaled, groaning and trying to
rise. Finally, he sat up, aided by Henri's firm grip. "Noire
stepped on my leg and rolled on me. I can barely move."
He admitted quietly through gritted teeth. He did not
want to confess an infirmity, certainly not in front of so
many servants, and now it seemed he was a side-show
spectacle! Lying on the wet ground, Lucien spotted many
colorful silk skirts and polished shoes among the
onlookers. "Damn."

"Poche! Set down the lantern, then get Doctor
Thomas," Henri ordered the child and smiled to see him
obey, enthusiastically jackrabbit dodging through the
crowd.

Lucien's brow wrinkled, "The doctor is still here? So
what is the problem? Is someone ill?"

Henri did not answer, still supporting Lucien's
shoulders. He grimaced to see Abigale running and
pushing her way through the crowd at the gate. "Prepare
yourself—" he began as the woman shrieked and ran into
the street.

"Oh, please, God, not her!" Lucien grumbled, swiftly
smothered in the woman's damp bosom amid tears and
the irritating perfume.

"*Mon Dieu!* What has happened? *Ma pauvre p'tit,*" she
petted and smoothed the tousled hair from Lucien's brow,
wailing endearments and unrealized fears between kisses.

Lucien caught her hand as she stroked his face. "I will
live. I am fine. *Laisse-moi!*" He struggled to move out of
her embrace. "Please, Abigale... no hysterics."

She began shouting for blankets and people to carry
Lucien to her coach. Her coachman would drive them to
l'hôpital.

Lucien felt his loss controlling the situation as others
bent to him, offering flasks or kerchiefs. Then, some

guests just patted his head in sympathetic concern. He despised this unsolicited attention.

Gripping Henri's muscled arm, *"Aide-moi,"* Lucien growled and pulled himself to his feet. The man supported him with muscles like an oak limb. Lucien let out a labored breath, glad to be upright and ready to move beyond the crowd. His pride now hurt more than his physical infirmity. He had no experience of being thrown by a horse. His horses were well-trained, as was he. Even as a lad, he had held a firm seat upon any animal.

"But, my love," Abigale rose to her feet with assistance and again fell against Lucien. "Please, you need attention. Look, you are bleeding."

Just then, Dr. Thomas came through the crowd carrying his medical case. He critically eyed Lucien and gently shoved Abigale away from his patient, taking Lucien's other arm. "Please, madame, he is my patient. Henri and I will attend to Lucien."

Abigale flapped a handkerchief and wiped her tears dramatically. "Please, you must save him! I love this man!"

Lucien cringed with that testament and the pain in his leg and back as he limped toward his house. The slight incline of the driveway was already almost too much to bear. But he stoically and bravely kept staggering with Henri and Victor.

"Merci. I might have died of embarrassment if you had not come. That woman is a lovely menace and worse than my wife!"

After assessing his patient's labored movement, Victor chuckled at Lucien's jest. "Yes, she seems rather overwrought by your mishap."

The crowd was noisy, people watching their downed host's progress and the wailing Abigale's theatrics in their wake. Lucien worked hard to adjust his gait, hurrying across the front yard and to the steps. Unfortunately, the jarring pain and his wounded leg undid his efforts. He stumbled and fell to his knees on the second step. Audible gasps and groans echoed among the party crowded about him.

Abigale was the worst, screeching, *"Mon Dieu!* Look, he is like Christ! Someone help him!"

Another man surged forward to aid the doctor and Henri, but Lucien held his hand up. "No! I am fine." He crawled to his feet, wavering, then gripped Henri, who hustled him quickly onto the porch and into the house.

He heard Abigale bawling again at the doorway. Then, with Doctor Vincent's surly growl, the traitor relented, allowing her passage into the foyer.

Lucien was nearest the parlor, the divan his target, when Abigale suddenly flung herself at him. He clumsily made the final steps using her as a crutch and fell on the velvety soft cushion with the woman under his arm.

She wrestled herself from his grip to sit beside Lucien. Concern in her watery dark eyes and ruddy and tear-damp face ruined the artfully painted cosmetics. She swiped his face with her wet kerchief, but Lucien shied away, catching her hand.

"Please, Abigale. Stop. You need to go now." He glanced around the room, noticing a few decorated candelabras illuminating the space, some furniture removed, and a few small tables set with food and drink. One lonely candelabra sat on the shiny ebony piano, its reflections almost ghostly in the dim light.

"But I can help you, my love." Abigale insisted, kissing his cheek and then sliding her mouth over his.

Lucien was used to Abigale's many kisses, but this one felt sincere, and his body betrayed him despite his infirmity. But he broke away from the kiss and the overly emotional woman. "You are in my home. You know I am married." He hissed and tried to grip her hands as Abigale began fussing with his shirt studs.

"It does not matter. You are mine since the very first moment I met you." She breathed passionately, sliding over to embrace Lucien again.

"How nice. But I know you for the temptress you are. Lovely, but not mine. I have a wife." Lucien moved to get up but fell backward, unable to find balance or strength.

Dr. Thomas stepped over quickly. "Yes, Madame, please return to the party. I must attend to my patient. Look, he has already soiled the upholstery with his blood."

Lucien caught the eye of Henri and then the lurking Esmeralda. Lucien's ire flamed. The rumors would spread like vitreous oil among the servants.

With a heavy sigh, Lucien pled, "Abigale, please take something to eat and drink, then go home. Or return to wherever you are staying. Farewell, Abigale." Lucien pulled out of her arms and stood. He was unsteady; spinning darkness swirled around his eyes, bilious in his belly, with a sharp darting pain from his back up to his head. Then Lucien swooned, falling onto the Chinese carpet.

Henri took charge then, picking up Abigale, carrying her outside, and dropping her in a heap on the flagstone walkway.

She shrieked in indignation. Then, catching the eyes of nearby guests, Abigale put a hand to her head and 'fainted.'

Henri pointed to her, "Andreas, put that one in her coach and get her out of here!" He colored ruddily, noting the other guests to say haughtily, "Imagine making a fool of herself like a common whore after too much champagne." Then, amid nods and whispers, Henri returned to the house, locking every door behind him.

"The trash is removed," Henri said, dusting off his hands with a smirk. He found Lucien was awake and lying with a comforter on the chaise. His left leg was propped on pillows, with his trouser leg cut away.

Doctor Thomas glanced at the tall man to demand, "I need more light, bandages, and whiskey."

Henri hesitated only a second. "For you or the patient?"

Victor's laugh was brittle as he said, "All of us could use some." He rummaged in his case, removing a cloth bag and a tiny indigo-tinted bottle. "Get me a teapot of boiling water, some rope, and more people to hold Lucien. *Vite!*"

Henri noted the groan and twist of Lucien's face, already in pain from the doctor's examination. "*Oui!*" He spun away, then nearly ran down his wife in the hallway to the kitchen. "Esme, please, I must—" he set her aside and passed into the kitchen. The swinging door almost hit her in the face.

"What happened to Lucien?" Esmeralda asked, doing a side-stepping dance with her husband as he searched the kitchen for needed items.

"An uninvited tart showed up. Lucien, in trying to get away, was injured." Henri slammed the cabinet doors and pulled open the pantry door. "Where is the good whiskey? I need a lot."

Esmeralda quickly set up a tray with the items she heard Vincent needed, even offering a hank of clothesline. "You look awful, and your shirt is soiled with blood. Is Lucien badly hurt?"

"I am unsure. Lucien's horse threw him in the street. You might ask the girls to bring him fresh clothes, a nightshirt, or a robe. I don't know if he can be moved upstairs. Lucien might stay in the parlor for a time."

Henri suddenly gripped his wife's hand. "Thank you, my bride. You are the best wife I have ever had. I love you more than anyone could do." He kissed her forehead, then picked up the tray, quickly elbowing open the door.

"I am the only wife you will ever have. I love you the same, my Hercules!" Esmeralda called him his former slave name, finding it still fit. She felt her heart rushing at the acclamation, for Henri was suddenly a romantic lover tonight. She watched him stride down the dark hallway, his white shirt sleeves billowing in his wake like a ship's sails on the high seas.

Then Esmeralda caught her reflection in the glass doors of the entrance to the dining room. Her cheeks flushed, hair frowsy in braids and ribbons, and the robe caressed her ample bosom. She felt pretty, like a new bride.

It was a good thing she had stayed tonight, intuitively expectant that she and a few girls would be needed for the guests who had yet to come inside. She glanced at the clock in the hallway, chiming for midnight. She held her breath, counting the bells, then relieved, Esmeralda returned to the kitchen.

A new day. Finally, things could be routine once more. Perhaps all that had happened so far tonight was her prescient dream. She still heard music and loud laughing from the yard despite the troubles. She hoped everyone would leave soon so the mansion's occupants could have peace again.

Now Lucien was bellowing in pain. But, no, the new day was arriving just as sad.

Esmeralda had heard rumors of Liliana having hysterical tirades and rants earlier in the evening. The young woman could not rest, pacing her room until near exhaustion. Yet Liliana once called for her maid to dress her to attend the party she heard outside. Then, angry that she knew nothing of it, she repeatedly asked someone to fetch her husband.

In a rare moment, Berthe had lied, saying Lucien did not come; the party was held by others for his guests. Then, with Doctor Vincent's dose of laudanum, Liliana finally slept.

Esme was also worried about the new baby and little Randolfe. The children were cared for by a wet nurse, Hilde, Berthe, and a maid. Liliana seemed so forlorn, with no want of her children in the last days, only crying for Lucien. Doctor Thomas said the poor woman was near apoplexy and suggested only bedrest.

Esme hoped that life here would be better again.

☙

Chapter 5—La Femme

The party was outside, not in the house, and the night seemed endless as Liliana restlessly tossed in bed. Her eyes were gritty from tears and sleep. She wanted peace and an end to the pounding war drums in her head.

It felt like years since she had been to a party or any event where she could be gaily dancing and charming her way about the room. She yearned to be part of the festivities. But she was a prisoner here.

Pressing hands to her still swollen abdomen, she felt emptiness, then recalled the painful days of giving birth to her son. *What happened to him? Where is he?*

As if in a dream, Liliana recalled people saying that she and the baby had died. But that could not be true, for she had breath... ached in every part of her being. She smelled the mint and lavender oil compresses and the strong cup of tea that had tasted bitter. *Did ghosts experience such things?*

If she was a ghost, she could go to the party, sliding in like a wisp of mist among the guests. Liliana wished she could hear what others might say of her. *Especially if she was dead!*

Her anger smoldered anew, recalling asking the maids to help her dress for the party. A burgundy-red brocade dress lay like something freshly killed across a chair and on the floor. Several pairs of dancing slippers littered the room. Yet she was still in her sweat-damp night-rail.

Liliana barely recalled holding her baby. She had cooed and sang a made-up lullaby while it screeched like a demon. Then, finally, Berthe took the child to the wet nurse, Hilde. At that thought, Liliana realized her breasts were leaking, the wetness soaked through the thin batiste fabric, darkening the bodice.

"Where is my baby? If someone has killed him, what use is it for me to live?" She sobbed again, "My husband is absent. I haven't seen him in a month. My Randolfe won't suckle and only screams when he sees me." She hiccupped amid the wailing. Then, trying to breathe, she stepped to the window and struggled to open it. She threw up the sash and inhaled the dewy, fresh night air, helping to clear her mind.

According to the clock on the mantle, it was well after midnight, yet festivities were still in the yard. People in brightly colored garb and jeweled masks idled among the red and gold-striped illuminated tents. They were like circus tents she once saw as a child. She wondered if Lucien had hired a circus to entertain her and the guests. Maybe he was elated by the news of their new child, and this was the celebration! She listened to the gay music, the singing, and the friendly laughter, wishing to be among the guests. Then she had an excellent idea!

Liliana spun around, opened her door, listened, and escaped her room. She padded quietly across the dark polished oak floors to the nursery. It was unlocked, so she crept in. The wet nurse was snoring in her cot in the small alcove of the room; the white cotton curtain partially hid her. Liliana noiselessly stepped to the large crib, spotting Randolfe.

He was a beautiful boy; dark curls graced his brow, and his chubby thumb was in his mouth. His round bottom was in the air with his legs bunched up. His bare toes were like white corn kernels, round and sweet. Liliana wanted to tickle them or pinch his dimpled, rosy cheeks. But she didn't want to wake him.

How long had it been since I held Randolfe? He had grown so much in the last few months. *Had I really been in bed that long, ill with my pregnancy?* She kissed his head and gently pulled the blanket over him. The toddler didn't stir.

Spying the lace and voile-covered bassinet, Liliana sped to it, moving the drape away. She beheld her infant. Again, another dark, curly-haired child, like Lucien. He lay with his tiny fingers gripping a brown wooly dog. His rosebud mouth slack in sleep.

"Ah, Tou-Tou, I have missed you!" She whispered, stroking the old toy, then gently pulling the blanket away. She had yet to see her baby since he was born. *Did he have the correct number of digits, arms, and legs? Did he have any birthmarks?*

Randolfe shared a small strawberry mark on his shoulder, like hers, something she shared with many of her Barre relatives, including her mother. She suddenly felt the ghosting of Lucien's lips on her birthmark and shivered despite the warmth of the bedroom and the smoldering fireplace.

She unwrapped the swaddling clothes and felt his bottom—it was wet. She removed his nightdress, took a cloth from his layette, and cleaned the infant's chubby body. For a newborn, he was a large baby with long limbs, a stout chest, and a strong neck. He lazily rootled along her neck and chest, and Liliana gave him a nipple. Her heart pounded as he latched on. Like a heated tidal wave, her milk let down as the infant suckled hard. It was a strange sensation, painful at first, then warm joy. Similar to making love for the first time.

At least Lucien had been kind and gentle for the first time. Liliana had heard the servants speak of such things and feared the act. But Lucien had calmed her "unrealized fears" and made her feel good, sore but satisfied. Lucien could be a wondrous lover when he chose. But he was a typical man, ready for rutting like an animal, usually not caring if she had pleasure. Sometimes, making love was a duty to submit to him. Occasionally, he would woo her, bribe her with promises, sugared almonds, or champagne, and soon Liliana succumbed.

She was never prepared for being a wife. She had no mother as an adolescent other than the negro nannies. As a youth, Liliana was of delicate health, often cosseted and doted upon. Her father, Girard, was mostly absent from her childhood until she was old enough to marry. A dreamer, Liliana was glad to leave her sad home and childhood behind.

The recent war had taken much from them, including Liliana's mother, who died of typhoid, and most of her older brothers, who died in battle somewhere far away. As a result, Liliana spent most of her childhood hidden, hungry, and desperately seeking any form of joy, food, or companionship. Thus, marrying Lucien, she had hoped for a lifetime friend and lover and a perfect life free from care.

Perhaps she was unlucky. Liliana knew the La Barre prophecy and omens; she was a second cousin, and her mother, Alice, was a former La Barre cousin. At least her father wasn't one of those ill-fated third sons. He was from the honorable Cachet family, which had cultivated a judge, senator, and ambassador who were part of her father's lineage. Girard Cachet had been a solicitor and was well-liked. But that did not mean fortune had shone upon them during the war.

Losing almost everything they had, she had been foisted upon the La Barre family, living on their immense river plantation. Although it was only moderately better there, the war affected the family and farm. But at least there was food and other children, and many women hid there. The eligible and able La Barre men, including the younger enslaved men, had gone to fight, leaving their families behind. So, for a time, she enjoyed the company of women and playmates and a few doddering old gents offering a penny for a dance or Liliana's kiss.

Shaking away the old lineages and sad life, she gazed upon her new son. "You are handsome, like your father. Damn him. But I promise you will be lucky!" She shifted the infant to her other breast, taking up a blanket to wrap about his relaxed body. "I shall protect you. Lucien can have Randolfe, and you will be mine. If Lucien continues to ignore me, you and I will run away. *Oui, ma petit homme. Mais oui.*"

Humming another silly lullaby, she stepped to the windows, wishing she could hear the music from up here at the side of the house. Liliana treaded quietly out the door, "We shall go see the stars, *mon enfant.*"

Filled with happiness, like a curious child, Liliana unlocked the French doors, went up the staircase, then stepped out to the catwalk that encircled the top floor with a short stairway to the crow's nest walkway above the attic.

The stars were elusive, partially hidden by the clouds. Everything was wet and dripping from the rain hours ago. The walkway planks were slick and cold as Liliana walked carefully barefoot. She shivered slightly in the chilly wind that swirled about the attic rooftop and the Garçonnière windows. The clouds hung so low she yearned to touch them. Liliana hummed the song playing below—a fun reel she would eagerly dance with Lucien.

She envisioned herself in the burgundy ball gown, the tiered skirts, and lacy petticoats flying, twirling about with Lucien. Despite his complaints about the silliness of such past times, he was an excellent dancer. She recalled several gay evenings, spinning about in his arms despite his sour attitude.

She spun, too, holding her son to her chest, feeling his warmth and lips upon her breast. Liliana inhaled the many night scents: blooming roses, freshly mown grass, budding apple blossoms, new leaves on the sassafras trees, and sharply scented bark—everything seemed enticing. She loved the herby sassafras filet seasoning for shrimp or crawfish gumbo, something she ate while living with the La Barres, for they had access to such things along the river and bayous.

Here in town, she ate eggs fifty ways to dullness. Their cook, Esmeralda, was capable and resourceful. Still, Liliana wished for other foods, not bland broths, egg custards or puddings, or overly cooked fowl with soggy vegetables, everything supposedly to keep her healthy while pregnant.

She yearned for garlic-buttered prawns and escargot like she ate in the fine restaurant in New Orleans that Lucien had taken her to on their honeymoon. Or the spicy andouille sausage the La Barres made! The newlyweds had a steamboat cruise up the Mississippi River—enjoying morning café and buttery croissants, the days napping, reading, making love; then the fresh fish dinners and wine, the nights of dancing, and Lucien at the card tables. Her husband was primarily lucky.

She didn't stay long at the game tables, finding it boring to watch the players, but she knew when Lucien had a good night. With his face radiant, Lucien would then make happy and tender love with her. But if it was a rough night, he might stay sullen and pace in the outer stateroom if he lost more than he could afford. Then, sneak in to make wildly fierce and painful, passionate love. Shocked by the difference in his temperament, Liliana asked Lucien to be gentle, not caring for the bruises or aching in her womanly parts. Even in the early days of their marriage, Lucien was both angel and demon in her bed.

But it had been many months since he had been in their bed. Now that the baby was born, perhaps her husband would return. She missed his warm, sleek, muscled body, smooth to the touch, like a panther—and a sin to enjoy. She flushed hotly, thinking of her husband.

But wasn't it Liliana's married right to enjoy him as much as he might take his pleasures of her body?

In confession, she had once asked the priest something like that. The poor man was near apoplexy, then coughing and sputtering so much that she left the sequestered curtained cubicle and ran from the church. She once had sinfully enjoyed reading the Songs of Solomon. The poetic words enticed lovers, and she learned to be her husband's joy and blessing.

Adam and Eve were made for each other by God's design. And if love were not a unique emotion, why did God make some people so beautiful or handsome to beguile the senses and make one fall in love? She loved Lucien beyond measure. But she did not care for his callousness and recent neglect.

Amid the cheerful music, she heard shouting from below and stepped to the banister to see an altercation. Several men were pushing and wrestling with each other. "Probably drunken louts," Liliana surmised, but she recognized Henri and Andreas among them.

Both servants, formerly enslaved people, were attempting to separate the fighters. They were tall and strong. She knew Esmeralda was especially endeared with her handsome husband, Henri.

But Liliana had recalled the stories of Henri whipped and beaten by Lucien's father for a slight mistake. And she had seen flogging at the La Barre plantation. Except those cruel men were a ragtag squad of Confederate rebels, who dragged all the enslaved men from the house and fields and beat them so they wouldn't run away. The women and other servants were made to watch it all. Two elderly men and a boy died that day. Liliana still had *cauchemars* of their agonized screams and the bloody wounds.

So when Liliana married into the Bonté family, she made Lucien promise not to beat their servants or ex-slaves. However, Liliana wasn't above rebukes or throwing something at the girls, who sometimes behaved stupidly. But that was all moot these days. She attributed her embittered moods and dreary thoughts to the recent lonely bedbound prison.

Liliana would change her fate and be happy again. Holding the baby upright, she crooned, "*Regard les étoiles, mon fils. Liberté!*" Liliana studied the night sky, looking for her favorite stars, but many were hidden by the clouds. A chill wind whipped around the catwalk, catching her gown and ripping at her hair, pulling some tresses loose from their braids and hair combs. She felt free of a sudden.

"It is just you and I, my son." She cried into his scrunched-up face. The baby let out a howl and flailed his fists, unhappy to lose succor.

Then she heard a woman's shrill voice above the child's wail, men shouting amid the distant music.

"Let me in! If Lucien is dying, then I must be at his side! I love him! I shall die with him!"

"What nastiness is this? Who is that?" Liliana leaned over the rail, clutching the screaming infant to her breast again, nearly crushing him. The shouting continued, but the wind snatched away the words.

In a gaudy emerald green dress, a woman fought with the men in the crowd. It was becoming quite a brouhaha down there. But all the while, the horrible woman kept screaming for Lucien.

Liliana was no longer amused. She shouted at the woman, "You! Tawdry peacock! Who are you? How dare you talk about my husband that way? *Chienne!* He is mine!" She shrieked.

Several people looked about, then up to see a woman in a white nightdress screaming at them from the attic catwalk. An infant also wailed in her arms. A hush came over the crowd. Then Liliana heard another commotion, and Henri ran to aid someone.

The woman broke away and fell upon the new man. He clutched her but looked sick and seemed to shrink from the woman's endearments of kissing and pawing at him.

Liliana witnessed the woman kissing the man as if her life depended on the act. Then, the man set her aside slightly, using her and Henri as a crutch to walk across the lawn. He limped and seemed frail. But then he looked upward when he brushed the tousled hair from his face.

Liliana's dark eyes met the fevered ones of Lucien. At that moment, she felt betrayed, now sickened by the passionate scene below.

"You traitorous, lying snake! You fiend... and spawn of the devil!" Liliana screamed *en Français* until her throat was raw. "Look at me... I have born you a son, and you have another woman now? *Cochon!*" She held up the infant above the rail. "I will dash both our brains upon the stones!"

The crowd below had increased in just the minutes since the fight began. An audible gasp rose to Liliana, with people shouting for her to jump or come down.

Her breath came in labored spurts, joining her child in sobbing. "*Mon enfant, je t'aime.*" She climbed up on the balustrade, her toes gripping the damp wood and iron railing.

People in the crowd below shouted in unison now, "*Non!*" Several crossed themselves.

Liliana searched for Lucien; his face shimmered in the lamp and torchlight as he called up to her.

"Liliana, don't be a fool. Come down from there!" Meanwhile, the woman in green clung to him.

"You cannot tell me what to do anymore! I am not your slave!" Liliana yelled hoarsely. She saw Berthe run from the porch and join the crowd with Henri. She waved at the old *nounou*, "I am free now, Berthe!" Then, holding the baby close in one arm against her chest, she sang to him, "*Ah, mon enfant qui es en mes bras, ah, mon p'tit biquet que je t'adore... Dors, dors...*"

A rough wind gusted about her, inflated the nightdress, and whipped her hair about her head like a cyclone. Liliana was over-balanced with one arm held out; she then slipped, pitching over the balustrade, hitting the third and second stories' roofs and eaves, bouncing and plummeting straight into the crowd.

Lucien barely moved away in time, but Abigale and others were struck and lying beneath his wife. He moved painfully, stepping and stumbling over the inert bodies to his wife.

"Why?" His voice was ragged with tears as he held her head—the beautiful tresses were soaked in blood. He smoothed away the blood from her face and kissed her. "What have you done, my love?"

One eye fluttered open. "You betrayed me, Lucien. I should kill you now." Liliana gasped.

"You almost killed me! I am glad I moved away!"

"I wanted to... Devil. I should have... never... married you." She took in a labored breath. Her eyes moved over

Lucien's face. "You were my dream... my angel, but it is all a lie. I will die today... and so does your son."

Liliana whispered against his cheek, "Meet your son... Jericho... my last battle—" Liliana was shifted to pull out bodies from beneath hers.

Her breathing became erratic, her eyes rolled and closed, then Lucien's fierce grip awoke Liliana until she cried out, "... never forgive you. I wish I had... never... met you. *Je te verrai en enfer, Lucien.* We are doomed to Hell."

Lucien, sobbing now, no longer caring about the display of emotions, mumbled, "But you are my wife... my life!" Then, he shouted, "How can you be so profane? I gave you everything. Now you will die unshriven. I will never live long enough to forgive or pray for your soul from purgatory... or my child's soul." Again, Lucien wept into Liliana's hair.

Chapter 6—Mourir

Doctor Thomas stumbled through the mass of people and then shifted Lucien aside from his wife. He tugged at the rumpled, bloodstained batiste nightgown, listened against Liliana's chest, looked into her mouth, and opened her eyes. He saw the bloodied infant held in her arm and hidden in the stained, belled sleeve.

"*Mon Dieu! Pauvre enfant*, I tried to save you only a few days ago! Damn! *Quel dommage*." He wrangled the infant away from the tight fingers of Liliana, then held him out to Lucien, "*Monsieur, je regrette... regardez votre fils... il est mort*." The doctor sobbed briefly as the child whimpered, and then a tiny chubby hand gripped Lucien's finger.

"He lives?" Lucien fell back onto the damp lawn, clutching his baby boy.

"It seems so, but I am sorry, his mother... *elle est mort*. Broken beyond repair."

"*Docteur!* Berthe ..."

The doctor rose to his feet and surveyed the crowd. "Where is Berthe?" Panting as he pushed away a few gawkers to see Henri and Andreas crying over an inert twisted body in a familiar black bombazine dress.

Vincent sped to them and kneeled on the wet grass. He gripped Berthe's wrist with shaking hands, then searched for a pulse at her throat. "What happened?" he demanded in a choked voice.

"Liliana fell on her. Berthe must have hit her head upon the flagstones," Andreas suggested.

"But she is on the grass. Surely it would not—"

"No, we moved her from the walkway," Andreas replied.

Vincent noted wet blood on her skirt. He raised the petticoats to peek and saw Berthe's foot and leg turned at a gruesome angle; the bones protruded like blood-blackened pickets, and her unnaturally bent spine and broken neck resembled a shattered porcelain doll. He gripped Berthe's still-warm hand and wept. "*Ma... Coeur*."

Andreas asked, "What of Liliana and the babe?"

"The mother is dead now... but how she could speak with half her brain exposed and a broken body, I don't know." Doctor Thomas wiped his eyes and nose on his handkerchief and said in a stronger voice, "The baby somehow is alive. Liliana must have cushioned the fall."

The two servants looked toward Lucien, rocking with the baby and weeping. They both knew the pain of his surgery earlier and now the death blows that struck the Bonté family perhaps had unhinged the man.

Lucien suddenly recoiled as a tall, handsome man bent over him in a gray evening suit. A loud exchange of profanity and weeping then ensued.

"*Ma cousine! Liliana! Pauvre belle.* You... rapscallion... parsimonious... philandering pig! You killed her!" The man sprang upon Lucien, then clouted him repeatedly on the head and shoulders with his walking stick's silver knob. Lucien then clumsily scrambled to one knee, still clutching the infant.

"How are you here? I never invited you, Carl!" Lucien held up an arm to fend off the attack. Then, turning his back to the man, he yelled, "Watch out! I have my newborn son here! *Votre cousin!*"

The men grappled over the child, with Carl wresting the squalling babe from Lucien. He then kicked his opponent in the upper thigh. Already wounded, Lucien fell and gasped in pain, subsiding in the wet grass.

Now concerned for his patient, Dr. Thomas stopped his weeping vigil over Berthe, trotted to Lucien, and put a restraining hand on the other man.

"You two men are hot-headed bulls! You should only fight in an arena with a matador!" he grumbled. But saw Lucien grit his teeth against a reply and the quick kick to his ribs from Carl Barre's polished boot.

"Enough! Can you not see Lucien is already wounded? Nothing you do will bring back your *petite cousine*, Liliana. Lucien is not to blame. Liliana took her own life."

Lucien rolled on the ground in pain. Then, shouted as Carl aimed another kick, "Enough! You win nothing by your assault!"

Carl Barre sheltered the baby in his arms. "I warned Liliana, like many others, including your father, that your marriage would fail—you would end up killing each other!"

"Ha! As if your marriage is so perfect. Yes, I know you have been with other women, too, so your self-righteous snit now is uncalled for. But, do you not see I am crushed by my wife's death? She nearly killed my newborn son in her distraught condition. As for us, we were happy enough! I loved my wife." Lucien wiped away tears.

Then, he growled in pain as Henri and Doctor Thomas pulled him to his feet. Supporting his body between them, Lucien continued. "Come, cousin, we have never had such animosity between us. Let us settle this inside."

"Cousin? Cousin! You are no longer related to us. It was only Liliana that brought our two families together again!"

Lucien ignored the milling spectators as he stumbled across the lawn to the veranda steps. He bravely spoke, "And for almost a century, our families have been friends and business partners, haven't we? But regrettably, my father, Claude, wrecked that partnership. But I have been honest with you and fair, and we have both prospered in recent years. Yes?"

Carl Barre's silver-edged mustache twitched as he wiped the tears from his cheeks. He shifted the baby in his arms. "Now, I suppose, we are related again through Liliana's children. Yes? Perhaps for this tiny babe... I might find some—" Carl paused, then looking at the dispersing crowd and the blanket-covered bodies being carried away, he snidely remarked, "It looks like you lost your paramour, too."

Lucien, grunting at his efforts, stopped near the steps. "What paramour? I had no such thing. You know me, everything is purely business."

"Abigale Gagner? You did not have carnal pleasures with *La Dame du nuit*? *La temptresse d' Orleans?*" He laughed. "You are a stronger man than I if you did not!" He passed the wailing infant to a maid from the house. "See to this wet fellow at once."

Lucien observed the young maid rushing into the house. Then, soured by Carl's remark, he spat, "*Tais-toi.* I do not wish to have my dirty laundry aired in public." Lucien hissed as he painfully moved up the steps with Henri and heard his name. He irritably looked about, grumbling, "What more will occur tonight?" then he blanched.

An ornately decorated page in deep purple velvet rushed up to the men, speaking rapidly in French,

"*Monsieur Bonté!* One moment, please, someone wishes to speak to you." The stout man looked away, then smiled, "May I present his excellency, the Grand Duke Alexei Alexandrovich Romanov." The man bowed low as an entourage, and an imposing young man marched through the crowd like the Red Sea parting for Moses.

The twenty-one-year-old Duke clad in a double-breasted coat with velvet lapels stepped forward nearer Lucien and his servants. His long, ruddy-cheeked face, wispy mustache, and high, broad forehead bespoke his young noble heritage. He commented softly in French, "Thank you, Lucien, for the impressive and passionate mystery play. It was quite convincing. I should like to meet the actress... she is exquisite." He gave an imperious nod and semblance of a wink.

Stunned that the Duke was here, Lucien suddenly erupted in tears. "That was not a play. It was my wife."

"Oh, so talented. *Trés amusant et ravissante, vous-êtes un homme chanceux. Bonsoir.*" Smiling, the duke came even with his page, murmuring in Russian, then amid his group, headed toward a carriage, his hand lifted in a half-hearted wave to the crowd.

The page turned to Lucien, "His Excellency would invite the ravishing actress and you, the lucky husband, to dine with him tomorrow at noon at the St. Charles Hotel." The man tipped his cap and then trotted away to climb into the carriage. The driver flicked the whip, and the impressive black horses trotted away.

Going into the house, Lucien again fell upon the divan amid the flustered servants, Henri and Andreas, Doctor Thomas, and Carl Barre. He laughed at their administrations of blankets, pillows, and cognac.

He shook his hand, shying away from the hot tea and the dripping, soapy towel Esmeralda produced.

"Please! Let me alone for just a minute. I need to breathe and think!"

He heard the other servants' whispered comments, some about his dead wife and more in awe of the Grand Duke. Somewhere upstairs, his son yowled like a scalded cat.

Carl Barre sat in a nearby chair. "So that was the Grand Duke from Russia? He looks like a puffed-up young popinjay. Hmm, I finally met someone famous then. Or does he have a doppelgänger for events like this? I heard many monarchs and nobles do that—protection from the crazed masses."

Lucien lay back with a sigh. "No, that was Alexi. I met him yesterday. Was it only yesterday that I met him at the reception? The Duke was supposed to have dined with General Custer and his wife, then see *Il Trovatore* with them tonight... no, last night, Lundi Gras. That was why I doubted Alexi would be here. It is also why I was so late in getting home yesterday."

Lucien took a fortifying sip of the cognac that Henri held and continued, "Every street yesterday was crowded or closed for Alexi's parade and all the pomp and folderol of his tour and visit to New Orleans. Tomorrow will be no better—probably worse, as the Duke has a procession in the carnival parade. Why do you think everyone wore his royal colors? Gosh-awful green and gold... and some fool added the royal purple. *Mon Dieu!*"

Lucien then accepted the refilled glass of cognac, joining Carl and the men. "Here's to another year of lunacy!" He gulped the drink, letting it course down his throat and heat his belly. "I am angry. I am among the wounded now. I need to be at the Carnival later today because I cannot miss the Duke in the parade; he is expecting me." Lucien worried.

"Is no one to say anything of the Duke's remarks regarding your wife?" Henri asked quietly, shocking everyone.

"Why bother? Liliana... is gone." Lucien coughed and tearfully said, "Someone, please put my wife in the front room dressed in her finest gown. So we shall have her wake. I do not care if we cannot get the priest here; she will be blessed nonetheless." He wept, then suddenly said, "Where is my son? Where is my nounou? My Berthe must care for him now."

Esmeralda howled, flinging her shawl over her head, and ran from the parlor.

Dr. Thomas coughed and said tearfully, "Berthe is dead."

"How? Who killed her?" Lucien rose partially upon an elbow, clenching a fist. "I'll have their skin!"

"Liliana killed her... fell on her the same as Abigale. All three died. You are lucky to still have your new son."

Dr. Thomas replied harshly. "About that, congratulations, you are a papa again."

Lucien subsided into fractured sobs, taking a cognac now laced with laudanum.

Peaceful oblivion came in the early hours of the morning. But as dawn came, so did the realization that Lucien was alone, a father with two infant sons, no nounou, no wife, or an amusing lover.

Epilogue—Then

Because of the injury, the scandal of his wife's death, and perhaps inspired by the affairs of the heart with Abigale, Lucien Bonté never made it to the Mardi Gras celebrations in New Orleans. Thus, Lucien would be absent from those craze-filled festivities for many years.

Within a few days after his wife's private funeral, he took his family and left on a train to Atlanta for business. After a few weeks, he took another train to Savannah, then took passage on a steamship to New York and another to Europe. It was his first oceanic trip in many years since his school days. He had two infant boys in tow, the wet nurse, Hilde, and an older governess to care for the children and him as he convalesced while crossing the Atlantic.

Lucien dealt with his businesses from afar. It was easier not to speak with particular associates, such as anyone in the La Barre family, especially that hypocrite, Carl. Liliana's cousins were still aggrieved by her demise. Telegrams and letters were the best communiques, less likely to cause a brawl, and easier to toss angry, spiteful correspondence into the fire!

Despite his children's familial association with the infamous La Barre family and their notable curse, Lucien vowed to raise them as his own, taking a new name while in France, Luc Rene Boulanger. Only long-time friends or associates knew his real name. His estate in Baton Rouge was closed. Primarily leaving Henri and Esmeralda as caretakers for the family and hosting occasional travelers. He didn't want to call it a boarding house or hotel, but his home was at least in good care. He sold the last of his father's homes in New Orleans, Shreveport, and Atlanta to finance his European trip and new life, also setting aside a hefty sum for his sons. He never liked those homes, which only brought up bad memories of his misguided and insane father.

His sons were dear to Lucien as he recovered from his injuries and heartache. Jericho (renamed Josef-Paul) and Randolfe soon became pleasant children, offering a little sunshine in Lucien's bleak life. Neither talked of their mother, as Lucien forbade it. Only Hilde knew Liliana. She was gone once the boys were weaned and four years of age. Lucien was kind, sending the young woman back to America with a new family bound for Canada.

Lucien would stay for many years in Europe, his heart no longer interested in the flagrant pastimes of his youth, nor did he appreciate the solitude without a wife, yet he enjoyed the freedom. But he kept himself on guard to affairs of the heart, never being close enough to another woman for him to want her or someone to love him.

He silently bore three lifetimes of guilt upon his soul: missing his nounou, Berthe, the only mother he truly knew. Then, yearning for the gamine loveliness and charms of Liliana Cachet, his depraved wife. Last, Lucien did not miss Abigale. He discovered too late that she was a greedy harpy in disguise, and his relationship with Abigale was scandalous.

Lucien's new goals were freedom and successful business endeavors, and he would teach his sons the same.

Many years later, he would finally return to Baton Rouge, a changed man, once again claiming his home and locally owned businesses for his sons.

Randolfe, his first son, took the *épicerie*—a French imports store and grocery once established by Lucien's grandfather. Lucien allowed his other son, Josef-Paul, to manage new real estate and collective investments and work in a bank. Lucien was the ultimate mentor for the boys, loving them both but a discerning and hard taskmaster as the youths grew up. Before he knew it, the young men were part of the Baton Rouge 'ton' and desirable young bachelors.

Weighed down by his guilt for the death of his wife and two other women, Lucien did not age well. Often drinking to excess, smoking opium, or taking laudanum for his pain and sleeplessness. Lucien was constantly plagued by nightmares and perhaps his wife's ghost, especially living again in the old Bonté mansion. Some years after his return, Luc Boulanger closed the top floors of the home, using it only as storage and removing the rooftop walkways. He planned to offer the mansion to one or both sons when they married and had families.

Because of the accident with his horse that fateful Lundi Gras night, Lucien had chronic pain and a leg and hip that never healed properly, causing him to limp and walk with a cane, later a crutch. He could never sit on a horse again. The pain often kept him home, and his handsome self grew wizened and curmudgeonly. He blamed much of his physical misfortunes on the curse of his wife's La Barre family. As a result, he steered far away from anyone of that lineage and urged his sons to do the same.

Both youths became handsome men—Josef-Paul was spoiled and an elitist rake. Randolfe, less so, being the eldest by a year and a half, always had wanderlust needing to escape from duties over his younger brother. The store was a good choice for him, as he spent many months away exploring the import side of his enterprises.

While procuring indigenous meats, rice, herbs, and other delicacies on one of his hunting trips, Randolfe met with a beautiful native Seminole woman, Singing Moon. The planned canoe and hunting trip into the backwoods of Louisiana was postponed as Randolfe spent time in the charming, isolated village. Moon's people were like ghosts suddenly appearing in the forest, like lost primitive tribes from a century before, magically dissipating into the mist.

For two weeks, Randolfe lived as Moon did in a simple cabin, gathered food, hunted for meat, fished, and learned skills for survival in the Kisatchie Woods. Each day, he fell deeper in love with her.

Finally, he dispatched a message to his father, asking to extend the trip a few months. The answer was no. Lucien was failing. Afraid to lose his new lover, Singing Moon, Randolfe brought her to Baton Rouge.

The exotically lovely Mona (Singing Moon) soon became the talk of the town, wearing beautiful clothes purchased by her lover and learning the ways of the 'White World.' Unfortunately, Lucien refused their marriage. So, the young couple eloped and returned to the woods. Randolfe retook his birthright name of Bonté.

Missing his son, Lucien turned to Josef-Paul for solace and gave his business affairs to the young man. A few years passed, and with the news that Lucien was at death's door, Randolfe again brought his wife and young son, Édouard, to Baton Rouge.

Upon Lucien's deathbed, the old man frightened everyone, crying that the ghost of his children's mother,

Liliana, awaited him. Then, in the last breaths, Lucien screamed that Madame Coeur had turned into a demon, breathing flames in his face. Berthe's banshee-like screeches accompanied him to Hell.

Randolfe inherited the mansion, being the firstborn and actually having a family. At least his father honored that claim. He returned to the store, ready to take on the business again, now needing a career in the city. He had the mansion repainted for Mona. His son finally had a nursery with a proper nounou to care for him instead of Édouard sleeping in a deerskin sacque hung by the stone fireplace in their primitive cabin.

Life was complicated this time in Baton Rouge, for Singing Moon missed her native lifestyle, their cabin, and her people. Instead, she was ridiculed and mistreated and soon became a pariah among women's circles. When she could have used kindness and friendship, she had none. So she escaped to her tribal roots, taking her newborn son, Reynard, and leaving Édouard for Randolfe.

Randolfe's many letters to Singing Moon went unanswered. Thus, he hardened his heart like he had learned to do under his demanding and cold-hearted father. Then Randolfe sank all his endeavors into his business, even eschewing his once fraternal friendship with his brother, Josef.

The grocery and import business prospered as Randolfe forged a new partnership with the La Barre family for fresh goods, honey, and meats. He hired a pastry chef to make bread and desserts in the current French style, missing them from his life in France. His shop flourished, and his son Édouard learned to please people but get a good deal from his business partners to make money.

Growing up, Édouard had many friends, including some La Barre boys. A distant cousin, Richard Barre, was nearly five years younger than Édouard, but the former schoolmates were best friends. Despite the occasional warnings that the La Barre boys were notorious cads and scoundrels, the youths kept their friendship. Randolfe never entirely understood what broke them years later... but suspected it was over a girl. The La Barre curse never seemed far away from the family.

Like Lucien, Randolfe sent his son, Édouard, to France to study international trade at the Université de Paris and learn to be a proper gentleman. But the youth returned to America as WWI began. Again, he was proud of his son, Édouard, a tall, sturdy fellow, handsome as the devil himself; this time, the exotic blood of the Seminoles and Creeks ran through the youth's body and soul. Randolfe could see the physical Bonté family resemblances, but Mona's blood made him robust and athletic. Fleet-of-mind, Edouard was interested in all modern things and justice—he was a fighter against wrongs but chose to stay out of the war.

Randolfe saw his son thriving. Then, over time, depending more upon Édouard and seeing him successful with their épicerie and boulangerie, the young man was allowed to court a wealthy young woman. Finally, when Édouard married Beatrice Laforêt, Randolfe felt he could retire.

Randolfe né Bonté-Boulanger retreated to the Kisatchie woods of northern Louisiana, finding his amour, Mona, Singing Moon among her people with a handsome youth caring for her. Their younger son Reynard was a wily, sharp native—fit and already searching for a wife.

By then, Randolfe had experienced everything he had ever wanted. Now, his dreams of Mona and Reynard were a reality, and he never looked back in remorse or sadness for his more extravagant but lonely lifestyle in faraway Baton Rouge or France. It was Édouard's chance for a charmed life.

Later

&&

On a fateful evening before leaving for US Army training camp in 1943, Barton Barre, then 20, met a young woman, Elise Boulanger, and her older sister, Elaine, at a War Bonds dance in Louisiana. The charming girls would be his pen pals during the war.

SSGT Barton Barre was later lost and severely wounded on the battlefields in Germany and presumed dead in April 1945, just weeks before the war ended in Europe. A lucky third son, he finally returned to his parents and siblings in Beaumont, Texas. Then, upon his recovery in the summer of 1945, he planned to visit his grandparents on the family plantation near St. Francis Ville, Louisiana.

Barton stopped in Baton Rouge to greet the girls before going "home" to the plantation, expecting a relaxing time to 'recover.' But his unplanned 'surprise' visit would set the stage for his fate. He would soon discover a strange family connection and a new love.

Inspired by the phantasms in "The Road Home," "Reunited" has a new generation of characters and familiar family names.

Reunited

Baton Rouge, Louisiana
Monday, June 25, 1945

It was getting late. Twilight was upon the land, and Baton Rouge had quieted for the sultry evening. I nervously sat with Elise Boulanger on a double wooden glider seat. It felt good to breathe deeply, catching the aroma of cooked food. Someone was grilling something, but it was overpowered by the heady scent of the nearby flower beds. A bird chirped in a tree, echoed by another. Crickets and cicadas clicked and thrummed a night symphony. The nocturnal sounds recalled my idyllic summer evenings at my grandparent's plantation along the Mississippi.

Embarrassed by my sweating hands, I swiped one on my trousers, and then I turned to Elise and took her hand. I couldn't help but smile at her lovely face, now cast in shadows. She was the most beautiful girl I had ever seen.

My daydreams of her while away were nothing compared to her natural beauty and the silent siren allure of her now. I wanted to kiss her.

"Can I kiss you, Elise?" I was shocked that I said it aloud but eagerly awaited her answer.

She looked up at me with surprise. "Do you really want to kiss me?"

"I do," I closely studied her glossy, full lower lip and blurted, "I want to very much. I think I might die if I don't." *Oh geez, talk about being overly dramatic! Still, it seemed to work!*

Endeared, Elise gasped and put her hand on my cheek; then, softly against my mouth, she whispered, "Yes, Barton, dear, you may kiss me."

I kissed her chastely, holding Elise's hand, feeling her mouth against mine. Greedily, I wanted more. Elise's mouth tasted like our dessert of cream puffs filled with vanilla custard and raspberries. I drew her in with my good arm, relinquishing her hand. Then, I found I wanted to plunge into the depths of her sweet kiss as if I were a hummingbird diving to the center of a flower in search of elusive nectar. I wanted to say that to Elise but couldn't get the words out, and I said instead, "That was kinda wonderful."

I could almost kick myself! Instead, now discomfited, squaring my shoulders, I leaned back against the bench seat. "I should have said, I mean—" I began, but Elise kissed me again but finished quickly.

"I know what you mean; I feel it, too."

I felt a pain in my groin, shifting away, growing uncomfortable now in my sexual awareness of the young woman. "What do you mean?"

Elise rested her head against my shoulder. "I feel our connection, too. I recall something you wrote to me once, that you felt tied to me with a string—"

I blushed hotly, then hastily replied, "Oh! I wrote that? I guess I was feeling lonely. Kinda dopey, huh?" *I read it once in a book and liked the line. Who knew classical literature could charm a modern girl?*

Elise lifted her head to look at me directly. "Barton, I have been feeling the same all along. I have felt connected to you since the night we met at the War Bonds dance. I sometimes dream of you."

I chuckled, feeling a self-deprecating mood rise to counter, "I hope they weren't nightmares."

✍

Elise sat silent momentarily, searching Barton's face, the glittering pale silver eyes, the cropped wavy cinnamon-red hair, then stroked the deep scar along his broad freckled forehead with a delicate finger. Then, finally, she quietly declared, "I saw how you got this. You were in an explosion. That was my *cauchemar.*"

✍

I shrank away from her touch and stared coldly at Elise. "Don't be ridiculous! How could you know such things?"

"You don't believe me?" She sat away from me. "It was just a few weeks after I had the dream that I received a letter from your parents. They were kind enough to tell me you were missing in action and presumed dead. My dream had felt so real that I wanted to write to them and tell them—"

I ran over her explanation. "Tell them what... that— that you dreamed of me?"

"No... not to give up hope. What happened to you? Please tell me." Elise took my left hand, which hung limply from the sling.

"How did you get hurt and lost? I even prayed to Adrian of Nicomedia... he is the patron saint of soldiers in war." She smiled slightly and scooted closer, "I am glad he heard my prayers."

I was stunned for a moment, wondering if I could retell anything of my experience. Elise's revelation scared me, and I hated feeling that way. I shifted away, pulling my almost numb hand from her grasp, and then took her hand with my good one.

"I was blown up twice that day." I glanced at my chest full of medals and bars, patting them with my wounded hand. "This medal was for bravery in action. I saved a British Captain after we were shelled. But I was stupid to do it, and that's how I was hurt and was blown up again... and almost died." I gulped, feeling the tremors rising, making me want to run away.

To think of those fateful minutes was like a nightmarish, cruel lifetime ago. I slowly recalled the experience, trying to edit out the most gruesome parts, but Elise accepted my bizarre story with nods and encouraging strokes on my hand. Elise's ebony dark eyes were glittering gems in the dim light on the veranda. But I knew they were tearful as she experienced my wounds and narrative.

Édouard Boulanger, Elise's father, was correct in that Elise was empathetic and a trusting, kind soul. Even though I stuttered, I could tell her everything, but it was painful. There was no bravado, just the honest and plain truth... just my bare fears and pain. I hadn't revealed as much when I talked with my dad about it. Yet, in those minutes, I felt a minor release from my wounded soul. When I shed tears and dashed them away brusquely against my shoulder, Elise used her handkerchief, dabbing at my eyes and cheeks. I felt like a baby.

I took the delicate hankie, finding it scented with the *Muguet des Bois* perfume I loved and embroidered with its flowers. I'd chosen a gift for her long ago if I ever were to make it home. Unfortunately, I had forgotten to give the handmade gloves and hankies to Thérèse and my sisters; they were packaged in the wrinkled tissue paper from when I bought them at *Lapin d'Or* in Vieux, France.

Hoping to cover the embarrassment of my tears, I rose to my feet, giving her back the hankie. "Elise, I have something for you... just a little souvenir from France. Give me a minute." Using my cane, I limped into the house's foyer but recalled leaving the duffle bag upstairs. Shaking my head, I returned to the veranda. "Oops. I have it in my bag. When I go up later, I'll give it to you."

"I don't need anything." Elise pulled me down to sit again. "You are gift enough for me." She sighed and put her head against my good shoulder. She let out another contented sigh when I put my good arm about her.

"I like this." Breathing in her shampoo-scented hair—like carnations: clean, silky, and seductive. I touched her glossy, ebony hair. "Pretty. I have wanted to touch your hair. It is soft like a cat."

Elise purred and smiled up at me. "Meow?"

"I like cats." I chuckled; my deep dimples fully engaged and charmed Elise.

"So do I." She matched my dimpled smile with hers.

"Hey, I remember you wrote about a poodle you once had. What happened to it?"

Elise sat up. "Chérie? Oh, she had to go to the vet for a dip—she got sand fleas last week when we were at the beach house. She comes home tomorrow. I miss her. Daddy despises fleas and filth." Elise smiled now as she scooted closer. "I hope you will like her. She is a darling little thing."

"I don't care for small dogs, much too yappy and loud." I probably sounded sour and a little cranky.

"Some are. But Chérie is my dog, and she is well-behaved and does tricks."

"I hope she knows how to turn into a quiet cat." I laughed at the weak joke.

Elise turned to me. "You aren't serious?"

I looked away to reply, "No. Dogs are okay, I guess. My grandfather raises Brittany Spaniels and Catahoulas for hunting."

"I think Brittanies are nice. A neighbor down the street has one. Catahoulas... aren't they a noisy lot?"

I turned to her again, glad Elise didn't take offense. "Yes. You should hear them when they tree a possum or corner a cat. *Mémé* turns the hose on the pack sometimes." I laughed, "Once, *Pépé*'s old hound Alfie treed me. I had a kitten in my shirt, and that dog would not let me down without a fight. So *Pépé* had to rescue me. He wasn't so happy about it either." I sniggered and wiped my eyes. "I think I got *un fait de pan-pan* for it, too." I glanced at Elise. "Do you know what that is?"

"Of course. My grandmother calls it 'ruling the child' or 'spooning' if the cook punished us. She is quite proper. My mother, when she was small, had a strict governess. Then, Mom went to a private school in France until she was seventeen. The rod was rarely spared, or so Maman said."

"Wow, I feel sorry for her. It's no wonder she is so... so you know... um," I weakly faded, not wanting to be rude to the prim Boulanger family.

"I know." Elise finished, then rounded to say, "But we are not all like that. Mom is the snobby one, and Daddy is the iron fist in the velvet glove. If you know how to get around him, you can win."

"Édouard is a little like my father. I can hardly ever win with him. So I learned to avoid an argument at all costs." I irritably shifted on the seat, knowing that my quick departure from Beaumont was because of a disagreement with my autocratic dad. But to find our families had a connection was weird.

"I am astounded that Édouard and my dad, Richard, knew each other as kids. Did you know that, too?"

"No, I did not. We should ask Daddy for some more stories. See?—We have so much in common." Elise giggled and snuggled up next to my shoulder.

Elise grew quiet, taking my hand and observing the pinkie finger stump and discolored, scarred new skin; she said somberly, "I am sorry that you got hurt."

"By your father? Nah, I am okay." I shrugged off the comment. "I can take it." I still removed my sore hand from Elise's grasp.

"No, I meant... hurt in the war. You were courageous and returned a hero." Elise fondled some medals and again touched the ragged scar on my forehead, stroking down my temple and cheek along the healed new pink skin. "If you are worried about your looks, don't be. I still think you are very handsome. And these will fade away like bad dreams."

Despite feeling uneasy about her close inspection, I hugged Elise's slim body. "And I think you are just as sweet as honey. I am not sure if your father likes me enough, though."

"I'll work on him."

I gripped Elise's hand, wishing it might be so. "Are you serious about what you said earlier tonight? Do you really care for me?"

"I do very much."

I kissed her palm and then kissed Elise on the mouth. "I think I may need to change my vacation plans," I mumbled as all the quick visions of a future with this girl swept through my mind.

"Why? What were they?"

Brightly, I announced, "I was only coming here to say hello and thanks for writing to me. But if there might be a reason, I should hang around a little longer... hm?" I winked at Elise.

Elise's smile was brilliant. "But where would you stay?"

"I was planning on buying a car here in Baton Rouge, then doing a little job hunting while I stay with my grandparents."

"You are?" Elise squealed, "Barton, do you know we have lots of oil here? Maybe you could find work on the rigs... or a refinery. Oh, that would be so wonderful! Would you really stay in town?"

"I might." I felt myself grinning cheekily. Initially, there wasn't a plan to get an instant girlfriend today, but Elise was growing warm to the idea, and so was I. Although I was looking for a different job as an engineer or designer, not a filthy roustabout on an oil rig like a guy with lousy prospects. I'd already spent a summer of my youth sweating my ass off working on an oil rig. Of course, I'd also worked damned hard for my engineering degree and minor in petrology. But that wasn't up for discussion today, even though Édouard Boulanger, during dinner, had cruelly pursued me for information like a hound on a scented trail. His plan was to denounce me as worthless and kick me out! Nope.

I yawned all of a sudden. "S'cuse me. It's been a really long day. I was up before five and caught the early train." I glanced at my new wristwatch; the luminescent dots quietly announced it was half-past nine. The Boulangers ate a very late formal dinner. I had been here all day, waiting for Elise to come home and then being entertained by her family before the meal. The worst was Edouard's Inquisition, which had brought us to an uneasy impasse. We ended our discussion only to finish the delicious dinner! Tiredly, I ran a hand over a sandpapery cheek. "I should get to bed and stop being a pest."

"You aren't a pest. But, knowing that you are across the hall from me, I might not sleep well tonight."

"I should say that. Although, I think I have had as much excitement today as I can take. I am not very good at surprises and impromptu stuff. I'm used to a different schedule as an Army Staff Sergeant. Funny, I could be up and fighting for two or three days in a row, and now, I am tuckered out by doing nothing."

Elise rose and pulled me up to stand. "Dear, it is expected since you are still recovering. But you certainly amaze me! I am glad that you came today. You can surprise me any day." She leaned toward me. "Would you kiss me again, please?"

I pulled her close. "*Oui.*" Smiling, I kissed her mouth and noticed that Elise had closed her eyes, and so did I— feeling the power of our innocent kiss swirling about us to where I could drown in them. I did not want to let her go. But I would be in trouble if I didn't curtail what was happening to my body.

I released Elise, "Let's go in... it's getting foggy out here," *and so is my brain*. I yawned again and thumbed away tears that sprang from my eyes. "Come upstairs with me, and I'll give you something I brought from France." I limped after Elise as she stepped lightly across the veranda and into the house.

I stopped short, catching the scent of pipe tobacco from the parlor and the sound of piano music. I moved around the corner to see the room was ablaze with lamps and glowing crystal wall sconces. Beatrice was at the piano, turning pages for Elise's sister Elaine as she played.

I found my feet following the sound, then stood at the edge of the parlor listening. Lovely blonde Elaine was quite good. But then I felt Elise at my elbow, and she tugged me away, motioning us upstairs. Curiously, I followed her.

I went to the assigned room and dumped half of my duffle bag on the bed while Elise arranged fresh towels and plumped the pillows on my bed. I found the crinkled packages and ripped them open because I no longer remembered which packet held the handkerchief for Elise.

"These are handmade in France. We had recently ousted the Nazis from a cute little town. And there was still a pretty little shop selling ladies' things. So I bought souvenirs for my sisters, Grandmère, stepmom... and you." I explained as I displayed the lacy hankies on the bed. I kept the lace-trimmed brocade satin gloves I had bought for Thérèse. "Take one."

"How pretty!" Elise cooed and sorted through them. "Which one did you choose for me?"

Honestly, I hadn't an inkling of a choice, but caught now, I glanced at the hankies. Most had embroidered roses on them, so I picked the most unusual one, with orange and gold Tiger Lilies. But then spied one with blue and purple flowers, "No, this is the one." I pressed it into Elise's hand.

"Lilacs! I love them." She held the handkerchief to her cheek, "It is a lovely gift... thank you for thinking of me. I will treasure it always."

I hastily shoved the remaining gifts into the shredded paper and dropped them in my duffle bag. "I am glad that you like it. I thought of you often. I am just sorry that I didn't write more. I never could think of anything good to say. My stepmother said I should only write about the good stuff that happened." I shrugged. "Not much good ever happened to me."

Elise kissed my cheek. "You are wrong, Barton. You survived the war, which is truly the best gift. Well, I forgive you. Knowing that you wrote to me and liked me was enough. Now, I cannot ask for anything more wonderful with you here. You made my day, and I am blessed."

Elise pranced about the room, tidying up, then spoke loftily, "Do you know it must be fate that you came here this week?"

"No, why?" I stuffed the remaining clothes in the duffle.

"I am lucky we didn't stay longer. We spent some of last week at our summer house at Lake Ponchartrain. Mom said the vacation would help take my mind off you. Yet, while I was there, I could only think of you. I wanted to show you the lake and the stars and row us out at sunset to kiss you—"

Charmed, I snatched Elise's hand and kissed it. "I am unsure I am worthy of your devotion, Elise. But I sure like it... a lot more than you might think." I sat on the bed. "But I need sleep. If I don't get enough, I get very grouchy. I wouldn't want to ruin our pleasant evening."

"Okay." Elise sprang away and called as she shut the door, "Sweet dreams, dear Barton."

Fait beaux rêves.

I sat for a long time before falling over on the bed, soaking in Elise's oddly familiar words, something my deceased mother, Charlotte, always said at bedtime when I was a kid. Exhaustion and pain sank into my muscles and bones. I felt the weakness as I hastily undressed, spreading my uniform on the chair beside the bed.

So much for being tough today; trying not to show my pain, I irritably pushed off the duffle bag. Having forgotten my pajamas, nearly naked, I climbed under the sheet, switched off the lamp, and lay for a spell listening to the ambient noises of the strange house, distant voices, and music.

I still felt Elise's presence in the room, smelled her perfume, and felt her in my arms. Finally, I carefully rolled over in the double bed, enjoying the satiny coolness of the lavender-scented fine linens, and soundly fell asleep for the first time in many weeks. Elise felt like home to me.

ও

I had a strange vision—it began pleasantly enough. I strolled along a tree-lined dirt road. The fields to one side were bright cadmium red-orange splotches of nodding poppies; the other had brilliant purple fragrant lavender swaying in the warm breeze. It looked like an expressionist piece and something I might try to paint. The trees' shadows were long and thin, interlaced across the roadway. I stepped from light into shadow and back again, feeling a chill in the shaded places.

Hearing familiar thunder behind, I saw American bombers and their escort fighters flying low over the fields. I could almost see the pilots and waved to them. However, the planes swerved away, and I continued the pleasant walk in the countryside.

But of a sudden, I felt a dark presence and then increased my pace, feeling as if I must run.

I ran.

My legs were strong, my muscles rippling, my lungs sucking air, dust biting my sinuses as my feet pounded the roadway. Then, decisively, I chanced a look over my shoulder. The trees' shadows no longer were across the road, but now they were twining snakes writhing and coiling in my wake. I pushed myself to the limit—my lungs burning and my muscles tearing as I ran. Then, hearing the thundering throbbing pulse again, I looked up behind and saw a dark machine approaching from above.

Bwoomm! Bbbbb-It-T-T-T! Bbbbb-It-T-T!

I ran off the road and rolled down into the ditch as I heard the explosive roar about me and stinging needles pelting me with flying dirt. I cried out as the shadow passed overhead, turning in the sky and returning to strafe the road again. One more pair of *Luftwaffe* fighters made another run across the lane and fields. But after this time, I saw people lying dead when I looked at the road. *Where had they come from? I had been alone!*

I crawled up the steep embankment to watch the evil *Luftwaffe* squadron rise into the air, heading across the bleak landscape. The poppies and lavender in the fields were blackened and burned. The people on the pitted dirt road had taken on the blood-red of the poppies, their bodies peppered with bullets. I fell to my knees and wept; I didn't know why. I didn't know these people, but they were dead—yet I was alive in this hellish place!

Just as ominous, a flock of ravens flew from the skeletal trees to settle on the road and fields to feast upon the dead. The enemy had reduced the serene beauty of the countryside to a hellish, macabre battlefield. No winners.

Crying, I felt a presence and shrank away, my skin prickling with fear and nervous energy; the hairs on my neck and arms stood up. My teeth chattered as an icy breeze wafted through the room. A white figure materialized next to my bed and reached toward me.

A soft crooning voice sang, *"Ah, mon enfant qui es en mes bras, ah, mon p'tit biquet que je t'adore... Dors, dors... mon p'tit agneau..."*

Something stroked me on the cheek and called me a lamb! I yelled and instinctively rolled away. Then, my hand hit something hard, and I heard a crash. The wisp of white vanished, as did the chilling sensation.

Light came from the room's doorway, and something tangled me in the bedsheet, almost naked with people staring at me. A white figure emerged from the light to approach my bed. I smelled her first—the lavender scent from my dream. Then my heart leaped in fright—I was awake now. The apparition was now confirmed.

Beatrice Boulanger bent by the bed to put a gentle hand on my arm. "Barton, dear, are you all right?"

I jerked away, still in the throes of the dream, then shivered at her touch. *"Mon Dieu...* everyone was dead." The words slipped out, and I nearly burst into tears again. But shook my head and leveled troubled eyes at Beatrice. "I'm fine... now."

Elise came in then, as did Édouard. They stood around the bed as I pulled the sheet to my waist. "I guess I woke everyone up," I stated the obvious.

"You did. Having *cauchemars,* are you?" Édouard chuckled but sobered when he caught his wife's grim look. "Bad dream, huh? Do you want to talk about it?"

"I'd prefer not to." I was more embarrassed than frightened. "I–I hate dreams like that."

Beatrice patted my bare arm, her eyes stroking the long stripes of scar tissue on my arms and left shoulder and the peppered, puckered skin on my broad-muscled chest. The recent wounds stood out darker in the garish light from the hallway. Then, decisively, she took pity on me and sat on the edge of the bed.

"Son, I cannot imagine the pain you have suffered or the horrific things you have witnessed. But you can always talk to us. We are your friends." She switched on the bedside lamp.

I looked away, hating to feel another's pity and weakness before strangers, let alone any family. I hated to be called *son,* like a small child. I sat up, leaning against the pillows, and pulled away from Beatrice again. "Thanks. I will be fine. Goodnight. Oh, I think I broke something." I leaned over the bed and saw a broken water glass on the wooden floor. "Oops!" I looked at Beatrice, "I'll clean it up."

"You will not... Elise and I will. You stay there." She patted me on a sheet-covered thigh and left the bedside, ushering Édouard out. "Give Elise and me a few minutes to clean up. Go back to bed, *chéri.*" She kissed her husband and sent him away.

I felt ridiculous and ashamed for the trouble. Yet the dream was still a wriggling worm in my brain as if trying to escape. The blackened poppy and lavender fields sprang up when I closed my eyes. I opened my eyes and saw that Elise was there at the bedside.

"You saw the ghosts, didn't you?" She bent to pick up the broken glass and dropped the pieces into a paper sack. "I told you they are real. Was it a lady in white?" She asked, swiping up the spill.

I froze. "I–I—what? No! No, I only had a stupid dream." I stared at her slender neck and the pale line parting Elise's hair where the silky ebony waves split into loose braids. I yearned to kiss her just there on that tender spot.

"Did she sing a lullaby? If so, that is *Madame Coeur,* the *Lady in White.* She mostly floats around the room singing. If one screamed in your face, then that is Old Berthe. She brings bad dreams. If it was a mischievous, laughing boy, that was Reggie. He does nothing harmful."

Confused, I shook my head. "Um, I—" I reached for her, wanting to hold Elise's hand, but then I heard footsteps coming up the stairs and tucked my hand under the sheet.

Beatrice lugged up the electric sweeper; she bent to plug it in and then vacuumed the rug and floor alongside the bed, picking up tiny shards of glass. I sat glumly, helpless, as I once did, watching the nurses work about me while I lay in the hospital bed. It was frustrating. "I should do that, Madame."

"No, you rest. You had a fright. I am almost finished."

I regarded Elise. "Does she do this for you?"

"Sometimes." Elise smiled and came around the other side of the bed. She took my hand as I released a grip on the linens. "I am sorry you saw the ghosts. I warned you. Old Berthe is a nightmare on her own."

"Elise, they weren't ghosts." I argued, then explained, "Well, maybe they are now. Everyone was dead. The *Luftwaffe* made a strafing run and killed everyone except me."

"That is horrible. Did you really see that... I mean, experience it over there?" Elise asked, her fine dark brows knitted with concern.

"Not quite like that, but they shot at me a lot. And I was blown up a few times and close to many other explosions. I am surprised I am not deaf by now." My last words were a shout over the vacuum sweeper as Beatrice switched it off.

I felt my face pale, and my stomach turned queasy. "I think I had better go to sleep. I have caused enough trouble. Y'all will toss me into the street!" Impishly, I pulled the sheet over my head and pretended to snore, making the women laugh. Then, hearing the light switch off and the door shut, I yanked the sheet off my head.

Lying in the darkness, I felt the tendrils of the evil dream snaking through my mind. I had not cared for the eerie cold sensation either. Then I did something I'd not done since childhood: turn on the bedside lamps and roll over to sleep with the sheet over my head. I didn't want to believe in ghosts, the lullaby I heard, or that odd perfumed icy breeze. I imagined it all—it was nothing but stupid, illogical junk in my weary head!

The Curious Case Of The Caddo Creature

Piney Woods, Texas
Saturday, October 29, 1955

Scoutmaster Jim Morton stood and held his hand up for silence among the Wolf Pack troops. The kids were excited about hearing ghost stories tonight and were energized by hot dogs, cocoa, and S'mores. He glanced at the pile of chocolate bar wrappers and knew that most of the candy never made it to S'mores. Thus, the boys were sugar-fueled. Their laughter was raucous and wild as the kids pelted each other with popcorn and marshmallows.

The usually calm man sighed with exasperation and yelled, "Hey! Quiet down! We have a special—" Jim whistled shrilly this time, getting most of the boys' attention. He glowered at Bobby Camden, lobbing popcorn at Francis Barre.

A fastidious boy, Francis Barre, stood and swiped off the popcorn crumbs from his uniform and wool jacket.

"Knock it off, Bobby. Mr. Morton is trying to tell us something." Francis said, annoyed.

"Yes... thank you, Francis." Jim held back a smirk and raised his hand again as several boys laughed and commented. "Yes, I have a special treat for y'all tonight. My friend Chester Long Foot is here to tell y'all some stories about his experience in the woods here."

"Oh, big deal." Larry Camden grumbled. "We wanna hear scary stuff. It's Halloween, ya know!"

Morton glanced at the guest sitting under the trees. The man nearly blended into the dark shrubbery. But the shadow surprised the kids as he appeared before the fire pit and stabbed a tall walking stick into the ground. Adorned with feathers, strings of beads, and trailing a hank of thick black hair and a bushy tail, the shaft stood quivering like a spear. A few kids shrieked and then laughed.

"Ooh, so scary!" Brothers Larry and Bobby sang together, making fun of the other kids.

In shadows under his wide black brim hat, the man's craggy face looked eerie in the partial glow of the campfire. Dark eyes sparkled, and a crooked hatchet nose rose from under the brim. The man wearily sat on a log across from the group with a labored exhalation.

Worn like a poncho, a torn blanket covered the man's shoulders and ragged clothing. He wore one mitten and a fingerless glove. The muddied boots looked ancient—scuffed, and the soles split, one boot wrapped with a rag. The man's smile was even scarier—crooked, yellowed teeth with dark gaps silenced the kids, as did his raspy voice.

"You will know scary after you hear my tale." He chuckled dryly.

Jim Morton refilled his cup with hot chocolate and sat near Chester. Before taking a sip, he smiled to say, "Yup, somebody's gonna wet their pants tonight!" He snickered. "Give it to 'em, Chester."

Sitting taller, Chester shrugged his shoulders, shook back his long silver-streaked hair, and exhaled loudly.

"It was on a night like this, cold, the sky full of stars and the moon peeking over the hills—"

"Mister Long Foot?"

The eyes speared the speaker and glittered with impatience. "What? You need to find a tree and tinkle, little boy?"

Everyone laughed. Walter Rusk elbowed his younger brother. "Sh! Petey, I wanna hear the story. Just hold it." Petey whispered to his brother, and Walter quickly announced, "He only has a question and doesn't gotta pee."

Everyone snickered.

"What is it?" Long Foot growled.

Petey looked about the group shyly but asked, "So how come you didn't start with 'Once upon a time,' sir? All stories begin that way."

"Baby!" Larry threw a pinecone at the boy, inciting further comments and squeals of laughter.

"This is not a fairy story about princesses, dragons, or knights. It is about what actually happened in the woods one night." Chester stood up, grumbling, "Maybe you are all too young to hear my tale. Let Bo or Jim read you a Goldilocks bedtime story. I better go home."

"No! Please stay!" Some plaintive cries echoed about the campfire. "We wanna hear it!"

"We want scary stuff!"

Chester's 'picket fence' yellowed smile peeked as he sat again, coughed, cleared his throat, and spat into the fire.

"It was a night like this, cold and windy; the trees spoke to each other in their swishing way. The birds were quiet in their nests. Except for the nighthawks and owls that prey on the nocturnal creatures of the forest." He held a mitten up to an ear. "Listen! For you can hear them even now."

He left a few breaths of silence as a timely owl hooted, and then Chester continued in a dry, deep voice. "The young boy, not much older than you kids, had a job to do for his father. He was to go before twilight and put out the snares for nutria, rabbit, squirrel, and fish, so there would be meat in the morning. Now, this boy—"

"Yuck! He ate squirrels?" Petey Rusk queried with wide brown eyes.

"I ate a squirrel once," Larry admitted proudly.

"Did not! It was a run-over, dead rabbit, and Dad found it!" Bobby retorted, then smacked his older brother on the arm.

"Sick!" Francis nudged his best friend, Benny Freeman, to say, "Larry always lies."

"Yeah, I know, he's a—"

"Quiet!" Assistant troop master Bo Eliot hollered.

Bo leaned toward Jim, commenting, "At this rate, we'll never get these kids to sleep."

Jim shook his head, finished the cocoa, and announced, "Hush, please, let's respect Mister Long Foot."

Chester nodded and tucked the blanket about his body. His breath plumed the chilled air as he spoke.

"The boy went quickly about his work, knowing where many animals had nests or hidey-holes. So, he placed the traps along the lakeshore and stream for the rabbits, nutria, and fish. He walked into the woods along the stream and set traps for squirrels and other game. Tired, hungry, and thirsty, the boy picked some berries, put them in his leather pouch, and stopped at the stream. He bent to drink the cool water."

The old man's hand rose to his nose, then whispered, his voice rising with each word. "But then the boy smelled something so horrible... and heard shuffling feet in the brush across the stream. Scared, he backed away into the bracken and hid, worried it was a bear."

The boys took an inward breath, now caught in the story.

Chester put his arms about his body. "The boy didn't want to be frightened, but a bear could be trouble. So he tested the direction of the breeze and pushed deeper into the thorny bushes, then sat still so the bear would not find him."

Motioning in sign, Chester walked his fingers as he spoke. "Soon, a dark creature padded out of the bushes and stepped into the water. It lowered its big furry head, and the boy heard it drinking. The animal lapped the water for a long time, then waded away into the stream, coming directly in front of the boy. The boy tried to be brave, but his knees were shaking—the animal was so close that he could smell him. If he could sniff the creature, it might smell him too in the bushes."

The storyteller took a sip from a canteen, then swallowed and let out a satisfied sigh. "The animal was only yards away from the boy, yet it was so dark in the woods that only a tiny thread of light glittered from the water. The moonlight caught the gleam of yellow-gold eyes. The boy knew it was an animal he had never seen before. It was indeed evil, a bad spirit, and something the boy did not want to meet."

The boys around the campfire shivered now, some clutched pillows or blankets or another boy's hand. Chester's smile broadened, "Hooked 'em!" He murmured and enthused, crouched down, telling his tale.

"That poor boy did not know what to do, but the animal did, for it leaped across to the other bank. A long-clawed paw struck the water like lightning. There was a loud splash, a roar, and the animal had a sleek trout in its jaws. The boy cringed and closed his eyes, not wishing to see the animal devour the fish, for he could hear the great teeth cracking the bones and slurping sounds as the fish disappeared down its gullet."

Chester Long Foot lifted his head and mimicked the creature as he continued, "The animal soon ran across the creek, sniffing along the bank, the shaggy head taking in great gasps of air. The boy sat in his hidey-hole, afraid that he might be the animal's next meal. He watched as it ran away upstream, panting and growling. The boy, still shaking, took the opportunity and crawled from the thorny bushes. Even though scratched and bleeding, he escaped into the forest."

Chester rose taller and smoothed the long tresses of his hair with his gloved hand. "Now that boy had lived there all his life, he knew the forest well, for his father, Bright Stone, had taught him much. But he became lost as the child walked farther from the stream and that animal. The trees were taller, the rocks were unfamiliar, and soon, he could not see the stars above the dense trees. It was the darkest place he had ever been, and he sat on a rock to think." Chester sat again.

"'If I go that way, I will run into the animal. I think I am too far from home if I go this way. Oh, what to do?' Tears came too easily, and the young boy was ashamed knowing he should be brave."

"So, he pondered, 'I should risk going the way I came. Maybe that animal or spirit has run away by now.' Wiping his eyes, the boy bravely turned parallel to his path, keeping far from the stream, and hoped he would soon find the trail he knew to go home."

"While he walked, he heard an owl, so the boy stopped to ask, 'Is this the way home, Great Owl?' But the owl only blinked at him and flew away in another direction. So, the boy continued through the creepy dark forest, hoping he would not run into any other nasty creatures or the big smelly one."

"Soon, coming to a gooseberry bush, he stopped and ate a few tart berries, thinking it would help him, but then a skunk came, and he backed away. The little animal was quite pretty, and the boy wished to kill it and take its pelt for his mother. But they were tricky and smart animals. 'I will only get skunked, and no one will like me anymore. Goodbye, Skunk.'"

The young scouts giggled as Old Chester continued.

"The boy walked on, but soon he heard odd noises and smelled the foul stink. 'Oh, no! The evil creature!' he cried and slipped into the bushes. He lay down and watched through the branches and leaves, hoping to see the animal leave."

Chester imitated, taking long whiffs of air. "The creature sniffed along the ground. It suddenly leaped upon something and then stood chewing what looked like a squirrel.

"'That is my squirrel!' the boy whispered. Then, as he looked about, he realized the animal was eating his snare bait and the catch! 'Father will be heartbroken,' he moaned."

"Yeah, my dad didn't like it when I threw my fish back in the water. I got clobbered for it," Francis whispered to Benny. However, he caught the dark eye of the storyteller. "Sorry, sir."

"Yes, the terrified boy worried his father might beat him for being lazy and coming home with empty hands. But then the wicked animal lay down near the thicket and licked its paws and face like a cat. Then, all of a sudden, it lifted its head and howled. The boy hid his face and wept silent tears. Next, he heard something nearby, digging and sniffing, and he moved as far into the thicket as possible, for the creature was coming after him."

◎

Francis took an inward surprised breath as Chester pantomimed the creature digging and hunting the boy. The man looked like an old chieftain from a Wild West show. But, in Francis's opinion, his black hat was ugly. It had a snakeskin band, which was creepy enough—he hated snakes. A string with many feathers hung from the back; the brim had a thick, dark fur trim.

Francis felt sorry for the man because he was so old and crippled-looking, with a pock-marked face and missing and broken teeth. He looked sort of hunched over and skinny. Maybe he was hungry, too.

But then Francis surmised many Indians were poor unless they worked in the movies or played in westerns on TV like Tonto—Jay Silverheels. His own cousin, Didier, was a mix of native heritages. Even though he worked as a game warden and hunting guide, he was poor as dirt, eating what he hunted, gathered, or grew.

Francis leaned against Benny's shoulder, yawning, tired from the busy day hiking with a heavy pack to this lake and campground. They weren't lucky enough to sleep in the cabins tonight—they were sleeping in tents and 'Roughing it.'

Then, glancing around the campfire to see his friends' faces aglow—everyone seemed to like this old man's story. It wasn't a ghost story like the boys wanted. The old man was like a fisherman, craftily pulling them all in on his bizarre tale. It reminded him of his great-grandfather, Francois, telling 'fish stories.'

Francis sat up again, shifting uncomfortably on the rough bark of the log, blew his dripping cold nose on a hankie, and shoved his hands in his warm jacket pockets, ready to hear more.

◎

"How is it that a beast can talk?" The storyteller asked the boys, but he did not wait for an answer. "The child yelled in fright as the creature finally dug its way into the thicket. It asked the boy, 'Why are you afraid, little one?'"

"'You will eat me!'"

"The animal sat on its rump and faced the youth. 'Do you taste good?'"

"The boy said, 'I don't think so.'"

"'What are you?' Asked the creature, 'You have little fur and no tail. How odd you are. Where are your claws and sharp teeth?'"

Chester laughed, startling the rapt audience to point a long-nailed finger at them. "'Ha! You are odd! You are not a bear or a wolf. You are weird. What are you?' The boy demanded bravely now and scooted closer to the hole in the thicket, ready to escape. The animal paced nearer, too. 'I am me.'"

"'I am me too. I am a boy. Little Long Foot.' echoed the child."

The scouts laughed and sighed, relieved.

"'Ah... a human boy? Like rabbits, I have heard humans taste good,' laughed the creature."

"'Oh no, I am like a skunk and taste bad, phooey!' The boy shrank from the beast's hot breath."

"The creature laughed too. 'I like to eat skunks, so maybe I will eat you!' The animal lunged forward at the boy and grabbed his arm. The beast's teeth were razor sharp and tore the boy's beaver cloak, then bit into the deer-hide shirt."

"'Ow! That hurts!' The child shoved at the creature. 'You stink and are a mean animal. It is no wonder no one likes you! Help!' The boy cried when the animal pulled at his arm. 'Why are you eating me?' The boy screamed as the creature licked the bloody arm. The beast licked its chops and sat again, eyeing the child with glittering golden eyes."

"'If you give me a gift, I will not eat you.'"

"Now, the boy stopped crying and rubbed his wounded arm. 'A gift? What do you want?'"

Chester leaned closer to the fire and put out his mitten-clad hand and glove, warming them on the orange flames. "'Give me your hand, and you may go.'"

"The boy stepped closer slowly. 'You want to shake hands with me and agree I can go? But what gift do you want, and do I get something too?'"

"The animal snorted and reared up on its hind feet, its claws sharp, and it said, 'Yes, give me your hand, and I will give you the gift of your life. You might live forever. If you are lucky!'"

"The boy was suspicious and looked up at the ugly beast, its eyes shining with their own light like a bright harvest moon. Its claws clicked as the creature shook its paws, and the boy wondered aloud, 'You are like a wolf, yet tall like a man, but you stink like a skunk and have terrible manners like a wild boar. You ate my squirrel! That was my morning meal! No, I won't give you anything. Go away!' With that, the boy threw a rock at the beast and scrambled through the hole in the thicket."

Chester gesticulated and spoke rapidly, "The child ran fast, tripping on pinecones and falling among the thick leaves and pine needles, but he jumped up and ran quicker. He could smell the beast's hot breath and hear its roar as it paced behind him. He veered left, turned right, zigzagged past boulders, and headed for the nearby stream he could now hear. 'I will swim away as fast as a fish. The wicked thing will not catch me!' The boy said and raced toward the water. He found a large branch barring his path along the way, picked it up, broke off the smaller twigs, and said, 'This will make a good spear. I will kill that animal.'"

Chester looked about the circle of faces, seeing the wide eyes and mouths agape, and chuckled. He jumped to his feet, shouting, "Then the animal broke through the underbrush and jumped upon the boy. They rolled over and over, the creature biting and scratching, and the child hit and stabbed at it with the sharp stick."

Chester swung his arms out. "The boy screamed as the beast bit off his hand, but he plunged the stick into the animal's heart with the other. The beast made a horrible groan and wailed. It thrashed about and dropped the boy's hand as it choked. It lay panting on its side. A great wound spurted dark crimson blood that flooded the forest ground and ran down the bank and into the stream. The boy stood up and retrieved the stick. He took his knife and cut the tail off the dying creature.

"The beast howled, 'Not my beautiful tail!' It moaned as it lay dying, 'What a cruel boy!'"

"The boy stood over the animal and said, 'You ate my hand. I thought you were going to let me go. You lied. I am glad you are dying.'"

"But the beast, in its last breath, shook and rolled into a ball as its bloodied black and silver fur faded to white and fell away. 'You have killed me, but I will live again inside you! Curse you, human boy!' It gave a loud grunt and died. The child, horrified, watched as the animal withered until it was nothing but bare bones, except they were human bones. He picked up the skull and marveled at the change from a wolf creature to a man."

"'This is a great mystery. I shall bring the shaman and father here to see this amazing thing.' He put the skull in his leather pouch, but it turned to dust, as did his hand lying near the creature's bones. He looked at the stump of his arm and saw it blackened, but the blood was already dried. 'How can I work with only one hand? My family and I will starve!' He asked himself."

"Little Long Foot leaned tiredly on the branch and tied the tail on it with a piece of sinew from his pouch— at least, the tail had not withered away. 'I will have something to show father, so he will believe me.' The boy felt something kick inside the pouch. Looking, he found a rabbit! He killed it. Then, he turned his face to the setting moon and found his pathway to home illuminated. 'I suddenly feel good and strong!' He ran along the traplines near the stream and noticed they were empty, the bait probably eaten by the wolf. 'Father will be angry that the beast ate everything.' But he had no more fruit or bait for the traps."

Chester paced as he continued, "The boy reached his village in the woods near the great Mother Lake. His traps there were empty. The people were rising, cooking fires were burning, and some women were grinding maize and acorns for porridge and making their morning broth. The aroma of the cooked meat soup and porridge made his mouth water. It surprised the child that it was morning already. He had spent the entire night fighting the creature in the woods."

"He ran between the twig and mud huts and animal skin tipis, excited to tell the story to his family. Then, as he poked his head under the tipi flap, there was a terrible scream. 'Mother?' he asked."

"His Mother, screaming, threw a gourd pot at his head; it broke but hurt like fire. The boy backed away. 'Father! No!' He cried as his father, flying out of his fur blankets, charged him. The man beat and pushed the boy away, ready to kill him with his knife. The boy looked up at his father with tears in his eyes."

"'Father! I am sorry I hardly have any meat, but please don't kill me for it. The beast stole all my bait and squirrels.' He put up his arms to hide and realized he wore black fur!"

"His father backed away, his face red and in great fear. He asked, 'How does this wolf talk to me? This is a great evil thing. I must kill it!' He pressed the knife to the creature's throat, and Mother ran to him. 'No! Do not kill it!'"

"'Why? It is an evil beast, but its pelt will—'
Mother interrupted, 'But it is our boy. Do you not see the creature wearing the pouch I made for my son? And look, there is a rabbit in it. We will not go hungry today.'"

"The boy looked up crying, 'It is me, Little Long Foot, Mother. But something terrible happened in the woods last night. An evil beast bit off my hand. I killed it, and now... I think I am one too!' The boy-turned-creature rolled over, exposing his furry belly. 'If you think I failed your task, you must kill me, father!' He cried."

"But the boy's parents, with pity, did not kill their wolf-child. This was the largest and most beautiful black and silver wolf creature they had ever seen but with only three paws! So, as a gift for sparing his life, the wolf hunted for his parents. They always had more food than they needed. For this, they protected their wolf son until they grew old and died. This story reminds you to be kind to Earth's creatures and your family."

The boys looked relieved, but the old man stood up. He dragged off his glove and mitten and put out his single hand, the other a naked withered stump.

Sharp shrieks from a few boys peppered the night.

"I am Long Foot. I am a wolf when the moon rises. Who would like to give me the gift of death and earn the gift of eternal life as a new wolf?" Chester whipped off his hat and shook his shaggy head, then snarled. "Who wants to fight me?" He then howled like a wolf!

The boys squealed, screamed, and ran away into their tents.

Bo and Jim laughed and stood up. "That was a great spooky story, Chester. It's better this year." Jim clapped a hand on the man's bony, hunched shoulder. "Thanks for taking the time from your lovely wife, Daisy, to be with us."

The man wriggled his glove onto his hand with his teeth, then tugged the mitten over the stump. Dropping the hat on his head, Chester tossed the black blanket over his shoulder. Shivering, he eyed the cold, pale moon above. "It's not a fairy story, so I must go... the moon shines."

Bo offered him a pint flask of whiskey. "Here, have a nip... this will take the bite out of the chilly night for ya!" He gave Chester a few chocolate bars and a five-dollar bill.

Chester eyed the proffered bottle and candy and shook his head. "Wolves, don't eat or drink that stuff, but I'd like a nip out of you!" The fellow snarled and pounced, biting Bo's arm.

Bo leaped away. "Oh, no! Don't turn me into a werewolf! I already have enough problems with five kids and a crabby wife—that would ruin me!"

Jim held up his hands. "Hey, don't eyeball me, Chester! You go home. By the way, have you been eating polecats? You stink!"

Chester swirled the dark poncho about his body with a lick of his bloodied lips and ran away. His shadowed figure looked more like a wolf in clothes racing through the woods.

"That was a close call." Bo rubbed the bite on his arm. He watched as Jim poured a bucket of water on the dying fire. "We better check that all the little squirrels are snug in their beds. We can't have anyone wandering away in the night. Chester might like a midnight snack. I'll sleep in the blue tent with the little guys."

Jim kicked the ashes and dirt over the last of the embers. "Hey, are you giving me the stinky tent? A fine friend you are, buster!" He put an arm over Bo's shoulder.

"Let's try our new first aid kit and treat that wolf bite." He noted the blood-soaked sleeve. "Dang, that old Caddo Indian, he got you good this time! Last time, it was the mumbly-peg game, and Chester's knife nicked you. So, do you still believe in his story? I know he's an old guy, but he told me once that he was born in 1879. But, of course, that isn't possible. He's just a loony old coot."

"Yeah, I believe it. But, oh no, look... the guy ruined my good hunting jacket! The wife ain't gonna like it." Bo complained as they ducked into the skunked, malodorous tent.

"Maybe we should get Mel Simpkins and his wife for next year's Halloween Camp. They do great impressions of Bob Hope and Lucille Ball." Jim laughed. The pair shivered as a sudden plaintive, unearthly howl echoed through the woods.

found Dead

California
April 12, 1968

The evening was perfect for a hike in the hills. In the distance, Edwards Air Force Base lay in the last brilliant glow of the setting sun, like a glittering jewel in the high desert basin. Jane, Ben Kinson, and their scruffy Otterhound, Itchy, were hiking the nearby hills. There was news of meteor showers and a lunar eclipse that night, so they were expecting the celestial shows. The hikers each wore simple knapsacks with rock climbing essentials, a sleeping bag, water canteens, sandwiches, fruit, and Ben had a bottle of Napa wine. Itchy had a hand-sewn orange pack carrying his food, water, and a sleeping bag. The proud, eager dog strode ahead of his family up the trail.

The couple was excited to have time off from their jobs at the hospital in North Edwards. Ben, a lab assistant, and Jane, an RN in the emergency ward, had a rare vacation week. So after the overnight hike, they planned to drive north to the wine country for some fun and R&R.

Suddenly, they heard a noise on the trail above them. Rocks and debris clattered down, followed by childish voices.

Soon, a pack of giggling Webelos passed them by. Each child stopped to pet Itchy.

"You're not staying for the lunar eclipse tonight?" Ben asked their leader.

"No, we have a quick tour at the base. At home, we'll try to catch the eclipse later with our telescope."

Itchy ate a few snacks the kids fed him. He loved the attention, but the boys and leaders soon hiked on, wishing all good luck and fun viewing the night skies. Finally, the trail was quiet again. Then, Itchy, with a bark, launched himself up the hillside.

Jane caught up to Ben. "Tonight, the stars will be marvelous, don't you think?"

"I hope so." Then he felt Jane's hand entwine with his. "Oh, you mean... that! I get it. Yeah, I brought something special for us."

"Oh? I can't wait. It will be nice sleeping under the stars... only the two of us."

"And Itchy."

"Yes, and the dog... too. But don't let Itchy sleep in the bag with us."

"I promise nothing, love. You can tell that fuzz-face he can't cuddle with us. I can't." Ben chuckled.

"We'll see," she inhaled deeply. "Take a whiff of that."

"Yeah. Wet dog and skunkweed with a hint of sage."

"No, the fresh air—it's so invigorating."

Ben sniffed. "Yeah, it is good up here, better than all that stale hospital air-conditioned air we breathe." He turned about to say, "You know we work in a sanitary hospital, yet I think the air we breathe is absolute pollution. The disinfectants, alcohol, people's cigarettes, and pipe smoke get to me. Then, of course, you get all the exhaust from the ambulances and trucks that pull into the ER bay. So, yeah, I'd say today is an improvement." As an example, he inhaled and exhaled. "Yeah, sweet fresh air."

"Miss Jane says you are a hippie, Benjamin Kinson." She threw her arms about his shoulders, climbing partway up his back, clinging like a monkey. "But I love you anyway, nature boy."

Ben's dimpled smile quirked up, and he turned his head, kissing her cheek. "Gee, thanks, Miss Jane. I am glad you are on Tarzan's side. You know I am dead on. I told my supervisor we should have an air quality control check. I'll bet we are all breathing toxic junk. Right?"

Jane squeezed him and dropped off to walk behind Ben on the narrow part of the trail. "Right. Still, I'm crazy for saying yes to your hikes and communing with God and nature. You need to go to church more often, buddy boy."

"Not for me. God and I talk just fine. Right, Itchy?" He patted the bristly head of his dog. The dog leaped ahead, scaling the steep climb.

An hour later, they achieved the summit of their goal. A partially flat hill with some scraggly trees, yucca, and shrubbery—a perfect spot to set up camp and make a pit fire as the sun set over the mountains to the west.

Entirely dark now; the stars were popping out all over the indigo sky. For moments, the pair stopped to breathe in the fragrant night air and exclaim over the constellations that appeared in the heavens.

Itchy ran end to end, inspecting their campsite, peeing on yucca, shrubbery, clumps of sage, and dried grass, then digging a few holes in excited glee.

"What is he doing?" Jane exclaimed, watching the exuberant big dog.

"He's making a bed for himself."

"A hole?"

"Yeah, why not? He's not allowed to dig in the backyard, so I let him do what he wants on hikes. He sees us making camp, so he's doing the same. First, he marks his territory, then finds a spot to keep watch. It's what any good soldier or scout would do."

Jane giggled. "You are a nut. So, were you really a Boy Scout, too?"

"Yeah. Eagle Class. Lots of fun."

Jane sat on a boulder near their campfire. "I guess that makes sense." She waved a hand at the dim camp. "This is your milieu."

Ben joined her on the rock and then poured wine into paper cups. "Yeah. But so is this," he leaned close and lustily kissed Jane. He entwined their hands as they sipped wine from each other's cups.

"Yummy." Jane licked her lips and tossed back her brunette ponytail.

"What, the wine or the kiss?" Ben winked and leaned in for another kiss.

After a seemingly timeless moment, they raised their heads and breathed deeply. "Both," Jane replied with a smirk.

"I guess we should eat our supper," he commented and stood, stretching his slim body.

Jane stroked his sleek form and patted his jean shorts-clad behind. "I am hungry for something else right now."

"Yeah? Now? Here? I thought when we settled later in our sleeping bag... um," Ben colored hotly, but his teeth caught his lower lip in a boyish grin.

"You are so sexy. Come ravage me on this rock!"

Ben undid his cut-offs, letting them drop to the ground. He kicked off the shorts and stripped off his windbreaker. "Lookout, here's Tarzan!" He pounded his chest and yodeled like the ape-man.

Jane climbed up the nearby boulder to a flat place. She laughed and watched Ben finish his 'striptease,' then shrieked when he pulled her lower to him. Before she could laugh or squeal, he kissed Jane and pulled her hiking shorts off.

They playfully wrestled about, backing up on the rock and kissing hotly, hands freeing them of clothing until naked as they were born; they had their way with each other.

Married less than a year, their little 'get-away trips' were mini-honeymoons—a real honeymoon they never had the money or time for after marriage.

Itchy, not used to Jane's squeals and shrieks while making love, seemed upset. The dog often interrupted them by jumping on the bed or howling outside their door. He was sure someone was being killed! Tonight was no exception, for Itchy leaped against the rock, having a fit, yipping, and whining. Ben finished quickly, hoping to appease the dog. Laughing, Ben and Jane came down the rock face to calm their dog.

Itchy was Ben's dog. But after marriage, the dog protected Jane. While on a leash, Itchy walked differently with Jane, behaving correctly and keeping pace at heel. Itchy was a mad, yapping, excited hound straining at his harness with Ben.

The pair quickly dressed as the chill of the night soon hit their heated bodies. They hunkered down around their campfire and handed around sandwiches. They had different fillings and, as usual, shared bites of Ben's alfalfa sprout-topped tuna and whole-grain bread sandwich with Jane's curried chicken salad. They reserved the peanut butter and jam sandwiches for breakfast. They shared bits with Itchy, even though he had finished a bowl of chow and several biscuits. The pair split a tangerine and apple and then reclined sated upon their doubled sleeping bags, sipping wine and eying each other with lustful looks. Itchy, satisfied, sprawled near the fire at the edge of his blanket. Soon, wheezing snores proclaimed the dog's sleepy state.

Ben took the chance to move closer, putting his arm around Jane. They watched the sky between kisses as the moon rose and witnessed the penumbra encroaching on the orb's lower quadrant. They snuggled close, breathing in the chilly air and watching the show in the heavens.

Amid kisses, Ben caught a glittering something near the darkened side of the moon. He broke away, "Hey, look there." Pointing, they observed something shiny, sputtering like a Fourth of July sparkler.

"Is that a meteorite?" Jane asked, then sat up to watch its progress. The glittering thing seemed to spin around in front of the moon, not on any falling trajectory like a meteorite; inconsistent in speed, it then streaked high overhead.

"It's a meteor in space and a meteorite when it crashes. But that thing is weird." Ben stated.

"Thanks, Mr. Wizard," Jane replied with a hug.

The sparkling thing left the rising moon's path, shooting across the sky in a southern direction into the darkness. They felt a chilling breeze swirl around their camp, filling it with dust dervishes. Itchy jumped up and barked into the increasing maelstrom. Then, the object went straight up. The trio watched for a long moment, only to see the phenomenon quickly losing altitude.

"Holy crud! Maybe that's a plane in trouble."

"Um, planes don't go straight up like that!" Jane replied, "Maybe it's a helicopter and—" then queried, "But why doesn't it have running lights? Look over there; jets are taking off from the airbase. They've got blinking red, white, and blue lights. That one doesn't. It is only a weird swirling red-orange thingy."

- 👾

Edwards Air Force Base, California

"Yeah, I see it. It's on a north-south trajectory now. We tracked it coming in over Needles and Victorville."

"Roger. I see it, too, tower... it's on..." Capt. Ricart spewed a set of coordinates, then laughed. "Nobody's gonna believe this, but it just stopped. The thing is hovering."

"What's it look like? Over." The tower asked.

"Not much. It's disk-like, but it changes color and shape. I can't tell how big it is. Sometimes, it almost blocks the bottom of the moon like a white shadow and then not, just a splinter against the eclipse's umbra."

"Do you think this might be a secret invasion of UFOs? Maybe using the lunar eclipse to sneak in?" The co-pilot, LT Devers, asked with a laugh.

"Nah, radar is seeing it. Don't be stupid. The aliens would be more covert or invisible if it was a sneak attack. Besides, there's no such thing as a UFO. Watch out! The bogey is moving again!"

"Whoa! The thing just went straight up. Holy Moly!" A blast of expletives came over the radio to the tower and the other jet fighter, then an apology.

"Man, it's got speed, that's for sure. I can't compete with it or follow it."

"Do you think the aliens know we're watching it?" Capt. Lowe, in the Charlie position, zoomed up nearer Ricart.

"Hell. Dunno. But if little green men can make stuff like that, they probably know everything we mere mortals do." Capt. Ricart chuckled at his remark. "Shit, Lowe, this is just weirdness to the max."

"I'm calling it... bogey... we can't..." Lowe replied amid crackling distortion on the radio.

"No, don't. Everybody will think we are crackpots. I repeat... that's a negative. Let the tower boys figure it out." Ricart ordered.

"I. Don't. Care. I see it, too. It ain't an enemy missile or ours. It has erratic movement, so it's got to be a bogey. My radar systems are working fine. Believe me... we don't have any experimental craft like that!" Lowe keyed his mike, waiting for a reply or comment, "Hey. You guys in?"

"Well, you better back me up on this... I ain't losin' my pilot's license or get written up for this one." Another huff and expletive came over the radio channel from the copilot.

Lowe replied, "I think it must be real. This is the third sighting this month of unexplained stuff. Last month, bogies were hanging around these hills and the airbase. The Colonel didn't believe us and soon spread rumors that people saw weather balloons. You know that ain't right. Maybe the ETs are observing us, too."

"Dunno, but the dang thing is moving downward now. I hope it ain't crashing."

"Oh, crappy day. Just what I need on my watch, a big wreck to investigate." Squelching and crackling noises from other mikes interrupted Lowe's comments and expletives.

Then, people in a cacophony of noise yelled from various sources in the tower and nearby aircraft, including a commercial jetliner heading south to L.A.

"United...–11 ... here." The radio crackled loudly, disrupting the pilot's breaking message. "Sorry for breaking... frequency, boys... Hey guys, are you seeing this? Over."

"Yeah. We got us a bogey! Hot diggity!" Simon, Lowe's copilot, yelled with excitement.

"Looks like a ghost! He's going down fast."

"Track it, Lowe!"

"We are—dammit!"

"Something split away... it... and... just went over us... We got... lots of turbulence! Wow!" Suddenly, the jetliner's pilot yelped, "United... to tower...It's on fire!"

"Hell, both blips just disappeared off my screen." Lowe sounded disappointed.

"Yeah, mine too. The sky is empty. Where is it?" Captain Mac Burlson, the airline pilot, remarked. "Tower? United... pan-pan... we..." the radio cut out and buzzed, "...systems damage... we lost George... request assistance... We've got 129 souls..."

"What just happened to the thing? Riggs ain't gonna like this." Simon sighed, echoed by others in the tower. "Shit. Is somebody gonna help that commercial... he's not looking good."

👽

Conditions Critical. Control lost.
Malfunction of guidance systems.
Repeat. D'Laynóxun down.
Need recovery.
No friendly species.

👽

Ben and Jane watched the odd light in the sky. It seemed to struggle as it partially hovered over the airbase and desert below them, then wobbled across the horizon and shot up high again. They also observed several aircraft nearby. One was a jetliner that dropped quickly in altitude and yawed, tipping wingtip to wingtip as if something invisible batted it out of the sky.

The mysterious object swept to the south this time, passing over them. They felt as if electric ants crawled over their heads and limbs. Their hair arose eerily in the air in a static array. Itchy howled and ran to a hole among the rocks. Cowering, he moaned.

"Man, what is that thing?" Ben ran to the edge of the hillside. Then, peering into the dark, they saw the object dip and roll in the sky, still fluctuating between a disk and a cylinder and not as big as they had perceived.

"That is not a meteorite!" Jane yelled. "It's a blimp!"

"No! That's a UFO! Cool!" Ben dashed to his pack for the camera. But by the time he got it out, trotted to the edge of the boulder-lined hill, and aimed, the sky was aflame with an orange mushroom cloud nuclear-like explosion. The pair fell to the ground as a hot wind roared toward them like a furnace blast.

👽

The Edwards AFB watch tower announced an explosion about ten miles south in the hills. It blossomed on the radar screen for three seconds, then was dark. Numerous fly-overs of the area showed no burn-marked terrain, crater, or debris from the crash. No radiation residue beeped on Geiger meters.

👽

"Recovering a crashed UFO will be an unprecedented event." News 10 announcer Rob Canady smiled into the camera. His microphone swung to the uniformed officer to ask, "So, what are your plans for recovery, Admiral Riggs? Do you think you'll find the bodies of spacemen?"

"Lieutenant General Riggs." The man corrected, sounding annoyed. "I shall repeat my previous statement in simple words so you and your audience will understand—this incident was not a UFO crash. They don't exist. Unfortunately, one of our aircraft had a navigational malfunction and crashed because of a pilot error. But yes, the incident and aircraft will be investigated and recovered."

The general stepped aside, but Rob followed, asking again while other news cameras and reporters barking their questions crowded in, their mikes readied for Rigg's snappish answers.

"Do you think anyone might still be alive?" Two reporters inquired.

The officer eyed them as if vermin, but now terse, answered, "Doubtful. Our aircraft had munitions. That, and the fuel, caused the massive explosion. Excuse me.

That is all I can say without further information from our investigation." The man sidled away, his hands held up as others crowded around him. The reporters' barking questions rose in volume as the officer exited.

"Hey! What about that jetliner? It almost crashed… who will answer for them?"

Two days after the UFO sighting

Air Force helicopter pilot Capt. Buster Langston pointed downward. "Look at that. Is that a dog?" His mirrored visor and white helmeted head showed no facial expressions, but his voice was full of curiosity.

"Big dog. Probably a runaway." Lt. Ron Anders responded as he tipped to look out the window.

"Out here? There's nothing for miles around." Navigator Cpl. Juan Costa scoffed and continued to regard his plat map of the suspected wildfire and crash site.

"True. But something is not right. The dog is running around in crazed circles. But, hey, I see a fire circle and a piece of orange cloth on a yucca plant. Maybe it's a signal." So the lieutenant theorized as Langston nudged the stick to head south over the hill.

"Could be. You gonna check it out?" Costa murmured, "I got a date tonight," glancing at his wristwatch. "Don't make me late."

"Might as well—it's us checking now, or someone else does it tomorrow. So far, we have gone bust looking for anything the past two days. So, I'll have the final say here. No use wasting more fuel." Capt. Langston then guided the chopper about the hill, coming in lower, easing down, and landing with a slight bump.

Costa slid open the door and warily looked out. The lieutenant, armed with a sidearm, and the corporal with a rifle, jumped to the ground. But then the dog ran away and disappeared over the hill's edge.

"Here, boy! C'mere!" Cpl. Costa shouted. He dashed after the dog.

The lieutenant grumbled as he paced across the hilltop, seeing a dead fire, singed grasses, flame-stunted shrubbery, and sagebrush. "This wasn't a fire caused by a crash. Damn it, there were people camped out up here." He plucked the blackened and melted piece of fluorescent orange nylon off the yucca. The yucca stem broke and crumbled into dust. "Wow! Weird. Look at this!" he turned about to shout for the corporal.

"*¡Ay Caramba! ¡Dios Mio! Caca!* This is so sick!"

"What is it?"

"You gotta see it because I can't explain it," Costa yelled.

The lieutenant trotted across the scorched area and skittered down the hillside. There, he saw the corporal bent over among some blackened rocks. "What is it?"

Costa glanced up at him. "This is really disgusting. Come look. Be careful! The entire hill is crumbling after the wildfire."

They traded places atop the narrow rocky area. Anders lifted his visor and bent down to look between the rocks. Pieces of blackened, jerky-like skeletal corpses lay wedged among the charred boulders. The dog growled and snapped at his invasive hand. He drew back quickly, "It looks like the dog is protecting the skeletons, doesn't it?"

"Yeah, but what is worse is the dog is hurt, too. The back and top parts are charred like the people! Looks like he was broiled. Do you think these people were up here when that UFO went down?"

Gruffly, Anders replied, "You know it wasn't a UFO—at least Riggs isn't calling it that. It's a tragic incident. I think these were campers, and they started the fire up here. This is miles away from the burning aircraft's trajectory."

"Ha, maybe you are right. But, you know, there wasn't any wreckage in a ten-mile radius within the flight path, and no actual planes or personnel were reported missing. Simon and Lowe told me that. So, maybe the flaming thing everyone saw skimmed this hill, killing those poor people and causing a flash fire."

Anders shook his head. "Whatever. It seems this time, we have actual casualties to report—civilians. It might be an interesting investigation with a link, whether it was a real crash or just a wildfire." Anders turned back to the dog. He reached a hand to him, "It's okay, buddy, we'll take care of you." The dog let him stroke his scruffy face. "I'll stay here, Costa, while you get the medkit, body bags, and the sling."

The corporal looked agape. "What for? You takin' the dog?"

"I'm taking everything. This is evidence of a bizarre and unexplained incident, maybe military or something else. The experimental craft possibly used a weird propellant. So these people are crispy critters, not the mountainside where we thought it crashed. It might get the LT General to change his mind about what happened here the other night."

"Yeah. If you say so, sir. Whatever loco thing you are doin', I'll help. Just don't make me pick up any green, slimy alien goo. Remember the Blob?—great movie!" Laughing, Costa shuddered but trotted off to do his duty.

Anders sat near the dog and dug in a pocket of his flight suit, taking out a fig bar. He broke off a piece, offering it to the dog. It finally took the tidbit and chewed. Anders felt under the singed and roughened coat of the dog to find an ID tag. "Itchy, huh?" The animal seemed to respond and nosed his arm for more food. "I hope you got some people left."

👽

Aid and Assist!
Aid and Assist!
B'Yéniza of the D'Laynóxun
Reporting from the tertiary orb of Star Navoutz,
D'Laynóxun destroyed.
The survival pod ejected 72 saweys from the crash.
The atmosphere here is hostile.
Terrible heat and caustic air.
No edible sustenance.
Survival nav suit disintegrated.
I have one more revolution around Navoutz.
Tell B'Valiatsu and our seed to remember me... and
plant a Foshako fruit so they will have life.
I will perish, the humble servant of Queen D'Andiféshasu.

👽

Later in the week
Angeles National Forest

Hikers enjoying the temperate bright spring day crowded the park paths. Some had radios, picnic baskets, and wriggly children. A few people had dogs that roamed freely along the trails. Several people with packs rode bicycles, ready to engage with nature on a lovely day.

Dilly had pulled away from his owner, Joel, who was still whistling for him farther back on the trail. *He didn't care, intrigued by an unusual scent just steps away from the main path. Dilly had never smelled such a thing. If he remembered what Joel called it, he'd eaten something similar looking at the beach— a jellyfish?*

This new stuff tasted awful and stinks worse. Dilly vomited the piece.

Yet, when he sniffed and pawed at it, the mush moved, making a high screeching sound like Joel's training whistle. Except Dilly did not understand the confusing command.

With a new harsh order, "Leave it!" A rough hand yanked his head away, and soon, Dilly was back on the trail, on his leash, heeling alongside Joel. Although Joel had looked at the smelly thing and said, "Yuck!"

Dilly usually enjoyed eating things that were yucky and stinky.

👽

Pain. I am missing an appendage.
A vile creature bit it off.
Why am I still here and miserably alive?
My sins to the Wondrous Creator must have been great.
Sadly, I am cursed.

👽

A family found an idyllic spot to peruse the forest and the hilly view while eating lunch. They spread a blanket and last week's *L.A. Times* upon the ground and then feasted on cold fried chicken, carrot sticks, chips, and cookies. The family dog, Boodle, enjoyed nibbling scraps from the kids. But soon, his attention turned to an odd sound.

He trotted into the woods and stood to look at a blob of something. The Blob emitted a horrible screech, but Boodle could not understand it. Barking at it didn't help, so he kicked some dirt on it and then scampered back to the family. However, the two boys were keen on an adventure and followed their dog back into the woods amid their parents' admonishment to stay close.

Poking a stick at the gelatinous glob, the children laughed as more squeaks and squelching noises came from it. Then, not listening to their father's shout, the boys were startled when their father pulled them away from their fun by their ears.

"Ow! Dad!"

"Ouch! Hey! Look at what we found, Dad!"

"I don't care. It is time to go. Clouds are moving in, and it might rain soon."

"But Da-a-ad," the pair wailed.

"Fine, show me."

"It's really a big gross-out."

"I can do gross." The father replied with a grin and resigned to follow his eager kids on their adventure.

♥

The trio of humans and the dog stood around the slimy goop on the forest floor. The tallest human hunkered down. He poked it with a stick and squinted at the mess. He took a square thing from his jacket, and a bright flash lit up the forest. The box spat out a square of paper, and one boy grabbed it.

"Okay, you're right. It is gross." The man kicked dirt and pine needles over the mess.

"It looks like a giant booger." One boy laughed as he threw a handful of leaf debris over the thing.

"Ugh, whatever it is, it's icky and stinks!" The other child made a face.

They heard a female voice shout for them. The father gathered his sons, and they left the disgusting blob alone. Soon, they joined the woman at their picnic site.

"I was just reading the newspaper. The reporters think the military plane crash last week was really a UFO." The mother aired her fears aloud, "What if aliens are in the woods here?" She shivered and hugged her husband.

"Now, Amy, don't believe in tripe like that. I've told you about those rag mags—all hogwash." He scoffed.

"Don, it was in the *L.A. Times*, so it must be real."

The boys chimed in as they packed up, "Hey, maybe that snot was a spaceman."

"What snot?" Their mother asked.

"Never mind, Amy, it was something dead the kids found."

"Oh, you boys are so—"

The voices faded as the family walked to the trail again.

♥

I expire.

The Beast of Snowy Ridge

A SUPERNATURAL NOVELLA

Chapter 1—The Hikers

Saturday, October 31, 1970
Snowy Range, Wyoming

Troop 296 tromped up the rough trail; loose, broken scree made their climb tedious and treacherous. Their nylon and aluminum frame backpacks creaked, mess kits in ditty bags clanked, canteens sloshed, and their boots crunched on the sharp shale and remnants of the last snowfall and ice. Quiet, they were not—no sneaking up on Troop 328 this evening for their Halloween weekend Bivouac. The climb from Snowy Lodge should have been only a two-and-a-half-hour trek. But because of the day's circumstances, it was not a fun or easy hike up the mountain.

The tired boys were eager for their supper. Once through the pine and lodgepole treed rise, cooking smoke trailed into the late afternoon orange-colored sky. A pall of smoke hung over the six tents already there. These were larger structures than the nylon or canvas pup tents the boys carried at the base of their knapsacks.

Several older boys from Troop 328 hooted and hollered their greetings at the group. They ran to Scout Master Ed Sharp and cheered on the tired kids. A few taller boys patted the younger ones or shouldered some of their equipment.

Ed ran a hand over his damp brow, sweaty despite the chilly air. "Man, I thought we'd be sleepin' rough tonight. Glad we finally found you all." He grumbled irritably as Troop 328's leader, Sven Amundsen, carrying firewood, loped into view.

"Hey, good to see ya!" Sven yelled back and dropped the load near a blazing campfire. Several smaller fires and an attended cooking fire with pots and pans steamed nearby.

Ed turned to his pack of nine boys, commanding, "Get your tents up pronto, then find a buddy and help gather firewood with the older boys. Don't wander far. Dinner should be soon." He glanced at his watch. "You've got fifteen to set up your tents."

The boys whined and tiredly stumbled into the camp area. They dropped packs, and some moaning fell to the ground.

Ed shook his head, disgustedly saying, "Man, we got some pooped pups here. These city kids are wimps."

Sven dusted off his hands and watched momentarily as many of his high school boys picked a young buddy to help. His assistant scoutmaster, Duke Hale, worked with a trio of their boys, erecting a mess tent in case of rain or snow. "So, what happened to y'all? You're almost two hours late. You guys were supposed to help set up this afternoon. I'm danged glad you weren't carrying all the food for tonight!" He stepped toward Ed and Lou.

Sven grinned widely, "Lost your compass again?" he asked Lou Wyandot, a 'den dad' and Ed's *ad hoc* assistant leader, for this camping trip.

"I wish." Lou colored ruddily as he and Ed dropped their packs in an open space near their boys.

Ed finished, "No, but we had a compass reading and trail marking lesson. Then little Joey Gustafson sent us off in the wrong direction so far west, we dropped the trail and had to backtrack."

"And you didn't correct them? That isn't like you." Sven admonished.

"Hey, lead your men astray—you're gonna pay," Ed growled in disgust.

"We paid for it, alright," Lou muttered. "I got a blister the size of Texas on my heel!"

Keeping Sven and Lou from commenting, Ed continued, annoyed, "We ran into some brambles and sumac along the way, so a lesson in poisonous plants seemed appropriate. Then Dickson fell into the creek. We had to take a break for him to change his socks and underwear, and then, of course, everyone needed to pee."

Ed tugged at his sweat-damp yellow leader's bandana about his neck, loosening it.

"Ya know, maybe I'm gettin' too old for these young whelps." He lowered his voice, growling, "They're a bunch of whiners and snot-nosed complainers, the lot of them." He heaved a sigh as he pulled off the tent from his pack and undid the ties. He and Lou arranged the canvas ground cloth and flung the shelter upon it.

"Sven, you wanna trade? I'll take your smart-mouthed Eagles any day." Ed smirked.

"Ha, then maybe you will be their biggest complainer. My guys are not for the weak-minded!" Sven adjusted his green khaki cap, shading his eyes from the lowering sun. The campground looked on fire as the sun blazed through the trees near the horizon.

Ed and Lou began pounding the tent stakes into the rock-strewn ground and pulling the brailing loops over them. Ed grumbled, "Nope, that's gotta be Blanding. He's the biggest whiner of them all. 'I've got a blister.' 'I'm hungry.' 'I gotta pee.' 'Hey, Mr. Sharp, how long do we hafta do this?' And the worst was Blanding complaining, 'My Mom said I can't,' whatever she said—" Ed shook his head and pounded extra hard with the flat side of his hatchet upon a stake.

"Sounds wimpy. Blanding, huh? Do I know him?" Sven considered the comments.

"Probably not. Kibby Blanding joined a few weeks ago. So this is his first camping trip and hike. His dad, Vernon, wants me to toughen him up. He wanted to pay me to give him a scare or somethin'. You know, put some hair on his flabby little chest! I don't like that mean tough love treatment, but maybe the kid needs it." He coughed and spat into the shrubbery.

Ed handed over the tent poles as Lou crawled under the flap to erect them. "My boy, Stu, he's about as tough as they come, but then maybe he is built to be an Eagle Scout or a great Marine," Ed stated proudly.

"I wish he were along. Stu might've kept Kibby Blanding marching on. Stu's a good harrier and pace-setter. You taught him well, Ed." Lou chuckled and crawled from the erected tent. "I hope his football team wins tonight."

"Me too. It would make this day all worth his absence." Ed stood and shrugged his shoulders and stiff back muscles, then complained, "Young Carlton, Lou, and I traded stints carrying Kibby's pack part of the way until the kid got the hang of carrying it himself. He had it packed all wrong—his canteen clunked him in the leg halfway up the hill, and then his sleepin' bag dragged behind. He sorely missed my lessons on packing yesterday at the lodge. He must've had a finger up his nose and his brain wandering around in Arkansas."

Ed shook his head to say, "When we stopped to re-pack, I made him bury some of his stuff along the trail. We'll get them on the way down. Can you believe he had a huge can of fruit cocktail, a box of cereal, and a tin of cookies? Then the worst, a bottle of prune juice in his pack!"

Lou and Sven laughed, but Ed continued, "Kibby said his mother made him take it if he got constipated. What a city kid, huh? I got just the thing for that—green gooseberries or bear berries. He'll be shitting his pants in no time."

"That's being nice. But, of course, knowing you, it'd be a gopher snake in the kid's sack!" Sven chuckled to Lou.

After adjusting the tent's guidelines and snickering, Lou loped away to assist his youngsters.

Sven watched and listened while Ed, still complaining, finished setting up his tent and started a small fire. He admired the older Scoutmaster despite his wicked humor and stabbing complaints.

Eldon 'Ed' Sharp could track a buck a mile or more into the forest—kill it, skin and field-dress it, and lug it back to his truck in no time. The man knew the Snowy Range, Medicine Bow, Big Sheep Mountains, and wild Wyoming forests better than most mountain men or park rangers. He could scale up and rappel down the rugged cliffs, sniff out good water sources, find food, make a shelter, and live off the land better than any tree-hugger survivalist.

Ed was a former Marine sergeant, having once served in Korea in the early days of the war. Much to his chagrin, a poorly recovered leg wound and a glass eye now kept him stateside and out of the current Vietnam conflict. Ed would have re-upped just for the adventure!

But the man was hard as bullets, still wanting to do something worthy—as if being a construction contractor wasn't tough enough. When Sven was a teen, he was an Eagle Scout under Ed. There was no tougher or wiser Scoutmaster than Eldon Sharp in these woods.

Sven wished he owned the same practical, keen woodlore and was as brave as Ed. The guy could probably do self-surgery with a damned stick! That thought made Sven laugh.

"What's funny, boy?" Ed raised a flinty eye and grimaced at Sven as he stood up, arms akimbo, hands holding his canteen belt.

"Nothing, sir. I'm just admiring your camping skills." He thumped the older man on the shoulder, then turned to whistle sharply. A few nearby heads popped out of tents, and some boys whistled back. "Hey y'all, we got supper soon. So get your tails back here. Let's have our stew and biscuits!"

Cheers echoed from the nearby dark woods as boys noisily crunched out, and some dropped their loads of firewood near the few banked campfires and joined the growing circle of scouts around the central fire.

When everyone stood around the campfire, they joined hands and sang their mealtime grace. Then, retrieved their mess kits and lined up for dinner.

A couple of older boys served supper. Ed hungrily sniffed the vegetable and hamburger stew bubbling in the large pot over the grill placed on rocks. A few lidded skillets sat buried in the hot coals, steaming with fragrant biscuits. A giant tree stump made a temporary table for wrapped corn-on-the-cob, plastic jugs of water and cider, and a box of the ubiquitous Scout treat—the makings for S'mores.

Sven was an excellent camp cook and had taught the boys well. Nearby was a plastic tub with soapy water, ready to wash their camp dishes. A few dunks in ditty bags followed by a bleach-laden hot water rinse cleaned their mess kits quickly. There was an area for hand washing and a latrine that the older scouts had dug earlier.

Amundsen was a competent leader, always hoping he inspired the kids to take charge, trade jobs daily, and be proficient in each duty. Everyone seemed cheerful doing their chores, for these also meant basic survival in the wilderness, besides knowing how to make their camp run well.

Ed smiled to see Sven and his troop helping the younger boys and the fresh blood, Kibby Blanding, settle with their meal.

~~

Chapter 2—Thief!

"**M**r. Sharp? I don't like this stewed junk."
Ed drew back as a metal cup appeared under his nose.
"What?"
"It's got peas and... peppers and stuff. I think there's some creepy meat, ground snake, or somethin', so I can't eat it. Mama said I can't eat weird things."
Ed raised his one steely gray eye, a frown on his face, and grumbled, "Too bad, kid. Sit down and eat it anyway since there ain't nothin' else." He shook his head at disappointed Kibby. "Hey, even if it was a snake, if you were starvin', you'd eat it."
He watched the chubby boy's shoulders slump as he returned to sit on a rock by the fire. Kibby Blanding poked through the bowl with a spoon and then got up to get another biscuit. Two biscuits per person, and Ed knew the pans were empty now.
Kibby then wandered to the makeshift table, peeking under the foil-topped empty pans, and snooped in the dessert-making box. Then, with a sad expression, he stomped his way again to the rock, his oversized, untied hiking boots flopping about. Kibby slumped on the rock and then dumped the contents of his cup on the ground behind him.
With a sneaky look at the other boys, he reached into his jacket pocket and withdrew something silver. Before Ed could yell or do anything, the kid squashed a sizeable chunk of chocolate in his face.
"The little thief!" Ed set aside his bowl and stood. There would be a payday for thievery. He stamped over to the boy and, gesturing with an outstretched hand, snarled, "Hand it over, Kibault."
The boy with watery, pale amber-hazel eyes looked up at the imposing scoutmaster. "Hand... What?" He mumbled through the mouthful.
"Give me the chocolate bar. You look like a guilty dang squirrel with your cheeks full like that." Ed hunkered down before the boy. Then, whispering, he gritted, "Scouts do not steal from each other."

"I didn't steal it. Mama gave it to me." The boy looked crushed but reached into his jacket again and pulled a pair of bars out. "See? She gave 'em to me cuz I get the hiccups if I don't eat right."

Ed rubbed a hand over his sand-papery two-day bearded face. "You sick? Got diabetes or somethin'?"

"No, but Mama said," Kibby's eyes clouded with tears as Ed snatched the bars away.

"I don't care what yer mama says, kid. I... I... don't cry. There's no crying while on a campout unless you are bleeding or have broken bones. Got it?"

Kibby wiped his nose on his jacket sleeve, "Y–Ye–yes, sir." Although snot ran down his upper lip, he nodded; the tears made tracks on his dirty face.

Ed felt remorse. But he knew control must be maintained over the boys. He should be a stern but kind and fair presence for them. These fragile city kids were not idiot buck privates to bust into shape in the Marines.

"Look here... you might have a piece tomorrow. We'll be making dessert here in a few minutes, anyway. I ain't gonna have you go into a sugar coma on candy. What would yer Mama say then?"

Kibby's smile wavered. "Um, not sure, sir."

"Fine, then. You go clean your dishes." He pointed to a pair of older scouts going to the wash bin. "See those boys? They'll show ya how." He patted the boy on the shoulder. "Scoot!"

Chuckling, he returned to his spot as Sven made his way around the fire circle to him.

"What was that about?"

"Aw, maybe a misunderstanding is all," Ed growled and sipped his metal cup with now cold coffee. Then, looked up at the Scandinavian blond giant, asking, "How many chocolate bars did you bring?"

"Hm, a box... there's about two dozen, I guess. If the boys don't go berserk tonight, we might have enough for hot chocolate at breakfast. Why?"

Ed handed over the candy bars. "I caught Kibby with these. He didn't eat his dinner and was stuffing himself with candy."

Sven's sunny countenance clouded. "He's a thief?"

"Maybe. Kibby said his mom gave him the candy."

Sven studied the face of his former scoutmaster and knew Eldon was troubled. He then glanced at the chocolate in the foil, commenting, "Maybe the kid is right. These are smaller bars than I bought. And this one has almonds." He passed the candy to Ed.

"Hm, well, the kid was so dad-gummed sneaky about snooping in the food boxes. So, who's saying if he's lying?"

"But, as usual, your eagle-eye might be right, so we'll watch. Somebody always loses something during these outings, whether by negligence or thieves. You and I also know about the wildlife running off with our stuff." Sven, chuckling, stepped away. He then announced clean-up time and told them to prepare to make their S'mores. Everyone needed a long, sturdy stick.

Ed rose, feeling creaky in the joints and embarrassed to come off so blustery. But dang it, if he didn't watch these kids, they'd get into nonsense. And that Kibby kid had just proved himself sneaky, like a dog stealing food from his master's plate.

Ed's worries about Kibby faded when he settled with a trio of the boys, helping them whittle long marshmallow roasting sticks. He noticed Kibby and two other boys were fascinated by an Eagle Scout's ingenious four-pronged carved branch. Soon, everyone gathered at the campfire, roasting marshmallows. Laughter and shrieks echoed through the woods as some boys lost their treats in the fire or went up in flames. Kibby seemed to do just fine; he ate four, then sneaked a fifth, dropping it in the mud.

Also, Kibby was bolder, pushing his way in for more, nearly knocking Tad Newsome into the fire. An older scout stopped whatever altercation might arise by letting the two boys have the few marshmallows left in the bag. Even though Kibby still looked hungrily and envious of the others with their desserts, they shared the package. Other boys were carousing, with a few bandying their sticks like fencing epees and screeching with laughter.

Ed grimaced, knowing how hard it would be to calm this wild lot after their sweets. If it were only the older boys, he would take them on a short hike to the lake or a higher elevation for stargazing. That would burn off their sugar-fueled energy. But that was a dangerous trek in the dark with the younger, inexperienced boys. He wouldn't lose anyone on his watch, not even fat and annoying Blanding.

With everyone sated with food for the night, they sat around the campfire as Sven plucked his guitar, Ed played the harmonica, and Duke strummed his ukulele. The troops sang some favorite camp songs. Kibby's choirboy soprano voice rose like a descant through the frosty night, surprising everyone. He took the ribbing without a fight.

Then, the leaders pointed out some constellations in the indigo sky, even spotting a stray meteor streaking across the heavens. The boys soon were fidgeting, and one scout offered to tell a scary story about the local murderous creepy creatures. A few jokes and laughs echoed around the fire.

Ed watched as the campfire's golden-red shades shifted over the campers' faces. Some wore caps or knit hats, while others had unruly curls waving in the chilled night breeze. Most now wore heavier coats, gloves, or mittens, their cheeks naturally flushed by the chill and campfire. A few grew drowsy after the long, tiring day and substantial meal.

Ed couldn't wait to climb into his bag tonight, although he would share the tent with Lou. Lou's two sons, Scot and Tim, were a year and a half apart. Tim was in his last year with Ed's troop, so he would move up to junior high next year. They were conscientious little Scouts.

Ed smiled, thinking of the many boys he had mentored, trekked with, and taught camping and woodsman skills through the years. He felt he was a decent bowman and an excellent teacher. In addition, archery was a fun scouting sport for target practice, hunting, or survival.

He enjoyed the quiet solitude of the hunt, silently slipping through nature's paths between trees and rocks, a tiny pang in his heart when he spied his prey. Ed could almost taste the danger, the animal's death, the blood, and the meat of the fallen animal. He would take a tiny breath, sight his arrow, and let it fly.

Yeah, once a sniper, always one. Korea and his military training had made him a bold, robust, silent, and victorious killing machine, whether with a machine gun, pistol, rifle, or bow.

Some of the older scouts in Sven's troop had been in his cub scout packs, including Sven. Ed was proud to have served his country in the Marines but was equally pleased to mentor competent, trustworthy, excellent young Scouts. In recent years, Ed had lost some older boys, former Scouts, over in Vietnam, a few posthumously awarded for their heroic actions. In Ed's opinion, any man who saw combat was a hero.

Ed's attention was drawn again to the campfire and the surrounding kids. He plucked a cigarette from the packet in his pocket and lit it... the tang of the lighter fluid and the crackle and hiss of the ignited cig gave him pleasure. He drew deeply, his first smoke in many hours. While on the trail, Ed never smoked.

For one, he was teaching the boys woodsman's skills. They needed all the oxygen and fresh air to keep their minds sharp. Even in the war, Ed rarely smoked until he could be at ease, nor did he encourage his men to smoke unless they were safe. The innocent scent of cigarettes could put them in danger, the enemy knowing they were just there! No litter of dead butts on their trail, either.

Ed exhaled the menthol-laden vapor, savoring the little head rush, the hot sting in his lungs. Knowing his troop was safe and content, he could now enjoy the beautiful night.

Yet, any sound beyond the campfire caught his ear. Listening like a hound, judging the distance of the noises, and trying to identify them. Mostly, it was birds, an owl, or a rustling nocturnal animal. Finally, spotting far too many yawns and drooping heads, Ed creakily stood up to announce bedtime. He caught Lou and Sven's attention as they arose as well.

"Hey, it's time to get some shut-eye. Morning comes early around here." Ed flipped his cigarette butt into the embers of the fire. Soon, the boys gathered around to sing their night song. The adults helped the youth by banking the cooking fires. Then, they ensured the camp was debris-free and hung their food storage high in the trees. The leaders taught lessons each time about conservation and protecting themselves and their supplies from nocturnal marauders.

The camp was quiet shortly—all the boys watered, tinkled, and were safely in tents. Tired as they were, there were few complaints and no roughhousing. Tomorrow, the troops would break camp, hike to Snowy Lodge near the ski resort, climb into the vans, and head home to Cheyenne. The one-and-a-half-hour drive to Cheyenne was relatively short compared to their hikes up and down the mountain.

So far, the weekend has been fun. It was a perfect winter camp with the dusting of snow last night on top of a previous snowfall. Better, perhaps, than the prior year's white-out blizzard. Although building snow shelters and teaching the boys how to make a campfire in the wind and wet was entertaining, sadly, it became an almost futile endeavor amid whining cold kids.

Sighing, Ed took another turn around the now quiet and orderly campground. Seeing the scudding clouds above, Sven met him at the banked cookfire. "Think we might get more snow?"

Ed cracked his knuckles, the cold making his thick fingers ache. "Maybe. The weatherman said there was a sixty percent chance of flurries. But then, who wants to believe him? He's wrong half the time."

Sven chuckled, "Yeah, but then he's right half the time, too."

"Point taken." Ed turned a bit, hearing footsteps behind him. "Hey, Junior, get back to bed."

Kibby looked nervously at the men. The boy dressed in waffle-weave long underwear, flannel pajamas, a down jacket, and boots with a tasseled red knit cap over his ears made him look like a chubby gnome. "I can't sleep. Can I stay up with you guys?" He took Ed's hand. "Please?"

Ed bent to the boy to reply, "No, son, we are all going to bed. Now, get back to your sleeping bag before you freeze."

"But what about the scary animals?"

"Animals?"

"Yeah, the bears, wolves, wolverines,... snakes, and creepy stuff. Don't we have to keep watch for the Terrible Beast of Snowy Ridge?"

"It's almost full winter, so the animals are all asleep, at least at this late hour," Lou commented, standing behind Kibby. "Besides, you won't find snakes in the snow, and the Terrible Beast was only Harry's silly Halloween story to scare you guys. Come on, Kibby, I'll take you to your tent."

Lou guided the boy to his lime green tent, helping him in and zipping and tying the flaps closed. "Night!" his voice was loud in the dark, and a couple of young kids echoed it from nearby tents.

"Man, that kid wears me out." Lou shook his head as he stomped to the campfire. "Do you think he will be alright alone in his tent?"

"If he has any common sense, he will stay put," Sven remarked.

Ed looked pensively at the pair before him. "Ya know what?—bring him into our tent. We've got space. Just make sure he's got his own bag. I ain't sharin' my sack with a pisser."

The pair chuckled, and Lou left to get Kibby.

Clutching his pillow, sleeping bag, and a small stuffed bear, the boy trundled behind Lou to their large four-man tent. Lou dropped the boy's pack inside and helped the child settle. With a sigh, Lou climbed into his bedroll, inflated his travel pillow with a few breaths, and flung the covers over him. "Night."

Kibby's scared, childish voice trembled as he replied, "Goodnight, Mr. Wyandot. Thanks. I didn't want to meet Harry's Beast alone."

Chapter 3—Night Watch

Ed took the first watch, only for an hour, to ensure everyone was settled and safe. Invariably, the weather, unfamiliarity of the forest, and perhaps because of the boys' innate curiosity, there was always some kid running off to roam into the woods or take a piss. The older and experienced scouts were wood-wise and did not venture far from camp. Ed had taken boys on midnight hikes in his day, but then it was a buddy system, so no one got hurt or lost.

It was never a wise idea to go alone into the woods. Only Ed's personal experience taught him self-preservation and cunning ways that he dared hunt alone. Of course, he had a few buddies, but he was a serious-minded huntsman, not out to shoot game for sport or get drunk and rowdy in the forest, like many men. Ed also did not put up with sloppy or chatty hunters. He only needed fresh, delicious meat for his family. Hunting was a life-and-death thing.

Ed, too, was exhausted right now. His maimed thigh ached for relief. He wished his wife Issie was here to rub liniment on it and maybe rub something else!

"Shit, a fine time for a boner!" He pressed down the hardening lump in his pants.

He was lucky his wife put up with his cranky self and his jaunts to the wilderness to hunt, fish, or take the Scouts out in the boonies.

She was an absolute peach, raising their two sons— each kid a unique, intelligent, talented, jovial pair of wiseacres and the joy of their lives. Also, Issie, a robust and outdoorsy woman, appreciated her stoic and resilient man.

Once upon a time, they were high school sweethearts. Then, when Ed served in Korea, they wrote copious embarrassingly sappy letters to each other. Issie also sent care packages of venison jerky, peanut butter cookies, and snickerdoodles, which kept Ed sane. Then, when Ed came home severely wounded and promising he'd quit the Marines, the dear woman married him.

Ed felt a pang flutter through his chest. Knowing now, years later, the discomfort was not a heart attack or murmur but genuine love and adoration for his dark-haired wife that made his heart patter. She was part Cheyenne, Shoshone, and Irish. A real beauty. A practical sort, Issie rarely was caught up in the wealth they did not have nor asked for much other than love and Ed's respect.

Ed was a mutt made of various crumbs of European ethnicities, primarily English and Germanic. His surname, Sharp, had once been Schapp in his great-grandfather's time. The stout elder man once was a skilled dairyman and butcher. Ed enjoyed good beef, and the hunt—blood and guts never bothered him. In fact, his blood sausage recipe was from Germany, a tradition passed down for generations. He changed it from beef to buffalo or antelope. Although elk and venison were family favorites in the recipe.

Instead of the grease-laden hamburger and tomato soup-based campfire stew they ate earlier, Ed could go for some tasty sausage or a venison chop for his dinner. The Scout supper gave him the gripes as Ed spat into the bushes.

Something moved there.

He peered into the darkness, now discerning he was not entirely alone except for his thoughts. Releasing the snap of the leather holder, Ed grasped his hatchet and slowly removed it. Then, studying the shadows, he stepped back to the banked campfire. Taking up a thick branch, Ed plunged it into the coals. In seconds, it burst into flame. He spun about, hearing cracking and rustling shrubbery. A sudden grunt and rush of breaking branches caused him to whirl again.

There, panting, its tongue lolled from a foamed mouth; the elk's frightened dark eyes were surrounded by white. Then, heaving a belabored sigh, the giant 6-pointer took a tentative step closer, its hot breath steaming in plumes. Dark blotches painted its thick, ruddy coat.

Ed smelled blood. He felt the hair rise upon his neck as they cautiously eyed each other. The animal was clearly frightened—something had attacked it. The buck could dash the few yards between them and gore him with the rack of antlers. Or it could bolt and crash into the tents of the sleeping kids, tangling itself in the guidelines or the clothesline strung between a pair of trees.

Ed could hardly breathe, wishing he had a pistol or the bow, ending the animal's fright at this moment. But a dying, flailing gigantic animal could be just as dangerous as one trying to escape.

He lifted the fiery brand, gently waving it side to side as he approached, making a soft hissing sound at the animal, hoping to get it to turn about and leave. Instead, the buck stamped a front foot. Its nostrils flared as it sniffed the charged air.

"Sh-sh. Easy... move on, fella." Ed spoke softly, "Get on... go on back to yer ladies there. Mama is waiting," he said, still approaching the buck. He noticed several long gouges in the dense fur where blood dripped down its hind legs.

The animal fearfully stepped back, its rear end disappearing into the bushes. It pawed the ground again with a snort. But then, the stag let out a huff and turned in the close confines of the shrubs.

The buck suddenly reared up and beat the air with flailing front hooves, then twisted about. The frantic elk kicked, and it disappeared into the darkness with a horrible gurgling sound amid crunching and breaking branches.

Ed's heart thumped in his chest as he witnessed a muscular, shaggy, dark arm encircle the animal. A horrid fetid stench assaulted his nose. He froze to the spot, afraid to move, run, or do anything. The noise of the attacker and the dying animal ended in mere seconds. The chill wind rustled about his ears and nose, already scenting the tang of copper-rich fresh blood. Ed could not move for a time.

Then, a sound came from behind him, a stealthy slink with the rasp of perhaps claws upon rocks and ice. Ed turned his head and held up the burning branch, wisely not moving his body much.

Large eyes glittered from the darkness, closer now than the elk had been. Ed chanced to breathe and turned slowly to face this new threat. He smelled the death and gore on the creature's hot breath. His only thought was, "What the hell is this stinking thing?"

The 'thing' sprang through the trees upon him. With sudden precision, Ed's head fell to the ground as his headless body flopped into the snow like an unstrung marionette. Then, the beast devoured the skull's contents with a loud crunch and slurping noises. The body suddenly flew into the forest with an effortless swipe of a mighty paw. The animal crouched low to the ground, sniffing; it peed on the fallen brand, sizzling as the flames died. Then, the creature swayed toward the tents with an almost effortless gait. So quiet for such an immense beast, it walked stealthily, sniffing at each tent with hardly a sound on its way into the shrubbery.

Kibby Blanding, hungry again and heeding the call of nature, crawled from the tent, surprised it was snowing. He waddled off into the shrubs to pee. Rubbing the salty sleep from his eyes, Kibby yawned widely and shivered in the crisp cold. He aimed the urine stream to hit what he thought was a snow-covered fallen log. Giggling, Kibby tried to write his name in the snow, like some boys had done yesterday. He took out a broken square of chocolate and let it melt in his mouth as he attended to nature.

As his eyes adapted to the dark, he saw the gleam of dark eyes in the beam of his flashlight. His hand fell away; he pulled the Scout's knife from his jacket pocket. Kibby quickly fumbled out the longest blade. Then, feeling bold carrying Tim Wyandot's pocketknife, Kibby bravely approached the noise in the bushes.

The reek caught him, and he retched. "Oh, geez-loo-eeze! What a stink!" He moved away from the mangled animal carcass as he heard a sound nearby, the crackling of brush.

"Who... who's there?" Shaking, he brandished the knife as his voice rose higher. "I got a weapon, so you go away. Yeah? Tim? Is–is that you? Don't you dare scare—" The rustling noise became louder as a rush of sound, heat, and foul stench overcame Kibby Blanding.

Chapter 4—Horrors!

Sunday, Nov. 1, 1970

Sven, troubled by bad dreams and odd noises in the night, finally kicked aside the quilted flannel sleeping bag. The rough canvas cover was slightly damp with condensation as his hand shoved it away. Yawning, he rubbed the crusted sleep from his eyes. He bent to grab his boots from the bottom of his bag and shoved his sock-clad feet in them. They were slightly warm, almost dry, and already felt good. He tugged on a thick knitted wool sweater and snatched up his knit cap.

The tent flap zipper was hard to move. Sven could only open it halfway. He slithered out of the shallow opening into a dune of fresh snow outside. Then, he rose to his knees and worked on the zipper, freeing it from the ice thickly slicking his tent.

He then looked about the still-dark camp covered in pristine snow. Glancing at his wristwatch to see it was not yet five, he yawned sleepily. He had planned on sleeping until six, then getting the fires going, some coffee brewed, and breakfast started when the kids got up at seven. The sun would finally shine among the trees to warm them by then. The camp was quiet now, and only his crazy self was up at this hour. The sky was still purple, dark, and frigid as the Arctic.

Sven glanced westward to see the snow-covered Medicine Bow Peak. Rising above the Snowy Mountains over 12,000 feet high, it glowed lilac in the dim morning. Stars still edged its profile. He pushed aside the wild desire and goal to tame those rugged peaks with his rock-climbing friends this winter. Those trips were in preparation and training for his ultimate dream of climbing the Alps in Switzerland.

Sven waded quietly through the nearly two-foot-deep powdery drifts, his footsteps marking the path to the camp latrines over the virgin snow. He breathed deeply while concentrating on his morning constitutional.

His nose suddenly crinkled—discovering an odor that didn't belong to the pristine morning. He sniffed an underarm and knew it wasn't him. He kicked snow over his mess and trod back into camp. As he passed Ed and Lou's tent, he knew something wasn't right. The flap and the zipper were open. No footprints led away from the shelter. He brushed snow from the entrance, kneeled, and peeked in.

"Hey, are you guys okay in here?"

Lou grumpily curled up in his bag, pulling the top cover over his head.

Sven waited for a bit, then pushed at Kibby's bag, letting out a gasp. "Hey, Ed! Kibby's gone!"

But Ed's bag proved unused, too. Looking about the tent, he saw their backpacks were still there, so they hadn't gone far. Maybe they got up and went to the latrines together. Somehow, they must have passed him in the woods.

"Where is Ed?" Sven asked as he glanced at the still neat bedroll and the kid's empty mummy bag. "And Kibby?"

"Hm," Lou rolled and blearily stared up at Sven above him. "Huh? What's up?"

"Ed and Kibault Blanding aren't here. Did you see them?"

Lou raised up on his elbows and drowsily looked about the tent. "They're taking a dump?"

"Don't think so. I was just out there." Sven patted Kibby's bedroll. "It's cold. Kibby hasn't been here in a while, and I don't think Ed slept here since his bag is still, in its case, not laid out. I doubt he'd be that busy so early to pack it away again."

"Now you're scaring me." Lou kicked away his covers and sat up, ducking low to avoid the tent's sloped side. "They've got to be around here... I mean, you know..." he hurriedly shoved his feet in boots and wrapped himself in his down jacket. "I swear I didn't hear a thing."

Sven backed out and stood up. Then, looking about the campsite, he commented, "There are only my footprints toward your tent and from mine to the woods. Look."

Lou rubbed his whiskered cheek, but then horror hit his flushed face. "Oh, hell, my kids!" He rushed about the group of tents and fell to one. Unzipping it, he peeked in, then sat back in the snow. "They're okay and still asleep." He re-zipped the flap and stood, then eyed Sven bleakly, saying, "Maybe Ed took a walk last night or... I don't know."

"Ed was limping last night, so I doubt he would have gone hiking, and certainly not with Blanding." Sven pursed his lips and touched his chin, thoughtful to say, "Unless Kibby tried to run away during the night. The kids did rib Kibby a lot yesterday. And Ed was kinda annoyed with him."

"For what?"

Sven's lips drew down. "I shouldn't say, but Ed thought Kibby was stealing candy. But I don't think so."

Lou looked pensive, then asked, "I think a couple of us should go look for Ed. Maybe he fell or something... Ed might be hurt. He's kinda old."

"Don't let Ed hear you say that. He'll knock you upside the head for it." Sven spat the angry retort.

Lou put his hands in his jeans pockets. "Not to sound like a wimp or anything, but I think *you* should go look before too much time passes. You are better traipsing through these woods than I am. Since you are the trail guide, take a couple of your best kids or Duke."

"Yeah, maybe so. I don't want to leave the boys, but I think it will be alright if you are here for a while. Let the younger ones sleep some more. But I'll get a few of mine up, and they can get the fire going and something hot to eat and drink. If the guys spent the night in the snow, they are probably freezing to death, and we'll need something hot for them in a hurry."

The men separated, each to their task. Sven, Duke, and four older scouts were ready within seven minutes. Duke and Sven wore backpacks filled with food, emergency supplies, a climbing kit, and ropes. Each wore heavy coats, one youth, a canvas poncho, and snowshoes. Everyone had a couple of water canteens and had rock picks or small hatchets on their belts.

"We'll send up a flare if it's bad. Otherwise, see y'all in an hour or two. Maybe less if we are lucky." Sven said to the worried Lou.

Lou stood with a pair of Eagle Scouts, watching them leave. As they tramped away from the campsite, the bundled search party looked like yetis. First, they circled the area looking for signs, then split, each leader with a pair of boys.

"Let's get the fires going and heat the water. We'll all need it." Lou directed as he chaffed his hands and stuck them again in his pockets after forgetting his gloves in the tent.

Sven's scouts were competent in starting the fire from last night's banked embers. Both speaking in whispered tones to each other, they then sat with Lou by the roaring campfire, watching the pots and kettles steam.

Mike Donner, a tall, gawky-looking teen, swallowed audibly. "Do you think something horrible happened to those guys? Maybe they got kidnapped or somethin'. Remember last summer there was a manhunt up here, looking for some escaped jailbird? Maybe they never found him."

Lou, gazing into the flames, responded, "Don't know. But you know Ed, he'd never just leave without telling someone. So something must've happened."

"I was like... wondering if maybe an animal got 'em."

In his parka and fur-lined hood bundled warmly like an Eskimo, Danny Flynn snickered, "C'mon, Mike. What animal, like what, a cougar? That'd be the only thing that could sneak in and snatch somebody away without a sound. I've seen a big cat grab a calf and get halfway up the mountainside before we could do anything. Dad's always on the lookout for 'em. It's too bad we ain't got a rifle."

"Yeah, maybe. But don't cougars hibernate? So maybe it was a bear or somethin' really... deadly big or—" Mike retorted.

"Bears are less likely to come out of hibernation. Besides, there'd be a big mess of blood and guts, and we'd find them buried nearby. So nope, it was a cougar." Danny spat into the fire with his assertion.

Tired of the teens' gruesome, sibilant argument, Lou held his hands toward the flames, enjoying the warmth as he added his opinion. "I think something more sinister happened. Or maybe that dumb kid, Kibby, ran away. Only that would make Ed take off like that."

"But wouldn't Mr. Sharp tell somebody, leave a note, or mark his trail like he taught us?" Danny queried.

"Maybe not. Not if it was an emergency, but then," Lou tiredly rubbed his whisker-stubbled cheeks, his eyes raised to the youths, "maybe Ed is still just a stubborn

Marine, doing his solo duty." Lou shivered again, both from the cold and the morning's realization. "I'm sure the guys are okay. Ed wouldn't let any actual harm come to Kibby."

"Ya think?" Mike echoed, nibbling at his thumbnail. His worried eyes looked about the camp, bouncing in thought as he counted the snow-clad tents. "The tents are all here, the food is still in the trees, nothin' is wrecked or messed up, so maybe it wasn't a bear."

Danny, thoughtful, asked, "What if we don't find Mr. Sharp and Kibby? Does that mean we are stuck up here until we do?"

Lou answered. "No, if we don't find Ed and Kibby, we'll still break camp and leave today as planned. Sven will let the forest service know we have missing men. They've got helicopters and trucks. If that doesn't work, they'll bring in the local sheriff and dogs to find them."

"Sir? Isn't that a bad thing... just leaving them? I mean, Mr. Sharp always says you never leave a man behind. That's the Marines' motto." Mike's voice quavered with the question.

Lou nodded, his dark eyes assessing the pair before him. "I know, boys, but sometimes, the good of the many outweighs the good of the few." Then, seeing them look puzzled, he added, "We've got the responsibility of the other kids to worry about. We don't have enough experienced people for a manhunt. And then, if we are stranded here waiting for Ed and Kibby to return, how do we tell the parents that some idiot kid ran off and is lost, so we all stayed to find him and got stuck? And what about food? We have barely enough to last another day out here."

Lou shook his head. "No, getting an experienced tracker to find them if the guys are truly lost is the right way. We can't risk anyone else's life."

He got to his feet, "On that note, let's get the oatmeal going. It takes longer at this higher altitude to boil the water. So we'll be the smart ones, burning the home fires for our heroes out there this morning."

Duke stopped following a trail of broken branches and littered bits on the ground. He glanced around, putting up his hand for quiet. The pair of boys, Fisher and Calvin, halted abruptly. Their eyes widened, noting the tension in their leader's stance.

"Mister... is it—"

"Sh." Duke's head turned as he sniffed. "Do you smell that?"

The boys sniffed the air, and Calvin whispered, "Yikes! What a stink. Is it a skunk?"

"I don't know, but it's worse. My dog, Bingo, got skunked once, I know—" Fisher was cut short by Duke's command.

"*SH!* There's something just over there—" He pointed into the darkness where the trees and foliage were so thick it resembled a cave's yawning mouth. "You two stay here while I check it out." He slipped off his backpack and, holding his walking stick and a flashlight before him, Duke cautiously stepped away.

The fearful boys stood in place, straining to hear and watch Duke enter the dark woods.

"HO...LY SH...IT!"

There was a retching sound, but then the floundering crashing of something heavy coming towards them.

Fisher stood his ground, a long, thick, sharpened branch at the ready, as Duke stumbled out of the underbrush nearby. The teen spun, prepared to stab or throw his weapon, but released a heavy breath. "Thank goodness, it's only you, sir!"

Duke, gulping air, fell to his knees. He coughed and vomited.

"Gross!"

Calvin kneeled and patted Duke's back. "Are you sick, sir?"

"Oh, my lord, I have never seen such a thing," Duke rasped between heaves. "Of course, I'm sick!"

"What is it?"

"I don't know, but it's bad." Duke sat back on his heels. "Oh, hell, this is a disaster."

"Can we see what you found?" Calvin made to step past, but Duke's gloved hand shot out, grabbing the youth's pant leg.

"NO! It's Ed, I think. I can't have you seeing horribleness like that!"

"Is he... um... dead?" The pair asked fearfully.

"He better be dead by the look of what I saw, but I'm not sure if it's him or something else. It's like a scene from a slasher film. Man, it's grotesque!"

"Cool!" Calvin crooned.

"Not nice, you gory goon." Fisher slapped Calvin's shoulder. He turned to Duke, "So what do we do now?"

Duke sat back, grimly wiped his mouth, and took out his emergency whistle under his jacket collar. He inhaled deeply and then let out three successive blasts, piercing the quiet morning. Finally, he leaned back on his arm and blew four equally long bleats. They waited and, from a distance, heard an echo of two bleats in response.

The boys, nodding to each other, knew the messages: *SOS* and *Everyone Rally Here*. The answer: *All right. Message received.*

"Mark the tree there, pointing into the bushes. I already did it at the site." Duke ordered the boys but grimly thought, *I did it with last night's supper and the bag of Gorp I snacked on.*

Calvin bent branches while Fisher laid a couple of rock cairns and sticks pointing into the woods.

The trio rested for several minutes as they heard the other search party's grunts and footfalls nearing.

Sven crested the slope and waved at the group. Then, huffing frosty exhalations, Sven and his boys arrived by Duke.

"You found them? Where are they?"

Duke sadly shook his head, "Not sure, but only you should see what I found, Sven." He pointed into the trees, "Walk east about twenty yards, then under the fallen tree, you'll see it. I hope you have a strong stomach!" Duke called after the brave Sven.

The four boys eyed Duke as he climbed to his feet. "Was it Kibby or Ed?" Charlie asked in a squeaky voice made dry by the cold. He gulped a mouthful of water from his canteen, waiting for an answer. However, a loud shout from the woods and running feet frightened Charlie, and he dropped his canteen.

Sven skidded on the packed snow and held his stomach. "Oh... Hell. Bear... shit!"

Even though alarmed, the boys snickered at Sven's announcement, as he rarely cursed around them.

He eyed them bleakly, admonishing, "Guys, I didn't cuss. I found bear dung." He coughed and blew his nose on a kerchief.

"Oh."

The boys, in echoing curiosity, asked and commented...

"So, what's going on?"

"Did you find them?"

"Are we done? Can we go back now?"

"I'm hungry."

Sven nodded. "Yeah, we're done here." He checked his compass, memorizing the coordinates, then removed a small can of fluorescent orange paint from his pack, shook it, painted the ground with an **X** and arrow, and marked a pair of trees. Then, dropping the can in the knapsack pocket at his waist, Sven steered the boys away. "Let's get back to camp. We gotta let the Rangers know what we found."

"What is it?"

"What did you see?" the repeated chorus of boys echoed as they hiked. "Tell us."

Sven and Duke followed behind the curious kids as they retraced their steps and soon were on the trail to their camp.

"Did you see what I did?" Sven quietly asked Duke.

"Terrible, huh?"

"The guy had no head. I couldn't let the boys see that."

"I know. I wasn't sure at first if it was Ed or a critter." Duke gulped audibly. "I got sick."

Sven rubbed his flat, muscled stomach, grumbling, "Yeah, I don't feel so good either. I think a bear got him and hid Ed there. I found a partial blood trail among some bushes out of camp. What about you?"

"Nothing but pure unmarked snow. But when we got closer, I smelled something worse than dead."

"I think the bear marked his kill. But, of course, the disembowelment didn't help matters any." Sven winced.

"Any sign of Kibby?"

"No, man. Nothing."

"So, what do we do now?" Duke asked.

"Like we talked about. Have a bite to eat for strength and break camp. I plan to run ahead of y'all down to the lodge and use their phone to call the ranger station. I'll tell them we have a dead man up here and a missing kid."

"Do you think Kibby is really missing? Perhaps he saw the whole thing and is hiding."

"I think if he saw it, Kibby would scream bloody murder," Sven remarked. "He was blubbering about a scalded pinky, blistered feet, and damp socks last evening. The mess I saw *was bloody murder*."

"You're right... It was a murder scene. You don't think a person did it, do ya? Ed seemed posed, like he was waiting for us. The body sitting up against the tree but missing the head." Duke ran a hand over his own neck and grimaced.

"I still think it was an animal. It took a crap on Ed and left claw marks on the body and tree. Even though disemboweled and shredded, Ed's body was half-buried in the snow and dirt. The snow last night probably covered the animal's tracks and most of the blood trail from our camp." Sven recounted with a shake of his head.

"So, what about Kibby?" Duke shivered. "I feel like a bum to leave him."

"He's probably dead too, buried somewhere in the woods like Ed."

"God, what a horrible fate. So, what do we tell the others?"

"I can't lie about it, but I don't want to scare the piss out of them, either." Sven sounded worried and sighed as they hiked through the deep snow.

"I know it's a fib, but if someone asks, we should say the guys returned to the lodge because Kibby was sick," Duke suggested.

"I guess." The men trooped behind the boys for a few minutes, and Sven called, "Hey, guys, stop at the aspen tree there. We're almost at our camp."

He rushed ahead to the boys. "Hi, let's talk for a second."

Sven leaned against the naked tree's white bark and eyed the boys. "You know I care about all of you, right?"

"Yeah." They echoed and shifted restlessly.

"So, what I am gonna tell ya is extremely bad. But we must be brave and help the younger ones get through the day. We will tell anyone who asks that Mr. Sharp and

Kibby left last night for the lodge. Kibby was sick. Got it?"

Heads nodded, but suspicion spiked in Fisher's eyes. "That isn't the truth, is it, sir?"

"No, but it is as good a story as we can say for the moment. Perhaps the pair were on the way down, but something happened. Something bad. We won't tell the others the horrible part. Okay?"

"What's the horrible part? That we can't find 'em?" Mike asked fearfully.

"Ed Sharp is dead, probably killed by a bear. That's the worst that I will tell you. We don't know where Kibby is. So, we will have breakfast, break up camp, and get off this mountain. Nobody will talk about this. We might find Kibby along the way to the lodge if lucky."

Duke pulled a shaking boy under his arm and said, "Look, guys, we don't want you all to be scared, but we must be careful. The bear could still be about, so we must leave quickly. Don't tell the others about the bear. Got it?" He nodded to Sven. "He's gonna hike down first, clear the way, and report to the rangers. After that, we should have an obvious trail and be safe."

"What if the bear gets Sven, too?" Charlie squeaked and sniffled.

Sven shook his head. "Not to worry, I have my bag of tricks right here. Pepper spray, a flare gun, and I'll whistle or mark the trail if I see the bear. You guys should be fine. Besides, most bears won't continue to hunt once they have a food cache. If it snows more today, it will hide out, eat, and sleep."

He smiled broadly, "Now, be brave and say nothing, except we found a message that Ed and Kibby hiked out earlier this morning."

Chapter 5—Morning has broken

Sunday, November 1, 1970

Men make plans, but nature perversely changes them. Before breakfast, the snow suddenly came harder, and it was a blizzard by the time the campers were ready to leave. As they packed their gear, the wind drove snow into their faces. Finally, the leaders gave up the plan to hike down to Snowy Lodge. Although Sven knew he could make it through the storm to the inn, he worried about the troops and canceled his earlier plan.

Mostly, the kids enjoyed the crazy weather, taking shelter in their tents to play or read, while only a few engaged in snowball fights. Some were glad they might miss Monday's school. A couple of kids whined about being cold and bemoaned that Ed Sharp and Kibby were probably sitting in the cozy lodge before a fire, drinking cocoa and waiting for them.

The Troop 328 leaders, as did the four boys in the search party, knew differently. They were all pensively quiet. Sven, moody as hell's fires frosted over, was restless, pacing in and out of the big mess tent that held part of his troop. He kept eyeing the storm, checking his watch, and grumbling like the dark clouds overhead.

The daylight dimmed with the encroaching violent storm, and soon, it was afternoon. The leaders rationed their food stores and ate cold burger bun bologna sandwiches washed down with hot instant cider.

Evening came with no relief in the storm, so they made do with oatmeal and SPAM. Lou retrieved Kibby's pack to find a box of fudge-flavored *Space Sticks*, more chocolate, and two PBJ sandwiches. The leaders doled out the sweets for tomorrow's trek, then helped the kids settle for the night, crowded now in the larger tents and no one alone in pup tents.

Monday, November 2, 1970

Lou and Sven crawled from their separate tents within moments of each other that morning. Then, each scratching, muzzy, and yawning stamped toward the camp's latrine through the deep snow. Lou eyed the taller, well-built fellow, admiring his effortless, long-legged gait and bedhead of golden curls. He stepped up to join him, self-conscious of his bony self and balding pate. They stood over the snow-covered trench, four feet apart, separated by a thorny holly bush. Neither looking at the other, they enjoyed their morning tinkle with little sighs.

"We got almost two feet of snow again last night," Lou commented, glancing about the dimly lit area, the trees trimmed with lacy white ice.

"Yup—looks like it," Sven muttered after a yawn. Finished, he put himself away and grabbed a handful of snow to wash his hands. Then, shaking off the melted stuff, he walked from the camp amid the swirling snowflakes.

Lou glanced at his watch, then finished, too. Emulating the woodsman and washing up with snow, he asked, "So, what time are we heading out today?"

Sven, loping away, turned about with a finger on his lips. He pointed. Lou caught up with him. He spotted an elegant scene framed between a pair of pines in the lavender shadows of pre-dawn.

A couple of white-tailed does were drinking at a rivulet coursing downhill to the lake. An enormous stag stood to watch as a few other deer milled about.

"Pretty, huh?" Sven sighed. "Just think, if we hadn't heeded the call of nature, we would have missed them."

"Yeah. Right." Lou responded and gulped, his heartbeat now steadying. "I'm just glad it wasn't a bear. So, we've got a couple more hours before sunlight hits these hills... we can go back to sleep, right?"

Sven inhaled, his barrel chest expanding and stretching the wool sweater and down coat. "Not me. You know it takes some effort to get wet wood to burn. We had only a little dry stuff left last night. So, let's get the fire going and some hot water and coffee started. By that time, the kids will be up. I plan to get us to the lodge before lunchtime. With all this snow, we gotta move as fast as possible. It'll be a hard slog. But we can do it, eh?" Sven buffed Lou's shoulder.

Lou shoved his ungloved hands into his jacket pockets, disappointed not to return to his warm sleeping bag, and trudged through the snow after Sven.

The pair worked quickly enough. Sven was quiet, but Lou was chatty. Something felt off, like the calm before a thunderstorm or tornado. Eerily calm. Not even a squirrel chittered a greeting, no birds peeped, and by now, there should have been several early morning mockingbirds, catbirds, and maybe a jackdaw or raven to break the silence despite the snow flurries. The deer at the stream had been the only evidence of wildlife around them.

Sipping the weak steaming brew, Lou stepped away and looked over their rocky plateau, hoping to catch the beginning rosy glow of the sunrise. Instead, dark clouds glowered on the horizon.

"Sven? Looks like more snow is coming."

Sven, whittling a stick, looked up and around. Then, smiling, he said, "Maybe we should break camp early while we have a chance. Hiking in snow flurries is better than trying to break camp during it. Maybe we can get off this mountain before the storm hits us again." He glanced at his wristwatch and said, "Yup, roust the guys out of their tents. Let's have a quick breakfast—oatmeal and instant cocoa."

Lou agreed and hurried along to his tent.

With a glance about the tent, Lou counted heads still there, glad no one else had wandered away in the night. He was not buying the story of Ed and Kibby hiking out yesterday before dawn. Or the idea they got up, walked to the latrines together and got lost. Somehow, they must have passed by through the woods.

Lou backed out of the tent and rose to his feet. He scanned the shady campsite. The scent of the refreshed fire enticed him to warm himself. A few boys were grumpily crawling from the tents. Some in only long underwear and boots wandered toward the latrine ditch.

He wondered now what the deal was. While Ed was a solitary guy, preferring his own company, he was a dedicated Scoutmaster. Ed wouldn't have left the camp without saying something or leaving a message. *Where did they go?*

Sven had been abnormally quiet yesterday after their search. Duke said little and avoided talking about Ed or Kibby. The boys with them looked scared and hardly said a word to anyone.

"Something stinks and it ain't a big lying Danish Fish!" Lou grumbled as he watched two boys argue over who took the most oatmeal and the last canned beans. "Come on, guys," he put a hand on each and sent them in opposite directions to sit. His stomach growled, and oddly selfish, he helped himself to more oatmeal than was his allotted portion. But Lou figured he was due for a full-sized part. The pot soon was empty as Charlie Hale took the last tiny glob.

The youth looked up with teary eyes to ask, "There's no more cocoa or oatmeal. Is this all we have?"

"Yup. Eat it and drink some hot *Tang*. It will fill you up." Lou offered, wishing he had something more substantial to add to the disgusting instant breakfast drink. He knew Ed always carried a flask, but Lou wasn't eager to paw through the missing man's pack. That still bothered him.

Why not take their backpacks if they were hiking to the lodge? Ed was a top scoutmaster, always prepared for any Doomsday event! The lack of communication or planned escape was unbelievable.

"Yup, something stinks."

He meandered over to their tent and crawled inside. Ed's sleeping bag and the rolled-up pad were tied to his backpack now. "'Curiouser and curiouser,' as Alice would say."

Lou peeked out of the tent to see if anyone was watching and then opened the top flap of Ed's pack. He rummaged in it, smelling soiled socks and the scent of mildewed old canvas. Lou found the prized aluminum flask, shook it, heard the delightful ping of liquid, then sipped the harsh whiskey and smacked his lips. He dug again through the pack, finding a plastic bag of jerky, another of dried fruit and nuts, and a foil-wrapped date-nut bar.

"What a bonanza! Jerky and Gorp are the hiker's best survival food. Now, why wouldn't Ed take them?" Lou wondered aloud. Hearing approaching footsteps crunching through the snow, he hurriedly slipped the food into his coat pockets. Then, he backed out of the tent but stopped at the harsh voice.

"What the heck are you doing?"

Lou stood up and turned to face Duke. He stepped closer, saying, "Did you know Ed left his pack? Don't you find that suspicious?" Then, he whispered, "Come on, Duke, what in the hell is happening here?"

Duke looked grim, then grabbed Lou's arm and steered him away to the edge of the campsite. "Look, man, you can't repeat this to any kids, got it?"

Lou, shocked, jerked his arm away. "I don't have to do anything. Where's Ed and Kibby?"

"Both dead. But we only found Ed."

Lou's eyes clouded and filled with tears and suspicion. Then asked, "How?"

"Bear. A big one."

"Shhhh-it." Lou sounded like a leaking radiator. "Where's Kibby?" He demanded with a gulp.

"Didn't find him... Probably dead, too."

"We gotta get the hell out of here. What if the bear comes back? We're an instant smorgasbord!" Lou gripped Duke's arm hard.

"Stop! Don't freak out! That's why we said nothing. Look, calm down. Go pack your stuff and help the kids. Even though it's still snowing, we are leaving soon. We've got to get everyone out of here. Got it?"

"Yeah, you don't have to ask me twice." Lou stepped away but stopped when Duke yanked his arm.

"What did you find in the tent?"

"Nothing."

"Liar. I smell whiskey on your breath. We all have to keep our heads. You can't lose yours now. We've got to keep the kids straight and under control."

"I found Ed's hooch. Not much there. Maybe he got drunk and wandered off. Ya think?"

"Nope, that's not Ed. It was only medicinal. I'll bet you found some other stuff, too, right?" Duke eyed the shorter man with derision.

"Just some jerky and Gorp."

"Give it up. We must share everything since we have only a little food left. So the sooner we get to the lodge, the better, right? But we'll need that food to keep the kids going today."

"What about the hooch?"

"Keep it for an emergency."

"This isn't one?"

"Not enough of one yet. Sorry, you can't drink on the way down. Now move it and help your boys break camp." Duke brusquely left Lou gaping after him.

Lou stuffed the wrapped bar deep into his jeans pocket. "Fathead. You don't talk to me that way."

The campsite was struck and emptied within the hour, their garbage packed, and the two troops filed out on a downward path through the woods. The snow continued, but it wasn't like yesterday morning, with a howling icy wind driving it in their faces. Still, big flakes littered their coats and packs, and soon, the group looked like snowballs sliding down the trail.

The boys understood it was essential to keep moving, so no one complained or goofed around. Instead, they held a steady pace, trudging through the snow. Their packs were lighter without the food and water stores from Friday and Saturday. Each had a handful of gorp, a venison jerky piece, a hamburger bun, and two water canteens. Not much food, but they would make it to the lodge by lunchtime if lucky.

Sven had abandoned the plan of jogging ahead, believing his boys might rebel and run amok without his steady influence.

However, haunted by the grisly image of the terrible condition, he found Ed, his former friend and Scoutmaster; Sven moved quickly along the trail. Nobody deserved to die like that. He also wished he could have carried Ed's body back with them. But keeping the falsehood alive was the best Sven could do to keep the boys and Lou in high spirits and cooperative.

～

Chapter 6—Trapped

The constant buzzing in his ears sounded like mosquitoes and a static-filled radio. No, not a radio. He shook his fevered head and rubbed his ears as pain radiated throughout his body. Everything was too loud. His breathing sounded harsh and labored as if he had run for hours. Yet, despite a nauseated, grumbly stomach, Kibby was hungry! But still too tired, he only flopped down on a thick nest of scratchy pine needles.

Kibby looked across the cave at his captor, a gigantic dark beast that sort of resembled a bear. He hoped it wasn't a Grizzly or Kodiak, also figuring it wasn't a polar bear since it was blackish brown. He should know what kind it was since he had visited the Denver Zoo last spring and had to write a school report about bears. Still, what he faced seemed like something else—larger and meaner.

He had been in the damp cave for a long time. Kibby thought it was only a hole in the earth, as roots and bugs were there. Mud dripped and pooled along a wall of the cave. He was toward the back, unable to see out or any daylight. Yet the shelter had a slightly fuzzy blue glow, not from any fire but something else he could not imagine or see.

The beast snored loudly, passed gas, and grumbled in its sleep. The boy wondered if he might slip by the sleepy creature and escape. But then he was afraid to wake it. There were deep scratches on the animal's hide. Some were old, scarred lines, while others still oozed blood. Maybe the bear tangled with a cougar!

Kibby wished he could escape because he also needed a toilet! Shifting his weight from side to side, he slithered along the mud floor of the cave. The closer he came to the beast, the sicker he felt. It rolled about as a massive paw with almost half-foot-long claws struck the ground. The wicked thing grunted in sleep as it faced him, blocking any escape.

Kibby stopped moving, then took his knife and chopped at roots in the ceiling, digging through the frozen mud, hoping for more air. At least it would be fresh and not stinky, but it would be cold. Although he had ceased feeling cold a long time ago. The cave was tolerably warm, and maybe the stinking beast helped keep it warmer. His stomach rumbled loudly, and Kibby stopped to watch his captor, hoping it didn't wake him. His fingers hurt from digging and were almost numb from the cold.

All Kibby knew was that he was peeing in the forest one minute, and the next, he was hanging upside down from a tree. His booted foot tangled in the branches. The animal had shuffled about for a time, digging in the snow and dirt below him and only occasionally coming to sniff him. Kibby played dead when it smelled him, even when the animal licked the blood from his arm and hand. He almost screamed, afraid it would eat him, but the thing disappeared, leaving Kibby to suffer.

Kibby hung there for a long time until the sun came up and the snow melted, causing the frozen branches to give way. Finally, he fell to the ground. Before he could escape, the creature returned. The animal gripped Kibby's foot in its mouth and dragged him through the snowy forest. It snowed harder as they went deeper into the hills.

Then, the creature pushed Kibby into a hole and left him alone. So disoriented, Kibby couldn't move, unaware whether it was night or day. Yet the animal seemed to abandon him until some hours ago when it tumbled down the rocks into the den.

The animal had sniffed him. Again, Kibby played dead, feeling lucky the bear had left him alone. It fell asleep near what he thought was the passage to the cave entrance.

Crouched against the damp wall, Kibby rummaged in his coat pockets, finding a partial chocolate bar. He had stolen this one! It was a chunk of chocolate for the S'mores. Greedily, he ate it. It was frozen hard and challenging to gnaw, but if Kibby held it in his hand, the chocolate warmed and became softer. He wished there was a fire... and marshmallows and cocoa. That would be good. But he nibbled on the chocolate, knowing he had to make it last. He put the remaining squares away in his pocket.

He yawned away tiredness and boredom; Kibby soon curled to sleep, wishing for his mother, hoping to see her rosy, apple-cheeked face in his dreams. Instead,

Scoutmaster Ed haunted his dreams, accusing him of stealing candy.

Because Ed yelled at him, Kibby took a giant bar to spite Ed. Of course, he would have eaten the evidence that night, but being scared to sleep alone in his pup tent, he never had the chance to finish it once he'd crawled into the leaders' warmer shelter.

He wondered where everyone was right now. Was anyone looking for him? Kibby hoped so. Although now terrified of the whipping he'd get for causing trouble. It wasn't his fault if he was lost in the wilderness—that was the bear's doing.

Kibby awoke again and stretched gingerly, still achy, parts of him raw and sore. He studied the beast nearby, wondering if it would awaken soon. The creature's snores had changed from a deep, resonant rumble to higher, raspy breathing, still punctuated by snorts and snarls.

Maybe this was the end, and now he would die—eaten alive by a bear!

The dense, dark pelt seemed to shudder and shrink slightly. A filthy, bare human foot with long toenails slipped from the fur.

Kibby gasped, afraid, wondering how another human could be in here. *Maybe the beast was shitting it, a leg and foot at a time! Perhaps he could kill the animal while it was 'doing its poop-thing' or crawl past it.*

But as Kibby moved away around the other side of the wall, keeping the beast in view, he saw something horrible. A hairy, dirty arm rose in the air, the hand gripping nothing yet seemed to search for something as its fingers sinisterly moved about. Another hand and forearm joined its mate, doing the same exercise, like a dance in the air. The long toes curled against the dirt floor, and suddenly, the fur pelt moved.

There lay a naked man. His hair was so long and tangled that it looked like a giant shrub. Very filthy, with a hairy torso and limbs, yet the pale skin glowed in the dimness.

Kibby watched from the back of the cave as the man went to his knees, then rose, but was too tall to stand fully erect under the dirt ceiling.

Kibby wanted to shout, happy that he was rescued. He hoped the man had killed the creature or something, but then the man-thing turned its head and stared into the darkness where Kibby hid.

"Come out, little worm... I won't hurt you yet." The thin man cajoled in a husky, oddly accented voice. "I'm not hungry enough t'eat a fat kid like you right now."

Kibby's gasp of disgust and fright caused the man-thing to find him. The man came and yanked up his prisoner. "You can't get out, ya know, little worm." He shook the boy and growled, "I don't like thieves or liars. So, you were gonna sneak out, huh?" He pointed at the slither marks near where he had slept. He grabbed the pocketknife, shouting, "You was gonna kill me, huh? You putrid little—"

With a roar, the man flung the boy against the far wall.

Lying stunned, already bruised and hurt, Kibby couldn't move. But this was worse—the man was still a beast!

Play dead, Kibby's mind slowly worked as he lay stunned.

"That game won't work with me. You ain't a possum, boy! But you is gonna be my supper later."

"No, please... not... that," the boy whined. "I'll be good... honest, I will."

"You's supposed t' be honest... a Boy Scout always is."

"Right, I am... a Boy Scout."

"Goll-darned if you's honest, though. I watched ya last night. You there shovin' them boys, all greedy to eat yer fill," the horrible man sniffed, "and you have been eating somethin' again!"

"I didn't."

"Ya did, Kibby-brat."

"You know my name?"

The strange man grinned—his mouth a wreck of broken and rotting teeth.

Kibby shuddered with dislike. "Can you please put on some clothes?"

"I ain't got none but that bearskin there."

Kibby now wondered aloud, "Is this a dream? Are you a real bear?"

The raspy laugh irritated Kibby's raw nerves.

"Nah, I's only a bear several days a month. Then I'm me."

"How can you be a bear? I mean—"

"How can I not?"

"But... hey, are you like a werewolf or a vampire?"

"No!" the thing bellowed. "I am *me!*"

"Well, you are weird. I want to go home now. I'm not having fun." The boy whined.

"Yeah? I hope yer done cryin' like a ninny-noodle! Ya gonna be good now?"

Kibby wiped his eyes and nose with a hand. "I'm not a ninny—I'm a boy. My Dad says boys, don't cry."

"Yeh? Yer nuthin' but a ninny all the way to yer yella-lilied-liver. I know yer kind. I seen them, boys, here alla the time. Some are really smart and brave. And some be plain stupid, too." The man sat cross-legged on the ground, not seeming to mind the filth or the cold, damp mud. "I et the stupid ones." His laughter sounded like a growling bear, then ended in a harsh cough.

Kibby gaped, eyes wide. "That is sickening!"

The man-thing picked at his teeth with a long fingernail. "Nope... it is life."

"I'd rather have a hamburger or hot dog."

"Heck, chil' I'd eat anything a t'all if I's hungry. Ain't had none of the burgers 'cept what them boys et already. And dog ain't so bad, kinda sweet and tender."

Kibby cringed and dared to ask, "How... um, how many people have you eaten?"

"Ain't kept no count."

"So, you've been here a long time, then. Are you lost? Maybe we can help you get—"

"I ain't lost. This here's my land. But you's been trespassin' on my homeland, kid! All those people out there are on *my* land!" The man flung an arm toward the faint light.

Kibby wiped the man's spittle from his cheek. "This is a public, I mean, a national park. Nobody owns it but the American government."

The man-thing rose and thundered back, "You ain't got to tell me that! I know it! They done stole it from my Pa and me!" Then, pacing, the man randomly struck at the roots in the roof and walls. Heavy dirt clods fell, a gush of water suddenly drenched the man, and he spun about screaming as if burned.

After wiping off the wetness and shrieking, "I hate it!" The man bellowed and jabbed a nasty, long-nailed finger at Kibby. "I really hate you, worm!"

Kibby's eyes leaked. Then he wet himself, now terribly afraid of the man-thing. "I never did a thing for you to hate me. Why do you say that?"

"It's 'cuz you got everything I always wanted, ya fat little grub!" The recluse tore at his hair; in a fit, he stomped about the dark shelter and cursed in a strange language, moaning and crying.

Kibby watched at first in horror, expectant that his life was now worth diddly squat. He was 'dead meat,' as Mr. Ed said when people were in trouble. But the more excited the man-thing became in his tirade, the less Kibby could understand his words.

So, it wasn't until he asked, "Are you the Snowy Ridge Beast?" Then, Kibby gulped, "I heard a story about you last night," he paused, his brow wrinkling in thought, "I think it was last night. What day is it?"

"There is a story about me?" The man-beast asked as he stepped near Kibby to bend down and breathe putrid excited exhalations in Kibby's face. "What'd they say? Talk, you little toad!"

"Yes, sir, there are stories."

"Sir?" he queried, "I ain't never been called that."

"Well, sir, I am hungry and cold and want to go home." Kibby looked about the dank, dim, smelly place to ask, "Is this your home, sir?"

"I ain't got a proper home, not for a hunnert year or more. Them nasty men from the guv-en-or-ship come and burn Pa and me out. They said we ain't got no rights to our land, what we got from our grand-pappy. But the In-Dee-Ans are the real owners to say it is our land. Not the American people like you, who know nuthin'."

"You know real Indians?"

"I am a real In-Dee-An, Arapaho, *Hinono'eiteen* through and through, so was my Pappy, and his afore him was a Cheyenne Chieftain. Although my Ma, a sassy German Fräulein, was full of sauerkraut, or so she said. Sour to the core. Ma and Pa never got on much," looking away, he mumbled, "so, one day, Ma got too sassy, so Pa eated her."

"Yuck! That is terrible!" Despite the horrible story, Kibby stood up and duck-walked under the lower ceiling to the man-thing, where he could almost stand erect. "Hi, Mr. Indian, I'm Kibault Blanding. I'm glad to make your acquaintance." Stooping, he offered a grimy hand to the man, who only glared at it.

"I told you my name, so what is yours?"

With a grumble, the man-creature replied, "*Hóún. Wo'teenox.*" Then, he admitted, seeing the boy's confusion, "My name is Bear Robe."

Kibby touched the filthy hand, but the man withdrew in alarm. "Nice to meet you, Mr. Bear Robe."

"I don't shake hands. I ain't makin' no deals wi' you, worm."

"Not a deal, just a polite thing to do. My Mom says courtesy and etiquette are the keys to making one's way in society. She knows what's good etiquette 'cause she was a Miss Colorado Beauty Queen once."

"Beauty Queen?" The man scratched his sparsely whiskered chin. "Don't reckon I seed one before. She purty then?"

"Oh, very."

The creature eyed him bleakly. "She must've been downright upset to spawn a fat, homely worm like you, boy."

"That isn't nice at all."

"I tell it like it is. Nothin' in this world is nice, other'n a full belly and a warm place t' sleep."

Kibby boldly stepped forward to touch the man on his arm. "I bet you'd feel better after a bath and a hot dinner." He nodded. "Momma says it always helps." He kept eyeing the entrance to the den, hoping to step nearer.

Bear Robe shook off his hand. "*Ja?* Mutti gave me a bath once—I hated it, I did. No reason to waste good drinkin' water like that."

Kibby stepped backward, gulping down a sick stomach to say, "Well, you need a bath because you really stink."

"*Ja?* Well, ye don't smell like spring flowers either, worm."

"So now that we are friends—"

"I ain't yer friend, worm." Bear Robe growled. "I don't make friends with my food. And you ain't a pet, neither."

"Did you ever have a pet? I've got a guinea pig and some goldfish." Kibby said proudly.

"Yup. A dog pup. A little fluffy critter that Mutti liked. A coyote got him. Ain't had one since." The man irritably rubbed his face as a tear leaked out. "Still hate coyotes, nuthin' but nasty thieves." He sat again, this time on the bear robe. He scratched himself like he had fleas, which caused Kibby to move away.

"So, do you read books? What do you do up here all alone?"

"I tried reading books once, just a bunch of weird marks. And stupid stories about your hero *prez-zee-dents*. Your chiefs have silly lives. I woulda whooped that Georgie's butt for cutting down a good cherry tree. But, nope, yer folks are plain tetched in the haid—*Verrückt*."

Kibby sat in thought for a while. Then, just when it seemed a long time had passed, and maybe the man was asleep, Bear Robe grunted and stretched.

"I gotta pee-pee, sir," Kibby commented, hoping for a reprieve as he grasped his crotch.

"Go ahead, then." Bear Robe waved a hand.

"I can leave?"

"Never said that."

After staring at the man for many quiet minutes, Kibby realized he could not leave for any reason. Fat tears leaked from his eyes. The man only watched the boy while still mumbling and fidgeting, idly scratching through the dark pelt of matted hair on his body and head.

"Why do you eat people?"

"Huh? Why not? It's decent meat most of the time. Although that old guy was tough and tasted off. His soft head meat, *köstlich*." Bear Robe licked his lips and grinned. "Good food."

With a sick stomach, Kibby then retched where he sat. "You killed some old man?"

"Yep. Buried the geezer to season him up. Besides, t'was more food on the hoof," he glanced up at Kibby with an evil smirk, "so I got a fat worm ready t'eat."

Kibby threw up again.

"Don't do that! Now you is stinkin' up my den!"

"I don't care! You're mean and smell worse than a dead skunk."

"Right. Good compliment, worm."

Kibby eyed him bleakly to say carefully, "As my dad would say, 'this is a Mexican Stand-off where nobody wins,' we're at an impasse."

"Don't know Mexicans, heard of 'em but not sure what yer sayin', worm."

Kibby observed the confusion on the man-thing's face, then stood, approached him, and boldly sat on the edge of the dark fur robe. "Do you have some food here?"

The man nodded. "You."

Kibby rolled his eyes and replied, "I meant something else to eat. Besides, don't you want me all fat and juicy? If I eat more, then I should taste better. Right? Just like in Hansel and Gretel, the witch fed the kids candy so they would be fat and tasty."

The dark eyes narrowed upon Kibby's pale face.

Kibby was close enough to see the man-creature's eyes for the first time. Gold-flecked around a big black pupil. As the pupil grew, the eyes darkened. Something was compelling about the man's eyes, though. Kibby studied the man-beast, noting the strong, long, sinewy muscles despite the man's almost skeletal frame. His stomach bulged tightly, and Kibby could only imagine the dead things inside there. The creature was far from being a man. Even though he could talk and walk upright, he seemed more animal than human. This intrigued Kibby. Maybe he could reason and argue with the man-thing to let him go or bribe him.

"Are you hungry?" Kibby asked kindly.

"Always."

"I've got a little something that I saved. Maybe we can share."

"I don't share nothin'. Give it." The man's filthy hand grabbed the air.

Kibby reached into his pocket, removing the chocolate bar. "Do you know what this is?"

"I saw it before. You Scouty-Boys eat that stuff. I never did."

"You want some?"

The man leaned over to Kibby and sniffed long and deeply, groaning and emoting, "Mmm...Sw-ee-ties."

"I need my knife to cut some." Kibby took back his pocketknife, but the man didn't complain. Instead, Bear Robe drooled in anticipation.

Kibby carefully carved away a thick chunk of the hardened chocolate and held it toward the man. "Here, let it melt in your mouth."

"Why?"

"You have rotten teeth, so you can't chew it. But it tastes very good melted."

The man stuffed it in his mouth, then drooled. "I li—like—it's *gut*." He said around the mouthful.

While Kibby had the knife, he cut the bar into chunks, leaving them in the wrapper, then pocketed his knife and kept several pieces of the bar. Thinking himself wise, Kibby sucked on a cube of chocolate until it almost melted, then swallowed it. He watched the oddly contorted face of the man next to him as he perhaps experienced the pure pleasure of eating chocolate for the first time. "Good, huh?"

"Yeah. Give me more!" Bear Robe snatched away some chocolate still in the foil. He stuffed the wrapped pieces in his mouth until his cheeks bulged like a chipmunk.

"Hey!" Kibby complained, "You're supposed to share."

"Ain't sharin' nuthin', worm." He grumbled around the mouthful.

Kibby scooted away a little when the man coughed, then gagged.

"Augh! UGH! You killt me!" The Bear man gasped.

Kibby ran to the other side of the den and watched as the man-thing writhed about on the cave floor and clutched his throat. His belly and body started convulsing, looking like he might split his skin and a strange thing might pop out! But Kibby quickly scooted around the flailing man, avoiding his touch.

Soon, he was near the cave opening. A long, narrow shaft of light seemed welcoming as he smelled frigid, fresh air wafting down the slanted passage. Behind him in the den, the man gagged and coughed. He wondered now what had caused it. "Maybe he's allergic to chocolate?"

He could not leave yet. His curiosity caught between watching the man die or live and what would happen next.

But then, there was an odd noise, and Kibby crept down to the cave again.

The man-thing lay, one arm outstretched, the fingers of a hand bloodied and clutching the dirt and stones, the other at his throat. Vomit and mess littered his chest and beard. Kibby decided it would be best to leave now. Maybe the creature was only 'playing dead' and waiting for the opportunity to pounce on him.

Kibby scurried away through the tunnel, clumsily climbing hand over hand like in gym class on the ropes, except this time, vines and roots helped him escape. He deeply inhaled the frosty air, coughed, and then shivered. His jacket bore the claw marks of the animal that had captured him. Then, not knowing what to do and leaving a warm place behind, he stepped outside, slipped, and fell on the slick, matted snow outside the rocky entrance.

Thoroughly cold, Kibby crawled, then dropped into the hole again, like Alice, to the dark lair of the wicked creature. He half expected the man-animal to attack, yet Bear Robe was silent. So Kibby moved into the cave and stood for a long moment, surveying the beast.

The dull gleam of a dark eye and blood dripping from the man's mouth and nose made the boy bold to act. He snatched at the dark pelt of the bear. Then, with a great tug, the wicked man-thing tumbled off and didn't move.

Kibby saw the glint of shiny red on the man's hairy chest. Then, using his knife to poke through the matted fur-like hair, he found a beaded stone necklace with a carved red stone bear. He cut the leather thong, taking the primitive jewelry, knowing some bits were turquoise and maybe worth some money! When they moved to Wyoming a few years ago, his father bought his mother an expensive Indian silver and stone necklace for an anniversary gift.

Kibby then ran like a thief to the passageway, dragging the bear robe in his wake. He pulled the foul-smelling robe about him, finding sewn skin sleeves for his arms and a hood for his head. It was over-large, but Kibby wrapped the legs and the clawed hind paws around his pajama-clad legs. Soon, Kibby felt heat rise like a bubble of bliss bursting in his blood when he dropped the necklace over his head, which slipped inside his pajama shirt. Before he knew it, he was up and out of the horrible den and breathing the cold air.

It was still early morning, and he wondered if it was another day. A couple of birds flitted about, squabbling about their nest. Kibby looked at them with a strange sense of expectancy, wishing he were tall enough to swat them out of the air. But then, he turned and plodded down the partially trodden path of snow under the dense trees, looking back once to see the den was in the shade of a large tree, and several bushes hid it from view. The farther he went, the cave disappeared into the snowy landscape.

He stumbled along, slipped a few times, and then was on his hands and knees, digging himself out of a snowdrift.

Kibby burst through the opening, then ran up the hill and over the next with an unexpected surge of energy. He stood still momentarily, sniffing the air and wondering where the Scout camp was.

His vision seemed blurry, yet a strange wavering halo lit up parts of the scenery. He wasn't sure why, but his head had been hurting for a long time, so maybe he had a concussion. The bear-man thing had roughed him up badly. Catching the scent of a campfire, despite his injuries, Kibby Blanding launched himself off the hill, tumbled, and ran through the forest, shouting, "I am here! It's me!"

However, the campfires were cold, and snow piled atop the blackened embers. He sniffed at them and held his frozen fingers out, still feeling faint residual warmth from the stones around the fire. He looked about the empty site; the only sign anyone had camped were the footprints already dusted with snow.

Flopping down, dejected, Kibby wept. "They left me behind! Traitors!" Wiping his nose with a hand, he realized the bear robe's sleeves had mittens, with the claws still attached. He slid his hands inside and instantly felt warmer. He pulled the leggings of the bear pelt over his boots.

Suddenly, he heard a whistle. His head spun, and he inhaled deeply, trying to find a scent. Then Kibby wondered about the direction of the sound. With a grunt, he ran down the nearby hill. Feeling good, nothing hurt anymore. He wasn't frozen and heaved a great sigh, which surprised him. A growl, a real bear-like growl, came from little Kibby Blanding! He kept running, afraid it was the Bear-Man thing behind him!

Snow flew in his face, up into his nose, and away from his legs. He used his hands and feet to pull himself through the deep drifts. He was soon a toboggan as he slipped and slid down the trail. He smiled, noticing footprints all the way, finding the right path. Mr. Ed would be so proud that he discovered his troop again.

Kibby ran for a long while, often sniffing and searching for signs that his troop had passed by the place. Then, finally, he could smell them: Mr. Duke's pipe tobacco, Ted's smelly socks, Tim's bubblegum, and someone must have eaten beans because there was an odorous trail he could follow.

Overjoyed that he was getting near his troop, Kibby bellowed. It was so loud it scared the hell out of him, and he plummeted from the path down into a shallow ravine.

Then he looked up and over, wondering what happened, and saw the scouts. In the distance, the trail curved on itself like a snake. He could make out several tall figures. Mr. Sven, for one, was leading the Scouts.

Kibby waved a furry paw but realized he was too far away for them to see him in the forest. So Kibby climbed back up another knoll and made the straight course to intercept his troop. He might even have fun scaring them, popping out of the woods, "Hi-YA!"

Chapter 7—Snowy Ridge Beast

Monday, Nov. 2, 1970

Sven stopped his downward trek on the trail for a moment. Then, finally, he put up a hand, silencing and stopping the kids behind him. Sven smelled something foul again. He looked about the thickly forested landscape, feeling his skin prickle about his neck. Now, he worried that there might be another gruesome discovery along the way. Perhaps the bear had buried poor Kibby! He listened for several moments, wanting to hear it again—the roar sounded like a bear and closer than it should be.

Duke stamped up to the head of the line. "What's up? Why are we stopping?"

"I heard a big... roar like a bear. And now I smell something, too."

"Yeah?" Duke sniffed the chilled air, then himself. "We all smell funky this morning. No time to wash up."

"That's not it." Sven shook his head and smiled wanly. "Maybe I imagined it all. I still can't get Ed's shredded body out of my mind. Last night, I dreamed he came after me. And little Kibby looked like one of those ragged ax-murderer Zombies, chasing us through the forest." He ran a gloved hand over his roughened cheek. "I'm still freaked out."

Duke nodded and pressed a hand on Sven's shoulder. "I understand, man. I got the heebie-jeebies, too. The faster we get out of these woods, the better. Let's get on it."

Sven, nodding acquiescence, said, "I'll take the rear, and you take the front. Maybe the scenery will be better and clear my mind."

Shrugging away the suggestion, Duke dutifully took his place, and with a whistle, the line of kids and men moved forward.

They hiked for an hour as the snow flurries worsened further from the hilltop camp. But the forest gave them a little cover and some peace. It was eerily quiet. Only the soft jangling of their equipment, the huffed breaths, and crunching boots announced their forward march toward Snowy Lodge.

They passed a couple of snow-topped rock cairns, be-ribboned markers, and a sign stating they had less than a mile to the lodge. Sven sighed, glad they had made it so far and without incident or spotting the tracks of the killer bear.

Genuinely bothered about the death of Ed Sharp and muttering under his breath, Sven asked the pale sky, "What in the heck am I to tell Issie? She'll have my sorry hide for leaving Ed behind."

He heard a rasping noise coming from the far right of their trail. He kept walking, but looking about and behind him, Sven swore he saw something shadowing them among the trees. "That's not good."

Groaning, Sven unclipped his hatchet, slid the tool's strap onto his wrist, and clutched the bear spray.

Sven, protected by the useful weapons, shifted his pack more evenly upon his shoulders, ready now for any invasion or attack. He was at the rear of the troop's trail and stopped. His shouts or the whistle should spur the group on. The kids, though tired, could dash the remaining distance to the lodge and get help. He only hoped that he could provide enough time for their escape.

Then, breathing deeply, he spun around to meet his shadow. "Come on out! I know you are there." He called to the darkened woods.

He had a hopeful thought; maybe it was Blanding finally catching up to them. "Kibby! Are you out there?" Sven shouted. The snow and the immediate shrubbery deadened his voice as though it fell to the ground without a sound. "If a tree falls in the forest and no one is there to see or hear it, does it make a noise?" He asked the brain teaser question. Sven always believed that the tree made a sound. Just like Schrödinger's cat was still in the box, probably alive.

He smiled weakly. "Come on, Kibby! No one is mad at you. It wasn't your fault."

He felt the prickles wriggle up his back and creep along his arms as he heard the rough grunt from nearby.

Ready to blow the lanyard-strung whistle, Sven spun about, and there, he caught the dark mass galumphing between the trees, headed straight for him! Sven's abrupt movement caused the pack to slip sideways, dangling, and he wobbled to stay upright.

Sven tried to yell, but the sound cut off in his throat as the colossal creature plowed into him, toppling Sven to the frozen ground with a rib-cracking clatter. The air in his lungs rushed out as the enormous animal bounced up and down on his chest.

Sven had a mind to inhale and blow his whistle between the painful bounces. It cut off quickly, but then an unusual thing occurred. The bear rolled its head as if in pain. Sven blew the whistle shrilly again. Then, hit it on the nose with the hatchet hanging from the wrist lanyard. With a groan, the animal fell away, shaking its head, then reached and flipped Sven with a giant paw.

Sven clumsily leaned on an elbow, shook his head to clear it, and sprayed the animal in the face as it lunged toward him. Then, taking a sharply painful inhaled breath, blew his whistle until he had no more air.

The animal backed away into the shrubbery. It banged its head upon a tree, clutched it with giant paws, and writhed about in the snow. Sven kept up the fusillade of shrill sounds until Duke and a pair of boys ran up to meet him.

"What in the hell happened? Did you fall?" Duke yelled and clutched his own head. "Knock it off!" He demanded as Sven continued to blow the whistle.

Taking a labored breath, Sven eyed his assistant. "It's keeping a bear away. It attacked me just moments ago."

"NO!"

"Yes!" Sven painfully sat up. Pointing into the forest, he said, "I just scared it away! It went over there." A trio of heads turned and saw the path of the escaped animal.

"Whoa! I'll never leave my whistle at home. That's one for the books! So far this weekend, our whistles have been a lifesaver." So amazed, Duke whistled through his teeth.

"Help me up here. I think the bear fractured some ribs. I can hardly breathe now." Sven complained in pain as the boys hauled him to his feet. "Get my pack too. Now I am glad I didn't have the waist strap on. I lost the pack when I fell. It would have broken my back when the bear hit and pounced on me." He grunted as the two boys lifted the pack onto his shoulders.

"I knew we weren't alone."

"You got big cajones, buddy, taking on a bear," Duke said with a laugh and a sigh of relief. "You could have been a goner for sure." He picked up the bloodied hatchet. "This too?"

Sven grinned lopsidedly. "I am a Boy Scout and always prepared!" He held up the spray and his trusty whistle. "I almost gave the bear forty-whacks with my ax, but I dropped it when it clobbered me and got only one." He retrieved the trusted tool and weapon.

"Do you think it was the killer bear?" one boy asked.

"I don't know. It was huge, though." Sven admitted, sounding winded, and put an arm about his ribcage for support.

The men and boys continued along, following the footprints of their comrades, soon joining them. Sven gave a silent prayer that he had survived while others had not. This story was undoubtedly bizarre and one to tell for his future grandkids, although his wife, Brigitta, would be upset.

Worried for their leader, the boys gathered around Sven, each taking turns supporting him. Some offered to make a litter with tree branches and a sleeping bag, but Sven knew he could tough it out. He could smell the sweet, hickory smoke of the lodge's barbeque restaurant. Man, he could go for that right now! But no, Sven must do his duty and report the deaths of Ed Sharp and Kibault Blanding.

Kibby sat stunned alongside the empty trail. His head hurt worse than when he awoke this morning. His eyes, tongue, and nose stung with peppery fire. Unable to understand why Sven didn't talk to him, he whined and cried. Instead, Sven fought him, blew his awful emergency whistle, whacked him with an ax, and sprayed something terrible in his face!

Kibby now wished for a whistle, an official Scout knife, or a big bowie knife like his dad owned. Maybe he could have fought the man-bear thing this morning. But his parents couldn't afford to buy everything Kibby wanted for this trip. Especially not 'some over-priced official Boy Scout gewgaws.' While wanting Kibby to be in Scouts and have some fun making new friends, his Dad 'wasn't made of money.'

Yeah, well, Kibby had promised to work extra hard in school and his chores to afford it all himself with the earned allowance.

But this was bad—he lost the Scout troop and probably all his backpacking stuff again. If he made it home, Dad would whip his butt raw for sure for the waste of money and losing his equipment.

Reluctantly, Kibby again trudged alongside the trail. He was no longer excited to see his troop. No one cared about him. He ran a little and stopped for a drink of water, lapping it like a dog at a sparkling brook. His eyes and nose seemed better after dunking his head in the stream. But his nose and mouth still hurt. He could now smell the boys again.

From a distance, he heard the boys' excited chatter, nearing the last of the kids on the road. He kept out of sight, no longer shadowing as closely as before. He recognized the lodge road now—a van with skis on top passed by the line of tired kids.

Keeping his distance among the trees, Kibby followed parallel to the road in their wake as the boys cheered and sang a marching song. They then half-carried Sven through the Snowy Lodge door.

Minutes later, Kibby trundled up the stone steps of the lodge and burst through the door. He stood tall and bellowed, "Ha! Ha! I found you guys! You didn't lose me!"

"BEAR!"

A multitude of screams and shouts echoed around the lodge foyer.

"Hot damn! It's the Snowy Ridge Beast!"

A sudden explosion, followed by a searing hot missile, hit the standing bear in the lower chest. It howled and growled and fell back against the open doorway, its weight breaking the door off its hinges. Blood and gore trickled across the roughhewn wood and littered the fieldstone lobby floor.

The giant animal, in pain, slashed out with a broad paw, with an even more tremendous roar. But then, he was silenced with another shot, this time to the heart.

Everyone stood in great fear, some silent, others weeping as the man near the lobby desk lowered his hunting rifle.

"Hellfire, yes! I got him! I got the Snowy Ridge Beast! I'm gonna get that big, fat reward!" The heavyset man boisterously gloated as others backed away from him.

Breaking away from his troop of boys, Sven carefully approached the fallen animal. The massive bear lay still in a pool of blackened blood. Then, the giant bear seemed to shrink and deflate in size. It was not the oddest thing, though—Sven spotted a tear in the bear's skin and the glint of something metallic under it. Even though others shrieked, he bent to the animal, pulling out a bloodied Scout's knife. Then, ripped and spread apart the animal's hide at the tear. Sven almost lost the lunch he never ate.

Kibby Blanding lay wrapped in the bearskin pelt. Dead. Shot cleanly through the heart and belly. An old leather string with stones lay on his bloodied chest. Clutched in one chubby fist, part of a foil-covered chocolate bar was now blood-spotted and partially melted in his hand.

Feeling ill, Sven backed away, passing the knife to a scout. "Here's your sneak thief, Tim. And maybe the Snowy Ridge's Beast." He rubbed a shaky hand over his tearing eyes to mumble, "Shit. I hope to God Kibby wasn't Ed Sharp's murderer. That will be another messy mystery to untangle! Poor kid."

Sven suddenly collapsed upon the silent hairy form of the grizzly bear robe and dead young Scout. His last words echoed in the lodge lobby among the onlookers. "Why did it have to be a bloody bear?"

"Yer Givin' Me The Creeps, Bro!"

Appalachian Mountains, Virginia
July 5, 1985

A trio of young men sat around a campfire, drinking beer and sodas and munching on chips and the last of their fish catches of the day. One man sat away from them, whittling a thick stick, murmuring imprecations and cruel wishes aimed at the other men.

They had been downright mean and rotten to him for the past two days of the holiday. Kicking him in the pants, both physically and figuratively. It was not a good day to fall out of the fishing boat, lose his new rod and tackle box, or be dragged out of the water by the seat of his split pants. While he was a hefty fella, built like a refrigerator that ate itself, he was usually good-natured and laughed about his jumbo size. However, today was not a day he wanted to remember. Nor was it something he could ever forget or forgive.

He fell overboard, which wasn't his fault. It was Newt's fault for gunning the outboard, and when the boat jerked, Bill suddenly unbalanced and tipped out. But there wasn't anyone to blame when he saw something horrible in the water.

Bill shuddered now, still feeling the snaking tentacle-like fingers and arms that reached out to him from near the bottom of the lake. He swallowed too much water; nearly dying was his excuse for what he saw.

Nope. There was a woman down there. Her long hair waved like the lake weeds, and her hands and arms floated and touched him. They grasped him. Her face distorted like melted wax on a candle, and with her mouth hanging open, an eel raced out to attack him! He grappled with the wicked-toothed creature and then got bit on the hand. He glanced at the bandana-bandaged wound, still leaking blood and hurting like stinging nettles.

That wasn't enough evidence for those stupid guys who laughed and said he was a big dope or must have hit his head on something. There were only fish in the lake, no eels, and no mermaids made of lake weed!

He shifted on the log and glared at the trio, still telling tall tales of their catches of the day like none of them believed what had happened. The men laughed and sent missiles of pinecones at him when talking about their biggest haul—three-hundred and forty-three pounds of Wall-Eyed Billy Basker!

Bill's fleshy face scrunched up as he sneered back at them, sending another foul curse. "I hope yer eyeballs fall out and yer teeth rot, so ya can't say nothin' more about me. Yeah, and yer ears get clogged up with wax and spiders, so you can't hear nothin'. Yeah. That's what you deserve. I told ya true... I saw a dead lady in the frickin' lake!"

What was supposed to be a fun Fourth of July weekend with pals had been, so far, unpleasant. Nobody shared their fish with him tonight, and since he didn't catch any, that was it. No dinner for Bill Basker. Although he had some jerky in his pack, he sat whittling and chewing away on the hard stuff until his teeth and jaw were sore.

"Nope, none of you are my friends, no more, no how." Bill rose to his feet, his joints sore and creaky tonight, which he could only blame on sitting around cold, in wet clothes. He was not a prepared Boy Scout, only bringing his sole pair of hunting/fishing boots, two shirts, a jacket, and the wet overalls he still wore. He forgot to pack an extra pair of socks and skivvies.

He clumsily circumnavigated the fire's circle, its warm environs, and coarse-humored anglers headed for his tent. At least he might get some shuteye.

Amid boisterous laughter and figuring it was about him, Bill thrust himself through the small opening of the tent, tearing the zippered seam and knocking down the center support. He flopped wearily on his sleeping bag, letting the nylon tent drape over his rotund form. Again, laughter and riotous hooting and hollering echoed in the campground.

"Dang fools. I'll show them. Tomorrow, I'm gonna catch the biggest fish, even if I do it with my bare hands." Huffing and puffing, Bill wriggled about to get comfortable. "I smell like the dang lake." He sniffed himself and wrinkled his lips in distaste. "Man, this is the last time," he snuffled and sneezed, then rolled to his side, putting the pillow over his head to shut out the jokesters, "... the last time I speak to or go camping with those guys... for good."

>»»▶

The chilly, eerie night often seems too long, and the morning comes too early in the woods. First, the courting night birds, hooting owls, and then the annoying creepy-crawlies sang shrill songs in Bill's ears until he hid his head. Then the sunlight arrived, with a loud elk trumpeting his herald song to the morning or the loon cackling to his mate about the spectacular sunrise.

All God's creatures were awake, so now was Bill Basker awake after a restless night.

Rolling to his hands and knees, still feeling creaky and stiff, Bill crawled from his tent. He got to his feet and plodded across the camp to the woods for his morning constitutional. He noticed the fire was only smoking embers. One of his 'former friends' lay slumped alongside a log. He didn't see anyone else. Still grumbling his discontent from his rough treatment yesterday, Bill noticed the lack of coffee or cooking food.

"Heck, I paid twenty bucks for a share of the food this weekend. Man, if they ate it all at their party last night, I'll—"

The sun was a golden orb in his eyes, dodging between the trees as he came out to the lakeshore. He stopped short of the water and didn't finish his thought. Their fishing boat was no longer pulled up on the beach but rocked out on the water. He wondered if the idiots did some early morning fishing. He cupped his hands to his mouth and hollered, "Hey, you guys! Catch anything?"

His voice only echoed around the lake and caused a flurry of loons and canvasback ducks to fly away in a noisy huff. No response irked him. He unzipped and took a piss on the shore, not caring that urine trickled into the lake. He waggled his weenie in disgust at the boat, expecting a crude burst of laughter. Nothing happened.

"Well, shoot. I hope the guys didn't leave me." Bill worried but squinted at the distant boat, hazy in the rising sunlight across the misty water. Something was not right. The craft seemed to list and bobbed about in tiny circles as if on a short mooring. The lake seemed placid, with hardly a ripple. Only a shallow wave approached the boat out there.

He tugged on the canoe that belonged to Caleb Cook. Bill clumsily got in after dragging it into the water, but it was stuck in the muddy shallows. He pushed with an oar, re-centered himself in the canoe, and finally pushed it deep enough for the craft to float. He smiled at the boys' joke that he was too fat for a canoe and kept paddling side to side, steering the canoe out to their powerboat.

"I got a fourth share of that boat. It ain't fair that they're hoggin' it all the time." After his dip yesterday, Bill was put to shore when the guys said he was too much weight—they might sink!

That really burned his cookies!

But now, here he was, paddling his way to rescue the idiots. Approaching the aluminum-sided twenty-foot boat, he realized no one was in it. Not only that, but a big dent in the port side also allowed the vessel to take on water. It was half-full. Yet the anchor rope and another pulled taut over the gunwale. He paddled around the listing boat, observing an empty bait bucket, two rods lying on the bottom, and the square orange life cushions bobbed in the boat's water. Something dark was splattered and dripped in various places.

When close, Bill grabbed the anchor rope and pulled— it wouldn't budge. He glanced toward the shore and wondered if this was another joke played upon him for his 'near drowning tale' yesterday.

"Hey, you guys are freaking me out! C'mon, the fun is over. Where are you?" He hollered. But only the slosh of the canoe and the clanking water-logged vessel was his answer.

He was afraid to get into the larger boat with the crushed side and water-filled bottom—it might sink. "But I can pull it back to shore."

Bill tried several times to pull up the anchor rope from different angles, but it wasn't budging, still drawn tight against the gunwale. Also, afraid to get into the water, Bill might never get back into the canoe without help and preferred not to swim the long way back in frigid water!

Bill cut the anchor rope with his *Dandy Pocket Knife*. He was glad, for once, that the TV commercial item was as sharp as advertised. Oddly, the anchor line did not sink—it floated like a dead fish.

He looked around again, wondering why everything was so quiet. No birds twittered. No ducks quacked—nobody was around. Then Bill bent over, grabbed both vessels' gunwales, put his face in the water, and opened his eyes, hoping to see a boulder or why the anchor was stuck.

He did not expect to see a bearded face, a foot under the water's surface, or blood seeping from empty eye sockets. The other rope was tight around the man's neck; another cord pulled tightly led downward into the lake weeds.

Gagging, he pulled his head from the water, almost capsizing the canoe. Bill closed his eyes and steadied the pair of vessels. Lake water spewed as he roared, "Holy Moly! Cat-Shit-on-Toast!"

It had to be Sean MacInnes, only he had a heavy dark beard. But the sightless face messed with Bill's mind.

"Screw it! I'm gettin' out of here!"

He pushed the fishing boat away and energetically paddled his canoe until it ran aground in the shallows. Then, frantically, Bill lumbered up the muddy embankment. Bill knew the fishing trip was over, no longer concerned for the other sinking craft with an expensive new outboard motor and fishing equipment.

Bill then plodded into the camp, shouting, "Hey, I just found MacInnes dead!" But his shouts fell on deaf ears. Caleb Cook looked dead to the world as Bill kicked at him, trying to rouse him from his drunken stupor.

However, Caleb's lifeless body rolled. His face was blackened and bruised. Bill bent over as a bright green snake slithered from Caleb's mouth.

Screaming, Bill backed away, falling on his blubbery backside. He scrambled away, but without grabbing his camp equipment or torn tent, he rushed over to the red *Jeep Cherokee* they had driven the day before.

Half expectant that the vehicle's engine was fouled or messed with, Bill, relieved, laughed when the *Cherokee* started with a throaty roar. He sped down the gravel road away from their campsite. But kept looking back in the mirrors as if he might be pursued. Bill sighed with relief—he was not followed—only the ghosts of the night and this morning haunted him. He drove to the ranger station to report the deaths and the missing man, Clyde Newton.

>»»▶

The newspapers would report the mysterious deaths and drowning of nine victims that the state police recovered days and months later. One body was the ghostly woman Bill had touched in the lake. She had been missing for three weeks when Bill saw her.

In some ways, Bill felt vindicated that what he witnessed wasn't a dream or his imagination. It was the real thing. Still, it was a nightmare.

So were the frequent nightmarish interrogation sessions by the various sheriffs, police, and detectives. Everyone accusingly pointed at Bill since his fingerprints were found on many items in the campground and boat.

"Of course, my fingerprints are there! I was fishing with those guys. And that's my tackle box and fishing rod, which fell in the lake!" He nodded to the muck-covered red and black tackle box and matching rod and reel.

Then, feeling like the TV show comedic German Sergeant Schultz, all he could say was, "I know nothing! I woke up, and everyone was missing or dead. And I tell you, I saw a dead lady in the danged lake! That's my story."

He would have time to think about it all and wonder if his curses had somehow come from a mysterious power in the lake or woods and killed his friends. It sometimes made him sick. But again, Bill counted the lucky stars that he wasn't a victim, perhaps of a serial killer.

>»»▶

The oddest mystery is that Bill could no longer live in the city, as his missing friends' wives, children, and girlfriends were hassling him. Most wondered why their handsome men were taken so young when homely and fat Bill Basker, the wall-eyed Tub o' Lard, had survived. Nothing seemed fair. He was friendless and always under suspicion.

Bill, curiously, was still drawn to the lake area and moved there. His new role as protector of the lake through a job with the Forest Service gave him some fresh perspective and responsibilities.

Bill Basker had lost enough weight a year later that no one teased him. No one called him Mama's Boy or Refrigerator Bill anymore. Now Bill was ruggedly good-looking and heavily muscled in his new khaki and green uniform. His hazel-green eyes twinkled, and his dimpled chin and cheeks were something cute that the gals liked. He understood the importance of a uniform, and the subtlety and allure of the outfit, like firefighters and military guys, were irresistible to women.

Yes, he had a new life. He had a girlfriend now, the head bartender at *Rigger's Hideout*. It was three miles inland from the ill-fated lake and campground just at the edge of the national park.

Bill continued to have the weird dreams, but somehow, they became the backdrop for another new career—the author of a mystery novel, "Death at the Lake," and his bar-room tall tales. When tourists were around, Bill was quick with a story for the price of a beer.

Turning to his new gal, he leaned across the polished pinewood bar top and kissed her. "Thanks, Patti." He admired her buxom chest in the tight green t-shirt and the tan hiking shorts, the tavern's uniform. Her tanned legs were muscled and sleek, ending in a pretty, heart-shaped rump. He enjoyed hiking with Patti, making romantic moonlit rendezvous in the woods, and savoring early morning eggs and coffee over a crackling fire.

Life was good as he sipped a fresh, pulled draft beer.

"So, are ya gonna finish the story, Bill?"

Smiling, he turned about on the barstool. Holding up a hand, Bill commanded the silence of the surrounding tourists and fishermen. "Sure. So, perplexed by the empty boat, I dove out of my canoe and swam deep through the water, hoping to get the anchor unstuck. But I found, to my horror, and I'm tellin' ya, I almost lost my lunch, right there underwater... was poor Sean MacInnes tied to the anchor, his face ripped to pieces and his eyes gone—chewed out by eels—"

"Yer givin' me the creeps, Bro!" Several disgusted and horrified voices joined the din! "Tell us more!"

Yeah. Payback is good!

CAT·O'·NINE·TAILS

A NOVELLA

☯

Chapter 1—To Be or Not to Be Finkel

SoHo,
New York City, New York
October 22, 1995

"**I** told you Finkel was dead this morning. He was flattened right out there near the curb in front of the apartment house. I know a speeding car struck him—tearing him to pieces so badly Finkel had no tail." Sniffling, Penny Stratton set down a pair of tea mugs on the kitchen table for herself and her sister, Louise Arnold.

Louise gestured at the black tuxedo cat sunning itself on the bay window seat across the room. "Are you sure it was your cat, Finkel, outside on the street?" she asked, blew on her tea, and took a cautious sip.

"It was! I cried and screamed like hell when I found him! The man from 2A heard me and came out to help me scrape him off the street! I even have his collar." Penny picked up the red nylon collar with a heart-shaped ID tag.

"Joe wrapped Finkel in newspaper and put him in the trash bin. I wanted to bury him, but where could I?" Penny sniffled, wiping her eyes and nose with shredded tissues. "It was a lousy end to a good friend." She sat, stared at her mug, and then glanced at the cat in the sunlight.

"What do you mean he's dead? The cat looks fine." Louise offered brusquely.

"Except that cat doesn't seem right. He can't be my Finkel."

Louise pressed Penny's shaking, slim hand. "Sure. Okay, fine. Maybe this cat belongs to someone else."

Stifling a shattered breath, Penny remarked, "I don't know. But later this morning, Finkel was on the balcony, crying to be let in. He ran right to his bowls and begged for his breakfast. Finkel did that every day of his life for over seven years."

"Most cats are smart enough, and they supposedly have terrific sniffers. So if he isn't your cat, maybe he's a stray and just adopted you."

"I miss Finkel. This cat looks just like him—he even mews the same."

"Why don't you call him and see if he comes?"

Penny made a wry, twisted expression. "You know little about cats because they rarely come when called."

"Do it anyway, just for your peace of mind. Then we can talk about something else," Louise suggested.

Taking an even breath, Penny almost sang, "Hey, Finkel, want some tuna crunchies?"

The cat stopped grooming its backside and looked up with interest. "Me-hew?" He jumped off the window seat, sauntered into the kitchen, and rubbed his face on Penny's leg.

"Well, that's different. Fink actually came and now is affectionate." Penny bent to stroke the cat's sleek, ebony head and tail. "I guess it could be Finkel. Maybe he had a close call this morning or saw the other cat get clobbered."

"Maybe that dead cat wasn't your Finkel. So now that we solved the mystery—"

Penny rose to get treats from the low cabinet where the cat sniffed the door. He jumped up and batted at the latch. "I had to put this child-proof lock on his food cabinet because Finkel kept breaking in and eating everything. I'd come home from work, and he'd be sprawled on the floor in almost comatose bloated bliss, with the chaff of his thievery around him."

Louise laughed. "Yeah, I remember we came home once with takeout Chinese food, and he looked blotto. What a mess." She leaned to pet the cat, but he scooted away, howling for his treats. "This is Finkel. He never let me pet him. This morning, the other cat you found was probably a neighborhood stray."

"Maybe." Penny tipped out a portion of tuna-flavored treats and dropped them in the cat's bowl. She straightened and watched as the cat gobbled the food. "I guess it is him. Still, it doesn't explain why the dead cat wore Finkel's collar."

Louise sipped her tea and snatched a peanut butter cookie from the dish on the table. Suddenly, Finkel was upright in the chair next to her, pawing at the plate of cookies. "Okay, maybe this guy isn't Finkel." She remarked, pushing the plate away from the cat's paw.

Penny scoffed. "Finkel ate almost anything, the fat brat. But I don't recall he liked peanut butter." Tears coursed down her cheeks again. "Oh, heck. I think my little brat *is* dead. Perhaps you are right about this kitty," Penny scooped up the cat and hugged him, "this poor guy is only a stray. Perchance, my Finkel has been reincarnated. You know the Hindu people believe—"

"Stop!" Louise shook her head. "You are making yourself crazy. You still have a cat even if this guy isn't Finkel." She mumbled through the bite of the cookie, "So, stop crying the blues, Sis."

Penny squashed the cat with love and kissed his glossy face. "Whatever. But what if he isn't the same cat? Should I still call him Finkel? Maybe he has another name."

"Call him Jerk-Face... or Smelly Butt. Whatever. Cats don't care what their name is as long as you feed and pay attention to them."

In tears again, Penny kissed the cat's head and set him down on the tiled floor. "That's not nice. Cats are smart. Finkel knew his name but had his own agenda, coming only when food was involved, just like now." She watched as the animal sniffed the empty dish.

"Whatever floats your boat, Sis." Louise took another cookie; sounding snide, she said, "At least you have the good Nelson cooking genes like Grandma Bev. These are the best peanut butter cookies. You could sell 'em! You know that might be a good job for you. I could get some clientele, spread the word—" Seeing her sister shake her head, Louise stopped. Sighing, Louise held up her cup. "Fine, be a stubborn, lazy ass. I need more tea with this cookie. I wish you would get real coffee, not that instant garbage."

Still caught between the reality of the morning that the cat in her kitchen might be a Finkel doppelgänger. Penny wondered if she had hallucinated the entire morning's tragedy—perhaps this was Finkel on his best behavior. She stood lost in thought until her sister's shrill voice brought her into the moment.

"Hello! Planet Earth to Penny—do you hear me?" Louise cackled a throaty laugh. "I'd like more tea, please."

"What?"

Louise stood, noting her sister's clumsy and slow movement as Penny looked dazed around the room. "Never mind. I've got better things to do than drink tea, eat your fattening cookies, and talk about dead cats."

Looking miffed, Louise tapped her sister's shoulder. "You know, Miss Airhead, you forgot to call or come to my party last weekend. I had a really nice guy eager to meet you. You really ticked him off. I've invited him three times so he could meet you."

"Party? When? I don't know what you are saying. But, of course, I wouldn't purposely miss a party."

"You did, which was rude. John was all hot and bothered to hook up. He is quite the catch: sexy, rich, and fun. You will never—"

Blushing, Penny shook her head. "Oh, gosh. Will you stop trying to fix me up with guys? I don't need anyone." Penny said and slammed down the whistling tea kettle. "I dislike your choices of men. Even Bryan gives me hives!"

"Hm, really? Bryan is as harmless as a butterfly. I think he is quite handsome and my lucky catch."

"Fine, you keep him. But I don't like how Bryan always tries to kiss my hand when he greets me. He calls me Sweet Cheeks and Penny Patootie. Those are hideous nicknames!" Penny shivered like a nervous chihuahua.

Louise kissed her sister's cheek. Then, with her mouth set in a grim line, she struggled into her jacket and said, "Bryan is only being nice. You are the weirdo, Penny. See ya. Call me later so we can plan." She grabbed her purse and rushed out of the kitchen.

"All right. Sure. Wait! Plan what?" Penny broke from her reverie to follow Louise to the front foyer door. "So, what should I do about that cat? Do you think he's lost? His family is possibly looking for him... maybe I should make a poster."

"Again, with the cat?" Louise shook her brunette, curly head. "Forget about today. Can you focus for a minute on something else?"

"Hm, yes, I can." Penny nodded and straightened her shoulders, trying to stand taller next to her statuesque, model-thin, perfect sister.

Louise's fleeting smile didn't reach her eyes. "You recall that Mom's birthday is in almost two weeks. She is expecting us to do something spectacular for her sixty-fifth. Dad already said we have *carte blanche* to choose the venue and food since he is too busy with his golf tournament gala." Louise primped in the hallway mirror, reapplying her rum-raisin-colored lipstick, and fluffed her hair against the butterscotch-tan suede jacket collar.

"So, what should we do besides the Bennett's reservation? We already know what Mom will want: the lobster bisque and tiger prawn salad." Louise said to the mirror.

Penny sighed in exasperation. "You know I am a vegetarian these days. Finkel is the only carnivore in this house. Bennett's is all surf and turf stuff. Somehow, a plain salad doesn't seem like party food to me. I'd like something more. We could have a party at the Bombay Palace. They have seafood and vegetarian entrees. Dad can have the chicken vindaloo that he likes there and—"

"So, eat a damn veggie burger! I don't care." Louise snapped. "The party isn't for you—it's Mom's birthday."

Chastised, Penny felt only a tidbit of remorse. But for most of her life, Penny was the second act. Louise was lucky—lovely, clever, and talented with two-year-old twins and happily married to a handsome and successful husband. Louise and Bryan Arnold could afford the costs of a party at the uptown restaurant. Penny worked an at-home minimum-wage job to stay afloat, plus her infrequent commission work to pay the pricy lease on her rent-controlled apartment, keeping herself fed and Finkel in cat food and litter. Her life seemed insignificant and of little consequence to anyone, including her family. Instead of having a house with a yard, Finkel's propensity to use the balcony planters as his toilet and playground was the best Penny could afford.

Penny still didn't understand how Finkel might have gotten to the street in front of the apartment building. Three stories were very high for a cat to jump or climb down from. So she would check for other escape routes since Finkel ended up on the main street when her windows overlooked the alley and the parking area.

"Forget it. I lost you in outer space! Again, I will do everything all by myself."

Suddenly, a door slammed.

Penny came back to the moment. Alone again. The room and hallway were empty, except for the black cat rubbing her ankles and shins. The cat followed Penny into the kitchen and jumped up on the chair vacated by Louise.

"So, Finkel, sitting at the table is new for you." She remarked, taking away the plate of cookies and tea dishes. Washing them, she noted the cat swiped a paw, dragging her sister's last bite of cookie. The cat ate the piece with great relish before Penny could say no or do anything.

She swatted him down from the chair. "Bad cat! No eating cookies. Stay off the table." Penny angrily flicked him with dishwater. The cat growled and ran from the room.

A moment later, she heard Finkel scrabbling in the litter box in the bathroom. "Good boy. Whoever you are, at least you are box-trained." She finished washing the tea dishes and some from last night's supper. After retrieving the newspaper and spotting what seemed to be her dead cat lying in the street, Penny's daily routine had gone awry.

Penny's first lucent thought was a panicked call to Louise, expecting some comfort. But then, while waiting for Louise's arrival, trying to dress, and crying jags, the imposter Finkel showed up on the balcony.

Since then, Penny's emotional roller-coaster took its physical toll. She couldn't think straight. She was suspicious but glad and relieved that the cat might be Finkel. Yet, she was doubtful. The mystery of the early morning had left her confused and extremely tired.

Penny, born with a congenital heart defect, then had surgery to repair it as a year-old toddler, still had a problematic condition now—she had a heart murmur with occasional tachycardia and dyspnea. She was a late-in-life baby to an alcoholic mother and father, which may have caused the problem. Most physical activity or emotional stress negatively affected her, causing Penny to faint or fall apart.

The family once had treated Penny as a wilting violet, fragile, but later a failure and a disappointing loss. The medications also made Penny a little goofy, prone to losing time and muddled thinking. This morning had not helped her situation—finding the dead cat, she screamed and fainted on the street. So, Joe Bartoli rescued her before a car flattened Penny like poor Finkel.

Even though it was not a major thoroughfare, their street had many taxis and speeding cars. The neighborhood had petitioned the city for speed bumps or more stop signs to slow the traffic. Several residents had already lost pets. A boy on a bicycle clipped by a speeding taxi had parents seeking a lawsuit. Next, it would be a dead pedestrian.

This morning's tragedy proved that the traffic was dangerous for everyone. Whether Joe scooped up Finkel or another cat, a being had died. Sadly, Penny paced into the living room, where the cat was curled in the rocking chair.

"I don't know who you are, but Finkel knew his place. This is my chair," she said, bending to pick up the cat. Penny settled in the padded chair and arranged the cat on her lap. Surprised that it was purring raggedly, she scratched his white bib, chin, and ears as the cat's emerald and gold eyes closed in bliss. "Whoever you are, I think I like you. Finkel rarely sat on my lap." The cat purred.

Penny reached for the stereo remote and put on her favorite classical channel. "Ah, perfect nap music, Debussy." She lounged back in the rocker, closing her eyes. With a few deep breathing exercises, Penny soon succumbed to sleep.

SHIVER IN THE DARK

Chapter 2—Little Buddy

Penny awoke the following day, surprised that the cat had kept her company all night. The "old" Finkel usually turned nocturnal, howling and whining, and sometimes was involved in mischievous destruction. She padded in slippers to the bathroom, expecting to find shredded toilet paper or a tipped wastebasket, but the room was clean except for the scattered tiny pebbles from the litter box. Penny kicked some of the mess to the side for pick up later when cleaning.

The cat perched on the wicker laundry hamper as she sat on the toilet, watching Penny with avid, brilliant green-gold eyes. Finkel's whiskers twitched as he sniffed the room. Usually, Finkel howled at the door, wanting in, and would leave again when Penny opened the door. Finkel was fickle. But this cat seemed to enjoy hanging out, for he was grooming the glossy fur, even stretching his toes and washing them. Penny couldn't resist chuckling at the fastidious cat. Finkel had never been so attentive to his coat. Penny brushed him daily, but the new Finkel did not need it.

"Oh well, maybe my Finkel is truly dead." Penny sighed, finishing her toilet duties, then flushed and washed her hands. The cat jumped to the edge of the vanity counter, intently watching as Penny brushed her teeth, combed her fly-away brown hair, and then pulled it into a wide barrette at her nape.

Penny performed her usual morning assessment, peering closely at her pale complexion, hazel eyes, and limp hair, then stepping back to check her figure. "I should be glad I am not butt-ugly, but Louise got Mom's good-looking genes. And I sadly got Dad's overbite, big ears, and a frumpy figure. On him, that looks good, not so much on me." She made a funny face in the mirror, but the cat yowled.

"What's up with you?"

The cat sidled up to Penny, rubbed her arm, and stood on tiptoes to nuzzle under her chin.

"Well, aren't you the love bug this morning? Extra tuna crunchies for you!"

The cat purred.

Penny finished washing up and wiped the counters and sink, the cat observing as if supervising. Then, switching off the lights, she headed to her bedroom to dress.

The cat sat in the darkened room for a minute but then let out a sad mewl, echoing in the space. Penny called, "C'mon, Kitty." Soon, she heard a thump and skittering noise as the cat dashed into the room, springing upon her bed. Penny couldn't keep from smiling at the animal's antics. Even if the cat wasn't Finkel, she enjoyed her pet's new playful and affectionate behavior.

The cat followed her to the kitchen, suddenly keeping up a yowling commentary while rubbing on the chair legs, his food cabinet, and her ankles. Surprised by the odd behavior, Penny gave him two scoops of kibble and a canned kitten milk dribble. While preparing breakfast, the cat kept her company, finally sitting on the kitchen stool near the table. Penny liked Finkel's seating choice—far enough from the counters or table and not underfoot.

"Good boy," she smiled at the cat. "You still look like Finkel. But you cannot possibly be him since you have manners. So I should call you by another name."

"Mm-row," the cat purred and blinked, content.

Setting her meal on the table, the cat, taking the cue, leaped onto the nearest kitchen chair, looking happy, purring, and watching Penny eat. She always discouraged pets near the table or begging, and no animals on the counters or in the trash. But this new cat acted as if it enjoyed their time together, staying close by. Hopefully, the cat won't repeat yesterday's action of stealing a cookie! She'd seen enough awful videos of cats eating from their owners' plates or grabbing food off counters when unattended. Penny could see the feline intelligence working, perhaps sizing up the situation. As Penny finished her cereal and juice and stood to clear the table, the cat jumped off the chair and ate again from his bowls.

☯

That afternoon, Penny heard a yodeled cry at the French door to the balcony. "Quasi-Finkel" crouched low, his fur raised, intently watching something. Penny saved her work on the laptop at her desk. She headed for the angry cat. "What's out there, boy?" She asked.

The cat continued to growl but batted at the glass. Penny searched the balcony garden—everything seemed as it should be. The begonias, pots of herbs, red-leaf lettuce, and tomato trellis were like usual. The lone yellow Adirondack chair was empty.

"Nothing."

But then, there was shifting among the tomato leaves and vines—a black feline face poked through, reached a velvet white-tipped paw, and batted a small ruby orb.

Finkel, hissing, madly sprang against the window, then screamed.

The cat outside sauntered over to peer in. Poor Finkel went into hysterics, repeatedly smashing against the glass-paned door.

The other cat sat looking smug. It looked like Finkel!—marked with the black coat, half-booted, white paws, and bib. Penny was afraid to touch her angry cat and closed the doorway drapes. But Finkel went under the fabric and continued his tirade.

Penny searched for the spray pistol she kept, discouraging disreputable behavior when Finkel acted like a brat. She spritzed the cat, but he was not dissuaded by his punishment. "Stop!" Penny pushed him away from the glass with her foot. "Behave!" Then he only hissed at her. "Bad cat!"

Finkel howled at Penny and the intruder on the balcony, repeatedly smacking the door with a paw.

"No! You are not going outside!" She peered out the glass; the cat now was on the wrought-iron railing, like a tight-rope walker pacing along the edge. Suddenly, it jumped.

Penny, shocked, couldn't imagine where the cat might go, as there wasn't another balcony close enough. Struggling to exit the door but keeping her pet from running out, Penny quickly slammed the door in Finkel's face. She ran to the edge of the railing and then spotted the intruder on a balcony below. And almost twenty feet to her left on the next brick row house—a very long jump!

The cat peering in a window again was already annoying a small dog. Penny knew it was Mrs. Merkel's dachshund, Bruno, barking like a maddened hound after a squirrel.

Still holding the water pistol, Penny changed the nozzle, then aimed and squirted the feline prowler. The water hit his butt, causing the cat to screech, flip in the air, then bolt across Merkel's terrace, leaping between the posts and onto a parked delivery truck. Penny, laughing but marveling at the acrobatic cat, watched as it streaked away down the back alley.

She glanced at her pet, finding him crouched at the window but no longer in the throes of a fit. While on the balcony, she perused her plants, gave them a drink from the watering can, plucked some withered leaves, and enjoyed their greenery.

As long as the warm weather was here, she could reap the bounty of her small garden. Sometimes, Penny brought in the last plants before the snow and frigid temps to finish their growth. Usually, she calculated the change in weather correctly and could cut back the plants for the season, allowing them to rest in her apartment until spring. There was a wide window sill over the kitchen sink. She often allowed seedlings to sprout or had herbs in decorated ceramic pots.

This year, she had a bumper crop of tomatoes, a leggy zucchini that bore a bushel of squashes, then developed rust and died at the end of September. Or maybe Finkel killed it by using the planter as a litter box!

Penny opened the slider carrying a pair of ripe tomatoes, sprigs of oregano and basil, and a few lettuce leaves. The cat peeked at the terrace garden, then scooted away as Penny entered, shutting the door. "You poor crazy thing." Soothingly, she said, walking into the kitchen to dump the veggies in the sink strainer. She bent to scratch the cat. He seemed more at ease but anxiously paced again to the door. "The other cat is gone." Although feeling her remark was futile, she noted Finkel sat upright and watchful.

☯

That night, there seemed to be more moonlight shining into Penny's room. She felt a sense of unease and shifted in bed, her foot kicking the cat. "Sorry, buddy."

Suddenly, the cat was over her, patting her face with a velvet paw. She put up a hand and sleepily dragged Finkel close under her arm. "Go to sleep."

When Penny was asleep, the cat wriggled out from under her arm. Finkel crept along the edge of the mattress to the brass foot railing away from Penny's feet. The cat basked in the pale moonlight with an audible sigh, its ebony fur shining deep purple and midnight blue. Then, with a couple of odd mewls, the cat slid from the bed and lay on the patch of illuminated carpet. Stretching each of its feet out as if in a meditative state, flexing its claws in and out.

The cat slowly rose into an arched form. Then, with glistening bright green eyes gazing up at the doleful moon, the eyes changed to pale citrine; the ears flattened, the limbs lengthened, and with a few painful twists, something else emerged in the darkest shadows in the room to meld with the changing feline.

A dark-haired man with pale green eyes the color of sea glass rose to his knees, stretched, and stood at the end of Penny's bed. Large hands gracefully patted his lean, lithe form. Muscles rippled as his narrow nostrils widened when he deeply inhaled the scent of Penny. "You smell like spice cookies." He mewed, "But my dear lady, you are still sad."

He softly padded to the window, finding it open a few inches. He sniffed and looked out toward the fire escape's empty ladders. His ears twitched slightly as he listened. "Someone has been here. I can still smell him."

Then he paced to Penny's side, keeping in the moonlight. Kneeling on the floor by her, he risked a gentle touch, fingering away a strand of hair over her eyes. "Your hair reminds me of Mrs. Merkel's mink coat, so shiny and rich in color." He whispered, leaning only a breath away from her ear and purring. "You should only have pleasant dreams. When you see the moon, think of me, your poor Finkel."

A frown passed across Penny's features, and then a sad, weak smile fluttered on her lips. Penny burrowed her face into the pillow, sighing as if in a pleasant dream.

The cat-man rose, snatching up a satin bedroom slipper; he silently stepped to the other side of the bed to lie alongside Penny. Breathing shallowly, he whispered again, "I have never forgotten you or your kindness. I love you still, dear lady. My Penny." With an arm over her hip, he snuggled into Penny's body. She seemed to enjoy the sensation and moved closer.

The man watched the moon as it passed away from the window. Then, as the light faded, he whispered, "I will come again to protect you. I have killed one enemy already for you. Remember me. Until next time, my dear Penny."

☯

Chapter 3—Caught in a Loop-de-Loop

October 24, 1995

Penny awoke early that morning to feel like a strong new woman. First, she inhaled the fresh air from the open window, equally surprised that the curtains were gently tossed by a breeze over the window seat. Then, stepping across the room to query, "How did it get open?" She scanned the nearby fire escape area, worried someone might have jimmied the window lock. She glanced around the bedroom to query, "Was someone in here?" She shivered at the thought of an intruder and from the chilly morning air. She glanced at the clock, noting it was earlier than her usual seven a.m. alarm. It was minutes after six, and she wondered why she was awake. Yet, she felt well-rested. Also, recalling no nightmares about poor dead Finkel or whoever that cat was in the street.

"Finkel? Are you here?" She called, remembering he had slept on the bed.

The cat didn't answer and wasn't anywhere in the room she could see. The bedroom was still dim, the early sun yet to rise over the building tops. She left the window ajar in case he had escaped again.

While Penny took a quick shower and finished her ablutions, she recalled last night's pleasant dreams. Still relishing the strange sensations of someone holding her close and stroking her as if she was a... pet cat—or a lover's caress, Penny smiled at her reflection. She also noted the sadness and shadows on her face were gone—she almost glowed.

"What did I eat last night that made me feel so good? No wine, not even any dessert, hm, how strange." Penny left the bathroom, then clothed and ready for the day; she stepped into the kitchen, half-expecting to see Finkel waiting for breakfast.

"Kitty? Here, kitty," she called and peeked into the living room, sure he was sunning himself or watching out the balcony door. "How peculiar. Oh dear, maybe he got out again!" Penny put on the coffee maker, using the cone basket filled with a blend of spiced herbal tea instead of caffeine-laden coffee. Her cardiologist preferred that Penny not consume too much caffeine.

With another glance about the apartment missing Finkel, she headed downstairs, suddenly enjoying the spritely step in her walk by taking the stairs instead of the smelly, tiny elevator.

She opened the row house's foyer door to retrieve a newspaper from the stack left for the building. She surprised her neighbor, Joe Bartoli, who lived on the first floor. He grabbed two *New York Times* and passed one to her.

"How are you feeling today?" he asked kindly, searching her face and figure with concerned blue-gray eyes.

"Me? I am fine. Why?" She smiled, surprised by his interest. He'd rarely talked to her in previous meetings or silently passed by in the hall or street.

"I am very sorry about your little cat, um... Farfel? What was his name again?"

"Finkel."

He gave a chortled laugh. "Oh yeah. I felt so awful about putting your pet in the trash that I took him out later and buried him in my garden on the roof." He put out a rough, calloused hand, squeezing Penny's hand.

Penny, shocked, asked, "Really? That was thoughtful, except the dead kitty might not have been my Finkel. Mine showed up later that morning on my balcony."

"No way! Are you sure?" Joe frowned. "How do you explain the animal wearing Finkel's collar? I took it off before I wrapped him in the *Times*. You were still passed out, so I put the collar in your pocket, and minutes later, you woke up."

"I recall a little of the morning, except the shock of seeing a dead cat I thought was mine in the street. And then to find Finkel's collar in my pants pocket, still bloody, with no actual memory of how it got there. Then I—"

Joe shook his head, interrupting, "I'm sorry, but I was called away later that afternoon and never got to tell you about the cat or check on you. Being on call at odd hours is inconvenient for recurring thoughts and usually messes up my plans." Then, grinning broadly, Joe put an arm about her waist, "But you know, we are neighbors, so I just had to help you."

Penny felt odd about Joe's encroachment on her personal space. She glanced side-eyed at him as he talked, noting the fine laugh lines at his eyes and the slightly graying of his glossy dark brown hair. Joe was nice-looking, not gorgeous storybook-hero handsome, but attractive. She heard rumors and saw a few women coming and going from his apartment, knowing he was a single man. The building's gossip circle said Joe had a revolving door of women visiting him.

"Might I see where you buried the kitty?" Penny asked, hoping to lessen her time with this chatty lothario.

He stepped back in surprise. "Are you sure? I mean, it's nothing fancy. I planted him next to my tomatoes."

"Please."

Joe gently ushered Penny toward the elevator with his hand on her lower back. "I really should take the stairs—the Lord knows I need the extra exercise," he chuckled, patting his slightly bulging but muscular belly, "but you don't need to scale six stories of stairs. Right? Not in your condition."

Penny firmed her mouth, wanting to retort that she had taken the stairs from the third floor. Nor for his inference that she was sickly. Then the moment passed as the elevator dinged, the door creakily rasped open. The pair barely fit inside, Joe husky and taller at close to six feet, and Penny bumped him with her wide hips. But they just smiled at each other.

"Good thing we don't have grocery bag carts, right?" Joe grinned at his query.

Penny was surprised by the kind and friendly Joe today. He was usually brusque, always in a hurry, or impatient. Rarely a kind word or greeting other than a nod or excuse as they passed in the hall. "Yes. I use this cranky old thing since it's easier to carry all my shopping bags up in one trip."

Joe elbowed Penny. "Hey, just call me, and I'll give ya a hand next time." The elevator jerked to a stop, settling with a clunk as the door squeaked open. "Here we are. Can you walk up a short set of steps, only six more?"

"Yes, I can manage them." Penny colored prettily, feeling warm at this courteous man's close regard.

"You sure? I can carry you up there." His dark eyebrows waggled suggestively, and then his face fell as Penny shook her head. "Aw, nuts. So I don't get to play Sir Galahad again today?" He dashed up the stairs and unlocked the door at the top. Waving Penny through the doorway, Joe followed her onto the multi-level rooftop.

Oddly blazing hot, the sun was fully up, yet a chilly breeze wafted along, causing Penny's bared arms to prickle. Joe was already leading the way past terra-cotta pots with spindly trees or trellised plants, little fenced areas, some with ornate pickets, others secured with rabbit or chicken wire. She smiled to see that there was a garden of Eden up here.

"This is wonderful! I never knew we had a rooftop garden. I only heard that Mrs. O'Hearn hangs out her wet linens up here."

"That she does, over there." Joe nodded in the direction, the pair finding two sets of pale yellow floral sheets flapping in the breeze. "But let me show you my garden, just past the pigeon cages there." He paced away on the brick walkway but stopped briefly to coo at the birds.

"Are these your birds?" Penny admired the pigeons in various dark gray, dove white, and lavender hues.

"No, they belong to my cousin Paulie, but I care for them. A couple of months ago, his family was evicted from their building. Some rich rat-fink landowners bought blocks of old row houses and planned to build 'dee-lux' condominiums for the rich and famous. It's a lousy deal for about a hundred families getting tossed out, right?"

"Right." Penny tripped on a black garden hose trailing from a spigot across the pathway to a raised garden.

Joe grasped her arm. "Steady there. Let me take you. Go carefully along here; piles of crates and junk are along the way. I try to remind the tenants to keep it neat up here."

Penny mutely walked with Joe's hand squeezing hers. "Thanks, Joe. So, this is all yours?"

"Just this part over here. Some tenants, yours truly included, made a bunch of gardens and a patio area up here some years back. We all chipped in for the picnic tables, a few loungers, and deck chairs. But then, we subdivided the rest of the roof into service areas for repairs, laundry, and walking paths among the gardens. You can grow almost anything here, except for 'Mary Jane'—grass... um, weed."

Joe chuckled, then continued proudly, "I'm Italian, so it's Roma tomatoes, peppers, eggplants, beans, herbs, and salad stuff." Then, pointing across the roof, he gave a tour. "There's Mrs. O'Hearn's plot—peas, green beans, flowers, herbs, and a big tub of potato plants. And Mr. Jackson is from Georgia, so he's gotta have his greens, squashes, and black-eyed peas."

Then, laughing, Joe pointed to a few other plots of raised spaces several feet off the blacktopped roof's surface. "Those high beds are for Ruben and Freda Rosen since they are elderly and cannot bend over or sit on the ground. Ruben is in a wheelchair and doesn't come up here anymore. So, when they need it, I help, especially carrying down their produce bags when Freda harvests the garden. I keep an extra walker up here just for her."

Joe kept up his tour commentary, talking chattily, almost in gossip, regarding various tenants' odd gardening habits or styles or the weird things they grew or had let the crops die out. "Just a darned wasted bit of real estate up here," he stated sadly, regarding the few dried, empty spaces.

Penny, all this while, wondered why she had never known there was a garden or this pleasant side of Joe. They shared a love of gardening and a kind regard for animals. Although she didn't think Joe had a pet. "I am so surprised by all this. You are another person, Joey B."

Joe spun back to Penny. "Joey B? Where'd you hear that name?" his voice was gruff. Then, seeing her widened eyes, he softened his tone. "Only my Nonna calls me that."

"I'm sorry. It just came out weird."

Joe reached for her hand and squeezed it. "It's okay. I like it when *you* say it."

Penny flinched and dropped his hand. "So, what about the cat? You haven't shown me your garden area yet."

Rubbing a hand around his neck, Joe nodded and paced away. "Right here." He gazed upon a fenced area with arms akimbo as if proud of his kingdom. Shiny hubcaps like scallops edged a red picket fence, with odd metal parts twisted into sculptures resembling figures and animals bordering the garden. A few hubcaps and metal armatures were bird feeders and birdbaths amid the neatly planted ample space. He opened the odd little gate. "I know the gate is silly, but it is barely wide enough for a wheelbarrow, and the pickets are tall enough to keep out most of the little kids and critters—Especially cats and squirrels. That crazy Barnes brat likes to run bonkers up here."

He took Penny's hand, urging her to a spot. "Here is your little pet. I planted him near the tomatoes, and there is a dwarf lemon tree there, too. But I made sure he'll get sunshine most of the day. I knew your cat liked to sit in your bay window and on the balcony. From what I can see from the alley, you have a pretty garden. You might want some space up here next season." Joe gently elbowed Penny.

Penny couldn't help the rush of tears at the kind sentiments. "Yes, this is perfect. Finkel loved... loves to look out the window. It's too bad he only had a corner view of the street from the bay window. The balcony, of course, is on the alley side, as are the other windows. Thanks for putting seashells on his grave. How did you know Finkel likes the beach?"

Joe shifted his weight on his feet, nervously wiped the sweat from his face, and answered, "I saw you walking him on a leash along the East River and once at Cooper's Beach on Long Island."

Penny stood agape for a second. "I don't understand. How could you? Were you following me?"

Joe growled, "Of course not. I didn't know you back then. It was only after Cooper's Beach the next year that I put it together that you were my upstairs neighbor. I thought, 'What a crazy cat lady, walking her kitty like a dog.' You know, it is a little nutty." Joe laughed.

"That was about the best Finkel ever behaved. He enjoyed walking on the beach. It was the biggest litter box in the world!" Penny laughed. "But that was some time ago. How could you remember me?"

"How could I not remember? My quiet mouse of a neighbor, whom I rarely saw or heard, was wearing a sexy sailor swimsuit and walking her cat. Finkel had a patriotic flag harness with little rhinestone stars and a red leash.

He wore a tiny red and white striped bandanna around his neck."

Penny sat on the concrete bench in the garden, giggling, and replied, "It was the Fourth of July weekend, so my sister made us wear patriotic stuff for pictures. But why didn't you ever say anything to me? You were nearly rude to me every time we met."

Joe shrugged and sat beside her, studying his timeworn black *Converse* hi-top sneakers. "I guess I thought you might be out of my league. I saw the people you were with, ritzy-looking folks. And that suit you wore sure resembled a designer thing I saw in a fashion magazine. So, that weekend, I was hobnobbing with my rich and famous cousin, Antony, staying in his fancy beach house. And that lady you were with? She looked and acted like a model right out of *Vogue* or something. The guy she was with looked like Mr. GQ." Joe shrugged, "So, what was I gonna do... go over there and chat you up? I'd then tell a load of lies to tempt you to 'my beach house for sangria or a martini,' right?" Joe snorted.

Penny giggled and smiled. She gently laid a hand on his muscular arm. "I wish you had. I had a lousy visit. That new designer suit was borrowed from a friend. My best time that weekend was walking Finkel and seeing the sights alone. I didn't know those snotty people my sister hangs around. I cannot talk about my fancy sports cars, polo ponies, or diamond-bling-bling stuff like they all do. I don't belong with that crowd of a hundred dollars a sip for imported champagne or whiskey. I feel lucky to have enough money for a five-dollar bottle of California Zinfandel! That's my monthly treat limit!"

Sighing, she continued, "As I recall, Finkel liked the beach too, better than staying at the fancy house my brother-in-law rented for the month. My sister had her stupid cockapoo, Cuddles, with them. The bratty dog did nothing but bark and chase Finkel around the house and yard. I had to climb a tree to get him down. Your invitation might have been just the fun I needed."

Joe cocked a dark brow at her. "Yeah? So... you would go out with a guy like me even if I didn't have a fancy house in the Hamptons or Long Island?"

Penny snickered at Joe's accented pronunciation of Lon-GAI-land. "Yes. I might. Like I said, I don't run with that ritzy crowd." She looked away from his dark, intense gaze. "But that was a long time ago. Dirty water under the bridge, as they say."

"Yeah." He glanced at his watch, then asked, "Did you have breakfast?"

"Um, no. I'll just have cereal and juice. Why?"

Taking her hand, Joe stood, "Come with me. I'll make you the best frittata you'll ever eat."

❧

Amid the stereo playing an Italian opera and a noisy white and coral cheeked Cockatiel, Penny almost put her hands to her ears. The first two were a cacophony, then add Joe belting out the Pagliacci aria; Penny wanted to run away to the quiet solitude of her apartment. But she sat at the kitchen table watching as Joe deftly prepared their meal.

He grinned at her frequently, seeming happy to treat his guest to a gourmet meal. Although some ingredients Penny wasn't sure she would enjoy, she patiently sat sipping a robust but tasty fruit-laden *Sangria*, which Joe humorously called *El Punchero*.

"I've never had Sangria before. I thought it was a Spanish drink, not Italian."

"It is, but I had little else to offer you. I am going to a Tapas party, a potluck thing this week, so the Sangria is my contribution." Joe came near and took a sip from his glass. "Hm, it still needs something."

"I don't know, it's very potent, but I like the orange slices."

"It needs more cinnamon, or—" As if Joe had not heard Penny's comment, he wandered to the cabinets, again searching the spice racks.

"So, what is your bird's name again?"

"Pappagallo, like Mozart's opera character, right?"

"Oh. I don't have much experience with opera. I am more into New Age or instrumental light classical music."

"No rock or jazz?" Joe asked, licking a finger, and turned to remove the cast-iron pan from the stove and shoved it in the hot oven below. "The eggs need a little time there, and then we can eat."

He opened the window over the sink, inhaled deeply, and plucked a sprig of green from the red clay pot on the windowsill. "I love this stuff," he sniffed the herb and put it under Penny's nose. "Smells good, huh?"

Startled at the intrusion and odor, Penny backed away and sneezed. "Oh! Was that rosemary? No, thanks, I am allergic." She grabbed a paper napkin from the ceramic red rooster holder on the table. Sneezed again and blew her nose.

"Oh, wow! Really? I eat this stuff all the time." He hesitated, then waved the herb, "So I guess no garnish on your frittata? How about some grilled anchovies marinated in garlic olive oil?"

Penny, still wiping her nose, shook her head. "I am not sure how much I can eat. I do not eat fish. I rarely eat spicy food, only Wan Foo's tofu pepper pot or hot and sour soup. I can barely eat very mild salsa with chips. My sister Louise says I am a boring person. I cannot eat the red-hot curry dishes at the Curry Palace. So I always get the mild vegetarian stuff."

"Curry Palace? I like their food, and I like Wan Foo too. But it all seems kinda bland. There are not enough herbs and spices except for the curried lamb with peppers and pineapple chutney. Yum." Joe peeked through the oven's window, "Talking about food, I am starving."

He leaned against the counter to stare at Penny for a minute. "It's funny how our timing was always off. There was hardly a word between us when I saw you, but now we are like dear old friends here."

"You are cooking my breakfast, which might have the neighbors talking." Penny offered with a slight smile.

His eyebrows bounced, and Joe laughed. "So, they might. I don't mind. I like you, Penny—you are a nice gal." Hearing the timer ding, he rushed to open the oven door. Joe carefully removed the skillet with hot pads and placed it on a wooden trivet on the table. "Look at this beauty. Man, I am starved."

Joe grabbed the warm, buttered bread, put slices on their plates, and topped off their glasses. He sat and stared at his food. "Not bad for a big dummy, huh? Looks good enough to eat, right?"

Penny laughed and waited as Joe doled out steaming portions.

"*Buon appetito!*" Joe pounced on his food, forking into the fluffy eggs, blowing, and taking a mouthful. Then, he woofed and yelped, "Yow, that's hot! Sorry, I've got bad manners. It looks and smells so good—I had to eat it." He quickly drank most of his wine punch.

Penny broke up the colorful square of eggs to let it cool and instead ate some of the bread. "Do you speak Italian fluently?"

"I was born here in the *Big Apple*. But later, I lived with an elderly aunt and my grandparents in Terminello, Italy. That's a mountain ski town near Rome. My uncle then took me to live with him in Milan when I was nine, where I worked in his *ristorante*."

"Ah, so that is why you can cook so well."

"*Cara Mia*, anyone can cook if they want to learn. Do you cook? What's your specialty?"

"I'm boring. I don't make adventurous gourmet food like this."

Joe laughed, "Girl, this is what everyday folks eat, nothing fancy. My Tio Bernardi wasn't the *haute cuisine* type of chef, either. He cooked simple rustic, tasty food that people liked." Joe ate more of the eggs, still talking between bites. "They're good. Please try the eggs." He shoveled happily through the frittata, then used the bread, scooping up bits of the oily anchovies from a dish, chewing contentedly.

Chuckling, Penny could not resist commenting, "You look like a happy big bull chewing his cud. If you like it, I will, too." She took a delicate bite. "Mm, the fresh tomatoes and red bell peppers are tasty. What is the meat in there, ham?"

"It is smoke-cured Italian bacon—*pancetta*. Our ham version is *prosciutto*, which is very salty and shaved thin." Joe helped himself to more eggs.

"I like the asparagus tips in here too."

"Those are not from my garden, like most everything else. Asparagus is out of season, so these probably are from South America or elsewhere."

"You know a lot about food. So, what do you do for a job? Are you a chef?"

Joe sat back in his chair, wiped his face and hands, and left the crumpled napkin on the table. "Um, I sort of do odd jobs. Right? You know, for the family."

"Oh, but you said you had an odd shift yesterday. I thought maybe you worked at a hospital or a restaurant."

"Yeah? Um… okay, it's like this, right?" Joe leaned on his muscular arms. He put out a hand to Penny. "See these callouses? My hands look like this for a reason, because I work my ass off."

"But you aren't working this morning like most people."

"Nope, and I ain't most people."

"What do you do? I promise I won't judge you. For an odd reason, I like you too." Penny smiled plainly.

Joe made a funny face and shrugged. "You want the lowdown, eh? Okay, girl, you asked for it. You'll probably hate me when I'm done. Then *arrivederci, Giuseppe!*"

He poured another glass of the Sangria and drank some. Then, as if readying for a fight, he cracked his knuckles. "Girl, I have no proper education, barely a sixth-grade elementary school learning. I learned life the hard way by working and experience in doing whatever it took to survive." He paused, eyeing Penny as she stopped eating. "Still here? You want to escape now?"

"Not everyone has a higher education or college. Many people make a decent life for themselves despite a poor education. You must have done something right since you have this nice and not cheap apartment. You wear good clothes and have refined tastes in music and food. Your wristwatch isn't a cut-rate knock-off, either. Those *Omegas* are expensive." Her eyes glittered as she suggested, "Maybe you have a generous family who cares for you?"

"Observant. Right. I like good things, and I've worked hard to get them all by myself. No Sugar Mama for me. Am I wrong to do that?" Joe queried sullenly. "No, it doesn't matter. I shouldn't defend what I like. Right?"

"No, of course not." Penny sipped the sangria, feeling the warmth seeping into her bones and tickling her heart.

Joe was more interesting than she had expected. He had a secret and seemed about to share it.

"I won't repeat what you tell me, Joe. I don't know many people and don't care about gossip. So, you are safe with me." This time, she touched his hand. Joe clutched it with a smile.

"Thanks. I knew you were a nice, caring lady." He cleared his throat. "Look, I'm no charity case. I live simply minding my business most of the time," he winked at Penny, "and I try to behave. But I help people wherever I can." Then, shrugging, Joe added, "The Good Book tells us that is what we should do. I was raised in the Catholic church, and my teachers were nuns and priests. So I learned what was right and wrong."

Joe sighed. "But, unfortunately, not everyone in my family believes the same. For them, they go to confession and blab, blab, blab. Then they leave like an absolved saint and walk out to do bad things within minutes. I cannot live like that. It's why my grandma and aunt protected me from such people, and so did my uncle. But when I was fourteen, my family made me come home to New York, hoping to get me trained in their business." He sighed but caught the interest in Penny's face.

"What kind of business?"

"Death."

"D-Death?"

"Yup. Part of my family owns a chain of mortuaries. So I sometimes drive the hearses for the funerals and... do some of their dirty work." He paused, took a breath, and looked at Penny squarely.

"You know, the day when I helped you? I had to pick up dead people from the county morgues and hospitals around the city and deliver them to funeral homes. I hate those jobs. Driving along the turnpike out of New Jersey at night, bringing a dead wife and her stillborn baby was a real heartbreaker." He wiped his eyes with the napkin and ate some bread.

"I understand. I would be sad, too."

"It's not the sad part that gets me—it's the death part. I swear that woman screamed from inside the box. It wasn't a proper coffin, just a particle board box like a shipping crate. I almost wrecked the frigging hearse!"

"Do you believe in ghosts or a paranormal afterlife?"

Joe crossed himself. "Let me tell you what, yeah, I do. Because I've seen some unholy shit picking up stiffs and working in the mortuary. After the last run, I told my uncle I was out. He called me a puss—um, not a nice name and refused to pay me for the day. But I've driven the last stiff. The next one will be me in the hearse's backend!"

"Well, somebody has to do it. I hope you usually get paid." Penny nibbled at a forkful of eggs.

"Oh, sure, I do. I no longer do much as free favors for my family. They're all greedy shysters and lowlifes, you know. Everybody's out to nickel and dime everyone to death. So when everything is done as a favor, I get pulled back in, and I owe somebody something again. No gettin' rich for a poor ignoramus like Joey B here."

"You sound like the people in the Godfather movie and the *Sopranos*."

"Yeah, my family isn't that far off the mark." Joe sighed onerously and ate the last of the bread and anchovies.

"Can you do something else?"

"You mean when I'm not driving stiffs or hanging around morgues like a ghoul?" He quickly swallowed and continued. "I was a garbage truck driver and a street cleaner for the city. I've done my stint in the city's motor pool, operating everything from construction equipment to ferrying around the mayor in his limo for a summer. I've driven taxi cabs, handsome horse cabs, and bike taxis. But you know, I'm getting too old for that schtick. So now, I gotta find something else to do."

Penny was silent while Joe left the table and retrieved his bird. He fed the cockatiel some berries, a piece of carrot, and the egg crumbs from his plate.

"You have a good way about you, Joe. I am sorry that you don't have a job now. But I am sure you'll find something soon."

"Yeah. I'm not worried. I can do lots of things; however, it is mostly minimum wage stuff that doesn't require any education." He sighed and held a piece of melon for the bird. "Good thing I have a fun buddy here who keeps me company and some friendly neighbors."

He winked at Penny. "Thanks for listening. I get pissed, I mean miffed, because I want to do something worthy. But, you know, I'm not smart." He smiled, "Wanna hold Papa here?" he held out his arm, "Just put out your hand like this—" The bird stepped from his arm to Penny's wrist, "There ya go. See? I knew he would like you."

"Wow! He has warm feet. And he is not trying to peck me."

"He only bites if you are mean or scare him." Joe passed her a piece of raw zucchini, "Give him this."

Pappagallo delicately took the proffered bit of squash and ate it. Then cocked his head, his dark eye regarding Penny. "Pretty girl. Pretty boy." And whistled and wiggled in time to his tune.

"He likes you." Joe leaned on his hand, watching Penny delicately pet the bird with a finger. "I like you too, very much."

"Is your bird singing the Ipanema song?" She hummed the tune as Pappagallo bobbed and whistled, too.

"Yeah, I'm a sucker for Bossa Nova and jazz too."

"I don't mind those genres."

"Good, another checked item on my list. I am just sorry it took so long to engage—you know... to meet you properly."

"Have we actually met before this week? Do you even know anything about me? Except for my cat." Penny asked boldly.

"I know a little. I've gotten your mail a few times in my box. So, I know you like computers. You are a graduate of NYU—I once saw an alumni invitation. So you are not a dummy like me. And you must do marketing or something, right?" He grinned and continued, "And the nasty rich lady I saw you with is your sister, Louise, right? And you like walking your cat on the beach. I once saw you walking Finkel around our block soon after moving in. But that was a long time ago."

"Ha! You are an excellent listener. You are also more observant than I am. I hardly know anyone, including you!" Penny sighed. "Either that makes you creepy, spying on me, or acutely perceptive. And maybe it makes me a little scared that I thought I had a private life." Now agitated, Penny rose from the chair, "Here, take birdie. I need to go home."

The bird flitted from her hand and landed on Joe's shoulder; he touched it and kissed its little head. "Penny! Don't be afraid of me. I'd do nothing to hurt you." He rose to his feet, putting out a hand.

Nervous and breathing roughly, Penny frantically headed for the front door. "I'm sorry. I–I... um, thank you for the meal. I've got to go." Penny opened the door to step out and bumped hard into the lady from upstairs, Mrs. Rosen. Suddenly clumsy, Penny grabbed the woman's arm to steady her. The lady screeched in surprise, clutching onto her walker.

"Watch where you are going—you–you... foolish tart!"

Penny gaped, "I am so sorry. I didn't mean,"

"Oh wait, is that you, Penny? I didn't recognize you, dear. But, honey, I have some dreadfully bad news—your kitty died in the street. I saw... a red Mercedes splatter him. He was in the middle of the street looking for a way to cross, but the car made a turn and hit him."

Penny grabbed her chest. Suddenly out of breath, she whispered, "But that cat died two days ago, and it wasn't even my cat!"

"What is this?" Joe grumbled as he stepped up behind Penny.

"I saw it happen only a couple of minutes ago. I was just now heading to the elevator to see you, Penny. Your little black kitty is dead!"

Joe barely caught the slip-sliding woman. "Oh, *mierda!* Not again." He stumbled and fell into Mrs. Rosen.

☯

Chapter 4—New Ways

October 24, 1995

"**A**re you better, Penny?" Joe asked with great concern, his face worried as he dabbed her forehead with a damp washcloth. "Mrs. Rosen told me you have a heart condition. Get you excited, and you faint. Is that true? I almost called the ambulance, but you were breathing, and your pulse was steady again, so I thought I'd wait." He kissed her hand, "I was afraid I'd lose you."

Penny's closed eyelids fluttered open. "Sorry. Lose me?"

"Yeah. I finally found the perfect sweet woman of my dreams. Then she dies in my doorway. Imagine how I felt, and you had just eaten my food. Makes me never want to cook for anyone again. You know? I thought you had an allergic reaction or something."

"No. I think it was only the shock of what Mrs. Rosen said about Finkel." But then, Penny choked on her tears, "Is—is it true... is Finkel truly dead?"

"Let me just say that another cat looking like yours is buried next to the last one in my garden. So I think a curse or weird shit is going on, ya know? So that's three dead cats... three days in a row!" He held up three big fingers.

"Three!" Penny struggled to get up, and Joe moved to help her sit up. "What happened to the third one?"

"Um, the second one. I found a black cat in the alley near the dumpster yesterday afternoon. The poor guy didn't have the exact markings like Finkel, so I put him in the dumpster. I probably should have buried him too, but he was a mess." Joe put a hand on Penny's shoulder, staying her on the couch.

"You wouldn't have a contract out on you? You're not Italian. So maybe it's Lefty O'Squinty or some Irish thug, huh? How about the Russian mob?"

"Don't be silly. Where are my clothes?" Penny asked, gathering the knitted afghan up to her chin as Joe sat beside her and hugged her.

"Don't worry. Your clothes are in my laundry. I gave you one of my shirts because you threw up all over your jeans and shirt."

"I did? Oh, lord. I really feel terrible now." She cried.

"I got broad shoulders, so just cry yer eyes out, okay?"
The pair relaxed for a long time, with Joe gently stroking
Penny's arms and shoulders, even whispering small
encouragements in her ear as she ran through cycles of
weeping. After a time, Joe asked, "I wanna make you some
lunch."

"But we had breakfast a little while ago."

"It's been over four hours. And Pappagallo ate more
than you did. Do you like soup? I have chicken noodle
soup...It's what the doctor ordered."

"The doctor?"

"A joke. C'mon, you go clean up that pretty face and
then come hang with me in the kitchen. Pappagallo will
also be glad to see you up. It's been difficult to keep him
quiet while you slept."

Joe led Penny to the main bathroom and closed the
door. "I'll be in the kitchen."

"Fine," Penny answered almost angrily. She washed
her face, blew her nose, and used the toilet. She repeated
the first clean-up moves, surprised that she was still
weepy. "I don't understand any of this. Why is Finkel
dead? I never let him out. Oh, no, my open bedroom
window. I never saw him this morning."

❦

True to his word, Joe had soup and toasted cheese
sandwiches ready for her when Penny joined him. "I
doubt I deserve all this kindness, Joe. I think I was rude
to you earlier." Penny said as she sat at the table.

Pappagallo spun on a perch near the table. "La-la! Oh,
la-la!" he whistled and sang.

"I'm sorry. After lunch, I should go home."

"Not a problem. But maybe you shouldn't be alone
now. You've had a shock." Joe patted her hand.

"What do you know? You're not a doctor."

"No, but in my experience, I might know much more
than you think. I've had my share of fainting folks since
it happens at many funerals. And a few people have taken
one look at their dearly departed and dropped dead as a
stone. So, I've had lots of first aid training, CPR, and I
can't stop helping people." Joe shrugged, then said softly,
"I can handle most of the fallout that comes my way. I
almost gave you mouth-to-mouth, but you were breathing
and just in shock."

"Then you are no idiot, Joe. Please stop calling yourself a dummy." Penny snapped. She looked away, now embarrassed. "I'm sorry, but you have been so helpful today that—" Penny sniffled, "... I can never repay your kindness."

"I never asked for anything, Penny."

The pair ate in silence until Joe noticed Penny had stopped eating. "What's wrong now?"

"I feel terrible."

"Sick? Is it your heart?" Joe scooted his chair back, ready to help.

"This is the second time I've lost my cat in two days."

"Three days," Joe muttered.

"I am heartbroken. I want to die."

"No, you don't. I won't let you."

"Why do you care?"

"Does it matter why I care?" Joe asked huskily and changed the subject.

"If you are embarrassed that you vomited on my couch and rug or wet yourself, don't be. People in shock or who faint do weird shit like that. It's a common thing." Joe shrugged.

"Now, I am really embarrassed. I *will* find a deep, dark hole, crawl in, and stay there!" Penny held her arms about herself, looking withdrawn and sad. "I'm not good around people."

"I'd miss you if you did that." Joe eyed her, then urged, "*Manga!* Eat." He waited until Penny nibbled the sandwich hesitantly.

"Sorry. I won't, Joe." She sighed and picked at the crust. "But thank you, this tastes good—perfectly golden brown... all melty and gooey... it almost makes me feel better. You don't have to be a hearse driver or mortician. You can cook."

"Probably not good enough for a restaurant, only a greasy-spoon diner or something."

"Still, it's a job."

"Yeah, something making less than minimum wage on crummy hours, and I'd be competing with emigres, taking their jobs away. But, nah, I'll find something soon." Then, after taking a drink of his *Pepsi*, he grumbled, "And it won't have anything to do with my stinkin' family. Most of 'em are so rotten, I could hate them. But I don't 'cause it's a sin."

"You are luckier than you think, Joe. Family can be a blessing. They help bring you up and support you in times of trouble. Your uncle and grandmother did that."

"Not so much in mine. The bastards only take advantage of a bad situation. And I doubt," Joe glanced at Penny, "you get much support from your family. I hardly ever see you with anyone. Although I saw that snotty sister of yours the other day."

"Louise? Oh, yes. She stopped by because I called her. After Finkel died, I was sick."

"Did you feel better after her visit?"

"No. Then, Louise wanted me to help plan for Mom's birthday." Penny sighed. "Yes, another thing I cannot afford to do is pay for half the party's expense. Mom will be sixty-five on the thirty-first. And deserves a special celebration. But Louise and I have not been able to agree on anything for the last two weeks. I was so distraught that day that I couldn't think of anything but Finkel." She finished her soup. "Thanks for the soup. Did you pick out the chicken?"

"I recalled you were vegetarian, so I made noodles and vegetable broth instead. I was worried you got ill on the eggs this morning. I hope you can handle cheese."

"I can eat eggs and dairy but choose not to eat meat. I allow my cat to enjoy it because he needs it. Did you know cats cannot thrive on a purely vegetarian diet? The enzymes and nutrients in the animal proteins are crucial to their health."

"Listen to you, Miss Science." Joe chuckled. "Yeah, I heard that somewhere, too. Pappagallo is the same... he needs a balanced diet."

"I only understand it since I created a marketing campaign for an organic pet food company last year."

"I was right—you are in marketing."

"I was. But the stress and pressures were too great, so I am only a part-time consultant. I build survey platforms and webpages now." Penny sighed, seeming exasperated or weary of it all.

"Impressive. I can hardly get past the startup home page on my computer. But, of course, it helps if one can spell. Big Dummy, here."

"Stop. You don't realize how unique you are, Joe."

"Sure. Rub it in."

Penny reached and took his hand. "I mean it. Perhaps we are a misunderstood pair. We have our secret strengths that surprise people. You surprised me today. I doubt I would have fared as well without you."

Joe's eyes crinkled and sparkled when he smiled. "I enjoy hearing that. I have had too few good people in my life. I can now count on my blessings that you are around."

"I feel the same. Still, I am astonished by your gentility and compassion. People these days are usually too busy to care about anyone else. Thank you."

Joe leaned across the table with a small smile to kiss her cheek. They stared at each other for a prolonged moment, and Penny kissed him. Joe got up, twisting around the table's edge amid the kiss, and pulled Penny into his arms. After several breathy moments, Joe lifted his head. "I have wanted to do that all day."

"Strange, but I did too. Especially on the roof when you were showing me your garden." Penny suddenly yawned. "Excuse me." She made to sit again.

"After these fantastic and bizarre events, I need a nap today. At home." She said, finishing her sandwich.

"Sure. I'll get you some sweatpants and take you home." Joe said quietly but smiled. "You could stay here until you feel better."

Penny kissed him once as Joe passed. "I'll be fine." Then she stepped over to the bird's perch. Pappagallo, rocking crazily on a swing, twittered his little song. "You are a cutie, too." She fed him a noodle from her bowl. The bird happily sucked on the pasta and a grape from the fruit basket on the table. Penny was soon amused by his murmuring thanks and mock kissing sounds.

"I like your bird," Penny said as she sat to put on the sweatpants. "Am I that fat that your pants fit me?"

"No, you are not fat. Those belong to my sister, Lucinda. Although she is sporting an extra ten pounds these days, carrying my new niece or nephew. You are about her normal size."

"I thought you led a playboy kind of existence, Joe. So many people have stories about the revolving door of women through your apartment."

Joe gasped, "What the heck kind of gossip have you heard, girl?"

"Mrs. Rosen called me a tart until she recognized me." Penny slid to Joe's side and demurely glanced at him, asking, "So am I to be one of your paramours or tarts?"

Joe laughed and hugged her close. "Hell, no. I've got nobody, just like you. I'm not a *donnaiolo*, you know, a playboy. Any woman you saw was probably one of my bossy sisters, cousins, or something. I haven't had a date in a very long time. Who wants to socialize with a hearse driver or grave-digger?"

"Not to be macabre, but you are now an *ex-hearse* driver. And I would like to go out sometime with you." She hugged him, then yawned. "But first, I need a nap."

Joe grabbed a bag of chopped fruit from the fridge and dumped it in the bird's dish. He took a bottle of wine. "Just in case I'm not home early, don't wait for me." He said to his pet. Then Joe ushered Penny out the door to the elevator. "As much as I'd like to carry you up the stairs, we'll take the lift. I've planned other activities for later."

Penny kissed him as the scraping door banged closed.

☯

But all of that was before the evening. After lunch, the couple took a nap together. Joe was sleepy, too. Penny must have worn him out crying and talking. She hadn't talked so much to anyone in months. After they awoke, she chattered about her recent career downfall and solitary life.

After losing the big agent job at the marketing firm, any friends she had made there had fallen away. She had no one. Penny spent most of last year researching to create her own consulting company.

She took no short-term projects where time constraints might create pressure. Instead, she did her work in her own timely way. It was quick enough for most clients. If they liked her ideas but needed a shorter turnaround time to implement, she subcontracted and coordinated with a few agencies, including her past company.

Other younger and more eager associates employed their talents to her ideas in a faster, pressure-cooker environment that Penny could no longer handle. The hours she accrued were less than if she had done the work independently. But her little business was helping small companies get a ground floor start-up. With her advice and experience, Penny's consulting agency was affordable.

The pair discussed a catering business for busy families over a supper that Joe cooked of steamed vegetables and pasta and a chocolate soymilk pudding accompanied by Penny's peanut butter cookies.

"I'll cook the main dishes, and you make the desserts. How about that?" Joe clinked wine glasses with her.

"I still have my consulting firm. Remember that I help little businesses get a start."

"So? Start me. By the way, what zodiac sign are you?" Joe asked, munching on a cookie.

"Cancer. And you?"

"Can't you guess? A jack of all trades and a master of none, right? My uncle said I am a stupid, lazy lump with jumping beans in my pants." Joe made a face and said, "Tio says I ain't got any brains for the long haul. So my family gives me odd jobs that are done real quick."

"Oh, Joe, that is terrible. I don't know much about astrology. Who is compatible with me?"

Joe took her hand, "Me," and kissed it. His gray-blue eyes smoldered. "I think this is the beginning of a beautiful thing, girl."

"You are lonely and watch too many movies."

"Not so much. But hey, I like movies." He began counting off his fingers. "I also love the opera and symphony. I can roller skate and ice skate. I learned to ski at age five; I was a hot dog by nine. I love car racing. My grandfather and uncle took me to the races a few times. Those fast Ferraris, the sleek Maserati and Alfa-Romeos, and their drivers were *strabilante!*" Joe mimicked the race, holding the wheel and then shifting gears as he growled like a fast engine.

"Whoa! Mr. Andretti, slow it down!"

"No, Andretti, how about Lorenzo Bandini? I love him!"

Giggling, Penny leaned against Joe. "Shh. Even though today has been terribly sad again, I have found some happiness. Thanks for cheering me up, Joe." She yawned. "But I think we should call it a night."

"Yeah?" he glanced at his wristwatch. "It's barely after seven." But he brightly responded, "Did you notice my watch has four time zones I can follow?"

"Oh? So what are they?"

"New York. Rome for my grandma, who is still with it even though she's in her 80s. And Los Angeles because I like California. One day, I'd like to try surfing there. I short-boarded in the Mediterranean near Napoli as a kid, but it was boring. The last time zone is Hawaii. Because I really want to go there and surf."

"You are definitely not an ordinary or boring guy, Joe Bartoli. Although I have noticed you are a chatterbox. I am not used to so much conversation."

"Oh. Sorry. Okay, we don't talk. We can do other stuff. Like, let's go to bed." He switched off the VHS player and TV, offering his hand to pull Penny up into his arms. "I think I like this kind of talking better right now." He kissed Penny, then his hands stroked along her shoulders, down her back, then her backside, boldly pulling her closer.

Panting for air, Penny almost choked, feeling the hardness in Joe's pants. Nobody had been so direct in a long time. She stopped Joe's kisses and put an arm between them, wedging him away. "I cannot. Not tonight, Joe."

"No?" His face was interested, and then he shut down. "Oh. I get it. I'm a big dummy... *alloco*, a jerk-face, right?"

"It's not what you think. I am exhausted. I need to sleep by myself tonight." She stroked his face, noting the dimple by his mouth and the dark shadow of his beard. "Besides, don't most men snore? I'm not used to that and will end up on the couch. And as you've noticed, this couch is barely big enough for the two of us to sit, let alone for someone to sleep on it. So, thank you for everything today, Joe."

She took his hard, calloused hand and led him to the door. "Goodnight, Romeo. I shall have sweet dreams of you. In the morning, after seven-thirty, you can call me. Maybe I can make you some breakfast this time."

The man looked disappointed, giving only a tiny kiss on her cheek as he left. But then Joe turned at the stairs, "What did Juliet say to Romeo? Parting sucks, right? For tonight, I will only dream of you. *Buona notte*," he kissed his fingers and blew the kiss. Then, he added, "Feel better, Penny."

❦

The hours since Joe's departure and Penny's later bedtime seemed to drag. She worked on a recent website project, saved the edited pages, and closed her laptop. She took a warm cup of milk to bed and lay under the fluffy comforter, reading a book. "I miss Finkel." She sniffled. "And Joe."

She turned off the light to lie in the darkness, hearing the sounds of the city—sirens, horns, loud booming music, and racing cars up her street.

"It's no wonder pets don't make it around here. I swear if I get another cat, it will go nowhere." She sniffled some tears again. "But that would be a prison for us." Penny closed her eyes and wished for peaceful oblivion.

Chapter 5—Come To Me In The Moonlight

October 25, 1995

A pleasant dream had tickled at the edges of Penny's mind, but thick darkness, oddly comforting and a little scary, bled across the peaceful scene. Unable to sleep again, even though it was shortly after midnight, Penny walked through her apartment, suddenly alert to any sounds or slight disturbances; even her nose went into overdrive, sniffing at a bitter scent.

She followed her nose, switching on lights as she went. The bathroom light was garishly bright. The cream and jade green tiles, almost glowing like fluorescent flowers, led her to the bathtub. Taking a deep breath, she gripped the rubber plunger by the toilet for a weapon and jerked back the shower curtain on the silent count of three. The plunger dropped from her numb fingers.

A writhing, giant, bloody, black and white patched cat was lying in the tub!

"NO! This is a freaking nightmare!" She screamed. Trying to catch her breath, Penny stumbled away into the living room. Horrible noises were coming from the bathroom. Sounds of struggle and things knocked off the shelf and edge of the tub.

Clutching her arms about her shaking form, she screamed as a dark-skinned, naked man emerged from the bathroom. She ran for the front hallway door but, on the way, grabbed the fireplace poker. She bravely turned to see the man standing near the kitchen.

He raised a hand dripping with blood. "No," his voice broke and was raspy. "I cannot be in the light. Please."

"Who are you?" Penny queried as the man lowered his head, shading his eyes, and suddenly crouched on the wood parquet floor.

"I am a friend."

"Some friend!" she scoffed and shouted, "Get out of here, you sick maniac!"

Trying to stand, still blinking blearily in the bright lights of the hallway and living room, he rasped, "No lights... then I will leave." He looked at her with large celadon green eyes rimmed with black lashes and tears. His skin in the light was not as darkly tanned, but seemed to have a velvety layer of black fur or velour. His hands ended with claws at the fingertips. A long gash bled profusely from an arm.

"I don't understand how you got in here." She kept her distance but pointed with the iron poker, "Just leave—whatever way you came in here."

He growled, "I need food. I am hungry." He licked his lips and two fingers. "I haven't eaten for two days."

Penny felt her heart creak, and tears ran down her cheeks. "Please leave. You are scaring me."

"Give me something... anything! I will go." He growled and shuffled closer.

Penny glanced at the coffee table, seeing the tin of cookies and near-empty wine glasses left from the evening with Joe. "I don't have any money."

"I don't want that. Do you have tuna?" The man licked his lips. "Please."

Penny frowned but circled the man at a distance, still pointing the fire poker at him; she took the long way into the kitchen. But then almost screamed again when he rubbed his face on the doorframe from the hallway, watching Penny with avid eyes.

"You should put some clothes on. Aren't you cold?"

"Yes. But I am hungrier." He partially smiled as Penny tossed a tiny can of tuna. He didn't catch it, only staring at the tin. "I don't like this kind. Do you have the tuna in a green can ... with the pretty orange-striped kitten?"

Penny sat on a kitchen chair. "You want cat food?" She leaned to the cabinet where she kept Finkel's food. She selected a tin and rolled it across the tile toward the man. "Are you saying you like this stuff?"

The man batted at the can. "Yes." But then he clumsily kicked it and ran after the can as it rolled down the hallway. He tried to pick it up, but his hands had no fingers, only blunt paws and claws. "Open this." He kicked the can again like a hockey puck down the hall to Penny standing at the kitchen door. He hid his hands. "Please," he mewled, "hurry... I'm... so... so... hungry."

Penny lifted the ring tab on the can and peeled back the top. Suddenly, she felt a sense of power surge and sauntered toward the naked man. He no longer looked as tall. Instead, he seemed stout, thickly furred, and muscular. His eyes were greener, yet they held Penny in watchful thrall. She held up the can. "You want this?"

"Ye-s-s-s!" The man hissed and ran after the can as Penny tossed it into the bathroom. She hit the light switch and slammed the door after he went inside. Then Penny ran to get a chair to wedge under the doorknob. But, instead of a fight, she heard odd sounds—slurping, wet licking, retching, and coughing. Then, a plaintive, echoing mewl, which grew to a howl.

"Oh my gosh, the guy is a nutcase. He sounds like a cat in heat! That's it! I'm calling the police!"

"Help!" The man threw himself against the door. "It's dark in here."

"I thought you wanted the lights off."

"No, just the bright ones. Help. Let me-e-e... ow...out!" The man howled and rammed the door again.

Penny picked up the telephone receiver, punched in 9-1-1, then waited for several breathless moments for an operator.

"Help! A crazy naked black man broke into my apartment just now." Penny gave the address and listened, then talked over the operator. "No, I am not hurt—Yet. But I have the guy locked in my bathroom. No, he's not a boyfriend. I don't have one!" As she listened, Penny amended silently, *'Maybe I have a cute part-time boyfriend.'*

But then Penny answered aloud, "No, I didn't hurt him. I am not armed, and neither is he. Just send someone to get the weirdo. Maybe he is an escapee in a black catsuit from Belleview. He asked for tuna and began yowling like a cat. Yes. I'm serious."

Penny held the receiver near the bathroom door. "Can you hear that noise? I'm scared. Send someone! Please come before he breaks out and does something horrible. Sure, I can stay on the line. Thank you, ma'am." Penny rested on the couch's back cushions, watching the bathroom door and hallway. The frantic yowling and hissing had changed to low, sorrowful mewling.

About five anxious minutes passed when Penny heard the distant wail approaching. She glanced at the corner window to see the reflective flashing red and blue lights pass on the main street, then heard screeching brakes. "Operator, the police are here. Thank you."

She was glad the precinct was within several blocks of walking distance, so the cops often responded quickly. Within a minute, voices and loud footsteps echoed up the stairs. Then, finally, a knock at the door and the shout, "NYPD! Miss Stratton! Open up!"

Penny giggled, "This is just like a movie." She pulled her nightgown and robe closed, suddenly ashamed to be caught like this, but bravely jerked open the door.

"Hello. The crazy guy is in the bathroom." Penny pointed toward the hallway.

"Are you alright, ma'am? Did someone attack you?"

"No, a weird guy scared me."

The officers looked suspiciously about the apartment, one motioning to the wine glasses.

"Is it someone you know? Is he drunk?"

"No."

"Were you robbed?"

"I don't think so unless you count giving him a can of cat tuna."

"You are serious?"

"Yes, officer."

"Where is the intruder?"

"In my bathroom."

The men stepped quickly down the hallway. One pounded on the door, then yelled, "Open up. NYPD!"

Watching from the other end of the hall, Penny said, "It's not locked. The door is blocked on this side, so he can't get out unless he breaks through the door or escapes through the transom window."

"Right." The first officer kicked the chair away. "Sir? Are you armed?" They listened at the door. "We are opening the door and coming in. Put your hands up where we can see them and get down on the floor. Do you understand?"

Silence.

The second officer said, "Playing a hard-ass won't help. Come on." He opened the door but stepped back, then oozed around the frame, holding his pistol ready. "Sir? Come out." He dragged the shower curtain aside and stated, "We've got blood here."

The first officer paced out to the living room. "Was there a fight? Because we found blood, but nobody is in there, ma'am."

Penny let out a shriek. "Don't tell me a dead cat is in the bathtub!"

The man eyed her suspiciously. "No, ma'am. Just blood." He considered Penny. "Did you maybe hit your head or fall earlier this evening? A concussion can make you hallucinate."

"No. I heard a noise and woke up a while ago. But there was a foul odor, and I followed it to the bathroom. There was a giant dead cat in the tub."

She glanced at the man, seeing his disbelief, "Officer, you must believe me. Something odd is happening this week. Because my cat has gone missing in the last few days. But then I found him dead in the street. Just this afternoon, it happened again. He was dead. This time, he was run over by a *Mercedes*. My neighbor upstairs saw it happen. Now, tonight, I again find the bloody cat looking like my Finkel—"

"Finkel?"

"Yes, my dead cat. Then some weird furry guy comes out of the bathroom and gives me a hard time."

"Dispatch reported the guy was black and naked. Is this what you told the operator?"

"Yes, sort of. Except the man wasn't an African-American type of black person. He must have worn a close-fitting black furry bodysuit or something. I mean, it's cold outside. How could a guy run around nude? Except I could see he was... sort of naked, like underneath the fur."

"Fur, huh?" The officer holstered his pistol, then took out a notebook and pen. "Could you identify this man in a lineup?"

"Possibly. The guy had thick black hair, slicked back from a widow's peak, sort of longish, and was around six feet tall... in fact, the man's head almost hit the top of the door frame. He was slim, sort of attractive, with light green eyes."

"So, did anything else happen?"

"Not really. I was so frightened that a naked guy was in my apartment."

"Did he sexually accost you or—"

"No!"

"Do you take any medication? Miss... like barbiturates or harder stuff? Like PCP or meth that might cause you to hallucinate?"

Penny shouted, "No, I do not," as she hurried to the bathroom. Then, she returned to the policemen, "See? This is the can of tuna I gave the guy."

"I saw it. It's empty. I also noticed you have a litter box in the bathroom."

"Yes, that is Finkel's. But he hasn't used it since he died this week."

"Why is he dead?"

"I just told you... My cat was run over in the street. Twice now. Yet another cat looking like Finkel showed up yesterday, I mean... two days ago. But he wasn't my cat because he was loveable and well-behaved."

Penny glared at the officers. "I can see you don't believe me. My neighbors saw it, and one neighbor has buried two cats killed out there in the street. Oh, and another is in the alley dumpster."

Upset, Penny gesticulated. "So, I would like some help here. I think someone is trying to make me insane or implying my life could be in danger."

She hesitated, "You know... like the Godfather leaving a horse's head in the guy's bed or a dead fish as a threat. Someone is leaving behind dead cats that weirdly resemble my pet."

"Do you owe money?"

"No."

"Do you have a husband or family nearby you could stay with for a time?"

"Not really."

"Here is my card, and this one is for help. You can talk to someone about the dead cats." The pair moved away to the door. "Since we didn't find anyone here besides yourself, we don't have many clues to follow. Get some rest, and I'll bet your kitty will be back come morning." The man offered with a smile. He tipped his cap, "Night, Miss."

Penny dolefully watched as the door closed and heard the men laughing as they left.

"I am not a crazy cat lady!" She muttered. Returning to the bathroom, Penny inspected the room to find fresh scat in the litter box. "That's weird. So are the blood and the scratch marks on the door. The creep messed up my door!" She cleaned the box, the tub, the bloody window sill, and the floor, feeling better from the activity.

Penny rested for several minutes in her rocker and took her blood pressure, finding it very high. "No wonder I'm nuts tonight." Penny swallowed a pill and retreated to her room, hoping to sleep.

❧

October 25, 1995

Later, Penny heard the stealthy movement in her bedroom and sat upright. She reached for her flashlight and squinted as the intensely bright beam struck the corners of her room. She saw the time on her digital alarm clock, which was 3:02—over two hours since the incident and the police patrol's visit.

"Who is there?" Her voice shook, but she spoke in almost a theatrical shout, "I know someone is here. You have two seconds to come out, or I'll call the police again. One. Two. Okay, three. Come out! Is it you again, naked man?"

She gasped as a dark shape leaped upon her bed and ran to her. "Finkel!" She shone the light upon the ebony and white cat. He blinked and shrank from the flashlight's beam. The cat then burrowed his head into her nightgown.

"How in the heck are you alive? Everyone said you were dead!" Penny scooped up the cat, studied his form, and hugged him hard. "You scamp! Where were you all day yesterday? We all thought you were dead!"

The cat purred raggedly but reached and patted her face with a soft paw, then licked her nose.

"You are never going outside again! I don't care how much you want out on the balcony. I cannot bear to lose you again, baby." Penny wept. The cat only mewled and purred, still locked in her arms.

The last few hours and the rest of yesterday were a blur and gross embarrassment. The humiliating scenes swirled again in her head. Not only did Penny faint, but she took down Joe and poor Mrs. Rosen as she fell. She awoke with a terrible headache and chest pains, lying on Joe's couch. She rolled over and vomited into a conveniently placed plastic bucket. Joe rushed to her side, kneeled on the floor, and gave her some *Tylenol* and water. Joe had put another fresh, cold washcloth on her forehead. The man had been overly solicitous all day toward Penny.

Penny now suspected that any affection she had experienced might have been a ruse to get her to relax and not freak out about her missing cat. Perhaps Mrs. Rosen was the only reliable witness because the police thought Penny was loony.

Pushing away from the depressing thoughts, Penny hugged Finkel close and fell asleep.

☯

Chapter 6—Guard Dog

October 25, 1995

Hours later, the day dawned noisily. First, a cat was screeching and pawing at Penny, followed by a reverberating pounding in her head. But no, that was the front door, and now the telephone rang. Penny groggily dragged herself up and grabbed the phone.

Joe shouted, "Penny! Is that you? Where the hell have you been?"

Penny grumpily answered, rubbing the sleepy grit from her eyes, "Of course, it's me. I'm in bed." She gasped as Joe responded with a laugh. "No, I mean, I just woke up. I am alone, although Finkel was here a minute ago." She inspected a sore hand, glancing at a line of fresh blood. "The brat just scratched me."

"What do you mean you are at my door?" Penny cringed, hearing another loud pounding. "Just a sec." Penny scrambled from the bed, pulled her robe on, and went barefoot after not finding her slipper's mate. She yanked open the front door.

"What is going on here?" Joe pocketed his mobile and burst in to grab Penny and hug her hard. "Why don't you have more locks on this door?" He let out a heavy, exhaled sigh. "I was so worried. Mrs. Rosen and the manager said the cops were here last night. Why didn't you call me? They said you had an intruder."

As he stamped into the living room, he nearly dragged Penny in his wake. "Are you alright? Did he hurt you?" Joe paced toward the kitchen to stare down the hallway. "What'd the creep look like? Did anyone but you see him? Did he rob you? You should have called me right away!"

Penny pulled from his grasp. "I am fine. Why didn't I call you? It was in the middle of the night. We both had a long and stressful day. I figured the police were better suited to answering an intruder call than my neighbors."

Penny sat on the sofa and arranged her robe around her knees, "I'd like to know how everyone knows my business."

"I told the manager you would have called me if it was important." Joe continued his inspection of the small apartment, noting the cookies and wine on the coffee table. "That's our stuff, right? So you didn't share cookies and wine with the intruder?"

"Of course not." Penny rubbed her forehead in irritation and remarked, "Joe, you've got to stop gossiping. I mean it. Next, I'll have my picture on the front of the *Enquirer*, with an article about being the crazy lady and her dead cat! No more stories. I'd like to have some privacy, Joe."

Amid Penny's rant, Joe went into the kitchen. He rummaged through the cabinets, pulling out items. "Do you have coffee? I can't find any. Maybe that will help you this morning. I know I don't function without at least half a pot first—"

"Joe, do you hear me?" Penny came to the kitchen door. "Stop making a mess. I don't drink coffee."

"No?" He held up a coffee filter. "But I found these... what do you mean you don't drink coffee?"

"I use those to brew loose tea." She came forward, not as angry as before. "Please sit. I have a jar of instant coffee. I can make you some."

"Blech. No, thanks, I don't drink the fake stuff." He shook his head. "I was going to make some for you. What about a cappuccino? I can bring you one or an espresso, maybe with cream or—"

"It's all coffee. My cardiologist doesn't allow me to have caffeine."

He suddenly pulled Penny closer. "I'm sorry. I never thought about that. How are you feeling?"

"I am alright for the time. Maybe a little confused, but oddly slightly better now that you are here." She patted his flushed face.

"All I could think of was to get to you. I should have never left you alone last night. Dino Ravello said the cops told him you were delusional or off your meds. Was that what happened? I kept the manager from spreading more rumors that you were on drugs. Okay? Then Dino told me the cops never found a guy here. Only a crazy lady that saw some man in a catsuit."

Penny shook her head. "I don't think I imagined the man. Besides, the creep ate the can of tuna I gave him, clawed my bathroom door, shit in the litter box, and bled all over the place. That is proof I wasn't alone."

Penny continued to pace about the kitchen. "I freaked when I found a huge bloodied cat in my bathtub. And a minute later, a big guy came out of the bathroom, but he was odd and cat-like."

"Do you think he killed a cat?" Joe cocked an eyebrow at Penny, putting an arm around her. "Were you having a nightmare? I've had some bad ones too. Last night, I dreamed a giant black panther ate Pappagallo."

He shivered, "You gotta think that some of these dreams or the weird stuff happening must have some truth. The supernatural cannot always be explained, but it is usually true. For example, Mrs. Rosen said this block of houses was built over what used to be the poor people's cemetery. Ya know, like in that movie, *Poltergeist?*"

Penny shivered. "You don't believe that gossip, do you? It's silly. Besides, poltergeists and the scary stuff in movies are not real."

Joe hugged her close. "I know about ghosts and evil people, so I won't let anything bad happen to you, Penny. Believe me."

"That is kind, but you don't know me."

Joe let out a long sigh. His dark eyes rested on her face. "So, let's fix what you think is a problem. I will stay by your side so we can learn about each other. We'll talk, and I can help you do stuff. No more problems. Right?" Joe's expression was earnest and hopeful.

Penny burst out laughing. "So now you are my big guard dog?"

"How about I'll be your boyfriend or something more permanent? I hate the labels of "only being your neighbor, friend, or *dog.*" Joe pulled her head closer to his. "I am gonna kiss your face here for the next few minutes... if you'll let me." He smiled, accepting Penny's delicate kiss, turning it into an extended, ardent, sex-filled declaration. Then, breathing raggedly, Joe said, "I believe we should do something about the casual boyfriend-girlfriend part. I want more than kisses."

Penny withdrew. "I am not in the habit of having sex with people I hardly know."

Joe pulled her onto his knee. "Baby, don't think about it. Besides, we've been neighbors for years. There is something more to what is happening between us. Right? I need you more than anyone I have ever wanted before.

I slept only a little last night, especially after the bad dream. So, I sat up and watched a movie. I also read some poetry and memorized them, hoping you might like them. I have no real schooling, so I gotta show you I have a romantic side. Right? I'm not half-bad at recalling the good parts of poems."

"Joe, you are a crazy man."

"*Io sono pazzo.*" Joe rolled his eyes and laughed.

"I can think of no other person I want near me today. But I am too flustered by all that has happened recently. So, maybe you hanging around isn't a bad idea. Can you fight? What if that weirdo comes back? I wouldn't want you hurt. Although the cat-man didn't seem aggressive other than wanting food."

"Don't worry about me in a fight. I don't play with weapons like my family, who think they're big shots and fight dirty. Me, I can beat anyone in a brawl." He pressed his slightly crooked nose to one side. "I didn't get a broken nose for being smart or pretty, that's for sure." Joe laughed, "I can be the biggest bully and your worst nightmare if you treat me like shit."

"Silly man." Penny patted his cheek. "Okay, no treating anyone like shit. Thanks for coming to my rescue again. I need breakfast. And we can look for Finkel. But first, I will get dressed." Penny stood and moved away, but Joe was right behind her.

"Didn't we both see Finkel dead yesterday?" He queried. "I buried him."

"Yes, but he came back about three this morning. Finkel slept on my bed until you pounded on my door."

Joe shook his head. "*Cara Mia,* we need a serious talk here. Your kitty is dead."

"He scratched me a while ago." Penny held up her wounded hand. Joe kissed it.

"I buried another cat earlier this morning. I didn't want to tell you. But there is something very crazy happening around here."

"Another cat?"

"Forget the damn cats. You need some food. You don't eat right. Your poor little ticker won't last much longer without proper food, less stress, and me."

"What about you?"

"You need all my lovin'. You like the *Beatles*?" Joe started singing the Beatles' tune, then announced, "I'm making breakfast. No, it's late, so let's have brunch."

Penny agreed. Suddenly happier with Joe's company, she stopped to wind the antique kitchen clock with his help and the stepstool.

Joe prepared a tomato and basil omelet with salad greens and tomatoes from Penny's balcony garden. He drank Penny's usual morning herbal tea and liked it. Penny felt much improved, eating wholesome, fresh food. Joe was a better cook, so Penny was already enjoying Joe's take on good eating.

Then Joe settled in the sunlit bay window seat to page through a magazine while Penny worked on a client's website project and made a few phone calls to her clients.

In the afternoon, Joe spent an hour in Penny's balcony garden, making new string trellises for the leggy tomato vines and pinching off the immature sprouting leaves to encourage the last small tomatoes' growth. Then Joe arranged plastic film over the area as a greenhouse, keeping out the chilly night air.

"Don't you need to go home? How is Pappagallo?" Penny, curious, asked, hoping Joe might leave. Joe's presence was comforting, but Penny didn't want to take advantage of the man's time and present good nature.

"Papa's fine. He has food and a classical music station on the stereo. Did you know that birds love music?"

"He seems to enjoy singing. And you have a golden voice as well. Not everyone can belt out Pagliacci's lament. Right?" Penny chuckled, using Joe's infamous phrase, 'right?'

"I'm no choirboy, but I do alright. In a pinch, I sing Ave Maria for funerals." Joe shrugged. He approached Penny's desk and stood behind her chair for a few minutes, watching her fingers speedily type on the keyboard. The screens flashed and whizzed past too quickly for him to read.

"Wow! You are good. I never saw anyone type so fast. I never learned to type in school, but I guess they have classes for it."

Penny, barely distracted, continued working but replied, "Yes, I imagine there are typing classes. Although everything is digital now. So basic computer skills might be taught in most schools these days." She pressed a few keys, and the website's homepage popped up. "There, that should be good enough for a starter. Let me just save and publish this."

"Does it bother you if I watch you work?"

"Um, not really. I'm used to doing this as a presentation and training for my clients. They need to understand how to navigate or update the site later."

Joe pulled up a nearby ottoman. "Can you show me? This is exciting."

Penny smiled. "Are you just twisting my chain because you are bored? I told you earlier that I am a dull person. Nothing exciting here."

Joe put his arm around her waist, pulled the wheeled chair closer, and kissed Penny's cheek. "No, I am serious. I am interested in your work. It is all mind-blowing to me."

After about five minutes of a website tour and Joe's repetitive questions, he asked, "Can we make a website together for a job?"

"We could. However, what do you want it to be about? What skills or products can you market? The best solution would be to put your resume on various local employment sites. Then you might find a new job."

"Yeah?" He drew back to study Penny. Then he waved a hand. "Nah, forget about it. I don't have the job experience anyone wants."

"I think you do, Joe. Besides, you could go back to school. Get your GED and apply to a trade school for something you want to learn."

"I could? Nah, school is not for me."

"Yes, that is the practical way to learn. You are not stupid, only ignorant." Penny moved back as Joe looked angry.

"I'm not ignorant. You sound like my old man." He tersely stated.

"You are *ignorant* because you haven't much education. But that doesn't make you *unintelligent*, Joe. There is a difference. Part of your problem could be dyslexia because you struggle to read. You mix up the word order. Am I right?"

"Nah, I'm just stupid. Even the army didn't want me." He rubbed a hand over his face. "Please... don't... um...

no, now you sound like everybody else. My ma and dad always said I was born retarded, and that's all. But I don't need you to feel sorry for me." He stood and whispered, "I'm sorry, Penny. I'm gonna go now. I've taken up too much of your time."

Penny took his hand and said, "No, Joe. You are a smart guy and catch on quickly. How many people can do all the jobs you have done? Besides, you seem to have the drive to please others. You are caring and helpful. You are a skillful cook and an excellent gardener. You have the gift of gab, so you might do well in sales or working in a store. Maybe a grocery store or nursery. You could teach gardening or cooking."

Joe sat again on the ottoman in awe. "You think so, huh?"

"I know so. Let me show you some recruitment sites here. Then we'll make a resume and post your bio datum."

Almost two hours passed as the pair laughed and worked, scraping together a decent-looking resume from Joe's extensive but brief work experiences. He even took over the laptop with Penny's instructions, filling in the questionnaires and posting his resume on a few sites. The process was slow, with Joe using the 'hunt and peck method' and two fingers stabbing the keys as Penny helped spell words and pointed to the action keys.

Joe sat back, rubbing his head and laughing after accomplishing the work. "My family would never believe what I just did. I look like somebody with some actual skills. *Il successone!*"

"You have plenty of talent and experience. Now you have even more skills to add and the confidence to continue." Penny stood and left the room, returning with cups of hot tea and the cookie tin. "Here's a reward for my skilled buddy."

Joe laughed, accepting the snack. "I think you should have been a teacher. Because you have the patience of a saint."

"Not really. You will do well, Joe, but only if *you* are patient enough to listen, learn, and finish the task."

He slurped the tea. His eyes were bright upon Penny's face. "I bet you'd be a good mama, too. You remind me of my grandma. Nonna could tease the birds out of the trees and train the rabbits and squirrels not to eat her garden. But she was feisty if you made her mad. Nonna taught me to read and write when the nuns said I was too stupid to learn."

"Was it in Italian?"

"What else?"

"So, you can read and write in Italian and English?"

"So, what? That's no big deal. I also know some French. We used to go to Switzerland to ski sometimes. Did you know they speak French, German, and Italian in Switzerland?"

"Joe, you underestimate yourself. You are a sharp guy because idiots don't learn multiple languages. That is another thing to add to your resume—I forgot you speak Italian. You could be a translator. You could teach other languages!"

Penny announced with wide eyes and a smile, "Honey, you could also read to others in different languages. Seniors, Alzheimer's patients, blind people, and kids need someone to read to them. So even if you started as a volunteer, it could become a paying job."

"You think? But I read too slow." Joe shook his head. "I sure got lucky finding you, Penny. That's it," Joe snapped his fingers, "you are *my* lucky penny I picked up in the street." He suddenly hugged Penny hard. "I am keeping you forever."

Misty-eyed, he gazed at Penny's face, then softly admitted, "I liked what you called me. Honey. That's *Miele* in Italian." He snuggled closer. "You like me better than I thought. I like you a lot more!" Joe kissed Penny.

The afternoon and evening progressed in companionable activities until Penny yawned.

"You look tired," Joe glanced at his watch, "it is already tomorrow in Rome and the afternoon in Hawaii. Maybe I should put you to bed."

Penny stood and gathered their cups and dishes from dessert. Joe had baked a coffee cake from Penny's quickly diminishing pantry supplies. "I hate to end the evening, but I am sleepy." She added, "So after I put these in the kitchen, we can say adieu."

"*Arrivederci. Buona notte.*" Joe replied, following closely behind Penny with a bottle of wine. "So, can we sleep together?" But seeing Penny's rolled eyes and gesture to the couch, he replied, "Or I suppose I could sleep there too."

Penny spun to him, almost knocking him over. "Joe, I am sorry, but... how can I say this without hurting your feelings? I am not ready to sleep with you."

"No? But we took a nap together the other day. I didn't pull any tricks, did I?" He pulled the short woman to him. "You said I was a good guy. C'mon, Penny, you cannot be alone right now. That weirdo is still out there."

Penny silently thought hard about the situation as Joe then blurted his idea.

"We'll have a PJ party. I'll make some hot chocolate and put you to bed." Joe said with a wink and an enticing smile.

"But where will you sleep?"

"My couch turns into a bed, and I'll sleep there."

Penny frowned. "I must be more tired than I thought. Why would you sleep on the couch bed if I am here?"

Joe's grin widened as he said, "Because, Princess, you'll be in my bed. You cannot be alone. I won't risk your life, *con pazzi in giro a piede libero*. Right? And I don't think I will get much sleep on your loveseat." He watched the play of emotions on Penny's face. "Just say yes."

"Yes, to whatever you said."

"Good. Go pack your nightie and the lady thingies you need, and let's go home." He turned about at the sink. "I'll do the dishes while you take care of stuff. Since you have so much tuna, can I take a couple of tins? I thought I'd make tuna salad for tomorrow."

Penny laughed. "You are always a step ahead of me when it involves food. Go ahead. I think you already know your way around my kitchen." Penny stood on tiptoe and kissed Joe's cheek. "Back in a few minutes."

❧

The rest of the late evening went well. In good humor, Joe set up Penny in his Mediterranean-style queen-sized canopy bed, complete with a cozy eiderdown comforter, bed tray, the promised cocoa with a cookie, and a nightlight. Joe switched on the TV and then handed Penny the remote.

"Anything else you need before I go to bed?"

Penny flushed hotly. "You have made me feel like a queen, Joe. I cannot think of anything else."

"You have towels and fresh soap in your bathroom there." He nodded to the doorway of the master bath. "Sorry, the towels are plain brown, not pretty green and pink like your towels," he shrugged. "I'm a guy, and my sister, Lucinda, helped set up my bachelor pad here when I moved in. So that's why everything here is brown and gold in my bedroom and bath. Besides, my whacko cousin Louie installed gold and avocado green fixtures when the apartment was remodeled in the seventies." Joe sniffed and sat on the end of the bed. "Sorry, it's a homely place, not pretty like yours."

"I won't complain. I think it is cozy and earthy, like you."

Joe's face flushed hot pink. "I am an earth sign, a bull, and stupid as hell like one," he glanced at Penny's gasp of a complaint. "I mean, I'm a stubborn guy." He reclined on an elbow. "But when I see what I want, I am very goal-oriented. So wave a red flag or your cute plaid PJs, and I'll come for you." He snickered and patted Penny's knee. "Are you sure you don't want me to stay in here with you?"

"Thanks. I should be fine. My guard dog is watching out for me." She leaned across the bed, stroked his face, and delicately kissed Joe. "You are still a good guy. Be patient with me; soon, you might have your wish, Joe. Good night."

Joe grinned and left the bedroom. *"Buona notte."* He said again and quietly shut the door.

A couple of minutes of silence ensued, but then Penny heard the clatter of dishes and clanging of pots, then a timid knock on the door. "Yes?"

Joe shouted through the closed door, "I forgot to ask, do you want red or green onions in your tuna salad? And this is important, *Hellman's* or *Miracle Whip*?"

"No onions, dill pickles, and surprise me with the salad dressing." Then, on an afterthought, Penny asked, "Is this a tuna pasta salad or for sandwiches?"

"A pasta salad."

"Then I also like green olives with pimento and both types of dressing. Plus, some dill weed, garlic, and onion seasoning, no raw onions."

"I thought so. You and I think the same. Except I like the red onions."

Penny heard the heavy footsteps retreat, then return. "What's up, Joe?" she queried, almost ready to tell the man to come in instead of the silly closed-door conversations.

"Brownies or chocolate chip cookies?"

"I am full."

"No, I mean for dessert tomorrow."

"I adore brownies—the fudgier, the better."

"Alright. That's good to know. G'night, Penny."

Penny switched off the TV and reclined against the pillows but expected Joe to return with more questions. Then she finished the cocoa and licked out the partially melted marshmallow stuck in the cup. Finally, she set aside the small tray on the bedside table, switched off the lamp, and snuggled under the covers. Even though the linens were fresh, Joe's scent remained in the bedroom. Something herby like sage or bay laurel.

Penny soon drifted to sleep, contented hearing the distant sounds of Joe humming and conversing with Pappagallo while working in the kitchen.

☯

Chapter 7—Intruder Alert

October 26, 1995

In the wee hours of the morning, Joe awoke, hearing his pet flapping around in its cage. He let out a held breath, hoping the bird would settle. But then Joe heard something else that made his blood run cold. A low growl, then a hiss. Pappagallo screeched and battered around in his cage.

Joe stealthily but quickly picked up his weapon, an old baseball bat, near the sofa bed. In the slanted moonlight, Joe perceived he wasn't alone. The cage clanked, then a clunk, and the bird's surprised shrieks of "Bad Boy! No! Bad Boy!" had Joe on the move. He hit the wall switch, which turned on the main lamp by the front door, and then raced toward the front windows.

"Put him down!" Joe yelled, seeing a dark shadow snatching the bird from its cage on the floor. "NO!" He bellowed as the man held the bird in both hands, as if ready to twist off Papa's noisy little head!

Joe swung the bat, hitting the man in the back of his legs. An unholy shriek sent shivers up Joe's spine. He bashed the intruder again on the shoulder, but not before the dark man fell to his knees and dropped the bird.

"Get on your feet, buster!" Joe growled at the groveling dark shape in the shadows of the room. Then, cautiously edging away enough to put on the light in the kitchen, he grumbled, "I'll hurt you if you do anything stupid." Backing uneasily, pointing the bat, Joe picked up the phone set and punched the emergency code. The operator engaged almost instantly.

"Hello! I've got an intruder in my apartment. I need the cops." He gave the address. "Yeah, I can describe him. Tall, dark-skinned, wearing a fur hat and um—" Joe squinted at the man, "the guy is some kind of freak, wearing a black catsuit. *Caca!* Penny was right. I caught the cat burglar!"

The cat-man rolled over to his hands and knees and moaned. He crawled into the patch of moonlight from the window, rubbed his shoulder, and licked his arm.

"Come quickly, this guy is a freak-show attraction," but then Joe dropped the phone receiver and hovered nearer the man. "Hey! You! On your feet, now, and sit on that chair!"

"The light... it hurts. Please—turn it off!" The man mumbled, hiding his face in the dark blue shag carpet, and moaned.

Joe snagged the sash from his bathrobe, then quickly wound it about the man's hands and one foot. "Fine, buster, you can lay there and cry the blues all you want until the cops arrive."

Stepping around the man, Joe kept some distance and picked up a limp Pappagallo. Then, kissing the lolling head and putting the bird on the coffee table, he shouted, "You asshole! Why did you kill my bird?" Joe kicked the man twice and raised the bat. Penny seized his arm.

"Stop! Let the police have him." Penny put both hands on Joe's bulky muscular arms, suddenly realizing he was only in his red underpants. An odd thrill ran through her as she beheld this unique, unexpectedly sexy man. But tears and shock happened as she saw the yowling man rolling on the floor.

"That's him! The same guy who broke in last night." Penny shouted. She drew closer and noticed the dark pelt all over the man. "What are you? How did you get in here, and why... are you here?"

"I didn't find you. I could smell you here. I came to see you." The man wept amid yowls and mewls. His tear-filled green eyes were pitiful. He scooted into the moonlight, his eyes turning crystal green as his limbs lengthened.

"Why are you here with him?" The man glowered at Joe but mewled, "Miss Penny, I thought you loved only me?"

Penny gasped, saying, "I'd never seen you before last night. How can I love a thief? And how in the heck do you know my name?"

Outside, the nearing sirens grew louder. "Hear that? The cops are on their way." Joe retrieved his bird and stood by the door, cooing and petting the ruffled feathers. "Why would you hurt my bird?"

"I am hungry. I smelled tuna," the man glanced at Penny, "real tuna, but I didn't find any but empty cans in the trash. He—" the man jabbed a hand in Joe's direction, "doesn't have the green cans."

"I told you I gave him cat food last night!" Penny then shouted. "What are you?"

Suddenly, the cat burglar sprang to his feet and dashed to the front window, the robe sash trailing loosely from muscular, shorter, furry limbs. In the dark shadows, he had a tail that lashed angrily. "MRRR-ORRRR!" The man howled, then hissed.

Glancing at Penny, he pleaded, "Watch for me. Come to me in the moonlight. I still love you." He dashed into the kitchen, scrambled onto the counter, shoved the open window wide, and fell out of the aperture, knocking off the old screen. There were loud clatters and a crash as something heavy hit the trash cans below. Joe and Penny watched as a sleek, enormous black cat raced away down the sidewalk and across the street.

"Did we just dream all of that?" Penny asked Joe.

"No, I don't think so. My apartment is a mess, and Papa is dead." Then, in horror, he looked up at Penny, "I told you I had a dream that a panther ate Pappagallo! It is true! That was the panther—Your cat-man!"

☯

The police arrived, and one officer was the same as the night before. Again, he eyed Penny suspiciously as the men questioned the excited pair.

"Okay, you say the guy returned... someone dressed as a black cat, yes?"

"Yes, a cat burglar," the pair said in unison. Holding Penny's hand as they sat on the sofa bed, Joe squeezed it. "Penny told me what happened last night, but I wasn't sure I could believe the story. Sorry, Penny." He glanced at his watch. "That was early morning yesterday when she told me about the creep. Shit, another day has gone by, and the lunatic murderer is still loose."

The officer wrote his notes carefully. "You think he is a murderer?"

Joe cradled the cockatiel in his hand. "The weirdo was going to eat my pet. He killed him." With tear-filled eyes, Joe added, "And who knows why the creep came here? He said he followed Penny's scent, so he obviously tried to break in upstairs." Joe eyed Penny to say, "Oh, oh. Maybe they should check your place, too."

"My gosh! Right. Will you be okay here by yourself for a bit?" Penny asked, then seeing Joe's nod, she left with the other policeman.

"I never thought the Cat-Man would come back. But Joe was worried, so I slept at his place tonight. I mean, now."

"Are you in a relationship?" The officer asked as they walked up to the third floor.

"It is something new—only this week. Joe Bartoli carried me off the street when I fainted after finding my dead cat a few days ago. It oddly seems as if a month has gone by. Yet, as I told you, I keep seeing a dead black cat... twice in the street and then in my tub last night, like I told you. So Joe has buried three cats that resembled my cat, Finkel." Penny unlocked the front door and allowed the officer to check the apartment.

The officer looked about cautiously. "So, you don't know Mr. Bartoli very well? Maybe he is the cat killer and your intruder."

"No! We both saw the man tonight. Joe hit him with a bat! Then the crazy man jumped out the kitchen window and ran away."

"As Alice said, 'Curiouser and curiouser.'" The officer replied with amusement. But curtly, stating, "I'll check your place while you stay by the door. If you see the man again, just yell."

Penny only nodded.

After some minutes, the officer returned. "Did you leave a window open in your bedroom and bathroom?"

"I don't recall that."

"Your bed looks tumbled, and the bedroom is tossed. Perhaps the intruder was looking for something. You should come with me to see if anything is missing." The policeman led the way, still with his revolver drawn as if expecting an attack. He used the walkie-talkie, asking for the other officer to join him.

Penny surveyed her bedroom with dismay. "Why would anyone do this?" Her temper simmered, spotting red graffiti on the wall over her bed. "Bitch and 'The F-Word' doesn't apply to me." She whispered sadly.

The officer only shook his head. "Sorry, Miss. But this guy is in worse trouble now because he has broken into two residences and threatened you both."

"Do not forget to add vandalism and murder!"

"Murder?"

"Yes, he killed Pappagallo, Joe's cockatiel. What a lovely little pet he was, too." Penny swiped away tears that suddenly flooded her eyes. Leaving the bedroom mess behind, she went to the kitchen.

Joe and two other officers crowded the narrow doorway from the entry hall. Joe pressed past them to rush over to Penny. "Sweet Jehoshaphat! What happened here?" He noted an open cabinet door with spilled cat food and cans on the kitchen floor.

Penny peered into the kitchen cabinet to say, "Obviously, the Cat-Man struck in here, too! Everything is a mess. All the tuna is missing!"

"How do you know?" The first officer asked, squeezing past the couple, using the flashlight, and exploring the cupboard. "Anything else missing?"

"Tuna treats. I had two bags of them and three tins of tuna pâté. What a nutcase!"

Joe pulled Penny aside to sit at the table. "Honey, please don't worry. The cops will find this guy. Besides, I'll bet the creep won't return because I clobbered him. He'd be stupid to come here again." He glanced at the kitchen clock, then his watch. "How odd. Your clock stopped at 12:13, and my watch says it's 1:22."

"What's odd about that? Maybe the batteries died." One officer asked, peering at the wooden clock.

"No, I wind that clock bi-weekly. Maybe I forgot to do it—no! I wound it yesterday! You were washing dishes." She commented to Joe.

The officers shifted restlessly. "Okay, so we've got your reports. Since the guy is missing again, we'll put out an APB. You probably aren't the only people he's attacked or annoyed. A street cop in this neighborhood has seen someone resembling the description, but only late like this, just after midnight. The cop suspected the guy was homeless since he was spotted digging in a trash can."

Penny rose to her feet. "I told you he was real. But please, don't report this to our neighbors or the newspapers—they'll twist the situation to make it a hot story. I'd like to keep my life private."

Joe suggested, "Let's clean up this mess in the morning. I'll check over everything. I can buy new locks for the windows and doors since yours are old and crummy. Then nobody will break in again."

Joe herded Penny towards the foyer door as they shut off lights and secured the apartment. She left with the officers, going downstairs to Joe's place.

"You'll stay with me. It's not wrecked too badly." Joe offered, keeping Penny close with an arm about her waist.

The couple saw the officers out of the building. Joe locked the two doors of the outside and the entry foyer. Then he waved them away as the cops slowly cruised down the street, their searchlights piercing the shadowed walkways and alley.

Joe shut his front door and snapped the two deadbolts' levers, locking everything tight, including inserting a security bar and wedge that wouldn't allow anyone to open the door from outside.

He spotted Penny crooning and holding something. "Are you alright? What do you have there?" He neared Penny as she spun to him with a smile. "Look!"

Pappagallo lifted his head and made a feeble squeak.

"Papa!" Joe gently took him from Penny. "Oh! You are alive!" Joe crooned to his pet in Italian.

"I think he fainted or hit his head. There's a tiny blood spot on his head." Penny touched the bird's head and neck with a gentle finger. "I think the Cat-Man scared him half to death!"

"But this is a miracle! I really thought my boy was dead!" He placed the cockatiel on his kitchen perch.

"Maybe he was playing possum." Penny giggled.

Joe offered a strawberry to Pappagallo. "This will help get him fit again. Poor boy!"

Joe put his arm around Penny's shoulder and squashed her to his side. "Again, you are a brave woman! And look how lucky we are—everyone is fine and dandy. We've just a little mess to clean here and upstairs." He boisterously kissed Penny's cheek. "Are you hungry?"

"Not really. But you always seem to have an appetite. So I'll join you if you make cocoa again."

Thirty minutes later, Joe brought Papa's dented cage into his bedroom. He locked the door and turned to see Penny looking nervous, wrapped under the covers.

"I don't think you should worry about your virtue. I am so tired that I might sleep 'til noon!" Joe yawned, stepped around the other side of the bed, crawled in, and settled. Turning toward Penny to say, "Thanks for indulging me. I don't know about you, but I am so wigged out from earlier that I might have a nightmare. So I feel better knowing you are here safe with me."

Joe kissed Penny's hand. "G'night." He smiled, clapped, and the bedside lights turned off.

Penny giggled in the darkness. "It's like on TV." Then she settled, ready to sleep, quiet for two breaths. "Perhaps you should be worried about your virtue, Joe."

"Nah. I'm good. Sleep is all I need. I'll hold you to a raincheck for later."

Penny lay quiet, almost counting the minutes, trying to calm her nervousness. She watched the glowing bedside clock's hands spin around another half-hour, nearing three a.m. As if Penny had read a sexy novel, an unusual sense of arousal warmed her belly.

She peeked over her shoulder to see Joe asleep. His long dark lashes brushed his cheeks, a cherubic look upon his face, and the tossed dark curly hair was arrayed upon his pillow. She rolled gently to face him, feeling safe. Penny said a brief prayer of thanks and felt that everything would be better tomorrow—she slept soundly.

☯

Chapter 8—I am Missing You

October 30, 1995

The last few days had gone much the same, neighbors finding Finkel dead in the street or alley. When Penny was alone one night, Finkel shared her bed only in the hours before dawn. Otherwise, Finkel was usually absent for the day.

Joe had buried three more cats resembling Finkel— oddly, one each day. He was concerned that a plot or some evil at work was trying to drive Penny crazy.

But Penny was at the point of believing that she would never have her pet, Finkel, again. She was ready to go to the animal shelter and adopt a kitten. Perhaps that would keep the wicked Quasi-Finkel from bothering her again. Other neighbors had reported that Finkel annoyed their dogs or showed up at their windows, crying to be let in. If the stray cat was clever, it would find another home, and Penny hardened her heart against the rabble-rousing, wraithlike feline.

While sorely missing Finkel, Penny didn't forget the daily issues of his misbehavior, usual aloofness, or the anxiety of burying another dead animal.

Since the break-in at his place, Joe was vigilant, no longer accepting that Penny should be alone at night. Joe had replaced Penny's apartment locks so no one could break them or jiggle the windows to open. He also repainted her bedroom walls, covering the obscene graffiti. That night, Penny confidently slept alone.

Neither had seen the Cat-Man since the last police visit at Joe's. That didn't mean that the creep wasn't around. Joe and Penny were wary in the evenings, especially last night when they had supper at Woo Fan's and caught a movie—*The Scarlet Letter,* Joe's idea of a romantic date. They were watchful, feeling as if something or someone had shadowed them. They slept together that night like roommates.

But Penny, requiring space and peace of mind, left early in the morning to work in her apartment upstairs.

Joe showed up an hour later bearing fresh, warm breakfast rolls, a *Thermos* of coffee for himself, and fresh papaya and pineapple juice for Penny. They had breakfast together and spoke of pleasant things.

The pair spent an hour looking at emails for Joe regarding job offers. Unfortunately, not much had come in. But Joe wasn't sad, saying how much he enjoyed spending time with Penny. Penny wanted more for Joe than being a cooped-up, bored boyfriend. She still needed time and space to do her daily work.

☯

At precisely 11:30 a.m., Penny grabbed the ringing phone on her desk, wondering who it might be. But then laughed, knowing it wasn't chatty Joe; he was working in his garden on the roof, preparing it for the upcoming cold spell. Whoever it was, Penny hoped they had good news. She needed something positive today after burying another Finkel copycat earlier that morning.

"Penny? Where in the hell have you been? I've been calling you for over a week now!" Louise's distant voice screeched.

Penny held the receiver away for a moment as her sister vented nastiness.

"I guess you don't believe in leaving messages on my machine. I will respond to voice messages if I have them." Penny paused, then interrupted Louise's tirade. "Are you done now? Can I tell you what's happened to me this past week?" Penny asked calmly.

"Happened? Oh, do you know about Bennett's? You know they canceled our dinner party at the last minute! Supposedly, there was some rat infestation or water leak. I don't know. They still want to charge us for the food they prepared for our party since it was ruined. So, I have no idea where to go or what we should do now. Mom is furious, and Dad has threatened to have a heart episode or go on a binger. He already has Dylan Hunt lined up to sue Bennett's restaurant. It's a big mess."

"I thought this was a surprise party?" Penny replied mildly and turned her chair to gaze out the glass door, watching the birds at the balcony feeder.

"It is, but I had to tell her, you know, so Mom could plan a fancy dress or her costume," Louise replied snottily.

"You, Louise, are a killjoy. That isn't a surprise party. I also can't believe you sprang a costume-themed event on people at the last minute! And, you know, I am not happy with you nagging me about these problems."

"You were supposed to be organizing this bash with me!"

"Last week, you said you'd do it yourself. It's always about Y-O-U, Louise."

"Bitch."

"Fine. I can see we are getting nowhere. So, Mom's birthday is tomorrow. Why don't we have a nice supper somewhere else as a family? Or perhaps Mabel, Mom's cook, can whip up her favorites. We still might get a cake, or did you already order one?"

"Are you listening? I've invited seventy people! I can't tell Mom there isn't a party and then call all those people! Are you insane? Are you on drugs now?" Louise went off again, creating five more reasons that Penny might have lost her mind.

"Louise. Shut your pie-hole!" Penny commanded loudly, using Joe's amusing but crass phrase.

A hiss and crackle of the phone helped Penny continue. "Thank you. Now that I have your attention, I might have some ideas—if you'll let me get a word in here."

With a sigh, Penny stated, "I know someone who caters. I created their website. All we need is a place. We could still do it at the folks' house."

"Absolutely not. The house is a mess. Really. The gardener quit last week, and the carpets in the downstairs rooms are being cleaned. The kitchen is being re-painted. We cannot do it there." Louise dared to burp, then sighed loudly, "Oh, shit. I'm dead here. So are you."

"That was rude. What in the heck are you doing?"

"I'm trying to drink myself into oblivion because when I tell Mom and Dad how we completely failed to produce a big extravaganza event, they will hunt us down and kill us."

"Thanks for including me."

"Sis, you are as guilty as I am for this mess. Especially since you haven't helped me one bit. I am not going down in a solo flaming wreck for this one."

"How nice of you. By the way, we should have been working on this for months, not a couple of weeks. That is on you, Louise. You are always too busy for anyone else but your own concerns."

With an eerie sense of presence, Penny turned to find Joe watching her. His hands were dirty, and he held a basket of dripping produce.

"How long have you been there?" she whispered.

"Since you told your sister to shut her pie-hole." Grinning, Joe came forward and kissed Penny's cheek. "Good for you. Hi, Louise." He brashly said as he passed by, going into the kitchen.

"Who is that?"

"My... neighbor, um... Joe. He brought me some garden veggies just now."

"Boyfriend!" Joe's laugh echoed from the kitchen.

"Boyfriend? Oh, I get it now. So while I have been working my ass off planning Mom's party, you are diddling around with some guy?"

Penny spied Joe's amused face as he returned and took the receiver with wet hands. "Yeah, sure, canoodling is more like it!"

"Oh, my God! Let me talk to my sister! What a rude ape!"

"Louise? Right? Let me ask you a question here." Joe waited for a breath as Louise then quieted. "I think you have a problem, right? You want a party for your... um, Mom, right?"

"Yes? So, what the hell—"

"I might have a solution, Louise. I have a very influential family with many fine talents and resources. So you need a nice big place and good food right away?"

"Okay, what do you have in mind, rude ape-man?"

"Do you know Michaela's Ristorante?"

"Are you kidding me? That is one of the premier restaurants in downtown Manhattan. So are you saying you could get us in there? But what would they serve us on short notice? And can they make what Mom and Dad would eat?"

"My cousin, Michaela Daniela, owns it and is the head chef there. She owes me some favors. If you give me an hour or two, I might fix your problem."

"Not *the Michaela Daniela Bartoli!*" Louise squealed. "Oh, that is too good to be true! What a dream! I could kiss you!—whoever you are!"

"It's true. But I will do this for you only if you do one thing for me."

"Great. What do you want? I know this will cost us a hell of a lot more than Bennett's. What else?"

"I want you to say these three words to your sister." He eyed Penny's blushing face. "She is a wonderful woman and deserves to hear these words from you. *I. Am. Sorry.*" He held the phone in the air.

Louise laughed. "Oh, only that? What a jerk-off. So, tell me how—"

"No, you screwed up. Now you've got two other things to say to Penny. First, I am sorry. Second, I love you, Penny. Now say it." Joe held the receiver to Penny's ear.

Penny laughed. "I appreciate it, Louise, even if you don't mean it. But really, Joe? You can get us in at Michaela's?"

He leaned over and kissed Penny's cheek to whisper. "Probably. But only if your sister doesn't act like a bitch." He stated loudly, "You hear me, Big Sister?"

Penny was tactfully mum, even when hearing Louise say, "Bitch? I'll show you a bitch!"

Joe took the receiver. "Nope, the deal's off if you cannot behave. So why are you punishing your parents and my little *cara*? You're a sadist." He chuckled and held the set away from his ear, then smiled at Penny to whisper, "I'm only pulling her chain, baby. She's gotta learn some respect, right?"

After a few moments, they both heard, "Well? Is anybody there? Did you hang up on me? What a stupid fu—"

Joe said, "I should hang up because, girl, you have a mouth like a New Jersey longshoreman. But, if we can get back on the topic here, I will aim to get a reservation for you. Now, what day and time?"

He grabbed a pencil and scrap paper from Penny's desk and carefully wrote the information.

To Penny, it looked like a four-year-old's rough scribble.

"Okay, give me an hour or two to fix your problem. And, next time, be nice when you call your sister." He hung up.

Penny's mouth dropped, "You didn't."

"Yes, I hung up on Louise. Respect. Now she must behave each time we talk. I don't really need an hour, but let her think it is a big deal. Okay?"

He punched a phone number, listened, hung up, "Wrong number... *idiota*," and redialed twice. "I'm used to my auto-dial phone at home." He listened for a moment, then launched into a fast repartee and discussion in Italian. Soon, Joe wrapped an arm around Penny's shoulder and leaned to whisper, "My cousin loves the idea. She had a cancellation and can move some people around. Plus, I can help in the kitchen as her sous chef. I'm jazzed because I'll get paid, too." He winked, finished the conversation, wrote a few notes on the paper, and hung up.

"Done." Joe folded the note and put it in his shirt pocket. "Can we make supper? I wanna teach you how to make eggplant parmigiana."

The pair gleefully entered the kitchen to work on their dinner for later. All the vegetables were from the roof garden.

Once the casserole was in the oven, Penny called her sister with the good news. While they had a party again, Louise was cranky about making all the calls to change the party address and time. Penny offered to take half the list, but Louise refused so she could be a martyr.

☯

The couple discussed the upcoming party over their parmigiana meal and egg custard dessert with Joe's wine.

"I still cannot believe you got us in so quickly. It is Halloween tomorrow. Usually, Michaela's has a big bash by reservation only. You are an amazing fellow." Penny fed him a spoon of custard. "Maybe I am luckier than you."

"Hm, I think we are even. You'd make a good sous chef. So, I think you've been holding out on me, faking it in the kitchen." He smiled cattily and tweaked her cheek.

With a smile, Penny said, "I am okay, not like you, Joey. I never learned much from Mom or Mabel, our home cook. My cooking experience was mostly trial and error or watching Julia and other celebrity chefs on TV and in videos. Haven't you noticed my library of cooking videos?"

Joe sat back and took Penny's hand, kissing the palm. "Your desserts are so far the best. You are more than okay. If you weren't a paying guest at the party tomorrow, you could also help us in the kitchen."

"So, tell me again, what is on the menu?"

"Since it is a party, Michaela never takes individual orders for food. Instead, she makes a tasting menu or a buffet. But don't worry, everything will be *perfecto* and *delicioso!*" He kissed his fingers.

"We'll have the antipasto salad and garlic-stuffed mushrooms. The main courses include shrimp scampi, spinach fettuccine Alfredo, traditional sausage and cheese lasagna, and chicken parmigiana. Everyone loves meatballs and sauce, so folks can choose from four freshly made kinds of pasta. Dessert is New York-style amaretto cheesecake or tiramisu and espresso. And according to your sister, she is having a big cake delivered. The only extra expense for your party will be the bar tab. That is not included in the deal." He winked at Penny.

Penny blushed hotly. "You still astound me. Will I see you at the party?"

Joey leaned forward, keeping Penny's hand. "You gonna introduce me to your family?"

"I'd like to. Besides, they should know it was you who made the party happen. And that you helped cook the meal."

"Oh. So, I am only the kitchen help? Ouch." He shied away and sat back in his chair.

"No! Joey, I want them to meet you—" Penny gripped his arm.

"You gonna tell them we've been... you know... goofing around?" He blinked pointedly. "Seeing each other?"

"Earlier in the week, I planned for you to attend the party. I didn't ask you since I had no details. I am proud that you are my... um... date. What do you call a boyfriend in Italian?"

"*Ragazzo. Sono il tuo ragazzo.*" Joey said with a smile and thumbed his chest. "I am your boyfriend."

Penny repeated the words. "And me? Am I your girlfriend?"

"*Si. Sei la mia ragazza.*" Joe said with a kiss. Then, sat back to say smugly, "*Va bene.* So now that it's settled—

we are officially dating. But I have to tell you more stuff about tomorrow."

Joe sipped his wine as he talked. "As you said, tomorrow night is Halloween, an annual party at Michaela's. Everyone is expected to dress up in costumes or at least a mask. The buffets are for everyone in the restaurant. There is always a pasta bar, various sauces, salads, soup, three types of bread, and a dessert table. However, your party will be on the patio in the back and have the menu I described. Some of the menu is from the canceled group."

Sipping his wine, Joey continued, "There are lights, fountains, and music for a very festive ambiance. Your family and friends will have their own buffet, servers, and a bartender. And as a favor to my cousin, I priced it at what you would have paid at Bennett's for twice the food. I know Bennett's serves those silly *Nouvelle Cuisine* thimble-sized portions. Michaela deserves to charge more than she does because everyone goes away full. I told her to consider it an extra fee for the late reservation. Besides, your sister deserves to pay more. Isn't your mother worth it?"

Penny shook her head. "Still, everything sounds wonderful. I have only seen pictures of the place and read rave reviews. Who doesn't love Italian food?"

"Oh, I forgot this bit. Michaela has a chef who makes little thin-crust pizzas for special parties. The patio has a wood oven, and they make the pies to order."

Accepting a hug and kiss from Penny, Joe continued. "The big deal is that I must help in the kitchen all day tomorrow starting at six a.m. But the pleasant part will be that I don't serve or help for the rest of the evening. The parties are carefully planned, so we rarely run out of food. If it is gone, that's it. And Bam! The kitchen is closed! Order a pizza to go." He shrugged, "So by seven p.m., I can be all yours for the party." He winked, asking, "So, what is your costume?"

"I have no idea. It has been years since I attended a Halloween party. What about you?"

"Are you kidding? I love dressing up for Halloween, even for the little trick-or-treat kiddies! I have a closet full of stuff. My sister, Lucinda, is a seamstress and makes clothes for a costume store and theaters. So, I have lots to choose from. Let's go see what we can find, hm?" Joe rose to his feet and took Penny's hand.

"I probably got some story-book couple costumes, too, like Romeo and Juliet. My sister, Francesca and I went as the fated pair. Then, my cousin, Violeta, and I did it the next year."

Penny locked her doors as they left the apartment, following Joe to the elevator. She asked, "But won't your family think we are... you know something... an item?"

"What? It's just a costume, *cara mia*. How about you be Super Girl, and I'll be Super Man?" The pair laughed as the door closed on their conversation.

Chapter 9—Masque

October 31, 1999
Lower Manhattan, NY

The festive evening seemed perfect as Penny sauntered about the flagstone patio, greeting the guests and sipping sparkling cider. She kept a level head, not needing alcohol to mess with her emotional and overtaxed state.

Her sister Louise and their mother were in their social elements, looking like queens of the realm on the crowded patio. Oddly, both wearing courtly garb, mother Barbra as the British Queen Mary, and Louise as the Queen of Hearts with her husband, Bryan, the Jack of Hearts, at her side. But Louise was still bossy and, so far, kept a wide path avoiding Penny, only interacting with a haughty attitude.

Penny glanced around the outdoor dining area to see her father at the garden bar, already rosy-cheeked and sipping a cocktail. He looked the part of a court dandy wearing an 18th-century peacock-blue velvet waistcoat, ruffled shirt, white satin short pants, and sagging white hose. However, the ostrich feather in his blue hat looked limp, often hanging into his blue eyes.

An argument must have happened because Barbra was dressed in a period other than his own. Dad should have been Britain's King George V, with his wife, the Queen Consort, Mary.

Obviously, Dad was having his own amusements, now handsy with a younger woman wearing cat ears, a leopard-printed leotard, tights, and matching knee-high boots. So sadly, Stuart Stratton was a society lush and womanizer at most parties. But supposedly always faithful to his wife. Penny no longer cared about her parents' social games.

Although Penny's mother, Barbra, was just as flirty. Laughing coyly with men and ensuring her surgically enhanced bosom was artfully displayed caused them to gape. Or perhaps it was the sparkling diamond choker and large sapphire pendant that caught their interest. Penny could not watch all that ridiculous flirtation. Louise was the same, whacking men with her fan when they admired the sweetheart-cut bodice and contents too closely.

Penny was glad her costume covered her figure discreetly, yet was comfortable. She never cared much about her appearance, knowing she wasn't a beauty like her mother and Louise. But the cream flaxen linen two-piece stola was modest. The dark rose woolen palla artfully draped over her shoulders with a swirl over her head was comfortable. Her hair, set in fat, loose curls, was held up by a bronze circlet of leaves and pearls with a gauzy veil. She wore strappy sandals with a low heel, dangling earrings, copper bracelets, and beaded cuffs. Penny felt very elegant, feminine, and mysterious. Most of the guests did not recognize her.

Yesterday, Lucinda was a magician with costumes, finding the right colors to accent Penny's skin and eyes and creating a unique, flattering style.

Penny had watched for Joey for the last half hour, expecting him to dress as a gladiator or Caesar—he had a great body for those clothing styles. The thought suddenly thrilled Penny and made her hungry. Passing the buffet, she snatched a stuffed mushroom, ravenously wolfing it down.

Her heart was fluttery tonight. The excitement of the party, the overly worried expectations if it would be a success or a flop, had become moot. So far, nearly forty people mingled, with about five more who had yet to arrive and had RSVP'd for the new venue.

She didn't feel remorse that her sister had to contact all the guests. But then, Louise only called a handful and had her husband's secretary and assistants call and take messages. Penny was also glad that the party was initially supposed to be a masked event or optional costume for the restaurant's 'Super Couples in Time' theme. Most people seemed ready for the occasion despite the change of venue. She didn't hear one complaint about the restaurant, only glowing praise for the perfect evening and party on the patio with delicious appetizers.

Now Penny was growing antsy, wondering how Joe would look. His sister certainly had pulled it off with Penny's costume of a Roman patrician woman. She was glad of the woolen palla, as the patio was slightly chilly under a clear, star-speckled night with an occasional breeze ruffling her stola and veil.

A man in a white Navy officer's uniform went by, sipping his drink, but quickly stepped back to Penny. "Well, hello, Lady Guinevere!"

Penny's instant dislike probably showed on her face, but she didn't care. "Wrong century, Captain."

"Ha! Who cares? Who are you, pretty woman?" Wrapping an arm about her waist, he leaned closer, grinning like a drunk jackal.

Penny, uncomfortable, wriggled away, "I'm co-hostess of this party. Excuse me, I must talk to my sister, Louise."

She tried to step away, but the dark-haired man whisked his ornate gold-braided hat off with a slight bow to say, "Since we are being official here, lady, I'm Admiral Cannon, and we are supposed to meet. I am your date tonight, Lady Penny."

Too close again, now with his arm about her waist, he whispered harshly, "Your sister, Louise, said you'd be here. I am glad we finally could connect. She's one picky gal without a drop of patience. No moss grows under her feet. She was angry since you had blown off several invitations for cocktails or dinner at her place. I am the same—I'm peeved you never made it. I don't like getting burned by no-shows." The man gripped Penny harder.

"But now, we can have a good time. Nice place Louise chose here, with perfect dark, cozy corners to get better acquainted." His eyebrows bounced upward, and then the cad grinned wolfishly at Penny.

Penny regarded the man, finding him older and probably on the make for only the night. Any physical attractiveness was soured by his attitude and innuendos.

"Sorry, our schedules haven't meshed. I don't need a date. Excuse me, I must keep watch for new guests." Blushing hotly, she twisted from his grasp to walk away, the veils and stola lifting delicately in the breeze.

"C'mon back here, let's party together. I'll get us some champagne! Not too friendly, are you? Well, shit... what a bitch."

After passing a waiter with cocktails, Penny glanced behind—the Navy man continued to watch her. It gave her the creeps, and she wished Joe was here now. He'd give the rude guy an attitude change with one look. Also, the previous week's red messages on her bedroom wall immediately hardened Penny's spirit.

Penny still felt oddly out of place. These people were the spoiled elite players. Yet they were greedily out on someone else's dime for a good time. The festivities tonight were costly, the food so far delicious and plentiful, and they had yet to sit for dinner. So now it was just appetizers, drinks, and greeting each other. So far, so good. But she didn't like her sister's choice of date or suitor. The 'admiral' was a lecherous jerk.

She again spotted her sister gripping the Jack of Heart's arm. Her smile was fake and simpering as she talked to a buxom woman dressed in a powder blue ball gown and her escort, a man resembling Abe Lincoln. Penny recognized the man—a business partner of their father. 'Abe' Matthew Martins was extremely lanky and lean—the stove-pipe style hat made him seem seven feet tall, towering over his shorter, chubby wife, Lizabeth.

Penny wanted to tell her sister to call off the creepy date, but Louise waved Penny over to greet them. So now it was inappropriate to complain.

"Look who I found... the Martins!" Louise motioned her to come.

Penny was relieved to see the Admiral talking to the bartender and another woman. Then, feeling safe again, she strolled toward the couple.

"Are you enjoying the evening?" she asked kindly of the wife.

"This is by far the best party of the season." She sounded excited and turned to Louise. "Louise and Bryan, this is a terrific idea you had, much better than Bennett's. That place is so boring they haven't changed their menu in a century. I deplore this new trend in dining, where everything is only a bite for twice the price. Yet the food is the same as always. How rude!"

She fluttered her lace-trimmed fan and batted her eyelashes at Bryan, saying, "You know me, the ambiance and something unique and delicious wins my loyalty. The service and food here have been exceptional so far. A delightful surprise."

Penny felt ire rise, her cheeks heating as Louise bragged about her choice of venue. Then Penny took the woman's arm. "Liza, if you are interested, I can introduce you to the head chef later. Michaela would probably like to meet you since you write restaurant review blogs."

"Oh, my word! You know Michaela Bartoli? Please, oh please, introduce us! I ate here before when her father owned the place. It was good then, but so much better now!"

"Yes, although I only met her yesterday evening and spoke with her this morning, Michaela seems charming and talented. My *ragazzo*... Joe Bartoli is her first cousin. Good ristorantes seem to run in their blood. Joe is also an excellent chef trained in Italy and is Michaela's sous-chef for tonight's dinner."

Penny was now the focus of the conversation and felt pride that she had revealed Joe's skills and role in tonight's event. She secretly was glad, as Louise's jealous remarks were suddenly cut off by others around them joining in the new conversation.

"It was only thanks to Joe Bartoli that we could reserve this place tonight." Penny smiled at the other couples and answered a few questions. "I would be delighted to give Joe and Michaela your business cards. Thank you. Have a pleasant evening." She accepted a few and tucked them in a tiny silk purse under her sash.

She sailed away from the group, leaving them to chat, glowing with inner pride, knowing she was helping the good side of the Bartoli family. Penny went to the buffet to get a plate with antipasto and mushrooms. She stood at a tall table near the salad bar, nibbling the bits and enjoying the food. She didn't want to fill up on heavier stuff, waiting for the vegetarian pasta dish Joe had promised he'd make in her honor. Michaela was also pleased to create something creamy and shrimpy for 'Barbra, the birthday gal.'

Penny had a warm feeling that perhaps she had found her match in life. In only days, Joe Bartoli had lowered her usual defensive radar, charming her with his kindness and gentility. He seemed honest and outspoken yet acutely on the point. She admired him for the toughness but practicality of his way of living. While he had some rough spots, Joe persevered and made himself a worthy person. Penny wanted to help Joe feel better about his lack of education and the possible learning disability. The guy was more capable than he would admit and a powerhouse when he wanted to be. No, dummy there.

This morning, they shared a cab to the restaurant. Although nervous, Joe talked eagerly about the menu and the work ahead. She was then introduced to the staff at the restaurant, with Joe proudly keeping his arm around Penny's shoulders as they greeted everyone.

She observed as Joe washed at the sink as if he were a surgeon, then put on freshly laundered and pressed black pants, a black double-breasted button-up shirt, a red kerchief about his neck, and a white and black checkered apron at his waist. In addition, he wore a black bandanna around his head, making him look tough, especially when he grabbed a large cleaver. Finally, he came to Penny, sitting on a stool near the prep counters, kissed her, and whispered, "Wish me luck, *Cara Mia*."

"You don't need luck, Joe. You are ready for this. Make your mark. But remember one thing, *Carino*, please have fun." She kissed him chastely and watched him proudly stride to the counters, ready for his chance in the kitchen.

He was skilled, then dutifully and cheerfully, working alongside his cousin and her crew of line cooks and four preparation crews. Four of the workers kept up a lilting repartee of Italian, which sounded like jokes, but Joe laughed at it all and gave as he got in the exchanges. Sometimes, they'd bombast each other in a less happy tone, urgent or demanding. Joe shone happily like the sun through it all, especially when Michaela commended and smiled at him as they worked.

Penny admired his muscular physique as Joe hacked and cut into substantial veal roasts, legs of salted ham, and whole chickens and then delicately trimmed the fat and bones with the quick skill of a surgeon.

After an hour of watching the staff prepare for the buffet, Penny left, blowing a kiss to Joe with the promise to see him tonight.

Now, she wondered if Joe still labored in the kitchen. The entrees and side dishes would come out soon. Perhaps then he would appear. Penny hoped Joe might enjoy cooking and feel confident in his abilities tonight. The kitchen was his milieu. She couldn't wait for the food.

She planned to take him home to her apartment later and let him have fun if he wasn't too tired. *Or could she have her way with him?* She blushed hotly at the thought of an encounter with Joe. He probably was fabulous, considering his enthusiasm, romantic gestures, gentleness, effortless charisma, and physical brawniness. Although Penny felt almost virginal compared to Joe's vitality and possible sexual experience.

Penny secretly admitted that she was falling for Joe Bartoli. But was hesitant to say it since it seemed too soon in the short time they had been together. Yet, how else could she meet and date someone if she mostly stayed home?

In the oddity of everything, she realized Finkel had introduced Penny to Joe. Or it was pure luck that Joe had found her unconscious lying on the street.

The music on the patio seemed to swell loudly, as did the noise of the party! Penny, shaking off the mental ruminations, felt someone come up behind her and put hands on her hips, then someone else stepped in front, shouting, *"Jammo, jammo, ncoppa jammo jà!"*

The familiar Italian tune, *Funiculì, Funiculà,* blared through the speakers as many partiers joined the Conga line and pranced around the patio, kicking their heels and singing the choruses!

Caught between two tall men wearing jeweled masks, Penny nearly stumbled through the steps, suddenly feeling dizzy, her heart thudding yet buoyed along in the throng of dancers. Sure she would fall, Penny didn't let go of the man's shirt ahead of her, nor the grip of the one behind as they circled the patio.

As the head and tail of the dancing parade spiraled between tables and the serving area, she spotted Louise, Bryan, and Penny's parents enjoying the dance. Penny twisted away, gulping and gasping for air, releasing the two men's hands. She wobbled unsteadily toward a chair, hoping to make it before fainting.

Where is Joe now when I need him?

As she stumbled toward the chair, a dark velveteen arm swung about her waist and plopped Penny in the chair. The person kneeled before her, offering iced water. "Drink this."

Familiar moss-green eyes glowed, but the face was hidden behind a hooded disguise. Gold sequins and golden piping outlined the mask, creating a sleek feline shape like an ornate black panther god.

Penny took a frightened breath, worried it was the cat burglar. But the resemblance quickly ended. The husky voice spoke with a lisp. Nor was the cat as tall or slim as her intruder. This costume had gold-tipped claws on the velvet gloves, and the gold trim accented what might be padded muscles down the body. A shiny golden spiked collar lay above the collarbones and across broad padded shoulders. The costume was impressive and probably expensive.

"Thank you for helping me. I almost fainted out there." Penny said as the cat person dipped a cloth napkin in the water pitcher and dabbed her hot cheeks and forehead. "Are you a doctor?" Penny asked, already feeling some relief.

The feline's head shook negatively, but the velvet paw continued to dab at her face as the other held her wrist.

"Do I know you?"

A nod as the Cat-Man abruptly stood up, his head swiveling to the right. Then, with a squeeze of her hand, the person jogged through the dancing crowd.

Penny lost her errant knight among the throng but felt better for the attention, still embarrassed that she had a physical problem. This was why she sought a solitary life, rarely leaving home other than when necessary.

Penny wondered now if Joe would be content being a homebody. The past days had been busy for her but not for him. She would never get better physically. The doctors had cautioned that she would have a shortened life with the heart condition, especially if Penny did not care for herself. Yet most physicians were surprised she had lived past sixteen and was now in her mid-twenties. Maybe with Joe around, she could at least be happier in the years she had left.

Tearfully, she sniffled and picked up the napkin dropped by the Cat-Man. She wiped her nose, even though it was rude. But it was that or the veil of her borrowed costume!

Penny watched the dancers break out of the last song, Dean Martin's Pizza Pie Tune. She never recalled the proper name, but the lyrics always amused her.

She could imagine Joe having fun belting out the words, too. But, unluckily, she had not seen or heard him singing among the crowd.

Glancing across the patio to the pendulum clock on the brick wall near the bar, Penny saw it was seven-forty-five. Dinner should have been served already. Yet the music still played, and people were now dancing to something slow. Sadly, the appetizers looked picked over, and near-empty platters and heated trays looked abandoned.

Penny rose to her feet, noticing that Louise and Bryan were dancing close together, unconcerned that the meal was late. She wandered through the dancers to the ristorante's rear entrance and the kitchen's back door. Knowing she had been welcomed twice already, Penny would check on Joe.

There was less kitchen staff now than this morning, and most were engaged in cleaning and storing away food and utensils. Penny spotted a man she had met this morning and waved. "Hi! Paulie!" The stocky man waved her in with a smile.

"How is your party?"

"Good, so far. Although I wondered when the main courses were coming." Penny hinted.

As he wiped a steel countertop, Paulie replied, "It just went out. We had a little mix-up, and the front restaurant got part of your order. But all is good now." He smiled widely, "When I looked out a bit ago, everyone was dancing, so nobody seemed worried that dinner was late."

Slapping the cloth on the steel sink, Paulie glanced at Penny, "So, are you having fun? You look beautiful tonight. Lucinda is fantastic, isn't she? Last year, she made me Cyrano de Bergerac—I was a hit." He grinned broadly. "Need a costume? Lucinda is the best."

"Yes, Lucinda's design is perfect for me. Since her rates, even with a discount, were beyond my pocket, Joey paid for it all. Or maybe it was a paid favor." She smiled at the memory of Joe's odd family stories. Then, looking about the large room, noting everyone busy, she asked, "I don't see Joe."

"No, he left almost an hour ago. We finished most of the food, so he wanted to join you. Haven't you seen him?"

"No. Unless Joe is dressed so cleverly that I cannot identify him. But Joe would greet me, I think. Was he dressed as a hero... maybe a black panther?"

The man frowned slightly but shook his head. "Perhaps not as you think." Chuckling, Paulie added with a wink, "Joe is a prankster, a big kid, so he probably has planned a surprise. Now you go on out and get dinner. Joe is probably there waiting for you. Enjoy! *Buon Gusto!*" The man patted Penny's shoulder and stepped away, shouting something in Italian to a pair of teen busboys.

Penny used the restroom. She glanced in the mirror, assuming she was a frazzled mess from dancing. But she could only admire the lovely costume as it graced her ample feminine figure. "Perhaps I was born in the wrong century. Rome seems to suit me." She washed her hands, then primped, tucking in loose curls and artfully arranging the stola over her shoulders. Smoothing on rosy lip gloss, Penny knew for once she was lovely. She chose a jasmine and gardenia atomizer from the tray on the marble counter, spritzing the scent on her wrists and neck, and jauntily exited the restroom, feeling fresh and feminine. "I hope I can find Joe." She murmured, filled with new purpose.

"Hey! There you are!" The loud, gruff voice echoed in the marble-tiled hallway.

Penny startled, almost fainted, but jerked about to see the Admiral bearing down on her like a battle destroyer. She was hauled into his meaty arms and roughly pressed against the frescoed wall.

"Thought you'd ditch me again? I don't take it kindly to be ignored." His hot hand squeezed her throat as his face descended, meeting Penny's lips with his. "C'mon, baby... kiss me. Let's get this party started."

"No! I don't know you!" Penny struggled and shrieked amid the sloppy kiss, not enjoying anything about this creep. He was not tender like Joe. Instead, the man's kisses were rough, unpleasantly tasting of pungent liquor and onions.

"C'mon, just call me John. I've got a cannon just for you, baby. Let's play!" He snickered amid another sloppy kiss.

She raised a knee, hoping to knock him in the privates, but he was tall and not in range, so she made ready to stomp on his foot or kick his shins as she squirmed in his arms. "Stop! I am not enjoying this!"

The Admiral drew back slightly and repositioned himself over Penny, "Think you're cute, huh? Think again, girlie." He plunged back into the intense kiss, one hand gripping her throat, the other sliding between the folds of her costume, capturing a naked breast.

"NO!" Penny screamed through the kiss, jerking her head away as far as possible. "Stop! Somebody help me!" Her cries were muffled when he put a hand over her mouth and dragged her outside.

Laughing, the admiral flung Penny atop garbage sacks and damp cardboard boxes of kitchen scraps near the dumpsters in the alley.

He stood over her, an evil smirk on his twisted mouth, as he unbuttoned his tight white uniform jacket and opened his pants. He bent toward Penny and growled, "This could be better if you'd be nicer to me. But if you want it rough, that's what you'll get, bitch. I'll play either way."

Screaming, Penny tried to crawl up from the trash pile, but the man backhanded her across the face.

"Not so pretty, now, are ya, spoiled bitch? You look like a slut to me."

"You don't have to do this. Please... stop," Penny wept and touched her split lip.

"I told you I won't be ignored by a slut or anyone." The man yanked her up roughly and ground himself against her body, pressing them through the refuse to the brick wall.

"You should have met me at your sister's dinner parties. Then maybe I'd be nicer. But tonight, you were rude to me. I won't wait—"

An unnerving shriek split the night air as fury was released upon the Admiral. A black, lithe form sprang above the pair, tackling the man and leaving Penny to fall to the damp ground. Penny screamed as the dark figure fought with slashing and evasively agile moves. It avoided the heavy blows of the heftier man. The Cat-Man kept up a screaming, hissing warning as it whirled aside from a kick that looked like something from a Kung Fu movie! The Admiral again spun and kicked at the aggressive Cat-Man.

The heavyset, sweating officer became lethal as he quickly pulled a jagged-edged knife from under his coat.

He kicked aside fallen trash with a cruel grin and cagily paced toward and around the Cat-Man. Penny saw his ruse—he was forcing the cat away from her.

Penny scrambled to rise from the refuse pile and palmed her way up the wall. She planned to run inside for help and call the police if only she could do it without notice while the men fought.

The Cat-Man did not have gold or sequins on his costume, but he was just tall and sleekly muscled like a panther, and Penny realized now he was her intruder.

"Oh, my heavens, you are my cat burglar!" She yelped and shifted away from the pair as they neared her.

The Admiral cast a brief glance her way. "Damned right I am. I figured I'd visit you if you wouldn't meet me at your sister's shindigs! I'm not fond of Louise, although she always has fun soirees with many women, ready to play." He chuckled, advancing again on the pair. "C'mon, kitty, I'm waiting."

"What? I wasn't talking about you... wait. You were in my apartment?" Penny blinked tears, rubbing her bloody lip on the veil at her shoulder. "But this cat kept coming to my apartment."

"Yeah, I caught him on your fire escape one night and beat him to a pulp. Or at least I thought I did." The man slightly rose from the attacking crouch to ask, "How in the hell did you survive?" He slashed again.

With a yowl and leap, the Cat-Man tackled the Navy man. Then, he held the Admiral's throat with razor-sharp claws. His voice, a guttural growl, "Yes, I still live. You have killed me four times, beast. But I will win this time. I have one more wish, and my life is finally forfeit to save another."

The pair suddenly wrestled, falling then rolling, flailing, scrabbling on the ground, punching, slashing, amid grunts, the admiral's foul language, the cat's screams, and howls.

Oddly fascinated by the fight, Penny was rooted to the spot. Then she heard shouts and saw several people running from the patio gate into the alley, including her earlier rescuer, the costumed panther man!

Then, with a shout, a tall man in a red cape with leather and bronzed Centurion armor ran toward the wrestling pair.

Penny recognized the brawny muscles of the tanned arms as the guard lifted what looked like a real sword with gilded eagles on its hilt. The swing's momentum was stopped above the cat figure as Penny ran to him, grabbing an arm. "NO! Don't kill the cat!"

A scream and shouts echoed across the alley as more people ran outside. Penny spotted Bryan at the back of the crowd, hollering, "Don't hurt John Cannon—he's innocent!" Then, another man urged others to chant, "Fight! Fight!"

"Please, the Cat-Man was here to save me from this other guy." Penny shouted at Joe, then screamed again, "Someone! Call the police!"

The Navy man rolled free amid the distracting exchange, swung his knife toward Penny's abdomen, catching her forearm, and twisted to slash at the Cat-Man's belly. Then, getting to his feet, he brutally kicked the Cat-Man. As the guard approached, John Cannon spun to stab the Centurion in the chest.

The wicked knife clunked against the edge of the metal breastplate, sliding over the rounded edges into Joe's ribs between the leather straps. The admiral, with a grunt, shoved and twisted the knife deeper.

Joe blinked for a second in shock. Then, as the Navy man with hands outstretched to throttle his attacker, Joe came alive again and ran him through with the short sword.

The Admiral looked surprised and laughed. "Yeah, I know who you are, too. Think you are a hero? You are nothing but a low-class, ignorant thug. I guess this bitch enjoys slumming. I'm wasting my time here." He kicked at the cat near their feet. "I hate cats, so I hope you both die!"

The taller man suddenly wavered, back-stepping, pressed a hand to his belly, coming away with blood as the sword pulled free. "Shit, there's a stain that won't wash out." His smile twisted as he nodded at the Roman soldier, "Neither will yours. You are a dead man, too... I got you good. No rental deposit returns for us."

Then, slipping to his knees, the Navy man looked at his assassin and the crowd. "Did you see that? He attacked me. I'm supposed to be the hero here... but I—" Before anyone could move, the man fell forward onto his face against the asphalt. Blood trickled from his mouth; his bloodied fingers clutched the ground. "Fu... you... bitch." The man mumbled and lay still.

Penny ignored the admiral and crawled toward the Roman soldier as he staggered and fell on his rump. The bloodied sword clattered noisily to the pavement.

"Joe! No!" She pressed a bloody hand to his armored chest. "Please don't leave me." She hugged him as he slipped backward, the crimson cape stained darkly with his blood spreading like a fallen flag on the ground. The red-plumed horsehair and bronze helmet fell away. She stroked his cheek and moaned, "Please stay with me, *carino*."

A loud snarl surprised the crowd as the Cat-Man struggled toward the trio. "I told you I would win." He slashed at the Admiral, shredding his white jacket and leaving bloodied marks. His eyes gleamed brightly; the body of midnight-black fur trailed dark blood and gore as he settled near Penny. He laid a paw on Penny's knee.

"Please, let me touch you both. I never wanted to harm you. I love you, Miss Penny."

Penny caught on a sob and lifted her head from Joe's shoulder. "You frightened me. I don't understand. What... are you? A cat or a man? Are you my Finkel?"

The large, panting cat laid his head on Penny's thigh. "Yes, to all. I was a man once, hated by everyone and mistreated. I wished to be powerful and free like a panther. And I was one for many lifetimes until I was hunted and taken to a zoo. There, I wished to be a man again. I had many zoo homes until the one here in this city."

The man coughed and continued rasping, "Then I saw you taking pictures of the animals and me one day. You were so pretty and kind. When you sat near my cage, your purse fell on the ground. You had pictures of a cat... You were hugging and kissing him. I wished to be that cat... except that one was orange, not black like me."

"Ginger! That was my cat eight years ago before Finkel." Penny looked at the man, now closely resembling an actual panther, "It was you? I thought you were beautiful, wishing I could hug or pet you."

"I know. I heard you. But then, I got my wish and changed into a cat, black like I am, and lurked about the zoo for weeks, hoping to see you again."

"I recall the zoo reported the new panther from South America had gotten out of his habitat," Penny murmured, wiping her bloodied face and tears with her veil.

"Hah, not a habitat—a cage! But like a house cat, I was small, and it was easy to escape but harder to survive on the streets. I missed my daily meat. Then, someone captured me. After a vet checked my health, I was sent for adoption."

The panther man's enormous paw flexed the toes as if kneading the air. "It was my dream to see you again and go home with you." The big cat's purrs rasped, but then he grimaced in pain.

"You gave me a wonderful life. I loved you. You gave me tuna… thank you." His pink tongue ran over a lip but caught on an enormous fang. He resettled and looked up at Penny as a deep rumble came from the sky. A few wet drops fell about them.

"It was my fate to be yours… but my time is up. I have one wish left, and then I can be at peace, Penny. My selfish debt's paid by saving you." He licked her tear-streaked face and bloodied hand. "I have always loved you. So, I tried to be a good boy. But my days are gone. I hoped I could give you my last wish before my life ended. But, it might be too late… this is my ninth life—" the cat man choked and lay coughing.

No longer afraid, Penny stroked the sleek, ebony, furred face, "I am so sorry. Why did I never know this?"

"No, I am sorry. I never meant harm. I am glad you have this man. He saved you." The panther rasped, then purred raggedly.

Penny bent to see that Joe was barely breathing, his lifeblood seeping into the pavement and mud of the alley. "Oh! *Carino!* Please don't leave me." Her hand stroked his pale face.

"Do you love him or me?" The panther whispered roughly, his breath only a hiss.

Penny wept openly as she said, "I love you both. But I have died every time I found my Finkel dead. I love Joe and will probably die of a broken heart. So why was that man chasing you?"

"No, the evil man was hunting *you*. He killed me four times whenever I tried to interfere in the past nine days. He was often at the crux of my death. Sic'd dogs on me in the alley, flattened me with his red sports car, threw me off the balcony, and beat me to death. I only wanted to protect you. I wished I could do better and kill him for you. Revenge can be sweet."

With a sigh, the pseudo-man whispered, "Please, remember me in the moonlight." A shudder ran through his wounded body. "Forgive me."

The growling sky let loose as raindrops pelted them.

"Finkel!" Penny cried out as the animal-man went limp. Then Penny felt her heart leaping in her chest like an animal kicking to get out. Gasping, she collapsed upon the panther and Joe. About the wounded people, the partygoers shouted and ran inside from the downpour, sirens screamed, and Penny was lost in the dark void.

Chapter 10—Facta Non Verba

Manhattan, NY
November 5, 1995

The oxygen bellows wheezed and clicked, pumping air into the comatose body. The figure was pale, like a lifeless, fragile doll, perhaps already in another existential plane. Joe Bartoli, in a wheelchair, had resisted the many orders by nurses to leave Penny alone. Instead, he kept her dainty hand in his, repeatedly kissing it and whispering in English and Italian to her. Joe prayed with all his heart to trade his life for hers. He was miraculously alive and recovering from his wounds from the fight five nights ago with John Cannon.

But Joe could only tell his side of the story of that night to the police today. Before that, Joe had clung tenuously to life after surgery and then suddenly woke up last night at midnight feeling as if he had only been in a violent dream. But he and Penny were the only survivors of that bizarre alley fight.

According to the police account from the witnesses, the Cat-Man turned into a full-sized panther, then morphed into an emaciated, naked dead man. He'd been brutally slain, gutted by John Cannon. Yet, in Joe's dreams, he felt the panther or Cat-Man was more than a house-breaking burglar or fiend, as he had previously thought. Penny had cried for him as well. Joe recalled hearing her say she loved him. That hurt.

Love was the issue here that might save or kill him. Joe had never been so infatuated or devoted to a woman as he had Penny Stratton. It was fate. It had to be an act of God or some weird magic that they had experienced these terrible things... yet he fell in love. He ached for her and hoped Penny would love him one day soon.

In Joe's mind, love was more than sex or an eternal Friday night date... it was a way of living that he had always dreamed and yearned for. A partner with whom he could share their joys, sorrows, good fortunes, or chaos. No more loneliness and worries that he was below average in intelligence—He needed a woman to love him, anyway.

No matter what, in the last week, Penny had insisted Joe was not stupid. He had a more challenging time because of dyslexia. But, during the two weeks Joe had known Penny, he'd discovered that life meant little without her. And with Penny, he felt safe, capable, and brave. Words that had once been lost along the pathways in his mind or clogged in his throat and unable to speak them suddenly flowed like sweet wine. He remembered everything that seemed beautiful when he was with Penny. She never declared that he was stupid like most of his family had all his life.

The pair had endured the storms, and without Penny, Joe suffered like tossed-aside detritus. He was nebulous in his feelings about the Cat-Man. But realized only today the real threat had been the man he killed—John Cannon.

Joe had seen the man dressed as a Navy Admiral. But unsure if he was an actual officer or in costume, he suspected the latter since he pestered women, schmoozing with them, and was a little too handsy. He even saw John approach Louise and pull her into a tight embrace; his hands roamed her figure while dancing. Louise had put him off afterward, seeming relieved when the cocktail waiter passed, freeing her from her hostess duty.

That was it. Penny had not been around to see any of it. Joe had hoped to sneak into a romantic corner and kiss her, making it Joe's reward for a long day's work. He had brought a surprise for Penny, hoping to pop the question that evening. He would have been proud to share his good fortune with the crowd of Penny's family and their friends.

But then John disappeared too. Joe only heard a distant scream, and then his senses became alert. He searched the patio for Penny and ran into the alley when Penny screamed again. After almost two weeks of hearing her cry or shriek when finding her pet dead, Joe knew this was different. Penny was in trouble!

Joe's gaze was now caught on the stark contrast of the purple and black bruises on Penny's neck and face and the dark indigo veins on the alabaster white skin where the IV needle was taped on her forearm. The other arm was bandaged from her hand to the elbow. She seemed almost dead. A ghost already. Joe could no longer feel the mysterious connection he'd had with her for weeks.

Hot tears welled in his eyes, stinging the tender skin from crying. He swiped a tissue under his raw nose and blotted the tears. "Oh, *cara*. I am so sorry I was late. I should have been there for you. Please don't leave me. I promise I will always be with you and protect you." He painfully turned his body to lay his head near her hip, still gripping her delicate hand. Then, after a short time, he fell asleep, content to be with Penny.

❧

Penny sensed tender touches on her face, hands, and body through the mist of her mind. She wanted to say something, but there was a choking object in her mouth and throat, and she couldn't move. At first, afraid, she was a prisoner—bound, gagged, and perhaps held for John Cannon's pleasure. The thought was disgusting, so Penny vowed to never allow herself to feel anything but hatred for him.

But no... she witnessed John die, face down in the mud of the alley amid trampled lettuce and kitchen trash. A terrible fate he obviously deserved. She rested for a time, relieved he was no longer a threat.

Suddenly, Penny's mind jumpstarted again, the images swirling and disjointed, watching both men fight and die, their blood dark and oozing out onto the ground. Wasted. And the Cat-Man? He died, too, the cat's big head in her lap. Her fear and sadness increased like the chilling rain that fell upon them.

Why did she lose everything she cared about? It wasn't fair. She would be alone again if the Cat-Man's incredible story was true. Finkel was dead, possibly forever. But the life debt... the wishes... what were they, and how had it all happened? Maybe she deserved the assault.

Penny winced in pain, her mind still caught by the gruesome, bloody scene.

Like a jolt of electricity, she remembered the feeling of loss, perhaps as the life or spirit left the panther and Joe. Knowing remorse now that she had not admitted that she was falling in love with Joe earlier in the week. She wanted a life with him... and Pappagallo, too. But how could that be? Joe was dead, killed in the act of bravery to save her. Everything was undoubtedly a big mess now... she would be blamed for the party's failure.

She had never had men fawning over her nor very interested, and no one ever fought for her. Finkel had been her love and constant companion, and perhaps if the Cat-Man's story was true… how could it be? Finkel had saved her life, too, from the clutches of John. She worried that John's death was upon her—Louise would blame her for that.

Silently, Penny couldn't help but yearn for the end of her miserable life. Since, unhappily, there was no one left to care about her.

The cool air in her lungs and the oddly scented mist enticed her to sleep. Penny hoped she never woke up again. Without Joe or even Finkel, she could no longer bear solitude. Her mind and body hovered in that mist-shrouded place.

Then pain settled in her chest like an uninvited animal, weighty with claws that dug into her heart, ripping it out and devouring it.

Hell and its wicked denizens claimed Penny Stratton as she saw the horrors of a dead Finkel again and a dying John Cannon. But the worst sin was the pale, bloodied face of the man she loved.

☯

The heart monitor's alarm woke Joe. He groggily looked about, startled, as a nurse and orderly rushed in.

The nurse briskly shoved Joe's wheelchair aside from Penny's bed as the orderly hit a switch on the wall above the bed. Another alarm and blinking light went on as a disembodied voice repeatedly announced down the hallways of the ward, *"CODE BLUE!"*

Joe gaped at the team rushing into the room, pushing a cart, and attending to Penny, their voices terse, urgent, and loud.

He rolled the chair to a better vantage point out of the team's way. "Please save her! I love her!" He shouted over the din. His raspy and weak voice didn't seem to make any difference.

Another man in a white coat came in, saw Joe, and ordered, "You! Get out. Back in your room, this is not a peep show. Unless you are family—"

Shocked by it all, Joe suddenly found enough air and energy, shouting, "I am her fiancé… I'm staying. Save her!"

"Fine. But keep your mouth shut and stay out of the way." Then, the doctor turned to his patient.

"What happened to her?" Joe demanded.

Joe impatiently waited for an answer for minutes. A nurse approached him, saying, "Your fiancée is in cardiac arrest. We are doing everything possible for her, but it's not going well." She patted his shoulder but bent nearer, "How are you feeling, Mr. Bartoli? You should rest—"

"I'll be fine. Just save my girl." He couldn't help the warble in his voice, now afraid to lose Penny.

"You are bleeding again. Please let me take you to your room. The doctor needs to—" The nurse bent to him, lifting his soiled gown away from the wet spot.

Joe tugged away from the nurse's hands. "No. If Penny dies, it won't matter if I die, too. I don't care. Leave me alone." Gripping the wheels, he rolled away nearer the bed. "I'm staying. Penny needs me."

He stubbornly watched as the team provided various treatments and performed life-saving procedures. But to his horror, he saw the heart monitor only respond after the electro-cardia shocks for mere seconds. Penny was failing... the other monitors' graphs were slowing, diminishing, plunging into what he supposed were the 'danger zones.' Then, the screen's graph flat-lined amid the warning alarms. Finally, after an injection of something unpronounceable, Joe prayed Penny would respond.

But she lay still like an alabaster statue. Cold and lifeless, like the stone. Taking her hand, Joe wept. The team members backed away from their patient, and he rolled closer to the head of the bed.

"Penny, please... don't go."

"Sorry. Please go to your room." The nurse ordered.

"No, Marina. I'm staying. Please do something... can't you help her? Penny!" Joe wailed as the orderly pulled his wheelchair away from the bed.

The doctor glanced at his watch, "Nurse, mark the time of death—twelve-thirteen p.m."

Shattered, Joe's heart leaped, making a loud thump, and he felt weak. Sobbing and choking on his tears, Joe squeezed Penny's hand. *"Cara Mia,* take me with you," he pled in Italian. Then he felt someone lean to him and squeeze his shoulder, speaking in Italian, cooing words of comfort.

He looked up to see his cousin Michaela.

"She sleeps with the angels now." She whispered. "Come, Nino, let me take you to your room. I'll call Father Pasquale, and we can ask him to bless Penny."

Sniffing and wiping his eyes with shaking hands, Joe weakly sat up. "You are right. She needs a blessing. But Penny was my blessing. My angel. I love her. How can I live without her? I should have died, not her. Everything I did was for her... everything."

Joe took the tissues offered by his cousin. "You are a saint too. Thank you for calling nine-one-one. We both would be dead without your help that night."

After wheeling Joe across the room, Michaela kissed his brow. "Not a big deal compared to you. My Centurion, you are always the guard of the family. I have partially repaid my debt to you after all these years. I love you. Only because of you can I do my job or have my business. *Grazie.*" She tucked her blue silk scarf more securely around her neck.

"You still hide your scars. But you are beautiful and shouldn't worry that others might see your bravery." Then Joe added with a heavy sigh, "Penny was like you, a fighter. She tried to save me, too. And that Cat-Man. I told you about her pet Finkel and the weird cat guy that kept breaking in. She loved her cat."

"Yes, a strange occurrence. But it is all over now. So please, let's go to your room. You must rest. I won't lose you, dear cousin."

"Yeah. It is strange. But why did I have to lose the only woman I really loved? Why? Penny was my dream... my perfect wife." He dropped his head and wept brokenly.

Suddenly, the monitor beeped. The orderly looked up from his duties of removing the life-sustaining equipment. "What the heck?" He peered about the room at the other nurse talking to the doctor. "Marina, um... something is happening here... the monitor is coming on again. I thought we turned it off."

Marina and the doctor turned about to stare, then came over. The physician put his glasses on and scrutinized the monitor. "We've got a pulse, respiration...

holy cow!" The doctor gazed at his patient, then the team, "She's still alive! Stat! Get me a—"

Joe turned away from his cousin to look at the team again, busy with Penny. "She's alive?"

"Yeah! Oh, my God! Yeah!" The orderly and a nurse echoed each other.

Joe wheeled himself near the bed again. "C'mon, Penny baby, you can do it!" He rooted like a cheerleader. "I love you, Penny!"

The monitor beeped loudly as the heart rate rose steadily and then evened out. It echoed like a bell's joyful peal in the room. The doctor quickly checked the vitals of his patient. But after some minutes, he backed away to mark Penny's chart. "Unbelievable." He murmured.

"*YAHOO!*" Joe yelled but then winced at the painful effort. Finally, he came closer, "I gotta kiss my girl."

He witnessed the changing of the ashen pallor to rosier cheeks. Penny's even breathing came this time without the oxygen intubation. "Penny, can you hear me?" He had eyes only for her, waiting patiently for many long minutes until she stirred, a slight frown on her face as her eyes fluttered open.

"*Cara Mia! Brava!*" Joe, amid Italian epithets, happily leaned to kiss Penny's cheek.

"Michaela, look! Penny is here again! It is only God's blessing. My angel has returned!"

Michaela stepped around the bed and stood between the doctor and Joe in his wheelchair. The nurse packed the crash cart, still shaking her head.

"*Brava! Bellissima!* I'm so glad you made it."

After coughing, Penny whispered, "I feel weird. What happened? Joe? You–you... are alive? I dreamed you died. So did Finkel. Oh, my poor Finkel—" Penny cried, but Joe gripped her hand and leaned his face to hers.

"I almost died, and so did you. I am sorry your Finkel is truly dead. But he saved us both."

"I dreamed you stabbed someone with a sword and—" Penny coughed.

"A... *Gladius*—my short sword. And yeah, John Cannon stepped right into my blade. But he stabbed me, too. Almost got me in the heart—*Bastardo*." Joe grimaced at Michaela's pinch.

"You... I watched you die, both of you and Finkel, too." Penny said groggily.

Joe declared, "We all died that night," amid tears, this time happier ones. "But somehow, God watched over us because only you and I lived. So maybe we were the worthy ones to save."

"No more Finkel?"

"No, I don't think so."

"*Bella*," Michaela pressed Penny's hand. "It was your brave act that saved my cousin's life. God had to save you, too. We were so afraid and sad. Joe was beside himself that he had lost you." She kissed Penny's cheek. "I am glad you are back with us."

Penny subsided for minutes, then asked softly, "Why do I know you, Michaela? I mean, other than when I met you on Halloween morning." She looked at the pale green eyes glistening with tears. "You. You saved me at the party."

"I only called the police when I saw the fight in the alley."

"No, you helped me. I recognize your lisp now and those jade-green cat eyes. You were the beautiful panther-man at the party."

"No." Michaela shook her head, glanced at Joe, and sighed. "*D'accordo.* Guilty. I enjoy dressing in disguise and visiting parties at my restaurant to ensure my customers and friends have a good time. I saw you almost fall and had to help."

"I am glad it was you. But it was weird because I kept losing my pet cat for the past few weeks. Joe buried many of his doppelgängers. So when a Cat-Man broke into our apartments, it scared us. I thought he was you at the party. I was afraid the cat burglar followed me."

"Sorry. I was inspired by Joe's stories about it all and couldn't resist wearing a cat costume like he described."

"You wanted to frighten her?" Joe asked with suspicion.

"Not at all. The Cat-Man sounded romantic since Joe said it loved you, Penny. But I was going for the superhero role of the Black Panther from the comic books. I love those champions of justice stories." She leaned closer, "I like to surprise people. Since I am tall and not very feminine-looking, I like to switch genders in costume. It's fun to play a hero. There are no heroines these days."

"You could have been Cat Woman," Joe suggested.

"No, Cat Woman is beautiful but wicked. I enjoy being on the good side." Michaela squeezed Joe's shoulder in a hug, then added, "We have enough drama and evil in our lives. I'd rather fight it playing the good guy." She kissed Joe, "I've got to run... it has been wonderful to visit you both. And I saw a miracle today."

Michaela stepped from the bed to grip Joe's shoulder, "My Centurion, you have a job in my kitchen when you have recovered from your heroic battle. Be well. Let's talk soon. *Ciao!*"

The effusive woman bustled out of the room as the doctor returned to his patient. He was gruff. "Okay, Miss Stratton, time for a nap. You need to rest. I am overjoyed you are among the living again. Later, I need to run some tests and give you a thorough check. Today was a miracle, so rest easy for a while."

He turned to Joe, "And you, young man, need a nap. First, have the nurse look at your wounds. Then, I will message your doctor that you should be rechecked. All that blood on your gown is not a good sign. Have a good afternoon." Then, speaking to the charge nurse, he briskly stepped away from the pair.

Nurse Marina appeared with a prepared syringe. "Just a little something to ease the pain and help you rest, Penny."

She injected the needle into the cannula port. Then, she plumped the pillows and turned down the blinds. Penny faded quickly.

"Come with me, Mr. Bartoli. I'll take you to your room. We'll let Jennifer try to keep you there." She smiled as Joe kissed Penny.

☯

Chapter 11—Epilogue

November 23, 1995

The following weeks were spent in recovery. Despite another surgery, Joe was quicker to leave the hospital than Penny was. However, Penny's odd and unique case had the doctors baffled. Her former heart ailments were suddenly gone. The x-rays, tests, and MRI scans showed a healthy heart—no more signs of the surgery, the scarred patch she once had, or the unusual condition. Yet, day by day, she improved. Penny's wit returned, and soon, she was impatient to leave the hospital after her deathly experience. Finally, the grief counselor and doctors saw her mental health had stabilized and proclaimed Penny was ready to jump into her routine life again.

Joe was happy about it all, yet mystified, as was Penny. Joe's near-mortal wound that John Cannon had inflicted caused two broken ribs, pierced Joe's lung, and cut the lower quadrant of his heart. Although glad to be alive, Joe silently suffered, feeling weaker than before and experiencing labored breathing, unable to be as active as before the fight.

Once Penny left the hospital, she was at his side, daily helping around Joe's apartment, making meals, and soothing his impatience in the slow recovery. The pair retrieved Pappagallo—following a few weeks of care with Joe's cousin, Paulie. The cages of doves and pigeons were gone, too, since the cousin could have them in his new home.

The winter set in. Mild for most of the month, without the usual precipitation or snow. The couple worked together, finished their harvest gardening, and prepped plants for the indoors or hibernation.

Thanksgiving Day was spent with Joe, quietly listening to music. Although Michaela and Joe's sister Lucinda both popped in for a brief visit, bringing delectable food from their homes, restaurant leftovers, plus freshly made cheesecake. The women intended to stay for a short while.

Penny retreated to the kitchen during the visit, saying she would watch over the roasting turkey and bubbling foods. But really, she avoided the women so that Joe could have his family time. But after a while, Michaela came in, snuck a spoonful of the cranberry sauce, and visited Penny.

"You know, I have never seen Joe happier. He is a changed man." Michaela snaked an arm about Penny's waist. "I agree with his choice of a life partner. He is confident, he even speaks more clearly and—"

"Really bored out of his mind. I cannot wait for him to get back to work." Penny commented with a sigh.

"Oh?" Michaela's dark eyebrows rose, "Maybe you are bored playing housewife then. I know Joe is capable enough."

"No. I don't mind that. But Joe needs more physical activity; it keeps his mind from getting lost. I cannot work with him hanging on me like a lost puppy."

"Unhappy?"

"Me? No, I am content being with Joe. But when he is bored, he's like a penned-up moose. He makes too much noise and racket, cleaning and rearranging the cupboards or fridge, fussing and fixing everything. Then he asks me a hundred times a day if I need anything. When it is I who should ask him to stop and rest! I make Joe relax when he gets winded or weakens in pain. That is a feat as well."

Penny shifted away, afraid to say her thoughts, but boldly did. "I think when John stabbed him, it did something else to Joe's psyche. Joe has become a one-directional gratitude machine, never stops, and always trying to be my everything, including a loveable guard dog."

"Really. And you don't find that charming? I would love to have a grateful guy at my beck and call for everything." Michaela chuckled and stole another spoonful of relish. "Man, this is good. What makes it so different?"

"Raspberries and apples." Penny smiled and sat at the table near the bird's perch to offer an apple slice to Pappagallo. She stroked his white breast with the bright yellow and orange collar. "*Bene.*" She cooed to the bird.

"You are also good with Joe's pet. Pappagallo loves Joe and seems devoted to you now, too."

"He's sweet. I still miss my cat, Finkel. But a cat and a bird are probably not a good pet combination." Penny ate a celery rib from the relish tray as Michaela plucked a trio of olives.

"I am so grateful for Joe. He saved me from that creep, John Cannon. Although, I only recall Joe dying by my side. And so did Finkel, you know... the Cat-Man that said he was my pet. Maybe I dreamed it all, and it was just a horrible scene of me getting attacked by a weird sex fiend. I feel bad that people died because of it." Penny sniffled and turned to watch the simmering pots on the stove. She was embarrassed by the flood of emotions crowding her mind and heart.

Michaela took Penny's hand. "Hey, that guy got what he deserved. Really, he did. Whether Joe or that panther-man or you killed him, somebody had to do it. At least there have been no recent assaults in this area since then. So maybe he was a serial sexual predator. It was only fair he died."

"My sister was angry with me because what happened ruined Mom's party."

"Don't believe that lie. The party was a success. I have had so much business since then. Everybody loved the food and the entertainment—A real catfight in the back alley!" Michaela chuckled and forked a pickled artichoke heart, devouring it.

"That's great for you. But because of it all, my sister and family disowned me. Nobody visited me in the hospital. So, yeah, I am a black sheep now."

Michaela gripped Penny's fingers. "I will tell you something I have never shared with anyone but Joe, my psychiatrist, priest, and best girlfriend. The rest of my family doesn't know what I will tell you now."

"It's okay... You don't have to tell me."

Michaela's dark eyes were intensely focused on Penny. "I do. Joe saved me, too, one night in my restaurant. I was working late, prepping for the next day's menu. When I went outside to toss stuff in the dumpster, a bum I had been kind to that week jumped on me."

"Oh, my gosh!"

"During the week, I had given him some takeaway food boxes, thinking I was helping him. But he got twisted somehow, and that night, he came at me with a knife demanding money. He grabbed me... I tried to fight him.

He smelled so awful," Michaela said, shaking her head but continuing.

"I tried to reason with the man, offer him more food or a few bucks. But he dragged me into the restaurant kitchen. Beat me. He held a knife at my throat and cut me for everything I said."

Michaela opened her sweater and blouse, then loosened the russet-colored silk scarf at her throat. "I still wear the scars of his abuse and attack. He raped me, then beat me again when I refused to open the register's lockbox or the safe. Finally, I ended up in the freezer behind a locked door. I almost died."

Michaela sniffed and wiped her nose on a paper napkin. "Joe had called me, wanting to go out that night. When I didn't answer, he came to the restaurant. He found the guy ransacking the place, even breaking up the marble counters to get the cash register out. So he attacked the guy and decked the creep with a single punch."

"That sounds like Joe. He has the heart of a hero. I can never repay him for his protection and kindness for the past two months."

"You don't need to repay him other than love him. Joe is faithful. When in love, he rarely gives up."

"I noticed." Penny giggled, then sighed. "Oh, Michaela, that is a terrible story. So, what did you do?"

"After knocking out the bum, Joe searched the restaurant for me and found the freezer door handle jammed with a rolling pin. He opened it and found me half-frozen, like a leg of lamb, hung on a meat hook. Joe saved my miserable life, and he saved my sanity."

Michaela smoothed back her glossy, curly black hair, then smiled to say, "So, the little thing about me saving you both that night was not about payback; it was necessary. I couldn't let a criminal get away again. Because that lout escaped while Joe rescued me. But I guess the bum was scared enough not to return."

Michaela absently fingered the ragged scars on her neck and chest. "The world doesn't need evil like that. I am only sorry that you were attacked at my restaurant." She re-tucked the scarf and continued.

"It was a fluke that I could provide videotapes to the police and detectives for Halloween night. I got new surveillance cameras for the alley and a couple in the restaurant that week. Lately, we've had a bunch of bums in the alleys doing drug deals and a black cat that kept coming around and messing in our dumpster!"

"Maybe it was Finkel! He was always in my trash." Penny and Michaela both laughed. "Thanks for sharing your story. I feel like I had a less scary experience than you. I am sorry, yours was hideous. Mine was an altercation... a simple misunderstanding."

Michael shook her head. "That was not a misunderstanding, Penny. The videotapes showed that man assaulting you in the hallway and the alley. You had no blame for it since John Cannon was a murderer. The police just a week ago found that John had a record of such attacks in other cities."

She leaned closer and squeezed Penny's hand, "I think your family has horrible taste in who they call friends. Right? So... please, no apologies. I will only accept your concern and want you to feel like we are sisters. Soul sisters. Joe has brought two mistreated, unloved women together, saving and loving us both. I feel lucky, and so should you."

"I do. But what about Joe? Have you talked to him about all of this? I know he feels very guilty for killing John Cannon. So far, his priest hasn't made him feel absolved. But Joe also has feelings of some righteousness for it." Penny sniffled.

"So far, the police have no problem with what happened, and I now understand why. But we both worried Joe might be arrested and imprisoned for killing John."

"Of course, I have spoken to him about it. Joe also knows all my dirty secrets, including the months I had what the psych doc called PTSD, like what the soldiers get after combat. I was frightened to be alone, yet hated to be touched. I couldn't sleep. I feared every man but Joe—and I could barely stand him." Michaela smiled tearfully.

"But that big lummox is the best friend I needed. He brought me silly videos, food, and tiny bottles of wine so I wouldn't drink myself into oblivion. He was my best buddy, helping my dark moods. We ate popcorn and watched Pink Panther movies and Tom and Jerry cartoons." Michaela giggled and stole another olive.

"Joe started going with me to the restaurant, ensuring I was never alone, always with a crew of at least three others. Most of the employees I have grown up with are like *mi familia*. So, I finally got back into my groove. That was rough, my first year owning the restaurant after my dad retired. He died a month later from a heart attack. Pops retired too late at seventy to have much fun. I wanted him to be proud of me. The break-in and attack set me back."

"I am sure he is proud of your accomplishments. Maybe your dad protected you from afar, sending Joe to help." Penny squeezed Michaela's hand, then released it.

"I want to feel secure with him. Joe still protects me like I am a fragile china cup. But I am afraid to let go of myself. I have never had a boyfriend as an adult. I am embarrassed to say I have loved no one, you know, in that sexual way. So, I don't know what he expects of me."

"To him, you will always be his delicate Penny. He is in love with you. Maybe I shouldn't say this yet, but I will, so you have no doubts. He wants to marry you. Joe already asked to have the wedding reception at my restaurant."

The taller woman came around the table, pulled Penny up, and hugged her hard. "I am so glad that you will be part of my family. I have missed having sisters. Lucinda is the best one for Joe. She puts up with all his fuss and goofy escapades. But you will find she is genuine and loves you, too. So you have a trio of fans here. And soon, you will be an auntie!"

"I am flattered. You two were the only ones to visit me. You and Lucinda brought me gorgeous roses, and so did Joe. Mom sent me a tiny bouquet of four daisies with a printed florist's card, 'Get Well!' Whoop-dee-doo. So, thank you. I have fallen in love with you all, too." Penny, smiling amid tears, hugged Michaela.

Joe came to the kitchen doorway. "Cara, when is dinner? I'm starving."

He smiled at the hugging women. "Did I miss anything?"

"Not at all." Michaela wiped a tear from her face and hugged Penny to her side. "We were having a ladies' chat with wine and eating her fabulous cranberries. Have you ever eaten such a delicious thing?"

Joe came in. "Yeah, I tried it. Penny's relish is the best. By the way, Lucinda had to go home. Hubby Man called with a surprise for her." He grinned, winking, adding, "And I know what it is, too!"

Looking giddy, Joe said, "Dave had a handmade crib delivered for the baby. Last week, he showed me a picture. Lucinda will love it."

Joe looked suspiciously at the pair as Penny snuck away to stir something. Then, glancing at Michaela, he asked, "Are you sure I didn't interrupt something important? I can leave. I'll set the table. No, wait, you'd be here. I'll go watch a rerun of the parade."

Penny went to Joe, taking his arm, "Joe, stay. We were talking about you, too. Everyone is concerned for our health." She smiled up at him."Sit. Let's talk about us. How are you feeling today?"

"Hungry." Joe side-eyed Penny. "Oh, you mean," he swallowed audibly. "Um, okay... I guess." He rubbed a hand along his side. "I still hurt here, especially after working in the garden."

Penny nodded, "I do, too. But then I think some of our pains are because we are out of shape. We must ease into our work again." She stroked his dimpled cheek.

Michaela was silent for a few minutes, letting the pair talk, then added, "You two are so perfect for each other." She held their hands together, saying with a catch in her voice, "I know this ordeal has been mentally and physically wearing for you both, but keep up the good chats. Please be patient with each other. Rome wasn't built in a day!"

Joe snuck a kiss on Penny's cheek. "I know, *cugina*, but I can't help but do more than sit on my butt."

"It's called recovery, *sciocchino*. You deserve a long rest, no worries, and no stress." Michaela put a finger to her lips, "No complaints. I will help you get dinner on the table, we'll eat, and then you two have the afternoon to rest. After dessert, allow me to do the messy clean-up. Yes?"

The trio set the table, and the Thanksgiving meal was soon ready. Joe grasped the ladies' hands, "I'll say grace." He spoke softly, reciting an Italian prayer, then added in

English, "Dear Lord, give us the strength to have a good life again. Bless us for the special time ahead when I ask my heart's desire to be my beloved wife…" hearing Penny's gasp, he opened one eye, "Sh."

Boldly continuing, Joe added, "Dear Lord, you saved us for a reason, and we give our lives and hearts to your service." He released Michaela's hand and made the cross genuflection, adding, "Amen. Thy will be done."

Penny and Michaela were both teary-eyed as Joe turned to Penny. "I called your parents the other day after leaving the hospital. I told them we were getting married. I said I didn't care if they wanted to be a part of it. But it might be important for you if your folks and sister came to our wedding."

"What? You didn't. No one has said a thing to me. Except for your cousin, who only today told me you wanted to marry me." Penny blushed hotly. "Joey, you always surprise me."

"Sorry to wreck your surprise, Joe. I wanted Penny to know how much we care about her." Michaela sighed. "You need to be together."

Joe squished Penny's hand, "I heard you, Mich, but it's alright because I would have asked her later today. I am sorry that the sex creep wrecked my first chance to ask Penny. I had your ring in my costume, ready to ask the big question. Mickie, I am glad you were here to witness our joy." He kissed Penny's cheek.

"Penny and I have discussed what we want to do for jobs. She needs something, and so do I. But we think you might like to be involved with our project."

A dark eyebrow rose as Michaela eyed the smiling pair. "Oh? And you want to work in my kitchen, too?"

Joe blurted, "Penny could do it because she makes great desserts, but that's not it."

"Go ahead, I am curious."

"Well, I told Penny last week about the homeless bums in the alley. And remembering your problem, well, this thing with the Cat Burglar and the Navy sex creep just brought all that stuff back to me. So we want to buy the butcher shop next door to your restaurant and start a soup kitchen."

"You are crazy. Why?"

Penny sounded confident as she spoke. "We both like to cook and enjoy helping others. But, unfortunately, your high-end restaurant is in the heart of a crummy neighborhood, fighting to regain its pride. As a result, too many transients hang out, do drugs, and sneak rides on the subway down the street. Your customers may be at risk. But we think the location is perfect for our plan."

Joe declared, "Penny did a little homework for the kitchen, you know... about permits and tax stuff. And you can help us there too. She plans to build a donation website to fund a soup kitchen and sack lunch meal outreach to these folks. And maybe we can get some help for the old vets, too. Those guys deserve better treatment than eating garbage and being a bum."

Taking a new breath, Joe rushed along in his explanation. "You already give care packages for people living on the edge like Mrs. DiMaggio. We think your generosity will shine, focusing on the unfortunate folks in the neighborhood. Maybe it will inspire nearby businesses to share their services or food." Joe ate a big bite of sweet potato casserole and said, "Everybody wins!"

The trio gave thanks again. Their second chances were like Finkel's nine lives—meaningful and love-driven. The horrors of the past months were over. Love and hope for a brighter future were in the air as Joe held up a wineglass to say, "*Al nostro successo!*"

Penny chuckled, then burst out laughing as the cousins ate their meal.

Michaela asked, "So you are happy about your plan?"

"Oh, yes. However," Penny turned to Joe, "I think Joey B has something more to say or ask me."

Amid chewing, Joe rolled his eyes and shook his head. "Nope. I can't think of a thing. But, man, this turkey is so yummy! For a vegetarian, you did good, baby."

Penny set aside her napkin and rose to her feet. "No? Well, maybe I do." She went around the table and put her arms about Joe's shoulders to whisper, "Do you want to marry me, or is this only your silly idea and talking big?"

Joe's eyes grew wide, and he jumped to his feet. "Oh, I am a dummy! Yes! *Si, si!* Will you be my forever wife?" He fell to his knees and hugged Penny. "I want you forever and ever and ever—"

Penny leaned to kiss him and said, "I get it. Thank you for asking. Yes, I love you, Joe. My heart is yours forever." She confirmed as Joe slid Penny's finger into a gold ring with a ruby. "I am yours."

About the Books

Author C.A. Portnellus hopes you have enjoyed these original tales and novellas. A bit of fun, some spooky or creepy parts, like old camp stories—they should endure re-telling!

Please check out the author's other books and series, *Sparrow Wars in the Garden of Bliss: A La Barre Family Saga*. Follow the La Barre family from the 1920s through modern times with the sometimes ill-fated or fortunate six generations. Each book is a war and peace theme through the decades with a glimpse into the La Barre family curse, followed by hope, faith, and love amid the chaos caused by their generational third-born sons.

Each book in the saga is a complete story. Still, the foundations for the following books are in order, with secrets revealed, layering the bizarre La Barre curse and legacy among the saga's generations of characters.

Once these thirteen books are published, the author hopes to roll back to the early days of the La Barres in sixteenth-century France, with the gypsy's curse, fresh and cruel, following the family to America and beyond for a few centuries. Might the author live long enough to do all the historical research and write two or more novels? One can hope. But for now, please enjoy these novels and sideways stories. Watch for more collections of tales and books in the series and others.

Find the published books via your favorite retailers or online bookstores. All are available in softcover and e-book formats. The books are noted here: *Published, ^In Publishing, >Written and in progress, coming soon.

__Prelude to War__—1928-1943 Follow the Barre families, both at the Louisiana plantation and in Beaumont, Texas, guiding their fated third sons through the Depression into the beginning of WWII. Coming of age, new, and rekindled love brings joy and romance to this nostalgic tale.

__Legends of War__—1943-1945 Witness a lonely American soldier's fight following D-Day until the war's end in Europe, ultimately breaking the Nazi's powerful Third Reich. While at home in America, the Barre and Boulanger families struggle to find happiness amid the demanding war and depleted stores.

The Road Home—1945-1948–Rebuilding family, love, fortunes, and trust following WWII. New surprises await the Barres.

Things of the Earth–Part I—1949-1953–Love, marriage, and a new family begin in the dusty oilfields of Texas. Again, the La Barre family curse is at work to tempt its latest third son.

Things of the Earth–Part II—1954-1964–Fame, temptation, avarice, and a lonely childhood for Francis Barre are part of the La Barre curse.

^ *Back to Earth*—1964-1967–The Barre family is in crisis. The Summer of Love in 1967 proves to be scandalous and sexy.

^*Raw Earth's Secrets*—1967–A brilliant but lonely young man seeks his self-worth in helping others while his family has splintered into something unexpected and dangerous.

>*Garden of Bliss*—1968-1975 The fallout of a famed son from the La Barre curse follows his heart, creating unique and close friendships among the Garden of Bliss Commune.

>*Days of Distant Thunder*—1969–A forgotten son, formerly of the Garden of Bliss in Oregon, finds his values challenged by battles in the American *Dirt Water Navy* in Vietnam.

>*Echoes of Thunder*—1971-1985–Characters from the Commune and Barre families reunite, supporting each other through heartbreaking trials amid war and terrible losses, yet find friendship and love their saving grace.

>*Thunderstorm*—1998-99–A character once from the commune falls in love with an upstart star NASCAR driver. Unusual and fateful events occur, fatefully tying the La Barre family with these characters.

>*Biting the Big Apple*—1998-2001 The curse follows La Barre generations and Commune friends seeking fortunes and fame in NYC and Oregon.

>*Sparrow Wars*—2001-2003–The last Garden of Bliss commune members seek justice as secrets are revealed.

>*Alpha & Omega*—Family secrets, lies, and odd connections piece together the families of the La Barres, their cursed third sons, and the fates of those around them.

✖

Here are snippets regarding the tales in this book...

The Lament of the Lady in White
This novella is a *sideways tale* from my book, "The Road Home," which only alludes to the historic phantasm characters, the *Lady in White* and *Old Berthe*. It is a ghostly tale from Baton Rouge, Louisiana. The lady later frightened the bejeebers out of SSGT Barton Barre. I have introduced these new characters as part of this mysterious family saga, and we learn about an odd familial twist and more of the La Barre Family Curse.

The Curious Case of the Caddo Creature. Happy Halloween from Cristiane! This was an unpublished ARC short story for my readers in 2014. They enjoyed this country yarn. It is based upon actual places near Bastrop, Texas, such as the Boy Scout camp, but it is fictionalized and is a *sideways tale* with characters from *Things of the Earth–Part II*. This short story is an abridged version in this compilation and is the first time in published print.

Found Dead
Based upon 'actual UFO sightings' in April 1968 by local civilians and Edwards Air Force Base, California. All characters, names, and written incidents are pure fiction and only for entertainment. Who knows if the UFOs were real or not? But this alien sighting is a mysterious telling.

The Beast of Snowy Ridge
Set in Wyoming's rugged Snowy Range Mountain park areas. The persons and Boy Scout Troops and their numbers are fiction. Also, based on my Scouting winter hikes and camping experience in the Colorado and Wyoming Rockies. Now I wish I had this tale back then to scare my friends!

"Yer creepin' me out, Bro!"
Entertaining and total fiction, Bro! This is one of those creepy camp mysteries.

Cat-o'-nine-tails
A modern-day bizarre and unsettling romance novella for cat lovers set in the Big Apple, NYC.

About The Author

Author C.A. Portnellus enjoys the arts: theater costuming, a writer, poet, musician, fine artist, and cook. An admiring critter lover—animals play many roles in her stories. Married to the best guy who indulges and inspires the artist/author's crazy hours devoted to creating. With a lovely feline muse of another generation producing these new books, Portnellus continues to fine-tune and write the La Barre saga and other short stories and novellas for adults and young adults.

Please leave reviews for the books on social media and where you purchase your books and other venues. You may contact the author by email: **csparrow.bliss@yahoo.com**

Autographed books are available from the author with discounted shipping.

The author's websites are currently under construction.

Thanks for reading and taking the adventure with author C.A. Portnellus.

Vie! Remplissez-le de joie!
LIFE! FILL IT WITH JOY!